Julie D. Jones was born in Bovey Tracey on the edge of Dartmoor and grew up near Kingsbridge in the South Hams in Devon. After finishing school Julie spent some time as an au pair in Bavaria. Graduating from the Gloucestershire Royal Hospital as a nurse, she emigrated to Australia working as a Nurse and also in the Music Industry. *Conspiracy of Souls* is her third novel following on from the release in 2017 of *Bound by Polaris* and *Devil's Realm* in 2019. Julie is a classically trained flautist and enjoys sailing and horse riding. She is married with two children and lives in the Blue Mountains near Sydney.

This book is dedicated to the wonderful people I met during my time living and working in Bavaria. It was fun to write the Bavarian scenes. Amazing memories of living in such a beautiful place.

With Love,

Jules

Es hat Spaß gemacht, die bayerischen Szenen zu schreiben. Erstaunliche Erinnerungen an das Leben an einem so schönen Ort.

Mit Liebe,

Jules

This book is in memory of all those brave souls who fought in an Armoured Division in World War II.

Julie D. Jones

MOORLAND FORENSICS – CONSPIRACY OF SOULS

AUSTIN MACAULEY PUBLISHERS™

LONDON • CAMBRIDGE • NEW YORK • SHARJAH

A CIP catalogue record for this title is available from the British Library.

ISBN 9781398416215 (Paperback)
ISBN 9781398416260 (ePub e-book)

www.austinmacauley.com

First Published (2021)
Austin Macauley Publishers Ltd
25 Canada Square
Canary Wharf
London
E14 5LQ

To my husband, Terence, for his dedication / commitment and his vast knowledge of forensic science. To the team at Austin Macauley.

Operation Barbarossa – July 1941
The Woods, Outside Riga, Latvia

The combined scream of six Jumo 12 cylinder in-line engines at emergency power overhead, in the early evening half-light, shattered the silence of the ancient conifer forest. The twenty or so anonymous souls working frantically in the long trench flung aside their shovels and fell into the mud almost as one. Simultaneously, their overseers dressed in the distinctive green and black field uniforms, with twin lightning flashes, instinctively swung the MG 34 machine guns skyward.

'Don't fire, they're ours,' yelled a squad corporal, as they anxiously watched the white-hot exhaust flashes of three Junkers JU 88 bombers skim the treetops and disappear rapidly towards the horizon.

SS Oberleutnant Claus Bobich strolled to the edge of the forest clearing drawing heavily on his last cigarette, instantly relaxing as the nicotine fumes swirled intoxicatingly through his lungs.

The unnerving crump of artillery, twenty kilometres to the East, gently rustled branches in the forest canopy, reminding him of the panzer unit up on the front line, which three weeks ago he commanded; he missed the cramped, acrid confines of the Panzer Four and the comradery of his crew.

You've been specially selected; you have the qualities for the job, they told him. It's only for a short time, perform well and you could be back with your tanks in no time, maybe with a promotion. *I joined the Waffen SS to kill the Ivans, not do the dirty work of Himmler,* he kept telling himself.

For a few fleeting minutes, his mind drifted back to the farm, to the family dairy business, wondering who was bringing in the herd on the green slopes of the hillside, surrounded by the mountains so close you could reach out and almost touch them with the high, snow-capped Alps, only a herdsman's cry across the valley.

'Where do you want the 34s?' shouted the Hauptman, jolting Bobich back to stark reality. For a minute he was silent, savouring the last of the cigarette, unable to dispel the mesmerising vision of home far away.

Finally, he stubbed out the butt in the carpet of pine needles and turned towards the approaching panzer grenadier officer:

'At each end, watch the ammunition, short single bursts only please Berndt. We'll need every round for the Ruskies.'

Preface

The soft lilt of Kipling's Poem carried through the sultry air:

> If you wake at midnight, and hear a horse's feet,
> Don't go pulling back the blind, or looking in the street.
> Them that ask no questions isn't told a lie.
> Watch the wall, my darling, while the Gentlemen go by!
> Five and twenty ponies.
> Trotting through the dark –
> Brandy for the Parson,
> 'Baccy for the Clerk;
> Laces for a lady, letters for a spy,
> And watch the wall, my darling, while the Gentlemen go by!

Urgency took over, to swiftly bury the bodies deep beneath the clay peat. Sweaty hands shook from frostbite and exhaustion, yet they were not about to yield until the task was done. The sound of the spade breaking the virgin earth continued unrelenting for an eternity, and by dawn, with black clouds looming over Dartmoor, the two young women were flung into the ground, grey earth scattered on top.

As the lonely figure headed back through the small wooded copse towards Manaton, silent prayers were offered, hoping the bodies and the dark secrets they held would remain forever hidden.

****

Dartmoor – 28 May 2018

'Go on, dare you.' Allyson laughed, brown eyes bathed in late spring sunlight, her auburn hair blowing against the strong westerly wind.

The ancient house stood foreboding and isolated, almost alive, partly concealed behind two huge oak trees with the monolith of Haytor not far away, casting a shadow over its very soul. Sensing the house calling out her name Allyson summoned the courage to enter the derelict building leaving her friends behind, each footstep deliberately cautious on the springy grass. What were the others afraid of? Bert Simms had been admitted to a psychiatric unit six months prior, no one lived on the property anymore, walking the worn floorboards would be an adventure. There was no reason to harbour fear.

The ancient wooden door creaked menacingly on its rusty hinges as Allyson carefully pushed it open to step carefully over the threshold; already catching the repugnant odour of death.

Her heart beating methodically in her chest, stopped momentarily, when an unworldly noise originating from the basement, penetrated her senses.

Allyson glanced behind, half-convinced of a presence in the dark recesses nearby, watching. For a second, she wondered if entering the old building was the right decision, but there was no going back. The lure of secrets concealed behind walls was irresistible. She had to keep going, to discover what lay ahead.

****

Dartmoor – 12 April 2019

The school class trip from Easden Down to North Bovey would never be forgotten, tainted with sadness when Rebecca Price and Nicola Fletcher vanished on the desolate moor without a trace.

'Here have some of this,' Rebecca urged, removing a small packet from the breast pocket of her school blazer, her laugh infectious.

'What is it?' her friend enquired with anticipation, unwrapping the paper to reveal two small, crudely made, white tablets.

'Ice, I nicked it from Dad's surgery.'

'You never?'

'Yes, I did. A present from the gentleman, along 'o being good!'

****

Chapter One
Present Day

The young vivacious reporter waited anxiously to begin, clasping the microphone tightly with both hands. The camera ready and on cue, she broke into a well-rehearsed dialogue.

'Now well over a year since the disappearance of schoolgirl Allyson Carter, police have discovered the body of a young female in a disused Dartmoor quarry, a short distance from where Allyson was last seen. Although it is premature to determine if the body is that of Allyson Carter, speculation is mounting that it could be the missing Plymouth girl. A team of forensic experts are currently on the scene of the discovery, well into a preliminary investigation. This is Mary Saunders on Dartmoor. reporting for television South West.'

****

A dank mist easing its way in off the Channel crept up the Escarpment, unchanged since Neolithic times swirling around the small forensic team, wraith-like in their white protective garb. An approximation placed the female corpse around the mid-teens, now in an advanced state of decomposition.

'I'd bet my house this is Allyson Carter,' SOCO Clifford remarked, rubbing his hands together to counteract the predawn chill. Arms folded he stood staring down at the muddy, crumpled form, straining eyes against the glare from two powerful floodlights.

'It's too early to tell,' Fiona Sinclair warned, without glancing up, totally absorbed in taking photos. 'What I can say is the bastard who did this wanted to make sure we wouldn't make easy identification. Take a closer look; you can see how the face has been burnt with a strong phenolic, possibly some form of creosote.'

'Nice.'

'We'll have to be careful moving the body into the bag; try not to disturb the undergrowth and earth,' Fiona cautioned. 'This soil could hold vital clues.'

'Any idea how long the body's been here?' the SOCO probed, his warm breath visible in the air.

'Not until we undertake some specific lab tests.' Fiona lifted up one hand of the deceased to study the fingernails. 'I don't work on assumptions.'

'Hazard a rough guess?' the SOCO persisted, eager to have something to report back to the Commander.

'No, I won't guesstimate,' Fiona concluded. 'The regional pathologist team will come up with a pretty accurate number when they go over the remains in the lab.'

The SOCO moved away, bored with proceedings. A preoccupied Fiona, fighting back the urge to throw up from the rising stench of putrefaction, once again ran an expert eye over the young female, observing any unusual or anomalous features.

'There's a media mob hanging around your car, you'll be lucky to get out of here alive,' Detective Chief Inspector Parker announced, making Fiona jump as his well-worn shoes had not announced his presence. 'Allyson's family already has wind of our discovery, demanding answers. Is nothing a secret around here?'

'Apparently not,' Fiona continued to examine the body. 'I'm inclined to think our victim was buried alive. There's evidence of soil under the fingernails. Possibly indicating she began scratching at the earth, in a desperate attempt to escape.'

'Not a pleasant way to go, like drowning I suppose,' Parker mumbled, baulking at the smell of rotting flesh. 'I'll catch you later for a more detailed report. I'm a bit squeamish around death, best for me not to hang around too long.'

He left Fiona deep in thought slowly tapping fingers on her camera, as he retraced his steps over the moor. William Parker was different from most senior detectives Fiona inevitably came across; he was certainly in stark contrast to Mick Rose, one of affable and easy-going nature. Sadness revisited Fiona, as she remembered Mick's death nine months ago, from an inoperable brain tumour; it would take a while for the family at Moorland Forensics to gain trust in their newly assigned DCI.

Maintaining her melancholy mood, Fiona worked in silence, alongside a tech officer, measuring and documenting parameters around the deceased. Scanning the immediate vicinity her keen eyesight spotted a small leather clutch bag, half concealed in the undergrowth, not far from the body, which was placed into a clear plastic bag and labelled.

With the systematic forensic protocol, she selected random samples of the soil and vegetation from around the site, also adhering to the body, placing them into plastic evidence bags which were sealed, labelled and verified by the assisting tech. As an afterthought, and for added insurance, the soil scrapings from under the fingernails were added to the evidence.

Leaving precise instructions on how the body was to be extricated from the burial site, Fiona weaved a path across the moors to her parked vehicle. She almost made good her escape before a microphone was shoved into her face by a male journalist, instantly recognisable as Tom Markham, self-appointed chief reporter and sole owner of the high circulation "Star" whose paper thrived on speculation and sensationalist articles. 'Fiona, can you confirm the body you've discovered is that of missing schoolgirl Allyson Carter?' Tom inquired briskly.

'No, it's much too soon to determine that.' Fiona fumbled for the keys to the TVR, which had the annoying habit of dropping to the bottom of her bag.

'But there's a chance it could be?'

'There's a possibility, yes.' Sliding into the driver's seat Fiona jammed her red sports car into gear, the rear wheels fighting for grip on the gravel as she accelerated onto the main road. This was the start of things to come. Public pressure would demand rapid and unequivocal identification of the entombed soul.

****

'I hear your sister's been found,' the young stable boy probed, pushing Jacob jovially. 'Bet she looks all twisted, face crushed in, ugh.'

Jacob Carter shrugged his shoulders, continuing to work the heavy farm machinery. 'Allyson was a slut, what do I care if they've discovered her body?'

'What happened to her? You must know something?'

'Like I said, she was a slut.'

'Bet you know who killed her, right?' The boy persisted with his torment, fishing for titbits to relay back to his friends. 'Some say the Monks got her in the end, as a sacrifice to the devil.'

'Just leave it, will you. She got what she deserved.'

Jacob Carter brusquely shoved the stable hand aside, heading towards the farmhouse. He didn't want any more complications in his life. Hearing his sister's body might have been found was far from pleasant tidings. Allyson's disappearance wasn't straight forward, the possibility of more awkward questions being raised was cause for concern, both for himself and ultimately others.

****

Moorland Forensic Consultants Facility – Bovey Tracey
– South Devon –
One Week Later

Nick Shelby, prominent government forensic pathologist and Home Office administrator stared down at the array of grisly photographs spread out before the small group gathered around the laboratory evidence table.

Recently returned from a well overdue holiday back to family in New Zealand, pleasant memories were fading fast, as his brain struggled to focus on the realities of the job at hand. He was more than happy for his colleagues to convey their initial findings, on what appeared to be a complex case.

'From Fiona's efforts and the initial police findings, it appears the body has been underground for several months,' James Sinclair began. 'There is a high probability the remains are that of missing Plymouth girl Allyson Carter; the location is accurate. We'll undertake a full autopsy. Indisputably, you can see the face is totally unrecognisable; there's extensive damage to nearly all major limbs, which might have occurred after death. The only way of identification will be through mainstream DNA testing and dental records.'

Fiona nodded, peering across at James for reassurance. 'Assuming this is Allyson Carter, what do we know about her disappearance?'

James flicked open a manila folder lying on top of a nearby high-performance liquid chromatograph. 'Allyson was last seen with a group of school friends heading across Dartmoor towards Haytor on 28 May 2018. They made a detour towards the derelict property, known as *Heather Muse*, former home of eccentric scientist and naturalist Herbert Simms. According to colleagues, Allyson was the only one brave enough to venture into the old house, that's the last anyone saw of her.'

'The name's familiar, Simms I mean. Wasn't he in the news a few years ago?' Fiona raised.

'Correct. Was Chair of some UN sponsored NGO junket environmental committee when convicted of fabricating evidence in scientific reports in support of so-called "global warming". Completely discredited he went downhill pretty quickly. Like so many so-called "experts" today, completely consumed by the fraud cult ideology of climate change.'

'Okay, we can assume a team of investigators searched the house shortly after her disappearance?' Nick questioned, picking up a photograph of the deceased.

'Yep,' James replied. 'However, everything came up blank, no signs of Allyson ever having been there.'

'Footprints, fingerprints, blood, physical evidence; surely they must have found some trace?' Nick quizzed.

'Nope, odd as it may sound, nothing,' James informed him. 'The place and immediate surrounds were quarantined for two weeks; they gave it a right going-over according to my contacts.'

'No body fluids? What about DNA?'

'I was coming to that,' James continued, a trifle annoyed at his friend's badgering. 'Heather Muse was abandoned when Simms was admitted into a mental institute. As far as we know there are no living relatives, so the place swiftly fell into disrepair. The occasional hikers used it for overnighters, but apart from a few tin cans, cigarette butts and sweet wrappers strewn around the place, the guys couldn't lift any meaningful fingerprints. DNA swabs taken at all the obvious points came up zero. Bristol was struggling to identify any gene material, even after multiple replications.'

'Yeah, probably would have been contaminated by environmental DNA or severely degraded anyway,' Nick remarked. 'What do we know about Allyson's family?'

'Wealthy, according to reliable sources,' Fiona advised, glancing at her iPad for clarification. 'The Carters have a substantial dwelling on the edge of Ashburton. Mrs Carter supports a lot of local charities; her husband is the temporary Vicar of St Pancreas, in the diocese of Widecombe. They have one son; Simon aged eighteen, who has a part-time farmhand job, not particularly bright by all accounts, lands himself in a bit of strife from time to time; nothing too serious, mostly petty theft.'

'Perhaps Allyson's disappearance was a form of blackmail,' Nick suggested. 'If the family has money, Allyson would be the ideal kidnapping victim.'

'Not according to the police statement,' Fiona commented. 'The Carters have categorically stated they did not receive a call or note from anyone claiming to be holding Allyson for ransom. Given this signed statement, the police immediately ruled out any form of extortion after Allyson's disappearance.'

'Of course, the Carters could have been lying,' Nick conjectured, stifling a jet lag yawn. 'Perhaps it would be a worthwhile exercise for Katie to meet with the Carter clan, to quiz from a psychologist's perspective.'

'It's a bit premature for that,' James chimed in. 'A firm identification is necessary before Katie gets involved. We still can't be certain this is the body of Allyson Carter. No jumping to conclusions until we know for sure.'

Nick let out another long drawn out yawn. 'I hope you realise; if we discover this isn't the body of Allyson Carter, we still have no proof if Allyson Carter is alive or dead, adding a tangible twist to give the media something to feed on.'

'Indeed,' James remarked. 'It would also leave us thinking who on earth this teenager is, giving us an even bigger cause for concern.'

'Not going to happen,' Fiona remarked with confidence. 'I'm certain this is Allyson Carter, there can't be that many bodies buried on the moors.'

The autopsy was scheduled for 10:30am. Nick Shelby, now officially in charge of the combined Moorlands and government forensics team, waited anxiously in the examination room, constantly checking the time on the overhead clock and fiddling with his protective garb and facemask. Behind him, stood James and Fiona engaging in idle conversation, DCI Parker and his colleagues were observing expectantly from the viewing gallery. A sizeable media gathering camped impatiently outside the building, ready to pounce.

After a few minutes, the body was retrieved from a holding cool room cubicle and wheeled into the centre of the room, the covering sheet discarded with a flourish. Nick Shelby spoke briefly into a tape recorder, then launched without hesitation, into a systematic external examination.

For the most part, the autopsy was quite straightforward; internal organs were sliced and examined, their weight recorded.

'You know this person only died within the last few months,' Nick informed his colleagues, carefully examining tissue samples under a high-power stereo microscope. 'Gut instinct tells me this body is unlikely to be that of Allyson Carter. Also, Allyson had a malignant kidney removed at age ten. This body still has both kidneys present.'

A silence descended in the room. Everyone naturally assumed the body was Allyson Carter, such a fast and concise verdict, totally unexpected.

James moved in to take a closer look, peering over Nick. 'Yes, from the overall general physical characteristics and tissue degradation I'd say this body has been out there only a short while, Allyson went missing nearly fifteen months ago. I second that opinion; this is highly unlikely to be the body of missing Plymouth girl Allyson Carter, backed up of course, by the indisputable fact, this corpse has two remaining kidneys.'

A murmur broke out from the gallery, then the room went silent.

Nick continued examining the back of the skull. 'Although our victim received a blunt trauma to the Cortex, this was not enough to kill them. The actual cause of death would appear to be from asphyxiation, probably from being buried alive. Once we start our internal examination, I'm confident we'll find dirt in the trachea.'

'What about the facial burns?' Katie interjected, hiding behind Fiona. 'When did they occur?'

'That's the interesting thing,' Nick replied, peering over the top of his safety glasses. 'It would appear our victim was dug up a few months after their initial burial, chemically disfigured and then buried again.'

'What a strange thing to do,' Katie commented, keen to learn more about the thinking processes of killers. 'A lot of effort, but for what reason?'

'Right, a bit bizarre,' Nick agreed.

'We'll be able to follow this up with soil and vegetation samples I collected at the gravesite,' Fiona enlightened. 'I am hoping to have some initial results back from a Department of Agriculture soil lab in Salisbury later this week. Then we can start a full analysis.'

After two exhaustive hours, the autopsy wound up, enabling Nick to start work on a report of his findings.

'So, who is this girl?' Fiona begged the question, peeling off her mask and gloves, before scrubbing her hands under running water. 'The age and gender certainly matched that of Allyson Carter. DNA confirmation is still a week away, but that will probably now leave us with the genetic profile of an unknown female victim.'

'This undoubtedly complicates things,' Detective Parker remarked briskly, watching the team head back into the central office area. 'The media will be turning the blowtorch on us to discover the true identity of this body, plus find Allyson Carter. Shit.'

'No doubt, we've certainly got our work cut out,' James concluded. 'Best we keep things under wraps as much as possible, for as long as we can.'

****

A noisy throng greeted DCI Parker, the Deputy Chief Constable and James Sinclair entering the hastily arranged press conference in the foyer of the Newton Abbot Racetrack, escorted by a trio of uniform police officers.

The DCC, flanked by the local Conservative MP, cleared his voice and shouted for order. 'Ladies and gentlemen, I have an important announcement to make relating to our current police investigation,' he began in an authoritative Novocastrian accent, effective in quickly silencing the hubbub.

'I can confirm the body found on Dartmoor ten days ago, is not that of missing schoolgirl Allyson Carter.'

The room erupted.

'Do we have any idea who the victim might be?' interjected a local business identity from the back of the spacious room.

'Not at this stage, as soon as we have a 100% identification our findings will be made public,' the DCC said again calling for order and raising his hands. 'I think it appropriate at this stage, in the absence of our Head of Scientific, to let our consulting forensic scientist Jim Sinclair handle any further questions.'

He moved aside to usher James forward.

'How long has this one been up there on the moor?' came a bullet-like question, fired by Tom Markham; as the owner of the local gazette, *The Newton Abbot* Star. Markham routinely enjoyed tormenting Moorlands by printing articles attacking their credentials.

'A few months,' James directed his answer in the path of a TV camera, to avoid any eye contact with their despised nemesis. 'I urge everyone to remain calm, but if you do have knowledge, technical or otherwise, however insignificant, which might assist our investigation you must come forward, thank you.'

'Give us answers now,' Markham persisted unfazed, getting up from his seat in the centre front row, his lanky, spindly frame towering over the people next to him. 'Come on, surely you don't expect us to sit here today and cop your meaningless responses, Sinclair? Basically, you've given us bugger all. No one in the public at large will feel safe until we know what's going on.' He scowled defiantly.

'I appreciate your concerns Mr Markham, but you'll have to make do with this brief,' James reiterated smoothly.

DCI Parker noticing James's flushed features and rising irritation intervened, taking the next two questions and deferring the finalities to the DCC. James made his excuses and pushed his way through the mob, making for a side door exit, where he was escorted to his car by two burly police officers.

He drove out into the back streets of Newton Abbott, parking near the first available pub. Ordering a double scotch he downed it in one hit, banging another twenty-pound note on the bar. James took it personally. On any other day of the week he could handle Markham with ease; this time he got right under his skin. At last, with a semblance of normality restored, he mulled over the day's events, unfortunately, reinforced by a news replay of the press conference on the overhead flat screen. An unequivocal name was required fast on the body in the freezer, to turnaround the ebbing emotions of the local community.

****

'Police have confirmed the recent discovery of a body near Haytor on Dartmoor is not that of Allyson Carter. This news has sent shockwaves through the local community who were convinced the remains would prove to be that of the missing Plymouth schoolgirl. A question now being bandied about is; who is this latest victim?

This is Mary Saunders, in Newton Abbott, reporting for television South West.'

Katie reached for her mobile, simultaneously flicking off the TV News. 'Matt, it's me. Can we meet up in Exeter tomorrow at ten o'clock to go through missing person files? I'll contact Will Parker to get the clearance.'

'Yeah sure, what's your plan?'

'We may be able to identify our body a lot quicker if we have an inkling who she might be, and to gain that knowledge means sifting through all the local missing persons' files, say over the past eighteen months.'

'Not just a pretty face,' Matt teased. 'I'm with you on this one, see you tomorrow.'

Katie hung up, hoping this new form of enquiry would assist their current investigation. Somewhere out there was a family without a daughter, desperate to know what had happened to her. There was also no immediate closure for the Carter family. Allyson could still be alive, maybe trapped in a torturous world, desperate to get out.

****

Matt and Katie trawled through a police database of persons officially recorded missing within a twenty-mile radius of Dartmoor, their disappearance occurring over the past twelve to eighteen months.

'I can't believe how many teenagers go missing, never to be found,' Katie remarked, fleetingly taking her eyes away from the computer screen.

'What you have to consider is; many adolescents who run away from home do not want to be located,' Matt informed her. 'It creates an added complication for police; lots of money, effort and resources go into searching for people who invariably don't want to be found. Worse still; some parents are glad they no longer have an extra mouth to feed.'

'Now this is interesting,' Katie remarked, fixing her eyes back on the screen. 'Two Manaton girls went missing around the time our body was allegedly buried; Rebecca Price and Nicola Fletcher, both aged sixteen at the time. Rebecca was the daughter of prominent Dartington GP Philip Price, Nicola's parents died in a car accident on the M4 three years ago.'

'Yes, I remember that case,' Matt acknowledged, downing the dregs of a takeaway cappuccino. 'Didn't the girls fail to return from a two-day hike across the moors, as part of a school excursion? I believe the senior detective assigned to the case received an anonymous phone call from someone advising the girls had been brutally murdered, their bodies dumped somewhere on the moors, but nothing was proven. A crank call?'

'So, the bodies were never found?'

'No one knew where to look,' Matt concluded. 'The girls absconded from the camp in the middle of the night. They could have gone anywhere. Police, volunteer and Army rescue teams combed a decent part of Dartmoor for a week; but without a trail, the likely hood of finding them, dead or alive, was slim.'

'Although, we *may* have accidentally just stumbled upon one of them,' Katie replied softly.

'Perhaps.' Matt shrugged. 'James or Fiona will organise DNA testing of both girls' relatives to establish a match. Could prove a tad difficult with Nicola's parents deceased.'

'So what else do you know about these missing schoolgirls?' Katie probed, amazed how Matt could remember dates and names, stored in the recess of his memory bank. 'Why didn't the story appear in the papers or on television?'

'For some reason, it was hushed up at a high level. I only stumbled across the information when I was contracted to network some Home Office computers. At the time I found it all a bit bizarre, but it wasn't my place to pry. Perhaps the police were following leads and didn't want their investigation compromised, who knows.'

'What other files do we have access to?' Katie continued, enjoying this bit of detective work.

'Not a lot, but we can search the online newspaper archives,' Matt replied, logging into another database. 'That will give us a bit more information to go on.'

Eventually, Katie and Matt returned to the Moorland office with their findings. Some of the facts printed out from the police reports had proved fruitful.

'Interestingly enough; Rebecca Price, Nicola Fletcher and Allyson Carter all attended the same high school,' Katie conveyed to her siblings, gathered together to hear her findings. 'An exclusive but low-profile institution set in twenty-three acres of land, on the edge of the moors; Abbey College. Originally affiliated with Buckfast Abbey it was handed over to the nearby Priory in the seventies. Fees are not cheap, according to the Bursar; families will spend up to thirty thousand pounds a year, to educate their children at this co-ed facility.'

'All three girls go missing and all three girls attended the same college; strikes me as too coincidental, considering the number of schools in the area,' James remarked. 'Katie, I think it would be helpful if you and DCI Parker, or one of his team, spend a bit of time at Abbey College to see what you can discover. Use your feminine wiles to persuade Parker it's a worthwhile exercise. There may be someone at the school who knows a lot more than they are letting on. I suggest you go through the place chatting with teachers, students and admin staff. Find out if Allyson was friends with Rebecca and Nicola, and if they shared a common interest.'

'It won't happen for a couple of weeks,' Katie replied, casually. 'The college is still enjoying their summer break. I'll put a note in my diary to head over there as soon as they are back on board.'

****

Katie Sinclair, clutching a takeaway iced coffee negotiated her way through the noisy, hectic throng milling around the Tuesday morning market stalls on the Kingsbridge Quay, toward a prearranged meeting in the Council car park with Will Parker. Dressed in a dark blue suit, tie loose at the collar and leaning, half dozing in the Autumn morning sun against the unmarked Jag, Will Parker was easy to pick out amongst the crowds of locals and tourists. Catching sight of the attractive blonde he quickly stubbed out his cigarette, ran fingers through thinning hair and made a half-hearted attempt to straighten his tie. He waved as she approached.

'Thanks for seeing me at such short notice.' Katie smiled.

'No problem.' The DCI donned sunglasses to repel the intense glare bouncing off the water, now at peak high tide and lapping tantalisingly against the top of the sea wall. 'Now what is this about, seeking information on the excursion Beckie and Nicola were on when they disappeared; I've gone through all the case transcripts and I can't say I came across anything of interest. What exactly are you looking for Katie?'

'What do we know about the two-day hike?' Katie quizzed, getting straight to the point. 'I mean; who organised the trip and what topic were they covering?'

'It was a combined assignment on Wilderness Education and History,' Parker answered. 'Doc Lansky, the History teacher, wanted his class to study old war graves in England and then compare them with deaths associated with the Holocaust. It was to deliver a more meaningful understanding of how the war affected so many people, not just those in Britain. The old boy wasn't prepared to provide us with any more information as he still blames himself for the girls' disappearance. I guess you would feel this way if you were officially appointed their guardians at the time.'

'And the other teacher or teachers on the trip, what did they have to say for themselves?'

'Monique Poyre was an education postgraduate over from France, on a short-term Government study exchange program, she appeared shocked, but look… her English was abysmally poor, she was way out of her depth. Don't know who granted her a visa. I reckon she never quite understood what eventuated.'

'Could either of them have been involved in the disappearances?'

Parker shook his head. 'No, not for one second do we think that's the case. Both provided DNA samples. You can also rule out any other student involvement, no one saw anyone acting suspiciously. Many locals still believe the girls are residing on the Continent, living the high life. Or victims of the white slave trade in a Middle East sheikh's enclave somewhere.'

'Yeah, but that's only a theory,' Katie continued, ruefully turning her gaze to the rows of small runabouts and dinghies moored in tight rows along the sea wall. 'What if they did something spontaneous to piss someone off?'

'No use jumping to conclusions. What are you trying to say: some nutcase came across them on the moors and murdered for fun?'

'It's possible, two teenagers don't just disappear Will. They would have left some kind of footprint. Most young people are on social media, yet their Facebook accounts have not been updated.'

'Precisely, if you want to disappear, you're hardly going to broadcast your movements to the world.'

'Yeah okay. I only hope I am wrong on this one, but the characteristics I formed on Beckie and Nicola don't fit two teenagers running away, something went horribly awry.'

The DCI reached for another cigarette. 'Let's see what we come up with Katie like I said, there's no use jumping to conclusions.'

Earth to earth, ashes to ashes, dust to dust.

Dear Lord and Father of Mankind forgive my foolish ways.

I seized the opportunity to take the very breath from their bodies, to offer as a sacrifice to the devil. I can no longer allow people to torment me through the sins of others, those who step in my way must suffer the consequences.

Am I to be punished for what I have done, or do you want more? Am I being considerate in erasing memories of the past so everyone involved can carry on without remorse?

Guide me oh Lord to the direction you want me to go in and I will walk that path with my head held high and the full purpose you stow upon me.

Amen

Chapter Two

The mud streaked Ford Mondeo choked, leapt forward, misfired and choked again rumbling to a complete stop a hundred metres short of Cadover Bridge, on the desolate high moor. A waning three-quarter moon emerging from behind dark clouds bathed the deserted, mystical landscape in soft, surreal light.

'For heaven's sake Bruce, don't tell me we're out of petrol, not here, stuck in the middle of nowhere.'

'Stop nagging, woman. The damn low fuel light's been on the blink for ages. How was I to know we were running low on petrol; I put twenty quid's worth in yesterday. Find me the torch in the glovebox. Wait in the car while I take the jerry can and look for the nearest farm. Someone around here's bound to have a few spare litres.'

Watching her husband disappear across an open stretch of moorland, Veronica Peters turned on the heater to steal a few minutes warmth before it cut out. Soon she drifted into a peaceful slumber. She thought about the coming days and the sightseeing planned around the area. She'd read captivating articles illustrating Buckfast Abbey as a must-see place to visit, where the monks still operate the Abbey as a functioning business. She also added Haytor to the list, to trek across the high moorland, perhaps getting to see where Uncle Tom Cobley rode to Widecombe Fair. Dartmoor and its surrounding towns and villages certainly had a lot to offer. Veronica looked forward to a few quiet days sampling the Devon countryside, including Sparkwell Park, near Plymouth and the basis for a popular movie called "We Bought a Zoo".

With these pleasant thoughts drifting through her subconsciousness, time passed slowly, and Veronica dozed peacefully, finally woken upon hearing Bruce's long strides heading towards the car, unsure exactly how long he'd been gone.

Pulling her wrap tightly around to counteract the cold she called out softly, 'What took you so long? I assumed you were never coming back.'

****

'Vicious attack,' James remarked, using a led torch to examine the crushed skull of Veronica Peters, slumped forward in the passenger seat of the white Ford. 'The instrument used must have been sharp and heavy. Where can we find the husband?'

'You won't get much out of him,' DCI Parker answered, indicating to a nearby ambulance, its coloured flashing lights illuminating the nearby area. 'The paramedics have administered a strong sedative; it'll be a while before we can question Bruce Peters.'

'Do we know what the couple was doing, heading across Dartmoor at this time of night?' James questioned, checking the film counter on his 35 mm SLR before reeling off a few photos of the deceased. Although willing to embrace most technological advances, James didn't trust digital photography for evidence documentation. 'Not the best time for bloody sightseeing, what do you say?'

'Apparently on their way to find a bed and breakfast,' Parker commented. 'They travelled down from London on a four-day break.'

James blew on his hands to keep them warm, the ambient temperature continuing to plummet. 'You would have assumed they'd have secured suitable accommodation prior to setting off on their journey. They obviously don't know this part of the world and how remote it can be.'

'We'll know more when Bruce is up to being interviewed,' Parker remarked, betraying no emotion. 'What's the verdict Jim, what exactly happened to this poor woman? Do you reckon it…'

'Look, I can only give you my opinion, I'm not a forensic pathologist,' James cut in, still annoyed at being summoned as a last resort. 'My sister's in Cornwall, so she couldn't attend. Strictly speaking, the duty patho is supposed to be here.'

'Yeah, terribly sorry about that,' Parker hesitated. 'Derek Ingalls is on compassionate leave and the emergency backup rolled his SUV on the Plymouth by-pass on the way up; quite a bit shaken I believe.'

'It looks like a random killing,' James advised, taking a step closer to the deceased. 'You can see where her throat was slit; one swift movement from left to right. I'm almost certain this occurred after her head was smashed in, a small blessing. There's a clean slice through the carotid artery, the instrument of torture was sharp, probably at least four inches in length.'

'Hence why there's so much blood,' Parker surmised. 'We're not far from Greenways Psychiatric Hospital. I'll drive over later to make sure no inmate has escaped, although it's highly unlikely. We normally receive warnings from the professor if he has concerns regarding a patient.'

James appeared sceptical. 'That place should have been bulldozed years ago. There's been enough scandal associated with Greenways. I'm surprised it's still operational.'

'One can only assume Professor Green makes sure huge sums of money get to the right people, enabling him to keep the sanatorium open,' Parker concluded. 'So far he has managed to dodge any form of closure, even when half the county has lobbied against him.'

'Typical.' James snorted. 'Let's call it a night and get the body shifted. We'll reconvene in the morning.'

****

'Poke around and see what you come up with on Veronica and Bruce Peters,' James instructed Matt, meeting up for lunch and a beer in the Bovey Arms. 'Veronica's attack was particularly brutal; her skull was shattered, and her throat slit. I'm also going to get Katie to flesh out a psychological profile on our killer. This may be a random attack; however, we could be dealing with a serial killer, in which case we've more murders to follow.'

'Leave it with me.' Matt downed his pint and ordered another. 'My guess is; it must have been a psychopath inflicting those types of injuries though, random or otherwise. Who rocks up to a sleeping woman practically hacking off her head, they have to be crazy.'

'One can only assume so,' James agreed. 'Although people do kill in a fit of frenzy, some not having shown previous anger in their lives. Let's start working through all our evidence, to see what we're really dealing with.'

'Obvious question. Do you suspect the husband?'

'Anything's possible, but there are easier ways to bump off your wife. Besides Bruce Peters wasn't covered in blood; conclusive of someone slitting a throat. We only found traces smeared on his hands and shirt, which supports his story of touching Veronica to see if she was breathing, and to boot no trace of the knife for what it's worth. If Bruce had been the one to commit the deed, there would have been more blood on his hands – literally.'

'Is there a slim chance Veronica Peter's knew her killer?' Matt probed.

'There's that possibility.' James signalled for another bitter. 'Although, I believe this was her first trip to Devon, which makes that fact highly unlikely.'

'Great, a complete lunatic on the rampage,' Matt concluded. 'A Psycho who goes around committing a crime for the sheer hell of it, nice.'

Katie strolled into the pub to join the lads, overhearing the last part of their conversation as she pulled up a chair. 'I just don't get it,' she remarked, picking up the beverages list and nodding to the barman. 'Either the killer was extremely fortunate stumbling upon Veronica, enabling them to commit the crime, or they knew where to find her. If the latter is correct, my theory is; the killer must have been following Veronica waiting to pounce, yet the statement given by Bruce Peters indicates he saw no other vehicle as they drove across the open moors. Our killer bashes a woman over the head, cuts her throat and vanishes, how is that possible?'

'This is Dartmoor we're talking about,' Matt chided. 'There are plenty of places to hide.'

'Even so, I do not believe the killer happened to stumble upon his victim in a random assault, I believe he knew where to find her,' Katie persisted.

'Impossible,' James jumped in. 'Too coincidental. For a start, no one could predict the car running out of petrol.'

'Of course not.' Katie sighed. 'However, if the killer happened to know where Veronica had come from and where she was headed to, she would have been an easy target.'

'I'm with James on this one,' Matt chimed in. 'There's no way Veronica knew her killer. For that to be the case, they would require an itinerary of her stay in the West Country and I doubt even Veronica knew her schedule for the trip.'

Halting briefly to sample the house pinot grigio, Katie continued. 'From all the research and studies I've undertaken on these types of killings, they often turn out to be well-thought-out, with the sole purpose of making sure their victim doesn't survive. I stand by the fact I believe this was a premeditated murder. The killer came onto Dartmoor wanting to kill Veronica Peters; they would have waited for the opportunity and then struck.'

'So where did they head to after the deed was done?' James quizzed. 'I expect they knew it wouldn't be long before the body was discovered.'

'The first place I'd start my search would be the Psychiatric Hospital,' Katie replied casually. 'Nearly all the patients at Greenways would have matching profiles associated with this particular type of crime.'

James scratched his head. 'I'll chat with Nick and get some DNA typing underway. Although I feel this is a waste of time Katie, Veronica Peters was in the wrong place at the wrong time, nothing more.'

'We'll see,' Katie muttered, draining her glass and contemplating another. 'I'll work up the killer's character profile and make it a priority. I know I'm right on this one James. Veronica Peters was a nuisance to someone and had to be silenced. The crime scene photographs show a precision cutting of the throat, this indicates it was not their first attempt, our killer has done this before, maybe on several occasions. Where's the menu I'm ravenous.'

****

'Any confirmed identification on our refrigerated girl yet?' Katie enquired of James, as he wandered into the office late the next afternoon. He exuded exhaustion; his demeanour enhanced by a three-day growth.

'Still awaiting dental records and other DNA results.' He made for the kitchenette to fix an instant coffee, before sliding in behind his desk. 'What's your verdict on the killer of Veronica Peters, any conclusion?'

'It's a tricky one, no doubt. I've sifted through the initial statement provided to police by the husband and some things just don't add up. I did let Detective Parker know. I have a hunch this killing was not random, yet it's unclear if the perpetrator did this as a one-off, or on a rampage. Bruce Peters may know more than he's letting on, he just might somehow be involved in his wife's murder.'

'Are you seriously suggesting Bruce might have arranged for someone to bump off his wife if he didn't actually commit the crime?' James quizzed. 'My evidence to date plainly states he was not covered in enough blood to have done the deed himself, he was patently in a severe state of shock at the crime scene, not typical of someone associated with slaughtering their own wife.'

'It's a possibility, but nothing's definite,' Katie responded calmly. 'Give me till the end of the week and I'll hand you over a full psychological profile.'

'I'm heading over to the Price family home if you'd care to join me,' James advised, rising to his feet. 'Parker would like us to follow up this avenue; his team is flat out on other related matters. He has a feeling our missing body could be that of Rebecca Price or her friend Nicola, in which case we have a lot of fast-tracking to do. It could be useful, having a female present. Let's organise some priority DNA testing. Preferably on parental or sibling saliva swabs. I felt it wise to start with Rebecca Price.'

'Okay, can you pass my jacket. It's certainly shaping up to be a busy week, bodies surfacing all over the place.'

Within twenty minutes of leaving the office, James and Katie approached the outskirts of Widecombe. The small village earning its title from the old Anglo-Saxon Withy-combe, meaning Willow Valley; the sprawling parish extending for many miles, encompassing dozens of isolated cottages and moorland farms. Celebrated in an old traditional folksong, featuring Old Uncle Tom Cobley. Katie, without fail, always attended the Widecombe Fair, ever one to celebrate local traditions.

The Price residence was an impressive three-storey, forties building in the P&O style occupying a commanding position high on the Widecombe escarpment, with sweeping views into the village and beyond to open moorland. James parked his vintage Land Rover near a modern stable block, where several thoroughbreds greeted them in unison.

'James and Katie Sinclair, Moorland Forensics, we were hoping to have a word with you in relation to the disappearance of your daughter Rebecca,' James announced, when the door was opened by an attractive middle-aged woman in riding jodhpurs and cream coloured jumper.

'You'd better come in,' Gillian Price advised, leading the way into a spacious lounge room, sparsely decorated in extreme modernist style in stark white; dominated by an absurdly large abstract painting. 'I've been watching the news and had a feeling you might be turning up. My husband's in his study. I'll let him know you're here.'

James and Katie made themselves comfortable on a three-piece, acid green designer lounge, waiting patiently for Philip Price to arrive. He wasn't impressed with unexpected visitors, projecting visible annoyance when he strolled into the room.

'I know this can't be easy for either of you,' James began, a little tentatively.

'What news do you have?' Price demanded, cutting straight to the chase. 'Can you confirm the body you've recently dug up is that of Rebecca?'

James shook his head. 'Not until we receive all results back from Bristol, which includes toxicology.'

'My daughter went missing almost six months ago Mr Sinclair and you turn up on my doorstep to inform me you may have found her body; what sort of reassurance is that.

Don't you think it'd be more apt to conduct your fucking tests before you turn up with pure conjecture?'

'We're just trying to piece together a picture on Rebecca's disappearance,' James explained. 'We now know the body recently discovered on the moors is not that of Allyson Carter, so our investigation is taking a new route. If we can establish the body is that of your daughter Mr Price, the police will re-open the case, with your permission of course. It is in everyone's interest to discover what happened to your daughter and her friend Nicola.'

'We all know who abducted my daughter,' Price fired back. 'Those bloody gypsies are guilty as hell. Ask anyone around here. Those lazy good for nothings were camping on the moors when Beckie and Nicola went missing. It doesn't take a bloody scientist to work that one out.'

'I imagine all this was told to the police at the time of the enquiry?' Katie spoke up.

'Of course, it was, stupid woman,' Price retaliated, his eyes narrowing to dark slits. 'Not that it did much good. The police only issued the bastards with a caution and instructions to stay off the moors. No formal interviews were conducted, incompetent bunch of morons.'

Gillian Price reached forward, offering her husband a reassuring pat on the arm, her way of attempting to calm him down and cull his rising temper.

'Did Rebecca ever mention she planned to run away?' Katie inquired. 'Was she searching for a new life away from rules and regulations?'

'Is your colleague thick or what?' Philip Price turned on James. 'Why would my daughter give up a life of luxury to roam Dartmoor? Beckie was an intelligent girl, she would never give up the lifestyle we provided for her here, and before you jump to any conclusions; no we had not rowed before she disappeared, we had a normal loving relationship with our daughter. As I'm sure all reports will also indicate; she had no issues at school and was well-liked by everyone.'

Snatching an oil-proofed coat off a nearby hook, Philip Price marched out the door, slamming it forcefully behind, rattling china plates on a nearby cabinet.

'You must excuse my husband,' Gillian apologised, clasping her hands tightly together until the knuckles turned white. Up to this point, she'd sat without commenting, listening to her husband's increased rage. 'Rebecca's disappearance has taken its toll on us all. Philip doesn't mean to be rude.'

'It's not a problem,' Katie sympathised. 'I was wondering if you might have a photograph of Rebecca, we could take with us today? It might help our investigation.'

'Yes of course. I'll go and get one.'

A few moments passed before Mrs Price returned with a colour photo of Rebecca in her school uniform. Rebecca was a striking girl, with long blonde hair and wide emerald green eyes. Her teeth pearl white housed evenly behind a rosebud mouth. 'This is the same photo we gave the police five months ago.'

'Do you think there is any truth behind your husband's accusations of the gypsies?' James quizzed, as Gillian Price resumed her seat in the living room. 'Or is there anyone else you can think of who might be involved in your daughter's disappearance?'

She gazed into James's clear blue eyes. 'I don't know what to believe Mr Sinclair. Since Beckie's disappearance, there has been much speculation, but so far no one has discovered anything of consequence. Try to understand my husband's frustration; he wants to know the truth, but no one's capable of providing answers. Every few weeks we get someone knocking on our door, claiming to be one step nearer in finding out what happened. We've exhausted all avenues, Mr Sinclair, I even had a session with a clairvoyant, but now we just want to be left alone. So sorry, but I think it best if you leave now. I don't have any more to say.'

'Your time today has been greatly appreciated,' James concluded. 'Oh, I almost forgot; could we please have one small item of clothing belonging to Rebecca. We promise to return it within a few days; and a police forensic officer will be in contact to get saliva swabs from both you and your husband, before the weekend.'

With the colour photograph firmly tucked away in Katie's handbag, alongside a blue silk scarf known to be one of Rebecca's favourites sealed in an evidence bag, the siblings returned to the 4WD.

Katie broke the silence as they drove off the moors. 'It must be a living nightmare for that poor family. Not knowing what happened to their daughter would be torture.'

****

'So you're telling me one of your most dangerous patients escaped three weeks ago and you didn't think to report it to the authorities.' James fumed, only two minutes into a telephone conversation with Professor Green, proprietor and Chief Medical Officer of Greenways Psychiatric Institute.

'You can't allow seriously ill patients to disappear out into the community, you have an obligation to keep the public safe.'

'We hoped he'd wander back when he felt the time was right,' Green replied casually. 'We can't permanently keep our patients under lock and key, denying them some element of freedom, despite what all the textbooks recommend.'

'Are you mad or just ignorant?' James fired back. 'We have a woman battered to death, not far from your hospital and one of your patients could be responsible.'

'*Could* being the operative word Mr Sinclair, you have no proof Timothy Stanley committed this crime, so until you do, I suggest you don't shoot off assumptions.'

'From what you've told me, Professor Green, Timothy Stanley has been the perpetrator of several vicious attacks in the past. I'd say he is *quite* capable of committing further assaults, wouldn't you agree?'

'Perhaps, but nothing is conclusive.' The professor had an irritating habit of clicking his tongue on the roof of his mouth. 'When Tim takes his medications on a regular basis, we never envisage problems.'

James gave a shallow laugh. 'Well the likely hood of your patient self-administering his tablets is very slim wouldn't you say. Come on, Professor, face facts; this man is dangerous. If it turns out Stanley killed Veronica Peters, you'll have blood on your hands. Now, where do you think it best we begin our search for Timothy Stanley? You know him better than anyone.'

'He won't venture off the moors, that I do know.' The professor's tone expressed boredom. 'Tim has an almost manic fear of confined spaces and crowds. He will keep

46

roaming the high grounds until he decides to come back to Greenways.'

'Oh great, so in the meantime, he could kill again.'

'If Tim did murder this woman; as you're so convinced, something would have triggered the killing. Tim is not the type to go up to a total stranger and beat the crap out of them. A lot of deliberation would have gone into the process, and it is highly probable Tim would have known the victim. If you can find a link between Veronica Peters and Timothy Stanley, you may be right with your speculations.'

'Am I meant to be comforted by that?' James shot back.

'Yes. Tim never acts on impulse.' Professor Green paused, before letting out a long sigh. 'You could be totally wrong with this one Sinclair. If I were you, I'd gather more forensic evidence. That's my advice.'

'Thanks, I'll keep that in mind.' James hung up, forcefully bouncing the receiver onto his desk, deciding the conversation was going nowhere.

****

'Jesus, you can't go around accusing Professor Green of professional misconduct Jim.'

A concerned Rudy Jenks confronted James the following morning during an unannounced visit to the Moorland laboratory. 'He's put in a serious complaint Jim, which could travel further up the chain, landing us all in trouble. Go easy for Christ's sake.'

'I don't actually recall mentioning anything about wrongful conduct,' James shot back, trying to keep his anger in check. 'Far too long Green has been allowed to run that

47

hospital as a half-way house, it's merely a money-making exercise for him.'

'Even if that is the case, your job is to get some leads on Veronica Peters' killer, not worry about Green's management skills. You're a gifted forensic scientist Jim, but there are times when you forget your place.'

'If you won't allow me to interrogate Green, at least assign an experienced police officer to do the job,' James requested. 'He might be deliberately sitting on vital information linked to Veronica's murder. I'd like all the assistance the force can give me.'

'I intend doing just that. All I ask is to be careful where you tread. We are encroaching on dangerous territory with these bodies on the moors. I'm desperate to keep our latest findings out of the national media. Does your team have any idea what's going on? Corpses turning up all over the place is a nightmare scenario. You've got to realise; I'm extremely concerned about the body you've yet to identify. Surely you've got some inkling of a candidate?'

James blew out his cheeks. 'I wish I did know Sir. We'll know more when facts come back from the Bristol labs, but until then we'll keep going over the crime scene evidence with the hope of picking up fresh leads. We want an identity on the young woman as much as you do.'

'I'll be requesting a full report as soon as anything turns up,' Jenks counselled, softening a tad. 'DCI Parker has been assigned on a full-time basis to work alongside your team, plus a guy I'm sending down from London; hopefully, with their input, we can come up with a breakthrough fast.'

James nodded. 'I'll keep you informed of latest developments, Sir.'

'Do your best,' Jenks instructed. 'If this gets out of control Sinclair, from the Chief Constable down we'll all be answering to the Home Office Secretary and the whole of the South West will come under scrutiny, potentially causing a lot of irreparable damage.'

****

'What do you know about this Timothy Stanley?' Katie ventured.

'Not a lot,' James replied truthfully. 'Don't stop yet, add a few more drops of Eriochrome Black T indicator and keep swirling,' James cautioned, closely scrutinising Katie's burette technique.

'What am I looking for?'

'The solution will go from red to blue when the EDTA has complexed all the metal ions. Almost there. I was hoping you could arrange a meeting with Professor Green to establish a thorough character profile.'

'I'll try, but he may not be willing to provide me with any relevant information, due to strict patient confidentiality practices. I'll also wager he covers things up, to prevent his reputation becoming blemished.'

'That's it. Well done, your first complex ion titration. Now calculate the Magnesium Ion concentration and compare it against the result we got this morning using Atomic Absorption.

What reputation? The Institute's well known in medico circles for its borderline practices, the trouble is; to date, no one's been able to catch him out.'

'How do you propose I advance on Green about Timothy Stanley?' Katie ventured, biting down on her lower lip. 'I would suggest he won't take kindly to being questioned by a forensic psychologist.'

'Will Parker has already had a few words with the Prof; while Stanley remains on the run, he's been ordered to provide us with all medical history, including relevant treatments and medications prescribed, therefore if Green proves abstruse, he can immediately be cautioned for interfering with a police investigation, simple.'

Katie smiled. 'That's useful to know. In that case, it might be an idea to drop over after lunch today, if he's available, and see what information I can get hold of.'

****

In a relaxed frame of mind, Katie drove over Dartmoor to Greenways Psychiatric Clinic and Institute, a leisurely thirty minutes from departing the office. Not having been there before Katie was struck by the stark, modernist concrete architecture of the complex, dazzling white in the mid-afternoon light, set sympathetically in the landscape and screened from the main road by rows of conifers. *Walter Gropius would approve, she mused.*

Martin Harley Green, MD and Fellow of the Royal College of Clinical Psychiatrists sat hunched behind a large untidy desk, working away on a computer as Katie was shown into his rooms. A well-groomed secretary, aloof and predictably officious, indicated for Katie to take a seat whilst the professor steadfastly hammered at the laptop keyboard.

Ten minutes passed before he deigned to look up and acknowledge her presence, fixing her with an amused stare.

'How lovely to meet a fellow mind analyst.' He chortled. 'Not many people can venture into the psyche like we can my dear, although many think they can.'

'A lot of our working knowledge comes from textbooks and the published literature,' Katie reminded him, not sure where this conversation was headed.

Professor Green let out a cynical laugh. 'What utter nonsense dear girl. We are trained to tell a lot from just watching a person, enabling us to work out exactly what they're thinking, do you not agree?'

'Yes, to some extent, but...'

'No buts, now what can you tell about me; just at a glance?'

'I don't know you,' Katie protested, not in the mood for mind games. 'I would require adequate time to study you in more depth before I could faithfully answer that question.'

Professor Green laughed again, this time more loudly. 'Perhaps, this skill is not stowed upon everyone. On the other hand, I can tell a lot about you Ms Sinclair; you are a very strong individual, but not without complications. I sense sadness from an event that happened a few years back, leaving you scared and wary of strangers; an event, taking place at University perhaps? I can detect deep anger and resentment, especially towards the opposite sex, correct?'

The doctor was so close to the mark that Katie felt a shiver creeping down her spine. 'We're not here to talk about me,' she reminded the professor, colour flooding her cheeks. 'I'm interested in learning more about Timothy Stanley.'

The professor propped his glasses more firmly onto the bridge of his nose. 'He's a bright lad is Timothy. I often

51

conjecture what goes on in that decidedly eccentric mind. I try guessing from time to time, but it's all too menacing for my liking.'

'How long has he been in your care?' Katie probed, prompted by a few observations made on her computer tablet.

'On and off for about five years. He's complex, but like I told your brother; Tim does not strike without being provoked. I find it hard to believe he might have killed that woman. To do something like that would be quite out of character for Tim.'

'What's his diagnosis?'

'Schizophrenia. Tim believes he has been put on this earth to help the devil. He hears voices; sinister voices that tell him he is evil and must conduct all things evil.'

'That statement alone tells me he's dangerous and quite capable of murder,' Katie said, with an air of contempt in her voice. 'What's treatment have you been giving him?'

'Primarily, psychotropic drugs, combined with counselling sessions. I get Timothy to treat the voices as friends and then he can try to focus on moving them aside to another dimension. It's not your typical case study stuff, it's what I picked up through many years surviving on the streets.'

Katie seemed surprised to hear this, causing Dr Green to lean forward, smiling broadly. 'Not all of us were born with a silver spoon in our mouths,' he mocked. 'Before returning to get my MD at Cardiff University as a mature age student, I experienced some rough years living on the edge up in Finland and Norway. However, it didn't do me any harm, try it sometime. You learn instinct and survival.'

'What else can you tell me about your patient?' Katie delved, with no intentions of sleeping rough on the wayward advice of Professor Green. She liked her cosy flat with all the latest mod cons and still harboured a fondness for Freud and Jung.

'Tim was victim to a troubled upbringing, being given up for adoption as an infant. Apparently, he got in the way of his parents' affluent lifestyle. There was no room for a child touring the world on luxury cruise ships.'

'So he went into care?' Katie surmised.

'All up about four homes, before the age of ten.' Green shook his head. 'The poor lad didn't really stand a proper chance. It is also worth noting; Tim has an extreme phobia of water. We have a hydrotherapy pool here, which he won't go within fifty yards of. Near drowning accident when he was about two.'

'Has anyone traced his biological parents?'

'It wouldn't serve a purpose. Look, I don't mean to be rude Ms Sinclair, but your questions aren't really going to help solve this unfortunate woman's murder. I'm happy for you to look at Tim's file, although it won't provide you with any more insight than I've already given you.'

'Perhaps you're right Professor Green, but I'll take a look at the file all the same,' Katie pressured, offering a sickly sweet smile.

Green surrendered and stood up, moving to a locked cupboard from where he produced a bound folder. 'Here you go, take your time. I'll keep typing my correspondence. I have a lecture to conduct in an hour, must press on.'

****

Government Forensic Centre, Exeter – Two Weeks Later

'All tests are back from Central Forensic,' Nick informed the others, gathered in his laboratory office annex, eagerly awaiting the results. 'We have multiple positive DNA matches, which definitely confirms the body found on the moor is Rebecca Price. The police are on their way to break the news to the fam...'

He stopped mid-sentence to take an urgent call on his mobile. When Nick finished speaking, he turned to his colleagues. 'Another body's been found on the high Moor, in the vicinity where Rebecca's remains were discovered. It's highly probable this one is Nicola Fletcher.'

'Let's head up there immediately,' James pronounced, rising to his feet. 'Damn it, this is so final for those families. Up until now, Mr and Mrs Price held a glimmer of hope their daughter was still alive, shit.'

A sense of urgency struck, the team moving silently and with purpose, gathering their equipment to take up onto the moors. With bad weather coming in from the coast it would be necessary to efficiently extricate the body as quickly as possible to prevent crucial evidence being washed away. Working under inclement weather conditions was never easy.

Within fifty-five minutes of receiving the phone call the Land Rover, with all four aboard, and piloted by James, turned off an unusually deserted North Road now bouncing and lurching along a narrow dirt track leading to the remote grave location. A light drizzle severely impacted visibility; it was not a day for admiring the scenery. A team of police officers, including Will Parker, waved as they exited the vehicle.

'Rather gruesome,' the DCI warned, stepping aside so the forensic team could get in close to the burial site.

Fiona grimaced, glancing at the deceased, lying face up in a shallow grave. Like Rebecca, the face had been partially burnt, making it unrecognisable. 'Who discovered the body?'

'A local hill farmer moving his flock down to lower pasture.' Parker covered his mouth from the bacterial-induced stench of putrefying amines, attempting to suppress a gag reflex in his oesophagus. 'Unfortunately, his sheepdog trampled the undergrowth, probably contaminating a fair bit of evidence.'

'Right, I can see the damage done,' Fiona remarked, considerably disheartened. 'Let's take a closer look at our victim to see what we've got.'

A police forensic photographer moved out of the way, allowing Nick and Fiona to kneel down next to the remains.

The corpse, obviously that of a young female lay in a distressed, upward facing, semi-foetal position.

'Not a shred of clothing,' remarked Fiona. 'Same as the Price girl.'

Lifting the body carefully and turning it a fraction, they searched for any signs of visible trauma or physical anomalies on the torso and limbs, their trained eyes scanning for bruising, lacerations and any distinguishing features or personal items such as jewellery, watches, wallets, etc.

'No broken bones I think; but definite signs of contusions around the breastbone and base of the skull,' she continued.

'I'll second that,' muttered a sombre Shelby. 'Asphyxiation again, do you think?'

'Not sure, no evidence of dirt under the fingernails with this one. State of decomposition appears similar to Rebecca; however, you can...'

'Check that out,' broke in Nick, excitement rising in his voice. 'We still have a stud earring in place, sapphire and diamond.'

'Yeah, looks like the real thing too. The face may be disfigured again, but whoever did this missed this butterfly tattoo,' added Fiona breathlessly, pointing to the top of the left buttock. 'We don't have any clothing, but I make that two physical identifiers.'

'You can add the four-inch appendix scar on the left lower abdomen,' added Shelby, as the body was turned over. 'And I reckon that will be enough to give us a name, hopefully by tomorrow.'

'If I'm not mistaken, these graves are quite a way from Easden Downs where the girls set off on their excursion,' Katie remarked, shivering from the cold. 'They certainly ventured a long way from the rest of their group.'

'Not necessarily,' Nick piped up. 'They may not have been killed here. There is the likelihood our killer brought them to this remote location after they were murdered. Further tests might bring something to light.'

'That's a strong possibility,' James butted in. casting eyes around the bleak landscape, whilst observing proceedings with interest from a respectable distance. 'I estimate this grave is about 200 metres in a direct line from where Rebecca Price was unearthed in the quarry. Funnily, just far enough away not to be picked up when the police teams combed the immediate surrounds two weeks ago. This is the perfect place to dispose of the remains, not many locals or tourists would venture along these tracks. You could easily get lost for days out here and not see a soul.'

'Come on,' Nick commanded, never one to participate in meaningless chatter. 'Let's get the body back to be lab. Those clouds are looking ominous.'

Forgive me, Father, for I have sinned. A woman died in the front seat of her car; an act created by my own hands. The blood ran freely that night.

Across the open moors, I staggered to wash away my mortal sins, in the meandering stream. I watched the deep red liquid seeping carelessly into the dark clay soil. Am I to be forgiven?

Please God, forgive me for my sins. I have death on my hands, yet I crave more. Life is so meaningless, what is the point of strolling upon this heavenly earth?

Guide me, oh Lord, help me to understand what possesses me to dim the candle of life.

Amen

Chapter Three

'What's so interesting?' Fiona queried, jamming a bunch of documents into her briefcase in preparation for an early evening departure.

'Came in the post this morning.' Katie flicked the old newspaper cutting across to her sister. 'There's no acknowledgement of who sent it or why, but it does sport a local postage stamp; *Torquay to be exact.'*

Fiona quickly scanned the article dated 17 August 1998, reading aloud.

'Tania Simms aged twelve, drowned in a Dartmoor reservoir the day before her thirteenth birthday. There were no suspicious circumstances surrounding her death. The Coroner reported death by accidental drowning.'

'An odd thing to receive,' Fiona commented, handing back the yellow-tinged cutting.

'Yeah, I might check it out, see what I can uncover,' Katie remarked. 'I think someone is trying to tell us something, as it was accompanied by a typed note;

'You may find this of interest and in connection with the bodies on the moor.'

'Hey, isn't the Simms's property supposedly the last place Allyson Carter was seen alive?' Fiona quizzed.

'Yes, I believe you're right,' Katie exclaimed, getting a little excited. 'I might drop down to the library to do some research on Tania's death. Anyway, was going to Exeter before five to collect that high sensitivity flame ionisation detector and a microcapillary column for the gas chromatograph James is screaming for. Who knows what snippets might turn up, in the archives?'

'Okay, but be prepared, this article could be a practical joke and totally unrelated to our current case,' Fiona warned. 'It's not uncommon for someone slightly unhinged to get a buzz from leading forensic investigations on a merry dance. Allyson's disappearance was all over the media in Devon and our new bodies aren't exactly shunning the limelight. There are a lot of weirdos out there with sick minds.'

Katie nodded in tacit agreement, donning her coat and exiting to the Courtyard, looking forward to a couple of hours vegging out in the County Library among the computerised files and away from the confines of the Office.

****

Glancing up from behind the returns section of the main desk, Sarah spotted Katie Sinclair emerging from the lift directly opposite. Folding the copy of The Newton Abbot Star and placing it to one side, Sarah smiled warmly as Katie approached.

'What are you researching today? Another juicy murder?' Sarah quizzed, constantly infatuated with local homicide cases.

'The death of Tania Simms.' Katie kept her voice to barely more than a whisper, afraid someone might overhear their private conversation. In her line of business, Katie was ever mindful of the necessity not to discuss sensitive information within earshot of the general public, the blight of social media a constant threat.

Sarah's eyes lit up. 'I remember my mother telling me that story when I was about ten. She warned me not to venture anywhere on my own, especially onto open moorland. Instead of reading fairy tales at night, my mother would scare me silly with stories of Dartmoor, delivering dire anecdotes of bad things during a full moon. No wonder I have difficulty sleeping, even to this day.'

Katie laughed. She'd met Sarah's mother on several occasions, finding her eccentric and decidedly alternative.

'What else do you remember your mother telling you about Tania Simms?' Katie asked, folding her arms with intrigue.

'Not a lot really. You want to visit Tania's old Gran at the Manners Nursing Home,' Sarah volunteered. 'Bit off the planet by all accounts, but still, in full control of her faculties, I believe. You just might get some juicy bits regarding Tania, and more genuine than any article you're about to delve through.'

'Thanks for that tip. I'll pop by one afternoon next week. Mind if I use the research room?'

'Be my guest, the key is in the usual spot.'

Katie left Sarah to continue reading the paper and headed towards the rear of the library. Without delay, she settled in behind a computer and was systematically scanning through newspaper articles from around the time Tania Simms first went missing. It was approximately one month after vanishing that Tania's body was discovered in a local reservoir by a fly fisherman, her naked body half-submerged amongst the weeds and debris near the embankment. The reservoir in question, Venford was located in the very heart of the moors; surrounded by rocky granite outcrops, close to the school chapel of Huccaby St Raphael, and near to Venford Falls. Katie from a young age, an avid student of local history, recalled many tales about this isolated region of the moors, particularly the confusion created by narrow lanes that wind deep into the countryside. Getting lost and facing death by exposure an ever-present threat for visitors and locals alike.

The small chapel built in the late nineteenth century granted the residents of this small community their own local house of worship, thereby avoiding the arduous (and often perilous) trek to Lydford.

A sad story unfolded while Katie digested articles published around the time of Tania's death. The family had been borderline poverty by contemporary accounts, barely scraping together a subsistence living on the meagre wages Tania's father Edward earned. Unwilling to go to school Tania spent her days roaming the moors, foraging for food. There were nights she would sleep under the stars, rather than return home to regular beatings from her drunken father. Edward Simms could hardly drag one foot in front of the other after a tortuous day in the quarries, seeking solace and refuge in the bottle. Locals feeling sorry for Tania would feed and clothe her, but no one trusted the wretched child. She would steal from those who showed kindness and fight with those who didn't. The authorities had given up long ago trying to help the family. Tania was known to many as "the wild child of the moors".

Her death hardly came as a shock to those who knew her. Some suggested she was 'an accident waiting to happen'.

****

'This just arrived for you by courier, soil test results I believe,' muttered Katie, tossing a yellow, official-looking envelope onto Fiona's desk.

Fiona's eyes lit up expectantly. After ten minutes carefully absorbing the contained report, she went in search of her brother, whom she located in the laboratory instrument room, head buried in the oven of the back-up gas chromatograph, engrossed in installing a new capillary column.

'Shit! You just made me burn my hand,' James erupted, not expecting this interruption. 'What's that you've got, it had better be important.'

'The Price burial site soil analyses back from the Agriculture labs in Wiltshire,' blurted Fiona, stifling a laugh.

'So?' James remained unimpressed.

'Okay – get this. They did a comparative qualitative and semi-quantitative chemical analysis and physical examination on the initial six soil samples I sent. Botanical material was not examined, and they didn't test for organics.'

'Why?'

'I instructed them not to. I wanted some comparative results quickly.'

'What methods?' continued James, his interest rising.

'Umm… it says here in the summary. Right, ICP/AES and Atomic Absorption Spectroscopy for both qualitative and quantitative, also standard classical wet chemistry for common cations and anions on the larger samples.'

'Sounds kosher. What about the physical examination?'

'Conventional high-power stereo microscope with digital imaging and polarising techniques. Looks fairly comprehensive to me,' added Fiona, continuing to peruse the report. 'Check this out; positive results for over 20 trace elements.'

'All right, what conclusions can you make?'

'Well, I wanted you to double-check the elemental profiles first.'

James donned glasses and quickly scanned the comparison table.

'Samples three and six have a similar profile, high Selenium content is unusual… And one, two, four and five are more or less chemically identical within reasonable limits.'

'That's what I came up with,' said Fiona, visible relief showing on her brow. 'Sample three is the fingernail scrapings, Soil Sample six, I got from the back of her throat. Microscopic examination confirmed particulate limestone and calcite fragments in both; which as the summary mentions ties in with the high Calcium, Magnesium and Carbonate levels detected.'

'Meaning…?' James was struggling to keep up.

'The other four samples are from the soil around and near the body. That tentatively indicates she was initially buried alive at one location, before later being moved to the second site at the quarry.'

'A fair assumption. Okay sis, well done. I'll fill in Nick and DCI Parker. In the meantime, do more tests on the samples. I want to run a thorough microscopic examination and possibly some GC/Mass Spec for organic and botanical particulate matter. We may get lucky and pin down some locations. I'll warm up the Scanning Electron Microscope as well. Doing anything tonight?'

Fiona reluctantly shook her head, envisaging another late night.

****

The climb up the steep hill to the abandoned Simms property presented a challenge even for Katie, who was fit and healthy. Her heart pounded in her chest.

Nearing the summit, she surveyed the surrounds, relishing in the view back over the plateau and all the way to the Coast, with breathtaking, azure glimpses of the Channel beyond. Approaching the derelict building she was immediately struck by its state of disrepair. The wooden window frames were riddled with dry rot, crumbling bricks were succumbing to the effects of a hundred harsh winters and paintwork, once bright and distinctive, was discoloured and flaking.

Katie read in a recent magazine the council had plans to demolish the neglected structures, the reason offered; no local estate agent was willing to take it on. Sure, the land had some value, but its location a fair distance from the main road didn't make it an entirely attractive proposition.

Harbouring no particular interest in the house itself Katie scouted warily around the established apple orchards located at the back of the property. Sarah had informed Katie Tania's grave was somewhere next to an abandoned tractor, close by the storage shed. She stumbled upon it by accident when her boots snagged a blackberry vine, revealing the changed earth underneath.

Katie glanced down at Tania's resting place, a small granite stone marked the spot with the words: *Resting where no shadows fall, God's own special angel.*

The words brought tears to her eyes. It was surely morally wrong someone so young had lived a tortuous life, only to die under such tragic circumstances. Could Tania be somewhere watching Katie kneeling down to take a closer look at her final resting place? A cold shiver swept over her being.

Katie was surprised to see a fresh bunch of flowers nesting on top of the grave; a mixture of freesias, daffodils and bluebells, held together by a frayed red ribbon. With Tania's family now living in Dorset and Granny Simms housed in a nursing home, she speculated who could have placed the flowers in such a lonely spot on the moor. Reaching out to touch a soft yellow petal it felt damp as if recently receiving water, yet it had not rained in days. Katie cast a furtive glance around the overgrown yard, her innate sixth sense detecting an alien presence close by. Rising to her feet she tried to keep the mind focused, no longer feeling safe or in her comfort zone. Heart racing she turned to head back down the heathery slope, rushing to put one foot in front of the other. There was something about the gravesite which unnerved. A hint of evil.

****

Keita Simms, at almost eighty-six, relied heavily on nursing staff for all her personal care. Medium length silver grey hair, matching the broad rim of her reading glasses, she glanced up with a toothless grin as Katie approached.

'Come to see an old lady.' She cackled. 'Not seen you 'er before dearie. Pretty maid, ain't you?'

Katie sat down in an armchair next to the old woman, unsure how coherent she really was and if the visit would be prosperous.

'You Tania?' Keita peered close, the odour of sweet sherry strong on rancid breath.

'No, but I've come to talk to you about Tania, your granddaughter.'

'She's a wicked child.' Keita coughed, wiping her nose on the sleeve of a blue cardigan. 'She's forever out on them wretched moors. One day that place will see an end to the poor mite. Winter on Dartmoor is harsh, Missy. Satan's armies rise up from hell and roam the moors at night, felling all who gets in their way. You be careful, the Devil's on the moors, he's out to get you.'

Keita rocked in her chair, letting out a high-pitched cackle, waiting for Katie's reaction.

'Do you remember what happened to Tania?' Katie asked, unsure if the old woman was living in the past or the present.

'Oh yes, I know what happened to her,' Keita remarked, eyes lighting up with excitement. 'The evil men in robes stole her from me; cast her aside to drown in the chilly waters.'

'What evil men?' Katie pressed.

'The ones who spend their days praying of course; not one of them is fit to follow God's teachings. Tania's great grandfather made them evil, mark my words those men are dangerous.'

'Where will I find these men?' Katie lowered her voice, suddenly conscious other people in the room were listening to their conversation.

Keita leaned towards Katie, her mouth only inches from Katie's flushed cheeks. 'They live in the old Priory, out Dartington way. No advantage will come of ye searching for their souls, no good at all. What they do is wicked, dark secrets lie hidden behind the Priory walls, and if anyone dares get too close, they will perish for their sins.'

Was there any truth in the old woman's story, or was she talking nonsense? Katie was undecided. It was hard to decipher her level of sanity.

'Time is no healer, my girl.' Suddenly Keita staggered to her feet, her voice transformed into a high-pitched scream. 'You keep away from that vast dwelling with its wicked ways. It's possessed by demons. The dark spirit will cast its evil spell on you, keep away I tell you.'

Keita collapsed back into her seat staring ahead, groaning in pain, rubbing her forehead vigorously.

'I think it best if you leave now,' instructed a young nurse, hurrying to calm the old lady. 'She's not been well lately and too much excitement will get her blood pressure up.'

Katie eased up from the chair, just as Keita clasped firmly hold of her right hand. 'Just remember what Granny Keita tells you: *watch the wall my darling, while the Gentlemen go by.*'

****

Fiona, scrubbed and in her garb, wheeled the second body they'd discovered on the moors out on a gurney to commence the autopsy; the one they now were 99% sure to be that of Nicola Fletcher. A team of forensic specialists all similarly outfitted in disposables, milled around ready to assist with proceedings.

'Not late, am I?' a male voice inquired, moving into the room. 'I hate narrow country lanes.'

Fiona looked up, surprised to see another garbed figure joining them, this one male, probably good looking she sensed behind the mask.

'Senior Detective Benjamin Crispin reporting for duty,' he said, piercing eyes shining above the top of his mask directed towards Fiona. 'I've been assigned the Bumpkin Case. The commander in chief wants me to oversee the case due to ahh… possible complexities.'

'You've been assigned the what?'

'You know, country bumpkin. That is what you lot are referred to isn't it?' Crispin sneered, playing to his audience.

Nick Shelby quickly intervened to come within inches of Crispin's covered features. 'I don't know who or what you think you are Detective, strolling onto our turf without prior permission from Forensics, but if I ever hear you refer to us as bumpkins again, I'll kick your sorry butt all the way back to the City. Now pass me the large scalpel next to you on the trolley; careful, that's the sharp metallic instrument used to slice and dice, just in case you're not familiar with surgical equipment. Act like a smart-arse again and I'll be using it on you, do I make myself clear?'

Appearing unfazed by this dressing down, Crispin smugly located the scalpel, which he placed into Nick's outstretched hand. 'So, can you confirm this is the body of Nicola Fletcher?' Crispin continued, his arrogance dominating the room.

Fiona ignored the question, peering closely at the corpse to examine a bruise on the left cheekbone. 'Now, this is interesting Nick.'

'What's interesting?' Crispin demanded, barging in and nearly knocking over an expensive microscope.

Nick lunged forward, quick reflexes saving the instrument crashing onto the tiled floor.

'Photo please,' Fiona instructed the lab assistant, standing by with his camera. He clicked away under her instructions whilst she continued with the assessment.

'There's evidence of sexual intercourse having taken place just before the girl died,' Fiona continued. 'See here, there's extensive trauma to the inner thigh. I'm inclined to believe only one male was involved in penetration.'

'Okay, I want vaginal swabs to check for acid phosphatase, hairs and foreign matter; also a full diagnostic run to check for foreign DNA,' Nick announced, turning to a female technician. 'Probably pushing it after six months decomposition, but we might get something.'

'Wow, this forensic stuff is pretty interesting,' Crispin decreed to no one in particular, not in the slightest perturbed at witnessing the dissection of a young female cadaver. He was feeling right at home in the sterile environment of unworldly instruments and murky odours.

Silence prevailed for ten minutes, the team continued examining and dissecting the cadaver. Every detail was openly noted and recorded.

'I demand to know if this is Nicola Fletcher,' Crispin broke in again, stifling a yawn. 'The media is circling around outside like a pack of bull sharks, demanding answers. Christ, woman, hurry up and tell me.'

'Detective, if you don't control your emotions in my lab, you'll be forced to leave,' Nick Shelby countered, once more reprimanding his visitor. 'Our Pathologist can't work any faster. We're systematically looking for clues and evidence to cause and motive here. More haste and we could miss something.'

Taking the hint Crispin moved to an adjacent trolley, where James was examining the stomach contents in a steel bowl. 'Honey. Can you smell it?' James announced.

'Not above everything else in this room,' muttered the interloper.

'I'll bet on it,' added James. 'Still mostly undigested, even after six months in the ground, astonishing.'

'How's that?'

'Probably due to the lack of fluid in the stomach at the time, and the naturally low water content of honey… net result being minimal or nil microbial degradation. See for yourself.'

'Anything else?'

'No, just honey,' James reiterated, enjoying the look of incredulity spreading over Crispin's façade. 'Weird thing to find considering the lack of grain or starch products in the stomach.'

'Honey from where?' Crispin moved a step closer.

'We might be able to narrow it down to a few possibilities with the right tests,' James continued, elbowing the Detective out the way who had encroached into his personal space.

'Depends on the integrity of what's left, it may not be worth the effort. The organics and flavouring components could be area specific. I don't know. My guess is there hasn't been a lot of work done to characterise honeys purely by their chemical fingerprint. I'll have to look up the literature.'

Crispin's eyes glazed over.

'Let's face it Detective, honey doesn't generate the same intense interest or snob appeal of wine.' James mused.

Nick retrieved his mobile, vibrating from about his person. After taking the call, he addressed the small gathering. 'That was Bristol with the DNA lab results. They can confirm what we already surmised; this is the remains of Nicola Fletcher, tying in nicely with the physical evidence already to hand.'

Crispin momentarily swayed, quickly regaining composure. 'Excellent,' he broke the silence. 'It's getting stuffy in here. A waste of time doing all this high-fangled stuff. Should have just waited for the phone call.'

Fiona, mentally drained, rolled her eyes, about to let loose when Nick pulled Crispin to one side, indicating for her to finish up.

'The autopsy was just a formality, but necessary regardless, to check everything,' Nick informed Crispin, firmly ushering him to the rear quarantine area where the crew were discarding forensic attire. 'I believe DCI Parker had organised the formal media briefing for 2:30pm, I suggest we get a move on.'

Nick leant against one of the arrays of stainless-steel sinks and again read the riot act, this time with a tone tinged with menace. 'Next time you want to step over the threshold into the world of forensics, think again. You may be assigned this investigation as a copper but if you ever interfere on my turf again, you'll be back on the neighbourhood beat so fast, your head will spin. Do you copy?'

****

'It's apparent you get a heap of unexpected deaths around these parts,' Crispin commented, idly observing Katie flicking through informal transcripts of the Nicola Fletcher autopsy. 'Guess no one's got anything better to do, huh.'

Katie managed a faint smile, only half-listening to his repartee. 'Looks like you got off on the wrong foot with my colleagues,' she announced, extracting the last chocolate digestive from the biscuit barrel.

Crispin dropped two capsules into the Moorlands espresso machine and moved his cup into position, savouring the addictive aroma as the thick steaming black liquid emerged. 'Got something up their bums that lot if you ask me, what they bloody well lack is a good old sense of humour.'

'Then you've read them all wrong,' Katie articulated, not bothering to look up. 'They're leading experts in their respective fields, at the very least dedicated to their line of work.'

'Conceited elitists,' Crispin continued. 'Forensics isn't that crash hot, damned sure I could master the finer detail in no time. Seen one body, you've seen them all.'

Katie ignored the flippant remark and tossed the file on to the lounge. 'Come on, let's get some fresh air. I think I can afford to shout us a drink or two.

You have to understand Devon is defined by its landscape. Stories of intrigue and mystery have been synonymous with

Dartmoor and Exmoor for the last thousand years and are entrenched in local folklore.

I'm betting there is one unresolved tale in particular that might actually entice your sceptical mind. However, change your attitude first. True Devonians are not stupid, so cut out these childish yokel references.'

'Yeah okay, sorry, to be honest, I was pissed off to be assigned this case. My boss in London sent me down here because I couldn't keep my hands off his wife. They were headed for the divorce courts anyway, so I don't know what all the fuss was about.'

Katie laughed. 'An obsession with married women, really? I'm well acquainted with someone who exhibits similar tendencies and believe me, it doesn't get any easier if you play around.'

Unbeknown to Ben, Katie was referring to her brother, who had the habit of getting into strife every time he slept with a married woman. Right now James was in way deeper than even Katie could imagine.

Crispin was quiet on the drive into the city. Katie deliberately turned the radio on high to prevent long conversations.

"The Carillion" was a snug little pub situated in a narrow-cobbled street next to Exeter Cathedral. Katie ordered two generous sized dry whites from the bar, bringing them over to the corner table she'd secured under a small bay window.

'Do tell me about this mystery,' Crispin begged, taking a long drink, keen to unwind from the tiring day.

'We're going back a few years, 1986 to be precise,' Katie began, enjoying her drink at a more leisurely pace. 'One bleak September morning, Hayley, the eldest daughter of Lord and

Lady Illbert-Tavistock went hiking across Dartmoor towards Dartmeet, never to be seen again.'

'From what I've heard people go missing all the time around these parts.' Crispin sniggered. 'What's so special about this case?'

'For a start, she was the daughter of the richest man in Devon,' Katie answered. 'Hayley was also very familiar with every part of the moors; it was inconceivable for her to vanish without a trace.'

'It could just be she wanted to disappear to get away from a wealthy, overbearing existence,' Crispin prophesied. 'On the other hand, did you ever consider a situation of blackmailing gone wrong. When this... who was it? Illbert-Tavistock, refused to cough up the ransom money the abductors did away with his daughter, case solved.'

Katie stared at the Detective, eyes projecting disbelief. 'No, I'm convinced something more sinister befell her out there on the high moor, but there were never any credible eyewitnesses.'

'Sounds like mere speculation on your behalf,' Crispin mocked, knocking back his drink, thoroughly enjoying the verbal joust. 'Perhaps Lord IT was up to his neck in dodgy deals, and someone exacted the ultimate revenge.'

'What are you saying? No, no. Lord Illbert-Tavistock is a well-respected philanthropist of the highest integrity. The Trust regularly distributes hefty sums of cash to local churches. He wouldn't allow himself to be caught up in underhand deals, and he would certainly pay any ransom money demanded. He would have done anything for his daughter. There's something else behind Hayley's disappearance. A local author Charles Whitely penned a book about Hayley's disappearance. Whitely now spends his life in and out of psychiatric institutions, suffering from extreme anxiety. I'd forgo a month's salary to discover what happened to tip him over the edge. I once tried to arrange a meeting, but he flatly refused, vowing never to let past demons cross his path again, whatever that means.'

'I recommend you indulge in a little detective work to feed your curiosity.' Crispin laughed, fondling the back of Katie's neck. 'Let me think about it, I may be able to assist. I can certainly get hold of pertinent details, but it may take a bit of time.' Ben rose from the table checking for his wallet. 'Can I get you seconds?'

Katie nodded. It was fun to be out with a handsome police officer, full of charm with devilish good looks. A combination proving hard to resist. She sat back, watching Crispin stroll to the bar and order another round.

'You're the lady who came to visit Keita Simms the other day aren't you, Katie Sinclair? I was the nurse on duty that day.'

Katie looked across at a young woman seated alone on a stool at the adjoining table. 'You've a clear memory.'

'Goes with the job I guess.' Lucy Whittaker, unrecognisable out of uniform, jet-black hair falling loose around her neck, vacated the stool and moved over to sit next to Katie, offering a brief introduction.

'I hope I didn't upset the old lady too much,' Katie apologised, fiddling with a beer mat. 'She was distressed when I left.'

Lucy laughed. 'She certainly had you fooled; Keita is a clever old thing. A Royal Command Performance no doubt just for your benefit. Nearly everyone who meets her for the first time believes she's away with the fairies. That couldn't be further from the truth. Go ahead and ask Keita anything; dates, times, facts about nearly every subject and she'll be spot on. There's nothing crazy about Keita, yet for some reason she wants everyone to think she's off her trolley, spouting that spooky Devil and hooded men stuff.'

Katie was completely taken by surprise. 'Are you sure about that?'

'Absolutely, come back to the Home next week when she's organising Bingo. You'll see a different side of our Kieta. Kieta the Chameleon we call her. I was tempted to let you out of your misery but didn't want to be on the receiving end of her wrath.'

Lucy stood up to leave. 'Keita hates visitors; says it makes her feel like a zoo exhibit. To deter people from frequently dropping by she goes into this crazy Lady Macbeth act. If you're around before lunch on Friday morning Ms Sinclair, I'll make sure Keita is on her best behaviour.'

'What was all that about?' Ben put down the drinks, his eyes following the young nurse out the door.

'I've been duped, by a woman in her eighties.' Katie reached for the drink, briefly allowing her mind to return to Keita Simms; now clearly exposed as a clever actress, pretending to be a decrepit harridan, a simpleton of working-class stock, barely able to string a coherent sentence together. Katie was mortified; all those years of study and intense hard-earned experience as a clinical psychologist had failed her, letting this one slip through her fingers.

Oh dear God, confession of another wrongdoing. A young girl drowned in the deep dark reservoir. I lie awake at night wondering what she went through. Did she feel any pain or was her death a peaceful slumber? We must all be forgiven for her death, especially the one who committed the crime. There are times when I believe I may have been the one to kill her, then those thoughts vanish.

So often I have blood on my hands, it is hard to tell which lives I have destroyed, there are so many, I begin to lose count. Even though I know my guilt, I still feel compelled to take more lives from this earth and provide sacrifices for all those past deadly sins.

Lord have mercy on my soul.
Amen

Chapter Four

'Up for a bracing walk on Dartmoor?' James asked, noting Matt struggling through the side door with a monitor and bunch of computer cables. Alone in the office since six o'clock that morning catching up on paperwork, now desperate to get out into the early morning spring sunshine.

'Yeah, why not, what's the occasion?' Matt dumping the goods on the nearest desk. 'Trying to keep fit, are we? You look like you've put on some weight. I note a slight increase around the waistline.'

James put up his fists, feigning a left jab to Matt's chin.

'I've heard the travellers have recently set up camp outside Princetown,' James explained. 'Drop-in out of the blue, catch them off balance, see if they know anything relating to the recent bodies? Romany Gypsies are shrewd, the ultimate survivors, it's in their blood to notice anything out of the ordinary. Besides, they're more likely to chat to us, than an official police deputation.'

'Okay, but still don't expect a friendly reception,' Matt warned. 'They might not take too kindly to the likes of us encroaching on their territory.'

'That's why I'm taking you along.' James laughed, rising to his feet. 'If things get nasty, you can protect me.'

The two men strolled out into the frosty morning to climb into James's Land Rover parked in the rear courtyard; opting for the battered 4WD in deference to Matt's only material indulgence a flashy, vintage, metallic blue Mustang. Definitely not a wise mode of transport for crossing the moors; if the travellers spotted his over the top sixties muscle car they would refuse to engage in any form of conversation, more likely to start throwing stuff.

Crossing through the Bovey Tracey roundabout, within a few minutes they were quickly within the confines of Dartmoor, James pushing the Landie at a reckless pace along a muddy, precipitous, unsealed road, oblivious to the protestations of his passenger.

He already had a rough idea where the travellers had set up camp, but it took a while to get to the remote location at the base of a secluded wooded dell. A carpet of bluebells led the way to where half a dozen or so rustic caravans were parked, some up on improvised concrete blocks. This in itself showed the travellers planned to stay a while.

Both men crunched across springy grassland, detecting the pleasing smell of a hearty broth wafting in the cool breeze from a black cooking pot stowed over an open flame. The Gypsies immediately ceased what they were doing, the small huddled group looking up, curious to know who had the temerity to invade their campsite.

'What you lot doing 'ere?' an elderly man shouted briskly, as the lads strolled nearer. 'We ain't doing nothin' wrong, just resting weary bones, clear off and leave us in peace.'

'We're not the authorities,' James reassured, keeping a close watch on a black Alsatian restrained to a nearby tree with thick rope. It barked threateningly, madly pulling at the tether. 'We want to ask a few questions in relation to the recent discovery of two bodies on the moor, we're forensic experts involved with the case.'

'Nout to do with us.' The man moved to loosen the tie securing the dog, a sardonic smile on his face. 'We never saw no girls, we ain't murderers.'

'Who mentioned anything about the bodies being female?' Matt fired back.

'A lucky guess,' came the nonchalant answer. 'A bit like roulette, I had a fifty percent chance of being right.'

'Think back, perhaps you saw them out walking on the night they disappeared last April, they were both wearing tracksuit pants and a school sweatshirt, easily distinguishable,' James continued, an eye fixed firmly on the guard dog.

'No one can survive these moors in dangerous weather. Damn foolish to have taken to the tracks on such a blustery night. It was the weather that surely killed 'em, or perhaps the men with the covered faces.'

'So you did see something?' Matt quizzed, picking up on the fact the man remembered it being a wild night when the girls disappeared.

'Even if I did, I wouldn't talk to the likes of you,' he replied gruffly, loosening the rope securing the dog, eliciting a knowing laugh from the group. 'Now make yourself scarce before I set Nasher on to you. He's yearning for some fresh meat.'

The man undoubtedly meant business, having every intention of releasing the animal if they didn't make a hasty retreat. Heeding the stark warning James and Matt retraced their steps back to their parked vehicle.

'They know something,' Matt stated, as they hopped back in the car. 'Trouble is, they won't talk.'

'I'll get in touch with Will Parker.' James shoved the Land Rover into gear. 'The DCI possesses an uncanny knack of handling an unruly lot like this; if enough pressure is applied. He's terrific at bartering. What they part with may not be of interest, but it's worth a go. I'm sure you're right, they've seen or heard something. What about "the men with the covered faces", must be some local gang that goes around murdering in cold blood for the thrill of it?'

****

With Timothy Stanley now safely back at Greenways Hospital in a secure lock-up unit, Katie had been permitted a visit under the proviso Professor Green remain in the interview room at all times. After returning to the hospital Timothy had refused to comment on where he'd been for the past few weeks, only providing information that he'd been somewhere on the moors.

'Before meeting with Timothy I'd like to take a look at his medication charts?' Katie instructed the professor. 'If I recall from our last visit, you mentioned there would be a medication review.'

Professor Green nodded his agreement. 'Yes of course.'

The paperwork was dutifully handed over for Katie to analyse. She sat for a while reading the medications prescribed, noting nothing out of the ordinary. Timothy was prescribed Chlorpromazine the main oral medication, which kept his condition in check. Katie gleaned there were rare occasions when Timothy became unmanageable, resulting in giving him a shot: a long-acting injectable antipsychotic medication (LAI).

'It would appear he's compliant taking his medications,' Katie remarked out loud.

'Oh, yes Timothy's a good lad.' The professor sounded cheerful.

Katie refrained from comment; Timothy could hardly be deemed as *good*, he had chalked up two previous convictions for grievous bodily harm, spending two years in Dartmoor prison for one brutal assault; his most recent victim an elderly gentleman, resident at a local nursing home. The pensioner suffered two fractured ribs, a dislocated elbow and numerous bruises; Timothy Stanley certainly not a pillar of the community.

After spending half an hour absorbing Timothy's medical file, followed by scanning a more detailed recent assessment on his current mental condition, provided by an independent consultant, Katie informed Professor Green she was ready to meet with Timothy face to face. Escorted into the small interview room by a security guard, Timothy Stanley wore an annoying smile. Emitting a shallow cough, he burped loudly before taking up residence in a high-backed chair and began tapping his knuckles firmly on the table.

'Where were you when you went walkabout from the Psychiatric Hospital a few weeks ago?' Katie began her questioning after the professor had conducted a brief introduction.

'Here and there.' Timothy stared into the depths of her blue eyes.

'On Dartmoor?' she quizzed.

'Yeah on fuckin' Dartmoor, where else am I gonna go, dumb bitch.' Stanley produced a crumpled packet of cigarettes from his jacket pocket, ignoring the "No Smoking" sign on the wall. He struck a match and lit up, exhaling the fumes irritatingly towards the ceiling. Katie expected the professor to draw Timothy's attention to the sign, but this didn't happen. Either he didn't care, or he knew not to antagonise Timothy. Katie surmised the latter.

Keeping her cool Katie continued, used to these types of interviews; although with Timothy she was unsure of his mood swings, and how he would react to certain questions. 'Did you happen to encounter a white Ford Mondeo parked near the Cadover turnoff, on one of your nightly excursions across the moors?'

'Nope.'

'Are you sure about that? My information is; you were spotted late one evening near the vehicle in question.' Katie was trying to call his bluff. There had been no such sighting.

'Then it must have been me,' Timothy uttered, now directing smoke from the cigarette directly into Katie's face, causing her to turn her head. Prone to asthma attacks, she was abhorrent of smoky environments, especially in confined spaces. She was sorely tempted to get up and walk out.

'I'd like to take some DNA samples if you don't mind?' Katie informed Timothy, rummaging in her briefcase to retrieve the necessary equipment. Although not her forte, Katie had assisted her siblings on numerous occasions with DNA sampling and more than capable of this procedure.

'I don't mind at all, we could also have a screw if you're up to it,' Tim mocked.

Katie drew a deep breath, before grabbing a couple of swabs. 'Open your mouth,' she instructed.

Timothy obliged long enough for Katie to get a sample from the back of his throat, then another from his nose. 'We done?' His tone was nonchalant.

'Not quite. I'm interested to know if you've ever met any of these females.' Katie showed him photographs of Rebecca Price, Nicola Fletcher, Allyson Carter, Veronica Peters and Tania Simms. The last photo thrown in as a wild card.

Timothy sat with hands in pockets and legs outstretched, a smirk on his harsh features. 'Yep, I fucked 'em all.'

Professor Green shifted uncomfortably in his seat. 'Just answer the question, Tim.'

'Just did, didn't I. How the hell would I know if I've seen any of them, my eyesight's poor, bloody glasses broke, and no one's bothered to fix 'em.'

'Tim, the psychologist is only doing her job,' Professor Green reminded him. 'Please try and co-operate, there's a sensible lad.'

'And what a pretty psychologist she is.' Tim laughed. 'I bet you like it hard and fast, am I right?'

Katie puffed out her cheeks, believing the interview to be a complete waste of time.

'Fine, I'll behave,' Tim conceded, watching her facial expressions. 'The third photo you showed me; I've buried that bitch between two trees near The Mire. I'll even take you there if you're lucky.'

'So you recognise Allyson Carter?'

'Betcha, screwed Allyson and dumped her body between the trees. Right little tart she was. Now if we're done, I'll be off.'

Timothy rose to his feet, before turning to address his protector. 'See you Prof, probably around teatime for my happy pills, unless you've got a worthier activity you want me to engage in.'

'Well I think that went very well,' Martin Green declared after Timothy had left the room.

Katie feeling the whole interview had been fruitless, thanked the professor for his time, before heading back to her car. She had no idea if Timothy Stanley had ever met Allyson Carter or if he was concocting the whole thing, but with all criminal investigations, there has to be a degree of official follow up.

****

'He's wasting our time,' James concluded, on reviewing the video of Stanley's confession to the murder of Allyson Carter. 'He's no more likely to have killed Allyson than you or me Nick.'

'Agreed, but the protocol is to follow all leads,' Nick replied, switching off the camcorder. 'What harm can be done by taking Stanley on to the moor for a quick poke around.'

James found himself laughing. 'Nick, we're not talking about a small playing field here. Dartmoor covers almost 1000 square kilometres. A quick look around as you succinctly put it could take days, even weeks.'

'Yeah, I know, but what else do we have to go on right now?'

'Not a lot,' James conceded. 'I guess it's worth a try. I'll speak to Parker and see what can be arranged.'

****

The rain teemed incessantly from the heavens as the Forensic Team set off across Dartmoor with Stanley triumphantly leading the way in his long black Macintosh, and army combat boots. He was not classed as "dangerous" when in a small group, so no tight police security was present. As a precaution DCI Parker had agreed to come along in the event things turned nasty, his back pocket housing a set of handcuffs and a police special issue Heckler and Koch automatic snug in a holster. Professor Green reluctantly joined the party on the off-chance Stanley experienced a psychotic episode, requiring urgent medication. He'd grumbled all morning he had more pressing things to do than take a jaunt across the moors.

'These psychotic episodes can be quite extreme,' Green informed the small group checking a phone GPS bearing towards Great Grimpen Mire, where Stanley claimed to have disposed of Allyson Carter. 'If he does get a bit manic, best leave him to me.'

'He needs locking up,' Parker mumbled under his breath, ready to use the Heckler and Koch if necessary.

The group set off from the quarry, along a narrow path heading towards Fox Tor Mire. With extensive local knowledge, they all knew to be mindful of the notorious "feather beds" which could drag the unwary under within seconds. A vast area of the moor was covered in these dangerous bogs, especially on the higher grounds where rainfalls were plentiful, and the granite shelves prevented water runoff.

'This is ridiculous,' James grumbled after they'd been walking for over an hour, painfully aware of the small blisters developing on his heels. 'Timothy Stanley has no bloody idea where he's headed.'

'You having problems keeping up with me, Doc.' Stanley smirked, moving over to where James sat resting on an old tree stump, inspecting his sore feet. 'Trouble with the young today; they don't get enough exercise.'

'Much further?' Nick prodded, equally frustrated, his old walking boots now leaking in moisture from the sodden turf. 'You sure we're heading in the right direction Stan?'

'Not far,' Stanley disclosed. 'See them two robust oak trees ahead, that's where we're going.'

Within twenty minutes, amid a torrential downpour, they reached the trees Stanley had pointed to.

'Where to now?' Nick shook water from his ears.

'You start digging,' Stanley instructed, throwing a small hand shovel in his direction. 'I *would* help you, but my back's playing up, old quarry injury. If you don't mind, I'll sit and watch.'

Nick mouthed obscenities. Picking up the shovel and moving between the two trees he forced the spade into wet slimy mud, bracing against a trunk to prevent slipping, as his boots fought to gain a firm grip.

'Looks like the earth has been disturbed here,' Nick called out to the others after a painstaking ten minutes had passed. 'Perhaps we're on to something after all.'

For almost half an hour the team dug hard, fighting frostbite and a loss of feeling in fingers and toes. The rain continued unabating, as thunder rolled in the distance, accompanied by the occasional unnerving flash of lightning.

Timothy Stanley sat watching, peering out from under a sodden wide brim leather drover's hat and puffing heavily on a cigarette.

'I've found something,' Nick yelled out. 'I think we've got bones.'

With practised precision, the team began to excavate their find, placing bone fragments on a groundsheet. 'These aren't human remains,' Nick scoffed, taking a closer look. 'Canine bones, if I'm not mistaken.'

Tim Stanley's laughter echoed satanically across the moor, intermittent between the claps of thunder. 'You've found old Buster. Never a finer dog could one ask for.'

DCI Parker held firmly on to Nick's arm, afraid he would swing for Stanley, as he tried to lunge forward. 'Come on,' Parker instructed his wrathful colleagues. 'Let's get back to the car park before we have another murder on our hands.'

Tim Stanley kept up an annoying banter as they trudged back to their vehicles. 'Apologies for sending you out into the insipid weather, next time I'll choose a sunny day and show you exactly where Ms Allyson is buried. Don't know about you lot, but I could down a hearty stew for tea, lots of lovely juicy bones.'

****

James picked up the laboratory phone on the second ring. 'Sinclair.'

'James, Margo Betteridge here. I understand your team have been making enquiries into who conducted the autopsy on Tania Simms, the young girl who drowned in a Dartmoor reservoir back in 1998.'

'Yes, we want to put the microscope over events leading up to her death,' James explained, delighted to hear from his old mentor; also a leading scientific expert, part-time government pathologist and head of the science department at the Royal Devon and Exeter Hospital.

'Well, in that case, you'll be pleased to discover I conducted the autopsy along with the late Pearce O'Malley.' Margo laughed.

'Thanks for the call,' James acknowledged, knowing full well as long-time confidant and trusted friend he could rely on Margo to willingly provide him with inside information, outside the usual, accepted medical professional conventions. 'Tell me, Margo, if anything unusual took place in relation to Tania's death you would have unearthed it, wouldn't you?'

'Absolutely,' Margo scorned. 'I conducted a very thorough autopsy to determine Tania's cause of death. Can't say I discovered anything to grab your interest. What's this all about anyway? Tania died a fair number of years ago.'

James explained how they were trying to establish if the recent bodies discovered on the upper escarpment could in any way be connected to the death of Tania Simms, as the new gravesites were in close proximity to the outlying boundaries of the Simms property.

'It does sound a bit suspicious, but I'm leaning towards coincidental,' Margo speculated. 'We both know how isolated the Simms's property is, my immediate assumptions are; a clever burial place, but it certainly doesn't mean your findings are in any way related to Tania's death.'

'What can you tell me about Tania's death?' James asked, phone pressed to his ear, his voice lowering a notch.

'We weren't sure if Tania was thrown into the reservoir or if she fell in. However, what we do know is Tania died from drowning. She was very much alive when she went into the water. Our findings to the Coroner stated it was a tragic accident as the police could find no motive for murder or a suspect. Case closed.'

'And you were satisfied with that outcome?'

'I guess I was,' Margo responded softly. 'We'd all like to discover hardcore evidence to convict someone of murder, but the truth is James, as you'd be well aware, that's not always feasible. We had no concrete evidence to indicate foul play, so death by accidental drowning was all we could record. Plus, we had knowledge that Tania was a poor swimmer.'

'What about bruising on the body or other signs of trauma?' James pressed.

'We found extensive bruising to the main torso and inner thighs. There was evidence of sexual abuse confirming my suspicions; Tania was raped. However, all evidence distinctly indicated the rape occurred sometime before her death, so the two didn't exactly coincide. The physical abuse did not contribute to her death. It was a well-known fact Tania endured beatings from her father, bruises on the body were inevitable.'

'Do you have any idea who might have raped Tania?' James knew his questions were treading on dangerous territory, but he'd known Margo long enough to know he'd be given a direct answer.

'We have our suspicions it might have been her father, but we didn't have proof. Edward Simms refused to co-operate with our investigation, and we didn't have the Court's permission to undertake any DNA testing. It emerged Simms was in cahoots with the late Judge Malcolm Frobisher, and we were warned off trying to implicate Edward in the death of his daughter. Frobisher threatened all sorts of legal action if we tried to take things further. Jim, we both know how ruthless Frobisher could be, God rest his hardened soul. He would stop at nothing to get his own way.'

James grunted. 'That man is probably still orchestrating shifty deals from the grave.'

Margo laughed. 'You could be right on that one James. Now, is there anything else I can help you with before I head off to the Northcott Theatre, for an evening of relaxation?'

'Yes, one more thing; you may be interested to know I managed to take a peek at the final Coroner's report put together shortly after Tania died. It incontestably states no signs of sexual intercourse; assault or otherwise, prior to Tania's death. In fact, it states Tania Simms was a virgin when she died.'

'What nonsense,' Margo said fuming, her voice rising. 'That was not the decree put down in my report. I know what I discovered James, and I know what went into the final report; Tania Simms was brutally attacked sexually, the physical evidence was quite clear. I also remember dropping the report up to the Coroner's office in Bristol personally whilst I was heading to a seminar in Cardiff. My final verdict was *drowning by misadventure*; however, it was vital the findings in the report detailed the sexual abuse.'

'So why would someone purposely go to the lengths of fiddling the Coroner's report?' James quizzed. 'That doesn't make sense. It also questions who got hold of those reports and why, sounds like an inside job to me.'

'Irrefutably someone had something to hide,' Margo declared. 'James, I know my findings were detailed and conclusive; perhaps you read the report wrong. It can happen if you were slightly fatigued. Maybe that's what *you thought* you read.'

'No, I read through it twice to check I'd got the right information,' James remarked. 'I'll get you across a copy from the Home Office first thing in the morning. Someone deliberately changed your report Margo, why on earth would they do that?'

'I'm not going to let this go.' Margo snorted indignantly. 'I don't care how many years have passed since young Tania died. I'm going to demand the correct results be written back into the Coroner's report. We can't bring Tania back, but at least we can ensure our report was accurately documented. That poor child suffered a lot in her lifetime and deserves to have factual evidence pertaining to her last days on earth, recorded in the appropriate fashion.'

****

Three weeks after the horrific death of Veronica Peters the forensic team filed their report releasing the body for burial. Her husband was offered extensive counselling, with the understanding it was necessary to fully co-operate with the police investigation.

Bruce Peters had given an initial police statement shortly after his wife's murder, now an official interview was convened at the main Plymouth police enquiry station in Crown Hill. Attending the interview was Peters' lawyer who had travelled down from London, a young uniformed officer, and Detective Chief Inspector Parker. Permission had been granted for James to view proceedings through a two-way mirror in an adjoining room.

'Mr Peters, was this trip your first visit to Devon?' DCI Parker cross-examined, taking a sip of lukewarm coffee from a thin cardboard cup.

'Yes, things work-wise had been mad for both of us over the last eighteen months. Veronica and I decided to get away from everything in London and spend a few days touring Devon and Cornwall. It was Veronica's idea to travel across Dartmoor; she was a big fan of Arthur Conan Doyle.'

'When you ventured on to Dartmoor you state you had no idea your petrol gauge was near empty.'

'That's correct. It's faulty and I've never had time recently to get the Mondeo properly serviced.'

'When the car finally ran dry, do you recall how long you trekked across the open moor in search of petrol?'

Peters took time to think before answering. 'I'd hazard a guess at just under an hour.'

'The farm you went to, can you recall who gave you the petrol?'

'A man, probably mid-forties, stocky build, thinning blond hair, plenty of freckles. Affable chap. Proper yokel with a strong Devonian accent. I had to train my ear to understand what he was saying.'

'That's interesting, because my officers have spoken to every farmer within a five-mile radius of your car breaking down, and not one person remembers having met you that night.' DCI Parker chortled. 'Would you like to tell us another story, with a little more accuracy?'

'I'm not lying,' Peters spluttered, turning to his lawyer. 'I did see a man; he gave me petrol.'

'Take it steady,' his lawyer instructed, offering physical support. 'You've suffered extreme trauma; I expect some recent events have become blurry. If there are some things you don't remember, that's fine. You don't have to comment.'

DCI Parker shot the lawyer a scathing look, before continuing with his forthright questioning. 'So, you are convinced you met a farmer who supplied you with petrol?'

'Yes.'

'Did you engage in any other form of conversation with this man? Did you exchange pleasantries? Perhaps mention your wife was waiting for you in the car?'

'I don't remember, I don't think we said much. I briefly told him my situation, but don't recall mentioning Veronica, he accepted the can and returned a few minutes later with it half full of juice. I thanked him, paid him ten quid for the trouble and left.'

DCI Parker consulted his summary of notes before continuing. 'Was it easy finding your way back to the car, I mean Dartmoor is a big place, Mr Peters. Even we locals get lost from time to time. I'm impressed you made it back to your car without spending half the night wandering around in circles.'

'I have an excellent sense of direction and a powerful torch, it was a bare twenty minutes down the road anyway,' Peters replied curtly.

'Impeccable I'd say, and very handy.' Parker fixed him with a smug look. 'I don't suppose you happened to notice a Psychiatric Hospital on your travels. A large white, modernist concrete structure, surrounded by high walls.'

'Are these questions really necessary Inspector?' the lawyer interrupted. 'What's it got to do with anything if my client noticed a few blots on the landscape?'

Parker ignored this question. 'Okay then, tell me Bruce; what sort of day did you and your wife have on the drive down from London? Your neighbours back in London tell me you often argued, a trifle embarrassing for the other apartment residents I'd say. A pleasant trip across the moors, was it?'

'We argued from time to time, what couple doesn't?' Peters snapped. 'I expect you fight with your wife at times, Inspector.'

'For the very reason of being inharmonious, I'm not married.' Parker smirked, tapping on the table with his empty cup, before tossing it in a nearby wastepaper basket. 'I tell you what, why don't we confiscate your personal computer Mr Peters and have our analyst look at all the data files. That way we may be able to uncover the truth behind your wife's murder. Big insurance scam was it?'

'I've nothing to hide,' Peters protested, once more staring questioningly at his lawyer.

'Then you won't mind us taking a look at your laptop, will you?' Parker grinned. 'If in the meantime you think of anything else that could be useful to our investigation, please let me know.'

Parker stood up to leave. 'Oh, one other thing, Peters, don't venture too far away. I'm sure there will be more questions we'd want to ask you over the coming weeks. I can recommend a lovely guesthouse nearby; they do a smashing country breakfast.'

Parker waved for the uniform constable to escort Peters and his lawyer back to reception and signalled for James to come in.

'He's lying, has to be,' the DCI declared, lighting a cigarette in defiance of smoking restrictions, and inhaling slowly as he and James replayed the interview tape. 'My people have conducted a thorough search of all farms in the vicinity and no one claims to have seen Peters that night.'

'Perhaps they don't want to get involved,' James piped up. 'It's not uncommon for rural folk to turn the other cheek. Can we at least confirm he did manage to stumble upon petrol?'

'Yes, there was petrol in the can when we discovered the body, but that means nothing,' DCI Parker concluded. 'Who's to say he didn't have petrol in the can already, only pretending to head off in search of some.'

'It's feasible,' James agreed, cleaning the lens of his glasses. 'Doubtless, his prints would be all over the can, but let's also see what his computer files throw up. It won't be a problem for Matt Tyler to retrieve any hidden data. I'll email him.'

Parker nodded, flicking ash onto the floor. 'I still think he's our man. Trouble is, we've got to prove it.'

'Therein might lie your problem. As I've already indicated; if Peters did kill his wife there would have been a certain amount of blood on him and his clothing when the police arrived at the scene. As I recall, there was none.'

'So you're adamant he couldn't have killed his wife,' Parker probed, frustration surfacing.

'It's highly unlikely. However, the question of him paying someone else to do the hit job is emerging as a distinct possibility.'

'Your Bruce Peters was not telling the truth,' Matt declared, placing a USB onto James's desk the following morning. His business records show he was in Devon for a conference back in May 2018, which coincidentally happens to be around the time Allyson Carter went missing. First trip to the county my arse, Peters was lying through his teeth.'

James picked up the phone to relay this message to Parker.

'I'll bring him in for further questioning,' Parker announced. 'I'm not sure why he'd lie about such a thing, but I'm determined to find out.'

Within two hours of receiving this fresh piece of ammunition, a second interview was underway with Bruce Peters, this time at the CID in Exeter. Visibly wrung out, Peters sat poised nervously on the edge of his seat, ready for a second interrogation, this time without his lawyer present.

'I didn't kill my wife,' Peters informed Will Parker bluntly.

'I don't recall asking you that question.' Parker leaned in towards Peters. 'What I want to know is; why did you lie about not having been to Devon before? Slipped your memory crossing the border, did it? Completely missed the robust sign; *Welcome to Devon.* Could be possible; it's only about four feet high and the same wide. Picture of a ship, which could easily go unnoticed. Perhaps you imagined you were still taking a leisurely drive through one of the home counties, unaware of the distance you had travelled.'

'Yeah, must have,' Peters replied complacently. 'I was probably driving with my eyes closed.'

'Don't be smart with me,' Parker retaliated. 'I can already do you for wasting police time. Now, why don't you come clean and tell me why you came to the West Country back in May 2018. Although Devon is a beautiful place, we suffer from harsh winters, often heavy snowfalls forming on the high grounds, not a lot of tourist attractions on offer, personally I prefer Devon during the Summer season.'

'I was here for a three-day conference,' Peters responded.

'What sort of conference?'

'A pharmaceutical conference if you must know. My job as a consultant academic pharmacist includes taking a professional interest in new drugs which are ready for release to the market. I write articles for commercial pharmacy magazines and the media in general. There happened to be a seminar held at the Greenways Institute, chaired by a Professor Green. I was keen to know more about two drugs in particular, which the pharmaceutical companies claim will have high anti-carcinoma potential.'

DCI Parker sat bolt upright. 'Had you met Green before May 2018?' he quizzed.

'No, no reason, we only corresponded through emails. He mentioned drugs for bi-polar syndrome had positive side effects for cancer treatment. I was keen to learn more.'

'So that was the first time you'd set foot in Greenways Hospital, last year for a three-day conference?' Parker pressed for clarification.

'Yes.'

'You sure about that?'

'Yes, I'm sure, what the hell is all this about?'

'You have difficulty remembering facts Mr Peters,' DCI Parker responded. 'If we have any hope in nabbing your wife's killer, you are to cooperate, understand?'

'Okay, so I may have fabricated the truth before, but I can assure you every word I am now telling you is accurate,' Peters declared.

'What opinion did you form of Green?' Parker questioned, leaning back in his chair.

'A bit weird, but he knows his medical stuff.'

'So why did you lie about having been to this part of the country before. What the fuck's going on there?'

Peters gesticulated for Parker to switch off the official recording of the interview. After an ephemeral hesitation, Parker obliged.

'Green sold me a batch of a new highly experimental anti-cancer drug, enough for two months treatment, in violation of certain provisions of government therapeutic drug regulations. I was afraid of being struck off by the General Pharmaceutical Council and losing my lecturing fellowship at the Imperial College if word got out. That's the honest truth, but I swear before God, I never killed my wife.'

Our Heavenly Father who art in Heaven, I buried another body on the moors and beg your forgiveness. I was trying to be worthy, yet I surprised myself by turning evil.

You of all people must understand why I do these things; to seek revenge on the past. I feel it is all coming back to haunt me, and it must stop.

So many people died under their regime, am I to continuously feel partly to blame when I was never there to see such atrocities.

Dear God, help me to move away from these dreadful memories. The only way I know how, is to kill everyone who learns the truth.

Amen

Chapter Five

James walked into the Bovey Arms striding over to the bar, where Tom Markham sat enjoying a quiet drink, taking in the fourth race at Doncaster on the overhead flat screen.

'What do you know about the disappearance of Tania Simms back in 1998?' James quizzed, ignoring formalities, nodding to the bartender for a pint of his usual lager.

'What's it to do with you?' Tom scowled, still fuming from the dearth of official scientific releases on the current murders.

'I was hoping you might fill me in on a few things,' James said, ignoring Tom's icy demeanour.

'Come on,' Tom screamed at the television, throwing his arms up in despair as he realised his horse 'a sure thing, mate', had just finished in last place; his two-hundred-note bet disappeared into thin air in a split second. It took him a few moments to focus back on James and his stubborn queries.

'Eh, the Simms girl? Not much to tell really, the girl went missing near the family home in the Mortenhampsted area, found lifeless three weeks later in a nearby reservoir. As you will already be aware: the official Coroner release was accidental death by misadventure. All up, we probably put out a one-column piece, as there wasn't much to report on.'

'I guess death by drowning is quite common; Tania was a sad statistic, one of many water-related accidents,' James spoke casually.

'Yeah, if that's what you want to believe.' Markham snorted, flicking the betting ticket onto the floor.

'Ah, so you don't believe Tania died from falling into the reservoir,' James pounced. 'Supposing she was murdered, who do you think committed the crime?'

Markham scoffed. 'Tim Stanley of course, he was doing odd jobs for Bert Simms at the time. Makes sense he did the deed. That screwed up, geriatric boffin may have even paid Tim for the privilege.'

'But was there any proof?' James probed.

'Us locals go on gut feelings Sinclair,' Markham stated.

'That will never put someone behind bars. Got any articles written about Tania's death?'

'There may be a few old papers lying around. Not sure why I'm obliged to assist the likes of you, but seeing you've encountered me in a reflective mood, I'll drop them into your office first thing next week. By the way, are the police reopening the Rebecca Price case? If you guys are, I could do with a juicy headline to sell a few papers. How about us trading information?'

'We'll see, it certainly looks like you need something to keep you busy right now,' James jibed. 'Can't have you spending all your days in the pub, you'll end up an alcoholic, all bitter and lonely. Oops too late, you already are bitter and lonely, and most likely broke to boot.'

James downed his beer in one quick movement, before making a hasty exit.

****

It was almost midnight when the three lads set off on their trail bikes towards the Greenways Psychiatric Institute on the edge of the escarpment. It was common knowledge within their peer group there were drugs on the premises and the boys intended to get their hands on a share. A detailed map of the building obtained covertly by one of the trio's brothers, indicated the exact location of the main storeroom where the supply of drugs was kept. A precision break-in plan was accordingly set in motion.

'Remember what I told you,' Jacob Carter warned his mates. 'The security cameras rotate every half hour, so bloody well keep down low and watch the angles. Billy the caretaker knows to let us in through the back door, we'll break into the East Wing once we get inside. Green sleeps upstairs in a separate apartment, he won't even know we're around.'

They parked the trail bikes on the edge of a muddy field, hiding them beneath a low hawthorn bush before lighting up a communal joint. With bravado reinforced by the psychotropic effect of tetrahydrocannabinol the lads ventured across to the outer perimeter of the hospital keeping in the cover of trees, aided in their mission by a low, dense cloud bank and a limpid, waning moon. They couldn't risk being spotted from one of the east-facing windows.

'Fuck you're late,' Billy informed them curtly when he opened the back-service door, allowing the three, now wearing ape masks and baseball caps, instant access into a dark hallway; forced to wait twenty minutes had blackened his mood. 'Now get what you're after and clear off. Green has left strict instructions to pull my automatic on any intruders, watch out, in case I take a pot shot by mistake.'

Billy gave a nasty snarl, pushing past them to return to his bedroom. The lads were unsure if Billy was joking but they weren't about to stick around and find out. The group moved swiftly and silently along the tight corridor in the direction of the East Wing, desperate to snatch the drugs and head home. They easily gained access to the wing before attempting to force the lock on the storeroom door, which eventually shattered, splintering the wood into tiny fragments. The back wall housed glass shelves lined with boxes of drugs, each one neatly labelled. The threesome seized the boxes, along with syringes and needles, placing them into two sturdy duffel bags.

'There's heaps more narcotics stashed up in the main surgery,' Jacob notified the others, throwing one of the duffel bags over his left shoulder. 'We might as well grab that while we're here.'

'Too dangerous,' Mick advised. 'Let's go, this place gives me the creeps.'

'Fuck no, you moron. We've come this bloody far, it's all or nothing,' Jacob said, standing his ground. 'Bailout now, Mick Parsons and I'll see your feet never touch the ground again.'

Reluctantly, the others followed Jacob to the main surgery, quickly locating the three plastic packets of heroin before attempting their escape. They'd almost made it to the main foyer when Jacob tripped and fell heavily over a cumbersome obstruction blocking the corridor. 'Shit, what the blazes was that?' he proclaimed. Rubbing his knee and sitting up he pointed his torch ahead, the powerful shaft of light illuminating a body lying slumped, face-up in a pool of dark red blood. Two eyes staring unseeingly at the ceiling.

'Fuck, he's dead, half his brain's missing.' Jacob gulped as the contents of his stomach welled in the back of his throat. 'Hell, what's going on, let's scarper. Looks like Billy carried out his threat.'

Flinging open the large glass front door, the trio bolted across the lawns and into the field beyond, only slackening pace when they reached the hawthorn bush to retrieve their bikes.

'We've got to get our arses off the moors as quickly as possible,' Jacob yelled to his friends, hopping on his machine and kicking the engine into life. 'Not a word to anyone about this, right? Something's gone down here tonight and they're not putting this shit on me.'

****

'Not a pretty sight,' James declared, stepping over a broken hall table, shattered glass and scattered magazines to get to the body of Timothy Stanley, under guard at a prudent distance by a uniform police sergeant. 'Shot himself in the head you might say? Certainly looks like it on first appearances.'

It was a little after two in the morning when James was roused from a deep sleep by a call from a distressed sounding Professor Green advising of the shooting. He claimed not to have heard gunfire, being alerted by a call from the security firm advising the front door was registering on the back to base monitors. He stumbled on the body on his way to secure the door, which was banging loudly in the wind.

'Perhaps Tim Stanley knew the past was catching up with him,' Nick Shelby surmised, studying the blood splatters on the wall. 'Not uncommon for someone to top themselves under those circumstances. But I'm not convinced it was self-inflicted... can't find a gun.'

'Did you contact Ballistics?' James moved around the body to take photos from various angles.

Nick nodded. 'Sure did, they're sending over Roger Tudor, I'm guessing he'll be here within the next half hour. He wasn't too ecstatic being dragged out of bed but promised he'd get here as soon as possible.'

When Tudor eventually arrived, he barged in through the main door like an angry rhino. Built like a rugby prop and known widely throughout law enforcement as "The Scarlet Pimpernel" due to a thick shock of red hair, permanently flushed complexion and heavily freckled countenance, he couldn't stand formalities or waffle, preferring to get straight in, do the job and go home. His demeanour came with an air of aloofness, he always wore a dark grey, tight-fitting suit as if on the way to a formal function, not attending the scene of a crime. With a wealth of "on the job" practical experience gained from many years with the Yard and the Met, Tudor now bartered his successful ballistic consulting services around European law enforcement organisations and anyone willing to shell out big dollars for his expertise.

'Take a look at this, fellas,' Tudor instructed, not bothering to greet his colleagues, instead holding up the deceased's head, as if it were a large coconut. 'From the angle, where the bullet exited the back of the head and the position of the body, there's no way this man shot himself. Someone else was holding the gun, that we can be certain of. I don't believe you have the firearm, that confirms it.'

Nick and James bent down to take a look at Tudor's explanation. 'Yep, that makes sense,' Nick agreed begrudgingly. 'Unless he was a contortionist there's no way Tim could have shot himself from the angle of the exit wound. Surprised we didn't pick up on that when we first arrived.'

Both men cast each other an embarrassed glance.

'Almost certainly the weapon was a small calibre handgun held at close range, judging by the exit and entrance characteristics of the round. Definitely 9 mm parabellum,' continued Tudor, as he scrutinised the single spent cartridge with a jewellers' loupe, enjoying the opportunity to display his technical savvy. 'From the characteristics of the firing pin indentation on the base of the cartridge, I reckon either a Browning High Power; or most likely the French MAB PA-15. The Browning's very easy to get hold of, getting a bit long in the tooth now, a perennial favourite of The Provisional IRA. The PA, very much a modern gun. Scarcer of course and a more elegant piece with a nice feel in the hand, but it's in the arsenal of some police forces. I've seen them offered around on the black market and internet. Very desirable due to its 15-round magazine; a formidable weapon. I'll put my money on the PA.'

Nick bit his tongue; afraid he would say something he might later regret. There was no doubt Tudor knew his stuff, but he was a complete arse hole when it came to building professional rapport.

'I'll send through my report by the weekend,' Tudor clarified, closing his worn leather case. 'Ah, here comes DCI Parker, I hope he hasn't parked his hack anywhere near my new Electric Blue Aston Vanquish; any scratches or dents and the police department will know about it. Cheerio chaps, if you find any stray slugs send them over to me; I don't want you mucking up the evidence. It wouldn't be the first time I've had to keep a tight rein on things.'

DCI Parker nodded curtly to Tudor before joining the others still examining the body. 'Couldn't you get anyone other than Tudor from Ballistics?' Parker grumbled, coming to stand next to James. 'That man is sheer hell to deal with. What was wrong with one of our own people?'

'Unfortunately, he was the only person to answer his phone,' James explained. 'Despite his arrogance, Tudor happens to be one of the best in the business. You just have to work around his obtuse personality.'

'Damn man's a menace,' Parker confided. 'Well, I'll leave you with the deceased while I go upstairs and interrogate Green; it'll be interesting to see what he's got to say for himself. I take it Tudor will be back in the morning to finish off his side of things, lazy shit spends as little time working unsociable hours as he can. I bet he was here all of five minutes.'

James grinned. 'He's happy with his initial deductions and will probably send a junior around in the morning to scrape together the rest. Tudor has learnt his way around the system, that's for sure.'

Parker walked off muttering under his breath, heading in the direction of Green's office.

'Professor Green are you aware of a gun being kept on the premises?' the DCI asked, entering the study without bothering to knock. Parker was not in the mood to exchange pleasantries, having been woken during a peaceful slumber.

His eyes were heavy with sleep, the back of his throat dry and his persistent backache doing nothing to enhance his darkening mood. 'Do any of your patients keep firearms?'

'This is a psychiatric clinic,' Green answered, nonchalantly moving papers to one side. 'I imagine many inmates mess around with guns. May I also remind you Devon is a rural setting; hunting rifles are not uncommon around these parts for shooting rabbits and foxes and recreational, of course.'

'You're not being helpful Professor Green.' Parker sighed, frustration obvious, as he sank into an old leather recliner. 'What about security, did you ever consider the safety of other patients if one or two inmates decided to keep firearms.'

'I am not law enforcement,' Green countered smoothly. 'If someone chooses to carry guns for self-protection, licensed or not, that's their business.'

'Okay, let's start again,' Parker continued, tossing a rolled-up piece of paper in the bin with an accurate aim. 'Can you think of any patient who might own a firearm?'

Professor Green drummed on the desk with the ends of his fingers. 'Billy Fowler would be my obvious choice. Had a long stint in the Royal Marines stationed in the Far East before being honourably discharged. He could quite happily blow someone's head off if they crossed him, that's why I gave him a part-time role as my caretaker, he's superior to any guard dog.'

'He sounds charming. Does he own a handgun?'

'Don't know. I assume he does from the way he talks of self-preservation.'

'What exactly are you treating Fowler for?'

'Post-Traumatic Stress Disorder, I've been trialling a new drug which has been working like a charm. Billy is coming on in leaps and bounds, he is turning into a pleasant chap with a charming personality.'

'Not if Fowler is the one who dispatched Tim Stanley,' Parker remarked coldly. 'Where might we find this Fowler fella?'

'He could be in his room or he might be out skinning rabbits, how the hell would I know,' Green snapped. 'Just clean up this mess as quickly as you can, I've got a business to run.'

'Why do you think someone would shoot Stanley?' Parker quizzed, expanding back muscles to ease the dull ache. He was tempted to ask Green for a few effective painkillers but dismissed the idea almost immediately.

'Your guess is as precise as mine; in my opinion, Billy Fowler was almost cured so I very much doubt he would let loose with a firearm. His neurotic episodes have been few and far between over the past few months. He'd served his jail sentence for GBH and was well and truly on the mend.'

'Bollocks, the man sounds dangerous, with every possibility of shooting anyone who gets in his way,' Parker retaliated. 'With a history like Fowler's, I doubt he'd ever be cured. One tiny relapse and bam, he'd get great pleasure out of blowing someone's brains out.'

'That's bullshit hypothesising,' Green snapped, standing up to tower over Parker. 'I know my patients better than anyone, when will you stop believing everyone with a psychological issue is dangerous?'

'The day you stop thinking you can cure every mental health patient in the county,' Parker scoffed. 'One last question: For such a high profile centre; I'm surprised most of your security cameras are fakes. I was dismayed to hear you only have active CCTV in the main corridors.'

'I believe in confidentiality, above all else,' Green retorted, an air of superiority to his voice. 'No patient would feel comfortable if they were being watched all the time.'

'Even though you keep an abundance of drugs on the premises, you don't consider security a necessity?'

'Not really, to any outsider wanting to break in they will automatically believe these cameras are recording their every move. Clever decoy if you ask me.'

'Not so clever if it allows someone to break in and steal thousands of pounds worth of narcotics,' Parker retaliated.

'Not all the packaged drugs are what they appear to be.' Green chortled. 'Most kept in the storeroom are peppermint sweets. I think you'll find whoever broke in for a fast heroin fix will be sorely disappointed to discover they've only managed to achieve fresher breath. I keep the "real" drugs safely stored, where only I know the combination lock. Now if that's all Detective Chief Inspector I must press on. You can see yourself out.'

****

James seethed with anger as he digested the front-page headline and story in the Star:

Bullet Sees the Demise of Timothy Stanley

According to an official police press release yesterday and one from the scientific team at Moorland Forensics, one

Timothy Stanley was most likely behind the recent spate of murders on Dartmoor, which saw young women savagely killed in a fit of rage. How could one man be culpable of so many homicides and manage to keep evading the long arm of the law for so long? Perhaps finally the Dartmoor community can turn their lights off at night and rest easy in their beds, knowing the perpetrator is dead. A round of applause for forensics and the CID; it's only taken them several years to catch their man. A job well done!

****

'Satisfied?' James questioned, slamming the newspaper under Markham's nose. 'Can't leave things alone, can you? No one is claiming Stanley to be responsible for any recent murders. To make a fast buck you always have to print blatant lies.'

'Yep, so true,' Markham confessed, throwing his hands up, as he leaned back in his chair, feet firmly planted on his desk. 'The thing is James my boy, Stanley was a monster. If he didn't commit these murders, he was bound to commit others. I think someone's done you a favour blowing his brains out. At least you don't have to try for a conviction – I rest my case.'

'You have an answer for everything, don't you?' James mocked.

'I suppose I do,' Markham chided. 'Here's the thing; I've now saved you and your little team a lot of hard work and money, I deserve to be congratulated.'

'How do you figure that one out?' James asked, blonde eyebrows raised.

'Well, even if I am wrong with my assumption on Timothy being a murderer, you can now write up your forensic report claiming Stanley did the deed and no one will be any the wiser. You'll no longer have to conduct your complex little tests, which I know can be expensive. You can put the spare cash towards a well-deserved holiday. Everyone will think you've detained the perpetrator and we can all get on with our lives, simple.'

'Interesting concept but a lousy one, especially if Stanley wasn't guilty of these crimes,' James reminded him. 'The murderer could still be out there, capable of striking again at any given time.'

Markham gave James a firm pat on the back. 'That's a risk you should be willing to take. Besides, people believe everything I print in the Star. Give me a final scoop and we can see an end to this sorry mess.'

'Not bloody likely.'

Markham grinned. 'If you change your mind, you know where to find me. By the way that vintage red you traded for me the other day was a ripper. I enjoy doing business with your little organisation Sinclair, very pleasing on the palette.'

James shot Markham a scathing look, before firing another question at him. 'How about you telling me, who you think killed Tim Stanley? You and I both know you have close connections with local criminal organisations, not to mention shady characters in general.'

'I have my suspicions, but a good journalist never reveals his sources.' Markham chortled.

'Oh, well that's okay then because you're not a good journalist,' James retorted, walking out the door, slamming it firmly behind him.

****

'We have to find Billy Fowler without delay to test for gunshot residue,' Parker announced to the small group gathered around the whiteboard in the Moorlands laboratory. 'It's highly likely he's our man. The Prof swears he has expert military capability in firearms.'

'Is that all? You'll bloody well want a lot more evidence than residues to make a conviction,' Nick remarked.

'I know, I know. But there are no other candidates at this stage, he's the best suspect. It had to be someone from the Institute. CCTV in the main corridor has ruled out the kids who broke in and lifted the drugs; looks like they were spooked by Stanley's corpse and panicked; at least we're pretty sure they were kids.'

'How's that?'

'They were spotted on trail bikes leaving the vicinity in a mad hurry after they dumped gorilla masks,' the DCI added, smiling, 'and we've got a sound handle on who they are. My lads are undertaking interrogations as we speak.'

'GSR particles can easily transfer from the victim so we can't rely solely on that as evidence,' Nick informed Parker. 'Fowler can concoct the story he went to Timothy's aid and that's how any residues were transferred.'

'I'll get you all the proof you want,' Tudor piped up, turning to Nick, his tone overtly condescending. 'It's my opinion you guys should concentrate on finding the automatic, and Fowler of course. We found the bullet lodged in a leather sofa near Tim's body. I can match the rifling marks on it to the barrel of the pistol, no problems at all.'

'However,' Tudor continued, waving his arms about, 'strong chance we'll get no powder evidence at all. From what you say this Fowler is ex-Marines. My guess is he's already ditched the clothing and showered and disposed of the gun as well.'

'Sure, but it would be handy corroborative evidence,' Nick broke in for the second time, trying to regain some technical credibility and lend support to the DCI.

'I agree SEM with energy dispersive x-ray analysis is 100% fool proof in conjunction with sodium rhodizonate testing. Your Bristol contractors I suppose might be up to the task… on second thoughts, I'd let Moorlands handle it. Jim's pretty skilled on residues with that SEM I spotted in the instrument room. Got all the relevant probe and x-ray attachments.' This was a rare compliment coming from Tudor.

DCI Parker pulled a face, the usual reaction to being told how to do his job. Tudor had an annoying habit of ordering people about, which never went down with the rank and file in police forces.

'I'll bring him in once we get a trace on him.' DCI Parker reacted nonchalantly. 'Green swears blind he has no idea where Billy Fowler is hiding, it could be weeks, even months trying to locate him. For all we know, he may have headed out of the county.'

'Not according to Green,' Katie exclaimed, handing over an email she'd just printed off. 'This report indicates Billy has limited knowledge beyond a two-mile radius from Greenways. His profile certainly indicates he has more than likely gone to ground somewhere local in the immediate short term.'

'What rot,' Tudor snapped impatiently. 'The man's served in Pakistan covertly on special ops for Christ's sake. If he's capable of that he's capable of travelling about the country, probably undetected with a strong knowledge of survival to boot. My guess, he's decamped into Europe and probably winging his way back to the sub-continent on a false passport.'

'Not necessarily.' Katie stood her ground. 'For the past five years, Billy Fowler has been living in and around Princetown. I don't think he'd stray too far until his confidence builds; it's moving away from his comfort zone. His profile states he wouldn't do that.'

Tudor muttered something inaudible under his breath, before retrieving his car keys. 'I'll leave you lot to draw conclusions on Billy's whereabouts, I'm due in Paris tomorrow for a briefing with geeks from the French Security Agencies.'

****

'Poor bastard never really stood a chance in life,' Fiona commented, dissecting the small part of Stanley's brain, which was still intact. 'See here, classic evidence of foetal alcohol syndrome. No wonder he had learning difficulties.'

She stood aside motioning James in to take a closer look at the cortex. 'Looks like Stanley would have died within six months anyway. This lesion indicates a small brain tumour, which would grow quite quickly. Best to test to see if it was malignant or not. The Coroner will want a full report on this one.'

'I bet the toxicology results will prove interesting,' James added, watching his sister placing the neural structure on the scales. 'My guess is Green would have been pumping him with all sorts of experimental drugs and I'll be intrigued to know what compounds they were.'

'Yep, that man is very shrewd. I am confident Stanley had no knowledge of the harm these drugs could do to him.'

'While you're sending off your requests can you also get the lab to dig out the old DNA patterns and results on the database conducted on the Tania Simms case?' James instructed his sister. 'I have my suspicions Tim Stanley could be our man, having killed Tania during one of his psychotic episodes. It would be great to put a closure to one case if we can.'

'I'll do my best,' Fiona promised. 'It all hinges on who the leading pathologist is. Some get tetchy if they feel it encroaches on their territory, never wanting to part with inside information without some accolade being passed their way.'

James grimaced. 'You'd think they'd be keen to solve the crime instead of putting up barriers.'

Fiona smiled at her brother's annoyance. 'It depends if it stops them climbing that hierarchy ladder. Forensics is a competitive game James, not everyone is as dedicated as we are, some are out for the bigger prize.'

'If Timothy Stanley did kill Tania Simms, they are welcome to take the credit,' James continued smoothly. 'I'd like to tie up a few loose ends, but I don't crave a damn medal in the process.'

****

'I've been working up a summary analysis of all four murders. Stanley, Price, Fletcher and Peters,' a confident Katie pronounced, fronting up for the usual Friday morning meeting in Nick Shelby's headquarters. 'Here are my findings, which might help to piece a few things together:

Tim Stanley's murder was not pre-meditated but more along the lines of self-defence. The killer we already suspect to be Billy Fowler, which matches my profile. Tim posed no threat to the killer, as he had no weapon. Upon encountering Tim, our killer acted through feelings of intense fear, helplessness, and panic. They felt threatened, afraid for their safety. Our killer was overly alert or wound up, most likely irritable with lack of concentration, easily startled and constantly on the lookout for signs of danger. I'd say they had a diagnosis of depression, anxiety, perhaps overuse of alcohol and drugs.

Reading Green's file on Fowler everything adds up, although Green in fact is pushing for justifiable homicide, claiming the killer did not intend to commit a violent act.'

'Crap.' Parker snorted. 'Billy Fowler knew what he was doing when he pulled the fucking trigger.'

'Don't panic, we're getting way ahead of ourselves seeing that Billy is still at large; and regardless, it wouldn't stand up in court,' James reassured the irate police officer. 'It's not beyond reasonable doubt. Any jury will have to dismiss it immediately.'

Katie waited a few moments before continuing. 'In connection to the murders of Veronica Peters, Rebecca Price and Nicola Fletcher I'm inclined to believe we may be seeking one killer.'

A few murmurs broke out in the small group as Katie raised a hand for silence. 'I can't be certain, but so far I'm coming up with a similar profile which has possible links. The profile on this person shows they could be a sociopath, someone with superficial charm and intellect. They strike me as unreliable, insincere, with a lack of remorse and shame. This serial killer is act-focused meaning the killing is about the act itself, the desire for that person to be extinct. Bizarre as it may sound; our killer did not get enjoyment from the torture and death of their victims; these killings were carefully planned. At a rough estimate, I envisage the killer to be mature in age. They show compassion but at the same time suffer from ASPD – an antisocial personality disorder.'

Convinced she had now grabbed the group's attention; Katie carefully chose her next words:

'All three murders display similarities to mass executions carried out in recent conflicts, particularly the Second World War where millions of Jews and patriots were tortured and murdered in pogroms and extermination programs by Stalin and Hitler... not to mention the more topical ethnic cleansing episodes of late in the Balkans of course. There could be a possible link between our murderer and pre/post-war Europe.'

Katie flicked off the overhead projector waiting for responses.

'So you think the person we are chasing, might have a Continental background, what about Pol Pot, you know the Khymer Rouge and you've got the Japanese Army atrocities in China and S.E. Asia; Tojo and his generals like Nakajima were clinical butchers,' Matt remarked. 'And lastly, you've got Chairman Mao? He tops the list for extermination by a country mile.'

A clever question, mused Katie, forced to quickly recheck her analysis. *Hell, Matt is more widely read than I assumed. Must be all the History Channel shows he watches.*

'No. I don't see any evidence of Eastern thinking or ideology in the way this mind thinks and acts.' Katie smiled. 'Indications are strong; my gut feeling says Eastern Europe.'

There was blood everywhere. He lay staring up at the ceiling, those eyes fixed on a cold emptiness. Did he see the bullet as it came straight for him or was his back turned in twisted distortion? The only one who knows is the one who fired the bullet, watching as he seized his last breath.

Dear Father, forgive them for their sins. I pray one day you will fix the wrongs and we can all live in harmony.

Amen

Chapter Six

'We've just received the preliminary DNA comparisons back from Bristol,' Nick announced, entering the Moorlands office first thing Monday morning, dashing inside to escape the cold, and a flurry of snow.

'That was quick,' Fiona responded.

'I put a priority on it, and it helped having plenty of fresh, uncontaminated Stanley DNA material. I just asked for a quick electrophoresis chromatogram and comparison with the old DNA patterns on file,' Shelby continued, flicking open a small notebook. 'They're running further confirmation tests mind you, but almost certainly Tania Simms was raped and murdered by Timothy Stanley. However, there is no match to Tim Stanley's genetic material with any of the small amounts of unknown DNA recovered from the Veronica Peters murder scene.'

'Okay, so we have a probable result on the Simms case, which I can pass on to Margo, however, we still don't know who attacked Veronica Peters or why,' James remarked, inspecting the water level in the coffee machine. 'Do we have any new leads to work off?'

'Our DCI wants another go at Green,' Katie advised. 'He believes Green may have been supplying Veronica Peters with prohibited drugs and covering up the evidence.'

'Parker would be best to wait until the full toxicology tests on Veronica Peters come back,' James warned. 'We don't want Green getting suspicious too soon. If he has been dishing out illegal pills, he'll be accomplished at covering his tracks. It's worthwhile Parker getting a handle on Green's internal operations before he tries to throw the book at him.'

'Try telling that to Parker.' Nick grunted. 'He's a splendid detective, but at times he reacts without really thinking.'

'Something Mick Rose would never have done,' Katie reminisced, missing the Detective who had been a firm friend to the Moorland team. She was still getting over his sudden passing.

'What drugs specifically would you be referring to?' Fiona asked, joining the conversation from the far end of the room.

'We believe Green was providing Veronica Peters with a drug he understood could cure a rare muscle tissue cancer, along with a variety of pain killers,' James informed his sibling. 'Once we know what those compounds are, we can try and get our hand on them to take a closer look at the adverse side-effects. They may have no bearing at all on Veronica's murder, let's analyse all evidence before ruling it out.'

'It won't be easy pinning the blame on Green,' Fiona informed her colleagues. 'Even if substances are found in Veronica's bloodstream, Green can deny all knowledge.'

****

James cursed under his breath spotting DI Wetherill striding towards him along the brightly lit corridor. Meaning to collect an oil painting left for him in Mick Rose's will, James had hoped his brief visit to the administration at Exeter Police, postponed on several occasions, would go without a hitch.

'Shame about DCI Rose, the department must have been working him too hard.' Wetherill chuckled, slapping James hard on the back as they drew level with each other. 'You know, the trouble is; the dear old chap was a bit too conscientious for my liking. He wasn't a bad cop, but his motivation was all wrong. I'm hoping his replacement Detective Parker will have more substance. Rose won't really be a great loss as far as I'm concerned. He lacked the sterner qualities to go after real criminals – perhaps weak sums him up.'

James thrust his hands deep in his trouser pockets for fear he would lash out at the senior police officer. 'Really Wetherill; you'd be advised to take a clear hard look at yourself in the mirror,' James retaliated, his tone chilled. 'One day you might be surprised at what you see staring back at you. Life in the Scrubs can be damn lonely.'

'Are you threatening me, Sinclair?' Wetherill shot back.

James held up his hands in mock horror. 'Me? Actually yes, if I can ever pin anything on you forensically I will. Tread carefully, Wetherill. The slightest fingerprint, a strand of hair, or tissue sample detected with your name on it, will go under the microscope. If you've been involved in anything underhand, I'll get you for it and that's a promise.'

'I applaud the challenge,' Wetherill sneered, giving James a firm shove. 'Let the fun begin Sinclair but I'm also warning you; forensic evidence gets contaminated if it falls into the wrong hands, not to mention continuity, what a shame if that were to happen. I hope your little lab has tight security, it's well known you have some pretty expensive equipment in that set up of yours, it would be dreadful if bad things were to happen: a few breakages, items stolen.'

James shot the departing Wetherill a murderous look. 'I'm not intimidated by you Wetherill,' he shouted, oblivious to those in earshot. 'I'm too smart for a low life scumbag, who spends life rummaging in the gutter. It's only a matter of time before you get caught. If I were you, I'd keep checking over my back.'

Smarting from the exchange and the brief adrenalin surge James marched off towards Rose's old office to look for the painting. He knew only too well the DI was dangerous and capable of carrying out his threats.

****

'Billy Fowler has been spotted on the moors,' DCI Parker announced excitedly, bursting into the Moorland office just after noon. 'Reports are coming in he's been seen sheltering in an old hut near Hound's Tor. We believe he's armed and dangerous, so I've arranged for a tactical squad team to head up there. Fancy tagging along for the ride James?'

'For sure, so long as you can guarantee I won't get my head blown off.'

Parker laughed. 'No such guarantee exists my friend, not in this game. That's a risk you're going to have to take.'

James, often one for adventure, decided to take the detective up on his offer. As part of the investigation team, he didn't want to miss out on the fun bits.

'Keep your scone down,' Parker stressed, driving into a small car park some distance from the remote Tor, noting the team of police officers already stationed in front of a makeshift barrier. 'Stay behind the police vehicles and don't move.'

James followed the concise instructions, his heart rate rising. Enthralled, he watched Parker join his men; advance cautiously, spaced well apart to 50 metres from the bottom of the rock formation. They wore the ubiquitous, special protective Kevlar composite vests and carried SAS issue Heckler and Koch MP5 sub-machine guns. For added insurance, a sharpshooter with an L96 military sniper rifle and attendant spotter with binoculars lay concealed under a small bush 200 metres in the rear.

'He's hiding behind the largest monolith stack,' one of the officers relayed to Parker. 'You can just spot his blue jacket waving in the breeze now and again from behind the bigger rock.'

'Give yourself up Billy,' shouted Parker, cupping his hands for maximum effect. 'You can't hide in the rocks forever. 'Throw the gun out and move to where we can see you, with hands up.'

Fowler reacted defiantly with two shots, the sharp crack resounding through the boulders; one bullet ricocheted off the granite missing an officer's cap by centimetres. He stepped back startled, instinctively letting off a short burst from his MP5.

'Throw it in, Billy. Killing more people won't help your cause,' the DCI yelled again, dropping onto one knee and frantically waving his team to take cover.

Another bullet flew through the air, this time striking a young constable in the chest. The hit saw him fall to the ground, cursing in pain from the concussive effect of a powerful 9 mm parabellum round against his vest.

'Man down,' Parker screamed. 'All officers are to move towards the rock if you see Billy, shoot. Keep it low around the knees. I want him brought in alive.'

The armed squad responded immediately, their military-style "cover and support" training kicked in, heading across the springy turf to assault the Tor. James watched as the injured officer was assisted by a fellow squad member to a waiting patrol car. His injuries were superficial, no real damage, but he was undeniably in a state of shock from the impact.

Huddled awkwardly behind Parker's Skoda James's toes began to cramp. He tried to keep them moving but eventually stood up to ease the stabbing pain. It was then he felt the cold metal of a gun muzzle pressed hard against the back of his head. 'Keep moving,' Billy instructed. 'One wrong step and I'll blow your brains out.'

Instinctively James followed the straightforward instructions, urging one foot in front of the other, Billy forcing him with a shotgun jammed in his kidneys across open moorland away from the Tor. He had no idea if anyone witnessed these movements, or if they were totally oblivious to the fact Billy Fowler was no longer where they understood him to be. James wanted to call out but knew this move would be very foolish. Billy most assuredly meant business, any false move and he would be history.

With a bitter chill hovering in the air, both men pressed on, walking further and further away from Hound's Tor toward the East, always a desperate Fowler, shotgun slung over shoulder urging his captive forward with menacing prods from his pistol.

James had no idea how long they'd been walking; he didn't dare glance down at his watch, but his legs were starting to ache in the calf muscles. With the sun slowly sinking in a crimson red Western sky, and the temperature rapidly dropping towards zero, his mind struggled to work out where they were headed. He guesstimated from their pace and elapsed time they might be heading cross-country towards Ivybridge but couldn't be certain; anxiously he scanned the early evening skies tracking the Pole Star to fix North. Surely a search party would already be out hoping to pick up his trail; why hadn't they seen or heard helicopters or even police dogs. Yet, that in itself would not be an easy task in the fading light. DCI Parker, knowing Billy was heavily armed and combative, wouldn't be too keen to put his men in harm's way. Most probably they had returned to headquarters to put together a master plan, although how long that might take was anyone's guess.

'Why don't you turn yourself in?' James ventured at last when Billy allowed them to stop and rest. 'If you shot Timothy Stanley in self-defence the law will take that into consideration.'

'Shut the fuck up,' Billy barked, lighting up a cigarette. 'You don't know nothing.'

'I'm a trustworthy listener. Why don't you tell me what really happened that night?' James pressed, a dry sensation welling in his throat; he craved water.

'What's it to do with you, no one's gonna take me seriously,' Fowler snapped, waving his military specification shotgun in the air. 'No one's fuckin gonna listen to what I've got to say, so shut the fuck up.'

'Try me. You're an intelligent man Billy. Twelve years in Special Services making it to Lance Corporal is quite an achievement,' James commended him. 'Only a fool is going to clam up and you're no fool.'

'Who the hell are you anyway? Don't fucking well try that good cop bad cop routine with me.'

'I'm not police, I'm a forensic expert, with no desire to join the police force,' James enlightened him. 'You fought for Queen and Country, for your comrades; far worthier than anything I have ever done.'

'That's what landed me here in the first place.' Billy grunted, digesting the news, his cold breath mingling with the cigarette smoke. 'We were forced to kill innocent women and children, and all for what? To end up screwed in the head with no real purpose in life.'

'Come on Billy. Who fed you that bullshit? Some politically correct, leftist activist cretin hoping to malign our service people in the media and render our defence forces ineffectual. That's the way they work. That's my guess. You're smarter than that. Innocent people are always collateral victims in any conflict. Has been for 10,000 years. It goes with the territory of a professional soldier.'

'Yeah right.' Billy maintained the fury but for the first time in over ten years, a tiny speck of doubt had just invaded his mental processes.

An uneasy silence reigned in the dank half-light, as James commandeered another opportunity. 'That automatic of yours, handsome piece. French isn't it?'

'How do you know, you a firearms expert or something?' Billy replied warily, slowly moving his left hand to cover the handgun jammed in his belt. 'Been with me for ten years... a PA-15.'

'You got it from a dead terrorist?' This was a guess on James's behalf.

'Fuck off. Nice and legit this one. Won it in a poker game from a Norwegian small arms weapons specialist in Chittagong.'

Before James could cobble together a reply, Fowler waved the gun at James's head forcing him to his feet to resume their relentless march across the darkened landscape.

'I didn't mean any of it to happen, the bastard set me up,' Fowler remarked, as they waded through a small stream, knee-deep in icy cold water.

'Who set you up?' James keeping his eyes firmly on the path ahead, aware any wrong move could spook Billy to shoot.

'Green of course. He told me he was scared of people breaking in, he ordered me to keep my gun at the ready. As sure as eggs; he arranged for Timothy Stanley to be wandering about the Institute that night, knowing I'd be on the lookout for intruders. It was all rigged. I've done enough killing in my past, I never meant to kill anyone that night. Green had it all planned, he wanted Stanley out of the way and got me to do his dirty work.'

'Supply a statement to the police,' James told him. 'It's not too late.'

'Trying to prove it will not be easy,' Fowler replied earnestly. 'Green wanted to get rid of Stanley and I was the stupid fool who was conned into pulling the trigger, no one will believe a word I say with my psychiatric history. Green's a sly bastard, I'll give him that.'

'Forensics can help, that's my job. I can help you clear your name.'

'Nope, it's too late for that,' Fowler snapped, producing a hip flask from his back pocket and taking a quick swig. 'Keep walking God damn it. We must get to the hut before the rain sets in. Count yourself lucky, I've not put one in your head already. One more death on my hands won't make the slightest bit of difference. Keep moving for Christ sake.'

****

'Any news?' Matt sat, arms folded on the side of Katie's desk, noticing dark circles around her eyes and a puffy complexion.

'Two days and nothing. What in hell's name are the police doing?' answered Katie, almost choking on her words. 'Why have they not located them by now?'

'The trouble is; Fowler knows Dartmoor well,' Matt commented, trying to choose his reply carefully. 'I was scrutinising his service file requisitioned by Will Parker. He would be very familiar with the terrain and potential hiding places; he spent some time here in training exercises for special ops teams.'

'Have they had any luck with James's mobile?' Katie pressed. 'I've tried a hundred times, without any response.'

'Yep, I can confirm it's completely lifeless. We think the battery has been removed; the tech boys can't get a position fix. Although it's probably still within range. Your brother's smart, there's every chance he's done that deliberately to save the battery, waiting for an opportune chance to get in contact and tell us his whereabouts. He would also know that any false move and Billy could turn aggressive. James is smart enough to play it safe, only phoning us if he isn't in any immediate danger.'

Katie's face lit up. 'So, James could contact us at any time, he's merely waiting for an opportune moment?'

'Maybe, but don't get your hopes up too much; my guess is Fowler has long since destroyed the phone. It'll be a battle of wits, both men are extremely resourceful.'

'Matt, any chance of a favour?' Katie's voice was beginning to crack.

'Sure Katie, anything.'

'I don't like going home at night by myself. Will you move in with me, just until they find him?'

'Of course, I will.'

'This whole thing's a nightmare, Matt, we don't even know if he's alive or dead.' Katie was unable to stop the tears that started to flow unimpeded in glistening rivulets down her cheeks. The past few days had been hell, with no positive end in sight.

Matt brought Katie in close to his chest, letting her cry against his broad shoulders. 'It's okay,' he reassured her. 'James is a fighter. He will do everything in his power to stay alive.'

'Yes, but some things will be out of his control. Billy has a gun; we can't pass on that. He's already shot one man, why would he spare another?'

****

Three days after the incident at Hounds Tor, with Billy Fowler still at large and pressure building on the police, DCI Parker summoned Martin Green to an urgent meeting at the combined search HQ in Mortenhampsted.

The visibly annoyed professor, frustrated with the constant disruptions in his normally meticulously planned daily routine, defiantly stood his ground, offering little in the way of meaningful co-operation. He kept stating he knew very little about the private lives of his patients as they were free to come and go as they pleased, not routinely requiring to be under lock and key. He also kept denying any knowledge of what happened the night Timothy Stanley was killed.

'I find it strange a man is murdered in the foyer of your hospital, whilst at the same time a considerable proportion of drugs gets nicked, during which time you're supposedly sound asleep upstairs,' Parker fired at Green. 'Quite incredible really.'

'Shit happens.' Green turned to smile at his solicitor.

'Shit you want to cover up,' Parker accused.

Green shrugged. 'I can't help it if I'm a heavy sleeper Parker. May I offer my condolences for you wasting your precious time today. Shouldn't you be next door organising dog squads and search helicopters or something? I'll be sure to contact you if Billy turns up, although I'd say that's highly unlikely, wouldn't you? The man's a crackpot. I hardly think he'll arrive on my doorstep asking for tea and biscuits.'

Parker ignored the sarcastic remark, instead firing another question. 'Did you plan the whole thing to the last tiny detail Doc? You must have realised Billy was capable of murder, is that why you gave him the loaded semi-automatic. Did you also suggest Tim stay awake all night knowing he'd come face to face with an armed and dangerous psychopath?'

'Don't know what you're talking about,' Green responded casually, resting his right palm on his right cheek. 'As I keep telling you, I was out like a light when Timothy Stanley was killed. I played no part in his murder. I knew nothing about any gun being fired until the security company raised the alarm and you lot arrived.'

'Interesting you suggest Tim was murdered,' Parker fired back. 'Give me more time my friend and I'll have you sent down for a very long time. Like I stated, it's my belief you told Billy to shoot any intruders that night, am I right?'

'Can't remember having that conversation,' Green stated, with a look of satisfaction on his face. 'But here's the thing Parker; I didn't pull that trigger and you'll have a hard time proving I had anything to do with Stanley's demise. Now I suggest you get yourself and your men back out on the moor and look for Mr Sinclair. You are wasting valuable minutes sitting here asking ridiculous questions. The longer it takes you to find Fowler and Sinclair, the worst it will be for everyone.'

'Wanted Stanley out the way, did you?' Parker tried desperately to keep his ebbing temper in check.

'No comment.'

'Okay, what about telling us where you think Billy has taken James Sinclair. You must know where Fowler hides out on the moors?'

'I've already suggested a few places to one of your senior officers but apparently, Billy's not opted for any of those locations. How in blazes can I possibly know what goes on in that guy's head? His mind is a complex one, I can only second guess at what he must be thinking.'

Green's solicitor pushed back his chair, rising to his feet. 'How about we call it a day Detective. If you've no further questions for my client I suggest we end this discussion, we're going around in circles. Without a doubt, you're trying to fabricate evidence.'

'Sit down,' Parker barked, through the fog of a chronic migraine brought on from three hours sleep in the last two days. 'I still have more questions; you can go when I'm done.'

The solicitor reluctantly obeyed, muttering obscenities under his breath.

'Why did you want Timothy Stanley, as they say, "removed from the scene"?' Parker gazed lazily at the ceiling. 'Had he stumbled upon one of your little secrets?'

'No comment.'

'Perhaps he was about to blow the whistle on the information you wanted kept under wraps. Is that why you had Billy blow his brains out?'

'No comment.'

Once more, Green's solicitor got to his feet. 'Enough is enough, Parker. It's obvious you're clutching at straws. I demand you release my client immediately.'

Parker leaned forward, his mouth only inches from the professor. 'You can go, but I'm warning you Green; I'll get you for something, it's only a matter of time.'

'Looking forward to it.' Green smirked, easing up from the table to head towards the door. Just before exiting, he turned abruptly, making direct eye contact with Parker. 'You know Detective Inspector, whenever our paths cross, you're quite tense. I've got pills to cure that. I can have some sent over to you. A quick diagnosis tells me you suffer from a form of anxiety, perhaps you're not sleeping well at night.'

'Don't push it,' Parker warned, following Green out the door. 'Get the hell out of here, before I arrest you for wasting police time.'

'Pleasure, but remember medications are available if you want them.'

Green's infuriating laughter echoed down the corridor as Parker reached for a packet of cigarettes.

****

The more James attempted to loosen the knots securing his wrists, the tighter they became until the binding started to dig deeper, cutting into the flesh. He felt a wave of pain followed by a rise of nausea until he could taste bile building at the back of his throat.

So far, little conversation had passed between the two men, Fowler appeared deep in his own world, not wanting to build a rapport with his captive. Often at night, as the sun set across the moors, Fowler would wander off, leaving James alone, to shout until his voice went numb and he collapsed from exhaustion, hoping someone would hear his cries for help. On one occasion a military helicopter discernible by its ponderous, muted basso beat flew slowly overhead its searchlights illuminating the entrance to the cave, James's cries utterly useless against the deafening throb.

The cavern was deep and narrow, concealed from the air by a small copse of stunted wind-blown trees and shrubs. The recognisable odour of decomposing flesh, which James hoped was from an animal carcass and nothing more sinister pervaded the dark confines. He tried to stay alert and focused most of the time, dozing only fitfully and in short bursts, trying to switch off from his unpleasant environment and devise a plan of escape; hoping for the smallest slip-up or opportunity.

Fowler provided James sufficient food and water, even allowing him to go for short walks, always at night and all the time with the shotgun no more than a few inches from the back of his head. James had a rough idea of their location within a few kilometres. He was convinced they were a short distance from the town of Ivybridge, probably not too far from a road, which saw a moderate amount of traffic. Alas, trapped underground and hidden, none of this was helpful.

With Fowler asleep most of the time, James would have attempted to overpower his captor or make a dash for freedom if it hadn't been for the tight cord confining his wrists and ankles. It had been five days now. He resigned himself to waiting, watching, hoping and praying.

****

'Katie dear, it's Margo Betteridge, I was heartbroken to hear about poor James, I can't begin to imagine what your family is going through. If there is anything I can do to help, please let me know.'

Katie held the phone close to her ear, struggling to hear against the freight train roar of a late afternoon hailstorm, marching in from the Coast and smashing against the laboratory roof.

'James is a tough old coot,' Margo continued. 'He'll be back in the office before you know it.'

'Let's hope so,' Katie responded, unsure what else to say.

'Katie my love, I hate to discuss business at a time like this, but I am interested to know if James ever mentioned crossing paths with a forensic biologist, first name of Keita, did a fair bit of work for the Home Office out of Aldermaston in her prime? She'd be getting on a bit now, I'm not even sure if she's still alive.'

'I can't recall him ever mentioning such a person, can I ask what this is about?'

'I recently discovered a final Coroner's report I worked on was grossly tampered with. We're going back a few years, 1998 to be precise. The case was that of young Tania Simms and I have my suspicions this Keita person was responsible for tampering with the report. I'm hoping Matt Tyler will be able to help me dig further with this investigation. I know my findings indicated young Tania was raped, yet someone has erased that information from the report, and I would like to know why.'

Katie caught her breath and gazed out the window at the hailstones rapidly carpeting the courtyard, her mind briefly distracted by concern for her brother, somewhere up on the high moor. 'Why don't you leave it with me, Margo, I'm sure you've a lot on your plate at the moment and I'm not particularly busy right now. I promise to contact you as soon as there is any news.'

Margo gave a hearty laugh. 'You're an angel. I'm certainly completely swamped under a backlog of work, so any assistance would be appreciated. Don't forget to call me as soon as you hear from James, I know it's only a matter of time before he'll be back safe and sound.'

Katie put down the phone, continuing to stare blankly out the window as the hail turned to heavy rain, now sweeping down the main high street, the day quickly turning to night. Her conversation with Margo had been disturbing. Why would someone alter a Coroner's report? To erase information was surely taking the side of the killer, in which case Keita Simms knew full well what happened to her granddaughter. It was also apparent to Katie there weren't many Keita's residing in the local area, it had to be Keita Simms Margo was referring to, only Margo wasn't aware of this. With her mind in overdrive, Katie picked up car keys, ready to confront Keita. Her psychological intellect wanted answers.

****

Katie ventured into the nursing home, knowing she was treading on thin ice. If James ever got wind of her imminent confrontation with Keita Simms, he would be ropeable, possibly unforgiving.

Normally, Katie kept work protocols and procedures on a strictly professional level, yet she felt passionate about Tania's death and wanted answers. What if Keita had played a part in her granddaughter's murder? Katie could hardly sit back and allow the woman to remain triumphant.

By-passing reception she went straight through, locating Keita alone in the small music room relaxing on a chaise lounge, eyes closed, lost in the enigmatic desolation of the Fourth Movement of Vaughan Williams' powerful Sixth Symphony.

'Keita, would you care to tell me who killed your granddaughter?' Katie fired bluntly, standing with her arms folded, only inches from the resting figure.

'I have no idea what you're talking about.' Keita slipped off the headphones, her eyes opening swiftly and meeting Katie's head-on. 'You, young lady, ought to learn some manners; has no one ever told you it's bad form to disturb someone during an afternoon siesta? Poor Tania died in a tragic drowning accident; it really isn't up for debate.'

Keita closed her eyes, indicating there was no more to be spoken on the subject.

'That's what everyone was led to believe,' Katie continued, her temper rising to the surface. 'What I want to know is; why you've been protecting someone who brutally attacked and killed your own flesh and blood, it doesn't make sense.'

'Everything was openly documented in the Coroner's report,' Keita remarked, clasping her hands together in a vice-like grip, still with her eyes closed.

'Oh yes, a Coroner's report, which you tampered with,' Katie shot back.

'Now how would I be able to meddle with such documentation?' Keita laughed, opening her eyes and moving into an upright position. 'I am a poor defenceless old woman residing in a nursing home, I never venture anywhere to cause such conflict.'

'You might be old now, but at the time of your granddaughter's death you happened to be a highly regarded scientist with a lot of clout,' Katie retaliated. 'You know Keita, I can understand how you fudged the paperwork in your previous role as a pathologist, what I'd like to know is why you did it. To defend a murderer is barbaric.'

Keita stole a sharp intake of breath. 'In order for this conversation to continue, I expect you to tell me something Ms Sinclair; how long have you known the truth? And by truth, I want to know how much you know.'

'My brother is the one who made the discovery,' Katie muttered, not sure she wanted to involve James in any part of this conversation. 'He ran DNA tests pertaining to Timothy Stanley, that's how we discovered Timothy killed Tania. If you knew all this Keita, why didn't you come forward and make a statement to the police? Instead, you chose to defend Tim Stanley, by altering the final Coroner's report. Tim could have been locked up years ago, letting justice prevail.'

'Justice for who?' Keita sighed, pressing the remote control to soften the music. 'My dear girl, life is not how it appears. We are not talking of a simple murder here; we are talking of a brother killing his sister.'

Katie stared in silence before Keita continued. 'Yes, Tim was Tania's older brother, living within close proximity, but neither knew of their connection. Timothy's real name is Timothy Stanley Simms.'

A hush descended before Katie continued. 'What happens next? Will you do the right thing and confess to knowing about the murder? I find it hard to believe you've been harbouring such a secret for all these years.'

'It was a burden, not a secret.' Keita sighed. 'And no, I am not about to speak out about my family's shame.'

'Surely you would want to bring closure for your granddaughter?' Katie urged. 'She deserves to rest in peace.'

'What's done is done. I think you forget Ms Sinclair I am about to bury another grandchild; Timothy was still my flesh and blood and in the eyes of God we must all be forgiven for our sins. Dragging up the past will not bring either of them back.'

'I have a right to let the authorities know you have covered up the truth,' Katie blurted out loudly, unable to restrain her rage.

'Do as you see fit.' Keita sighed. 'I am a frail woman now; my life is not worth much in this nursing home or in a prison cell. Remember Ms Sinclair, I have lived with my decision for decades, could you live with yours? They say some things are best left well alone, why create a future which belongs in the past.'

******

'Margo, Katie here, I did come across the scientist woman you were talking about. To be honest, Keita is quite senile. Nothing of interest would be achieved regurgitating events long gone. If she did alter your Coroner's report it might not have been deliberate, could be she was getting premature onset of dementia and made a mistake. I believe she was close to retirement around the time of the initial investigation but was brought in as a consultant on the case as a one-off, due to lack of experienced staff in the Coroner's Office. Rather embarrassing if you ask me.'

'Well, this isn't the answers I was expecting. However, it does seem a bit trivial for me to be getting so hot and bothered over things. Not to worry, I'll let this one pass, but thanks for your assistance.'

'Pleasure.'

Katie hung up the phone, reaching for the lab report matching Timothy Stanley's DNA to the death of Tania Simms. It sat in the out tray in reception ready to be mailed off to the Home Office in Bristol, a job James would have done, had he been around. For several minutes she toyed with the stamp ready to go onto the envelope. Eventually, she removed the document and placed it in the shredder, before compiling a short email:

Subject: DNA matching Timothy Stanley – linking him to the death of Tania Simms.

Hi James, FYI, DNA results have been posted to Bristol. Can now put a closure on the Tania Simms case. Margo is aware of all updates and has signed off on the case, no follow up necessary. Katie.

Opening the desktop drawer, Katie removed a mini bottle of Bacardi. She downed the contents in one hit, before covering her face with her hands. She hoped to high heaven no one would discover what she had done. Was her conscience finally clear or in a bizarre twist of fate had she now become part of a young girl's murder, playing her role with as much guilt as Timothy Stanley?

'What you got for me today?' Professor Green snarled, snatching the small package from the pimply faced youth moving up and down in the doorway to counteract the icy northerly rolling down off the moors. 'Let's hope it beats the last lot of shit you brought me.'

'This ain't shit, it's quality stuff, quite powerful, so be careful who you're giving it to, Granddad,' the young lad indignantly replied, firmly holding on to his mountain bike in the event a hasty retreat was required. He was wary of Green and how he might react.

'Don't give me any lip.' Green tore open the parcel to inspect the contents. 'If I'm satisfied this is the real deal, I'll have another lot next week. You tell your boss that.'

'Right you are, gov.'

'Well?' Green snapped. 'What are you waiting for? Get out and close the bloody door, there's a gale blowing out there. I don't want the likes of you hanging about.'

'I heard about Stanley,' the gawky, malnourished youth remarked, making no immediate attempt to move. 'Shot in the head at close range by all accounts. Very messy way to go.'

'Yes, the bastard just couldn't keep his bloody mouth shut,' Green snarled. 'Keep your gob closed too lad, or you'll end up in the same place. Now fucking well piss off, before I carry out my threat.'

****

'I thought it might be beneficial if you were to chat with Professor Green once more,' Nick suggested of DCI Parker, having called a meeting to go through the investigation. With James still missing, Nick was feeling the pressure. 'I met with Tudor to go through the Ballistics report and there's no way in hell Timothy Stanley shot himself, accidental or otherwise What's your take on things, Will?'

Will Parker pulled a grim face. 'I had intentions of meeting with Green again, but the commander has requested DI Wetherill be assigned to the Stanley case. According to Jenks, I have a big enough workload with the schoolgirl murders. Sorry Nick, but I am no longer the chap to turn to, DI Wetherill is your man.'

Nick scoffed. 'If that weasel uncovers anything, he won't tell me. My suggestion was to systematically search Green's hospital to gather as much forensic evidence as possible, a request I've asked for, yet not received.'

'I'll have a word with Wetherill, but I can't promise anything.' Parker let out a long drawn-out sigh. 'I doubt he'll oblige unless pushed.'

****

Nick rapidly flicked through the file Will Parker handed to him, his temper flaring.

'This is bullshit,' Nick said fuming. 'A crummy transcript between Wetherill and Green, which sounds more like a sociable banter between friends, than an official police interrogation. It could be the Guardian interviewing the Leader of the Labour Party. I assume you have read this Will?'

Will nodded. 'Oh yes, ten times or more to see if I missed something of importance, but sad to say, it still sounds like crap.'

Nick scanned the relevant page again before reading the words out loud:

Wetherill: 'Thanks for seeing me today, Professor; sorry for the inconvenience all this has caused.'

Green: 'No problems Rod. Glad to be of service.'

Wetherill: 'Any idea who shot Stanley?'

Green: 'The only person who springs to mind is Billy Fowler. He was up and about that night and certainly knows how to use a loaded firearm.'

Wetherill: 'It sounds plausible.'

Green: 'The trouble is Rod; you'll have a hard job catching Billy. He's likely to hide out on Dartmoor indefinitely.'

Wetherill: 'Yep, this could be a long drawn-out process; one the local Constabulary won't want to shove money into. Never mind, just make sure you call me if Fowler does turn up.'

Green: 'Definitely. Cheers for now.'

'Cunning bastards,' Nick said enraged. 'Between the two of them, they have practically dismissed the case.'

'Looks that way,' Will agreed. 'Oh, before I forget, Professor Green wanted me to pass this on to you.'

Nick grabbed the small white envelope and ripped it open. His face turned crimson as he read the typed note;

In my capacity as an expert medical practitioner, I have become accustomed to spotting a Cocaine addict. Do not worry Dr Shelby, your secret addiction is safe with me. I can obtain quality coke at a very reasonable price if you require a little tonic. Even the best of us succumb to temptation.'

Nick tore up the paper and tossed it in the bin before turning to Will. 'Thanks for dropping by, I'll give you a call by the end of the week.'

Last night Beelzebub paid a visit. His power grows day by day. I sat in my old chair rocking back and forth. We shared a little wine and laughed at all the wrongdoing.

Silently, in the depth of night, I rocked back and forth. I cried, I laughed, and I shed a tear.

Am I remorseful for my sins? That question I cannot answer. I wonder if there are times, I should seek redemption, offer up prayers in the hope I can be forgiven. Then it all comes back to me and I know what I must do…

Amen

Chapter Seven

Katie switched off the office overhead television and reluctantly returned to the half-completed report on her laptop. For the next half hour, she sat staring at the screen, trying to marshal her thoughts into some coherent sentences, but they wouldn't come. Eventually floating off into a half trance-like state, she was jolted back to reality by the piercing warning buzzer of the courtyard gates opening. Switching focus to the CCTV video she spotted her sister exit the red TVR and enter the laboratory directly via the back-delivery dock.

James had been missing for over a week and each new day brought with it increased anxiety. A hastily cobbled together police task force and scratch volunteer teams continued to systematically comb the open moors, probing for clues as to where Fowler and his hostage might be hiding, but frustratingly no definite trail or evidence of the duo had surfaced. A couple of police dogs briefly picked up on a strong scent, but it was lost almost as quickly as it was discovered, disappearing near a fast-flowing stream.

'You look like you could do with a stiff drink,' Fiona commented, joining her sister in the office after checking the status of an overnight gas chromatograph run on some illicit methamphetamine mixtures. 'I was thinking I could handle a scotch, care to join me?'

'Actually, I wouldn't mind a port.' Katie flicked the paper clip she had been playing with into a wastepaper bin. 'Somehow most things seem pointless at the moment, my attention span is bottoming near zero. The latest news reports are suggesting Fowler may have skipped the country already; and who knows what's happened to James. The Deputy Chief Constable is starting to sound negative, the bastard. They can't throw in the towel yet. I'll bloody well go up there and search around myself if I have to.'

'I know this is a particularly rough time, but I'm confident James would want us to keep going with our current investigations,' Fiona encouraged her sister, as she drained the contents of a vintage port bottle into two 50 ml beakers, passing one across. 'He's certainly not a quitter.'

'Yeah you're right,' Katie acknowledged, taking a gulp of the deep red liquid, before passing Fiona a small notebook size piece of paper in a plastic slip. 'Take a look at this, will you? Got this charming little note in the morning post; it claims the Headmaster of Abbey College was sleeping with Allyson Carter. Tell me what you make of it.'

Fiona carefully inspected the note. *'Mr Miller is nothing but a sleaze. He paid female students to have sex with him, including Allyson Carter. The little pervert wants locking up.'*

'Could be a prank,' Fiona declared, studying the note once more. 'Kids often try and blacken a teacher's name; they see it as a joke. This might not have any real significance with our current enquiries.'

'Yes, it may well be a spiteful attack, regardless I might follow it up. Can you run DNA testing on the note Fiona?

There's every chance it was written by a school student, apparently, Abbey College keeps DNA records on all its pupils, a very wise move.'

'A wise move? What are you saying? How is it possible that any parents with half a brain would consent to any school having that sort of invasive power? You can forget about that. No way. How would you feel about having your DNA genome profile on record in who knows how many obscure government departments, NGO's and private institutions?' Fiona shot back, scornfully. 'I really don't think DNA testing is warranted in this instance. It's a powerful diagnostic tool, I reckon too powerful, ideally used sparingly and in conjunction with other techniques. A lot of people don't understand the social implications and assumptions; and the technical difficulties inherent in DNA analysis. Talk about using a sledgehammer to kill an ant. Just think about it. The outcomes for society are potentially Orwellian, particularly when governments almost universally are rushing to embrace facial recognition technology; and other digital surveillance systems.'

Fiona paused her lecture for a quick breath. 'You could be convicted of a crime from one high molecular weight chain of DNA found at the scene, when in fact, you were never anywhere near it.'

'Fingerprints then, maybe?' offered Katie timidly, suitably rebuked, kicking herself for forgetting her sister's well-founded reservations and deep distrust of DNA diagnostics and databases.

'Maybe I can sandwich it in between some HPLC programs.'

'Lovely. I'll get in contact with Detective Parker to notify him of the note, he's bound to want to interview the Headmaster to at least clear his name. I'm popping out for a short while but am contactable on the mobile.'

Left alone in the office Fiona procured the note and headed out to the lab, closing the quarantine airlock behind.

Settling in behind her brother's desk she located the wire-bound volume titled "Moorland Forensic Consultants – Certified Laboratory Manual and Procedures", and went straight to Section III – 3.01, under the heading "Physical Evidence".

As the material in question was a notepaper, she opted for a silver nitrate solution sprayed directly onto the torn paper specimen, designed to capture any prints in situ rather than attempting a "lift" with adhesive tape. After two hours, Fiona succeeded in visualising and photographing two coherent, almost perfect patterns. Now it was up to Regional Police Forensic technicians to interrogate their extensive database.

Completely wrung out Fiona chose to call it a day. Katie hadn't reappeared; most likely detained somewhere, with no intentions of returning to the office until morning. Fiona would call her on the way home. A microwave curry and glass of wine beckoned. She mentally flicked through her classic jazz LP collection, maybe some early Modern Jazz Quartet...

Getting into the TVR, she was startled to spot the tall, hunched figure of Tom Markham through the security grill, hanging around outside the courtyard, behind two green rubbish bins.

'Shame about James, anything I can do?' Markham enquired, stepping in front of Fiona, preventing her driving through the gates.

'You can stop printing crap and use that rag of yours to assist the search,' Fiona retorted, winding down the passenger window and reaching into her bag to retrieve the morning edition of The Star. 'Your journalistic skills are starting to lack substance, Tom. I see you've popped us onto page twelve. Are we no longer worthy of front-page news?'

Grinning from ear to ear, he leaned through the window, grabbing the paper, flipping it open at page twelve and reading aloud; *Jim Sinclair – Forensic Scientist – feared dead.*

'The police are yet to discover the whereabouts of Bovey Tracey biochemist, Dr James Sinclair who disappeared, presumed kidnapped during the recent Hounds' Tor firefight. With extensive searches underway on Dartmoor and still no sightings of the missing local identity, one can only presume the worst...

'I don't see what's wrong with that, it's well written, straight to the point, what more do you want Fi?'

'There is no evidence James has been harmed,' Fiona fought back.

'There's no evidence James is still alive,' Markham retaliated. 'Look Fi, eventually, you must come to terms with the inevitable. Count your losses and move on. In fact, if you are contemplating a suitable replacement, I know just the guy, Rex Sheldrick, he lives near...'

Before Tom could finish the sentence, Fiona lunged at Markham through the car window, sending him toppling backwards over the Sulo bins and into the bushes surrounding the courtyard. Not stopping to see if he was injured, she accelerated through the gates, wildly fishtailing the TVR down the laneway at a maniacal pace, past the Old Mill and across the bridge out of town.

****

'How are you holding up?' Ben asked of Katie, as they sat enjoying a quiet drink at a pub in Teignmouth.

'Okay,' Katie managed a faint reply. 'It's been a stressful week, and still no clear indication of how it's going to end.'

'Positively, we hope.'

'The longer James is stuck out on the moors the more likely things will turn ugly. I really don't know how much more of this I can take.'

'It's never easy,' Ben remarked, staring down at his empty glass. 'You almost resign yourself to the fact they may never return.'

His face held a tortured expression as if he had gone through similar angst. Katie was about to comment when her mobile started to ring.

Only speaking for a second or two before hanging up, a slight smile crossed her face. 'That was Fi, she's headed home for the day, but not before shoving that conceited Tom Markham into a holly bush.'

'No more than he deserves.' Ben sniggered, signalling the barman for a refill.

Katie was about to speak when her mobile rang again. So much for a quiet night. She accepted the call, not recognising the number. For several minutes she fell silent, listening to the voice on the other end. Finally, she spoke, her tone frosty.

'Why should I be pleased to hear from you? I assume you've heard the latest news and are now pretending you care.'

Ben listened in surprise; he had never heard Katie sound this enraged. Both fists were formed into tight balls and her eyes narrowed.

'What is it you want Drew?' she quizzed. 'Perhaps start by telling me where you are, hopefully not close by, as that really would piss me off.'

Again silence, whilst the caller continued their part of the conversation.

'You call out of the blue, then you want to meet up.' Katie was trying to keep her voice low, with little success, already attracting attention from a group of men propping up the nearby bar. 'Don't do this to me, Drew, not now, not ever. You made your decision over five years ago, now go live with that.'

Katie ended the call, before switching off her mobile and tossing it into her red leather handbag.

'Old flame?' Ben inquired.

'Yeah, something like that. Now tell me, Ben, how are you settling into the Devon way of life? Met any nice women yet?'

'Just one. The trouble is, I've not yet found the courage to ask her out.'

****

Katie heard the commotion well before she realised what was happening. Ready to head up the high street to buy lunch she heard cars pulling up on Bovey Heath outside the courtyard and the babble of raised voices. Pressing the rear gate remote she glanced out the window to see two police cars, and a convoy of the press, including Tom Markham pushing a microphone into James's pale face. Will Parker shoved Tom out the way as Nick Shelby made a clear pathway to the rear entrance. Matt was the last one in, herding the press out and closing the gate behind.

It was an emotional reunion.

Katie gave her brother a firm hug, which lingered for several seconds. 'Thank Christ you're okay,' she announced, the tears pouring down her face. 'James, we didn't think we'd ever see you again. You were lucky to escape... Gee, you've lost weight.'

James managed a feeble smile through a week old, ginger facial growth. 'Actually, I didn't escape I was set free,' James explained to his sister. 'Our old acquaintances the Dartmoor gypsies had been watching Fowler foraging for food and spotted me walking in front, the shotgun stuck hard in my back. They waited until they calculated Fowler was off by himself, before coming to my rescue. The ropes were cut, and I was taken on horseback to the main intersection. I had no chance to thank my rescuers, who vanished in a gallop of hooves. By the way, where's Fiona?'

'In London at a media conference, but I've already phoned her with the good news,' Nick explained, stepping forward to pass his friend a strong coffee. 'Here, get this into you. I'll be outside helping Will with the mob.'

'You're not seeming too worse for wear, apart from needing a large steak and a half bottle of red,' Matt ribbed, giving his colleague a friendly shove. 'No sign of Fowler, from what I gather.'

'Nope, and it's highly unlikely he'll be caught if he remains steadfast up on the moors,' James commented, slowly sipping at the double espresso.

'Oh, they'll flush him out eventually. The main thing is you're okay. Wasn't the same without you around, welcome back, I'll even shout you a couple of beers.'

'Sounds great. However, before we go anywhere, I've requested an investigation update from Will and Nick. Feels as if I've been away for years, I'd like to catch up on all the news. Give me a yell when they get rid of the media. Just want to crash for a few minutes.'

Watching James slowly disappear upstairs to the bedroom and struck by his emaciated features, Katie phoned for a takeaway.

****

Nick Shelby and Will Parker standing in front of the smartboard watched on with amazement, as James voraciously attacked a third double cheeseburger.

'The Commander is pressing for progress on the murder of Veronica Peters. He wants the perpetrator apprehended as soon as possible and we're to make it a top priority,' Will Parker announced.

'Reasonable request,' James agreed, through a mouth full of French fries. 'Her murder was brutal and out in the open. I guess he's not too concerned with the death of Timothy Stanley, seeing that was conducted behind closed doors.'

'Oh he'll want that sorted as well,' Parker commented. 'The DCC is leaning on him pretty heavily; they're allocating extra manpower to the effort. Our dear friend Wetherill has been up to his usual tricks, but the Commander is now holding him accountable. Oh, and... I finally have a warrant for Green's Institute, and as we speak a team of senior officers are on their way to conduct a thorough search of the premises.'

'Well, we can definitely rule out Bruce Peters as the culprit in his wife's murder,' Nick chimed in. 'We've rerun all possible scenarios with task force detectives, studied all the forensics including blood spatters, tissue samples. Bruce is in the clear and lacking a motive at this stage, I would be surprised if he *was* linked to the death in any way. I spent three hours with your sister going over his psychological profile and we both concur he is still in shock over his wife's death. He's not presenting as a murderer.'

'So what's missing?' James pressed, shifting slightly in his seat in the Moorland reception. 'I still can't believe this is a random killing. Too coincidental for a start, and such a gruesome death indicates the killer meant to do a precise job. It shows someone had it in for the poor woman.'

'Exactly,' DCI Parker concluded. 'Therein lies our answer, so far we've been focusing on Bruce Peters and his background, but what do we actually know about his wife, nothing.'

James gave a low whistle. 'We've missed the basics on this one. Matt, see what you can find out about Veronica Peters: friends, associates, work colleagues, hobbies etc. The only thing we really know is she had cancer, but that isn't a reason to kill someone. What did her mobile phone records produce Will?'

'Nothing of interest. Text messages to local accommodations, a call to Buckfast Abbey and one to the nearby Priory. Bruce Peters told us his wife was a deeply religious woman, wanting to visit the Abbey during their trip to Devon. He believes she made the calls to find out the opening times.'

'Possibly.' There was a hint of scepticism in James's voice. 'Well, I'll leave those investigations up to you Matthew dear boy. If you dig out more stuff from the hard drive of her computer, we may just get the answers we are after. Now, if that's it for today, I suggest we all head to the pub. I for one am desperate for a drink.'

****

'Mr Miller, what exactly is your relationship with the female students at Abbey College?' DCI Parker launched at the Headmaster, watching him shift uncomfortably in his black swivel chair. If someone could be charged by wearing a guilty façade, Larry Miller would be serving life.

Miller turned bright red. 'I am a pillar of this community and have habitually been a professional in my field,' he scorned. 'I also happen to be happily married, so if you're accusing me of indecent behaviour, I can assure you it's not the case.'

'I ran a background search on your last position as head of Torview School in Torbay,' Parker fired. 'The information they provided me with was you left suddenly due to personal reasons, would you care to elaborate a bit more on your sudden resignation?'

'No.'

'They also went on to say that although you were a proficient teacher, with a fine academic record in the humanities, they wouldn't re-employ you or recommend you for any future position, why is that?'

'Wouldn't have a clue, but if you can't find any hard evidence against me or a current police record, you're wasting your time,' Mr Miller retaliated.

'I'll keep digging.' Parker sounded harsh. 'What I do find interesting is how you managed to secure this job. You must have friends in high places.'

Mr Miller took a sharp intake of breath. 'I happen to be a very experienced teacher. Why is it the local constabulary spends so much time and effort dishing up dirt on people instead of tracking down real criminals? No wonder crime has increased over the years.'

'It's the bigger fish we'd rather fry Mr Miller,' Parker responded. 'Trouble is; some little fish get netted in the big pond. Before I go, I do have one last question for you; exactly how many of the female students here at Abbey College have you been sleeping with?'

Mr Miller rose to his feet. 'Get out before I call security, and have you physically removed. I have never laid a finger on any of my female students. I will be demanding an apology and will certainly be reporting you to your superior.'

'Commander Jenks can be contacted on this number,' Parker informed Miller, dropping a shiny business card on the desk. 'Hold off till I get back to the office before you call him, that way he can give me a proper talking to, face to face.'

'Get out.' Larry Miller had turned a deep purple, the blood vessels rising poignantly on his neck.

DCI Parker decided it best to leave before the poor chap suffered a coronary. He was not in the mood to administer first aid.

****

Katie found Ruth Miller in her front garden, watering some small saplings behind a sandstone wall. Katie was surprised to see her in a wheelchair, legs wrapped in a blanket. The day which had started out warm and sunny was quickly disintegrating to the first blasts from a North Atlantic Low moving down from Iceland and building to gale force in the Bristol Channel.

'I'm sorry to turn up unannounced,' Katie apologised, placing her card on Ruth Miller's lap as a way of an introduction. 'I was hoping to have a word with you about your husband. I am investigating the disappearance of Allyson Carter, whom I believe was a pupil at your husband's school?'

'I'm not sure I'll be much help with your enquiry.' Mrs Miller peeled off her gardening gloves, throwing them into a disused wheelbarrow parked nearby. 'Would you mind helping me into the house, it's getting icy out here and I'm prone to catching chills.'

'Not a problem.' Katie smiled, taking a firm grip at the back of the wheelchair and carefully pushing Ruth Miller up the ramp to the front door. 'I must say you keep your garden immaculate, Mrs Miller you have some of the finest roses I've ever seen.'

Ruth smiled. 'Yes, I manage to get about fairly well, despite my impairment. Something my mother took during pregnancy they said. I'm a bit of a green thumb. The only thing that stops me from getting out into the garden is extreme weather.'

Following Ruth's instructions, Katie found the way to the sitting room where a welcoming log fire was crackling in an open hearth. 'I'm afraid my husband is working back late, parent-teacher night,' Ruth explained.

'Does your husband often work late Mrs Miller?'

'Quite often, and please call me Ruth. It goes with the territory of being a Headmaster. Why do you ask?'

'There are rumours going around your husband has been sleeping with female students,' Katie began, a little hesitantly, hoping Ruth wouldn't become too emotional. 'Were you aware such talk was going on throughout the local community?'

Instead of Mrs Miller turning on her visitor, she burst out laughing. 'Oh is that all you've come to tell me. You had me worried for a tick.'

'Doesn't it concern you at all?' Katie ventured, openly perplexed.

'My dear girl, Larry has no interest in the delights of the female form whatsoever, Larry's of the opposite persuasion.'

Katie stared, without managing to utter a response.

'Don't look so shocked.' Ruth smiled. 'I've known for years, Larry is gay and it doesn't bother me, we have an amicable arrangement... you could say; so I don't see why it would worry you. Come, I'll fix us some tea. It looks like you'll need plenty of sugar in yours or even a drop of brandy.'

A dumbstruck Katie followed Ruth, who deftly wheeled herself into an expansive open plan kitchen. The bungalow had evidently been renovated to accommodate Ruth's disability.

When they were back in the sitting room sipping hot tea, Katie felt ready to continue with the questioning.

'Did your husband ever discuss the disappearance of Allyson Carter with you? It must have been a traumatic episode for all concerned.'

'Oh yes, on several occasions we tried to fathom what happened. Larry and I found it odd the young woman could vanish without a trace. Larry spent days being interviewed by local police and a team of investigators sent down from London; there was no worthwhile information to be offered. Larry also held meetings with all the teachers and some students, but nothing came to light.'

'I imagine it didn't do much for the reputation of Abbey College, bringing with it a lot of unwanted publicity,' Katie surmised, accepting the offer of a second brew.

'After Allyson Carter disappeared, a number of parents, some of them high profile local identities opted to take their children out of the School,' Ruth Miller explained. 'Then, of course, we were hit even harder by the disappearance of Rebecca Price and Nicola Fletcher, right from under the teachers' noses on a school excursion. You can imagine how that went down within the community, even holidaymakers gave the College and its precincts a wide berth, afraid their children would vanish without a trace. There were rumours the Head Abbott and Priory Council were under instructions from Rome to close the College permanently if things got worse. It has only been in recent weeks school enrolments have picked up, thank God, but unfortunately not at the pace we had hoped for. Oh dear, I do hope your investigation won't see things spiral downwards again. I've read the local papers and seen the news about bodies being dug up on the moors. We really don't hanker after any more dramas.'

'Let's hope not.' Katie tried to sound positive. 'I don't suppose you knew much about Rebecca and Nicola?'

'Very little. Occasionally, my husband would come home with funny quotes from the students, but he generally never gossiped, we had a strict rule he was not to bring any problems home. Despite Larry's sexual preferences, he's a respectable man and a gallant teacher,' Ruth verbalised with force. 'Sadly he was suspended from his previous headteacher post at Torview School in Torquay, the locals didn't want a gay headmaster, fair enough I suppose. People can be cruel at times, Ms Sinclair, very cruel. What you have to remember though; is an individual's sexual choices does not deem that person to be a child predator or murderer. Now if that's all, Ms Sinclair I really must have a lie-down. I get very tired throughout the day. Good day to you and I hope your visit has been worthwhile.'

****

'What a day,' Katie proclaimed, crashing onto the Moorland reception lounge. 'Spending a day interviewing students at Abbey College makes me frigging glad I didn't take up the option of a BA, Dip Ed after the A levels.'

'What information did you pick up about Rebecca and Nicola?' James pressed, eager to keep their case bubbling away. 'Students with first-class reputations no doubt, judging by the privileged upbringing they both had? It's obvious both families had plenty of the folding stuff. I've managed to glean Nicola was raised by her Grandparents, who now live in a luxury property on the outskirts of Ilfracombe.'

'Actually not quite what you'd expect,' Katie said, kicking her high heels into the far corner of the office. 'Both girls were, how can I say it... unruly to put it mildly; often playing truant, knowledgeable of nearly every swear word on the planet and some that aren't, and both were heavily into illicit drugs; users and pushers. As we've already established from the toxicology results; confirming a heavy use of illicit substances, but we had no idea the girls were drug peddlers.'

'Where do you think they were getting the drugs?' James asked. 'It sounds to me their involvement in the trade *may* have got them murdered.'

'I have my suspicions,' Katie continued. 'One student accidentally let slip Rebecca worked part-time for a local pharmaceutical manufacturing company: Milton and Bailey. I ran a quick check with my contacts in the industry; small but very profitable niche market manufacturer who mostly supplies into France and the Low Countries. Cutting edge, low volume, high margin stuff.'

'Don't know them.'

Katie fished around in her handbag and produced a small diary. 'Here it is, ah... highly specific immuno-suppressants and programmed design of modified opiate-related narcotics. Not much on the web. It's something worth checking out further.'

'Good work, have you passed this stuff onto Will?' James enquired, constantly aware they were working with the police, not against them.

'Yep, I gave him a call shortly after I left Abbey College.'

'I think it best if I break the news to the Prices informing them of the fact their precious daughter was a drug pusher,' James volunteered. 'After all, they have a right to know and I don't want them finding out from the local press, Mr Price holds no prisoners. I'll run it past Parker first, just to make sure he's okay for me to pay the family another visit. Did you learn anything else of interest?'

'Ah, now this is probably the most interesting piece of news in relation to Allyson Carter; a number of Allyson's friends claim she had a rare type of Haemophilia. I have yet to establish the exact facts but plan to do some extensive research. One particular friend is adamant this is related to Allyson's disappearance, although how, I have no idea.'

'Did you establish if Allyson hung out with Rebecca and Nicola?' James quizzed.

'The girls knew of Allyson, but they weren't great friends, my assumption concludes their disappearances could well be unrelated.'

'Perhaps, yet nothing can be ruled out.'

****

With an email clearance from Parker, James drove the short distance through the Devon countryside onto the edge of Dartmoor for a hastily arranged visit with Rebecca's parents. In the car, he kept running over a little speech, swiftly cobbled together at the last hour on how to broach the subject with Mr Price. He braced himself for an icy reception.

'Were you aware your daughter was into drugs?' James inquired, sitting opposite a poker-faced Price in his meticulously outfitted study.

'What school kid doesn't dabble in a few illicit substances?' Price fired back at James, his temper already starting to show. 'Even if Beckie did experiment with occasional drugs, there's no proof any of this has bearing on her death.'

'I'm not implying it does,' James answered smoothly, briefly distracted by the view over Widecombe with its dominant church spire. 'We're just trying to establish what may have led to Rebecca's murder. Do you have any idea where Rebecca might have obtained any substances? Ever heard of a company called Milton Bailey, pharmaceutical manufacturers?'

Price shook his head. 'No, can't say I have. What type of drugs are we talking about; weed?'

'Cocaine and ice mainly, you'd know all about those; you're a GP, aren't you? Both can be fatal as an overdose, worse in combination. Sorry to ask, but is there a chance Rebecca stole from your surgery? I imagine she'd know where most drugs were stored.'

Price threw back his head and laughed. 'Are you mad, Sinclair? Do you seriously suggest we keep cocaine and banned amphetamines on our premises? That's a criminal offence. I happen to be one of seven GPs in my practice, Sinclair. Regardless, if even the smallest quantities of licit drugs were going missing, I can assure you our Practice Manager would want a thorough investigation conducted. Mrs Collins is like a spider over a hole when it comes to the practice and everything in it. Even a top marksman couldn't get past her. Now if that's all, I do appreciate you coming to tell me all this, Sinclair but I doubt it's going to help find Rebecca's killer.'

Philip Price shook his head, eased himself up from behind the desk and walked slowly over to an open bay window, staring down at the early afternoon tourists throng, cramming into the picturesque village. After a minute's silence, he turned around.

'My wife and I had no idea Beckie was into drugs, and if we *had* known, I would have kicked her sorry backside, it's certainly something I don't take lightly. We can't undo the past, but we can sure as hell try to find the person responsible for my daughter's death and seek some form of justice. I demand you and your investigative team start working on real evidence, not hearsay, not returning until you have something credible to tell me.'

****

'Err, you're not going to like this one,' Fiona informed her siblings. 'The two fingerprints I got on the note sent about Bruce Miller's involvement with female students are a 100% match with that of Allyson Carter. Her prints were on a national database of kidney cancer patients, would you believe. Bloody amazing.'

'It can't be Allyson's prints,' James remarked, taking the results Fiona held in her outstretched hand. 'In fact, it's impossible.'

'Well, not impossible,' Fiona commented. 'We haven't found Allyson's body. For all we know she could still be alive, and this latest development kind of proves it.'

'Not if the note was written some time ago and someone sent it as a decoy to complicate matters,' Katie broke in. 'There's no telling who actually *sent* the note.'

'True,' Fiona confessed. 'However, I am ninety-nine percent certain the note *was* scripted by Allyson Carter, who *mailed it*, remains a mystery.'

'Here's another unknown to throw into the equation,' James added, his brain constantly in overdrive. 'I got Bristol to run a second, more extensive toxicology screen on the liver samples from Rebecca and Nicola. It took a few weeks and the guys weren't sure at first. They sent the extracts to the UKAD agency for confirmation by a second Mass Spectrometer, but trace metabolites of Midazolam showed up in both girls. It's a bit of a puzzle why they consumed this drug, as we all know the effects of Midazolam. Why on earth would they take something to make them drowsy when they were in the middle of a school camp, keen for excitement and activity?'

'Any signs of forced ingestion?' Katie inquired.

James shook his head. 'Nope, they digested them willingly.'

'Err, maybe not,' Fiona informed. 'Perhaps they thought they were taking something to boost their energy levels. Someone could easily have mixed the medications or it may have been by injection.'

'Quite possible,' James agreed. 'But why?'

'Sounds obvious to me,' Fiona continued. 'As a way to drug the girls, rape them and dump the bodies, they were easy targets.'

'Yes, but that also means they most likely knew the person who supplied the drugs, and this, in turn, means they knew their killer,' Katie broke in.

'I think we're jumping ahead of ourselves here,' James reprimanded his siblings. 'Let's stick to the facts and get more forensic evidence on this one. Theories are great, but they won't stand up in court.'

Dear Father, allow me the confession of all my bad behaviour. I have urges I can no longer control. Is it wrong for me to feel this way? Will I eventually get well, or will I go on to create an even greater evil?

Killing seems so easy, perhaps a way of enjoyment. To end someone's suffering must be a remarkable thing. If I am not mistaken, perhaps I am not so evil after all, perhaps I am on this earth to destroy for the nobility of mankind.

Maybe, I will look upon myself as some sort of hero.

Amen

Chapter Eight

An unkempt Susan Carter, still wrapped in a dressing gown, even though the sun was at its zenith, cautiously opened the door of her Ashburton residence, straining her eyes against the midday glare at the visitors standing before her.

'Are you here about Allyson?' she quizzed, absentmindedly. 'You'd better come in, sorry about my appearance I didn't get to sleep until 3am.'

After brief introductions, Katie and James followed Susan along the brightly wallpapered hallway into a retro-style country kitchen.

'I've spent the past few weeks interviewing some of Allyson's closest friends,' Katie began, sitting down at a messy breakfast bar, strewn with dirty plates and condiment jars. An accurate assessment of the woman sitting opposite had already formed in her brain: *Early forties but looks fiftyish, heavy smoker probably handmade, hard liquor drinker definitely closet, a giveaway from the flushed spots on her cheeks. Disinterested in appearance and low self-esteem. Add the poor eating habits and we have the profile of an individual in a slow but steady decline.*

'According to a number of Allyson's closest friends she had a rare type of Haemophilia,' Katie continued, unsure how Susan would react to this revelation.

She didn't respond with voice, appearing preoccupied fumbling around her cluttered kitchen in search of cups.

'Don't worry about the tea, please,' Katie instructed. 'We don't want to put you to any trouble.'

'Utter rubbish, a strong cup of English tea is the antidote on a blustery day like this,' Susan Carter scolded her visitor. 'It won't take me long, be patient dear. You're like Allyson, frequently in a rush.'

'According to the statement you provided to the police when Allyson disappeared, you failed to mention your daughter's rare blood condition, Mrs Carter, why was that?' Katie quizzed.

'I didn't see it as significant,' Susan Carter replied casually, making little headway in her tea making quest. 'I was obviously distressed, and it must have slipped my mind.'

'What special precautions did your daughter take, Mrs Carter, given this rare medical condition? I assume she was well versed on what to do if she cut herself?'

'Being a Haemophiliac never stopped Allyson living a normal life,' Susan Carter responded. 'She wasn't an invalid in any way, besides, in today's world it pays to be strong, don't you think?'

'Yes, but it can be quite distressing having such a medical condition, especially to someone young. To help our investigation we are required to know as much as we can about your daughter, Mrs Carter.'

A silence prevailed before a frustrated Katie continued. 'I could make contact with Allyson's GP, I'm sure I'll get a clearer insight once I digest Allyson's medical notes. Perhaps there were some psychological issues relating to her Haemophilia you weren't aware of.'

'I would have thought those details to be confidential.' Susan Carter clanked down three Cornish ware mugs on the ceramic worktop, pouring in boiling water. 'I'm not sure my husband will take too kindly to your prying into our daughter's private records, Ms Sinclair. We're a strongly Christian family: as you know my husband is the Vicar of St Pancreas, an upstanding pillar of the community. As a family, we like to keep our private affairs confidential. Haemophilia is hereditary, if my husband's parishioners think he might be a carrier, it could damage his reputation. They may look upon him as some sort of freak.'

Halting briefly, to clear a space on the bench and failing in a valiant attempt at adjusting her appearance, the vicar's wife continued her discourse. 'My husband is only in the role on a three-year assignment whilst the regular Vicar is on extended leave. It has taken many months of hard toil for the congregation to accept him into the community. I've learnt, to my misfortune, that Devonians don't customarily salute newcomers, especially those not born and bred in the area. You should know that.'

'I don't see any of this as a major concern.' Katie tried to be tactful. 'Many people live with a wide range of medical conditions, it's quite normal.'

'Even so, I'd prefer you not to disclose this information to all and sundry, for fear of repercussions.'

Katie got the distinct impression Mrs Carter was more concerned about her status and profile within the community than her daughter's actual disappearance or well-being.

'We understand Allyson was quite high-spirited,' James alleged, pushing aside his tea and joining in the conversation. 'Did this bother you?'

'Of course, it bothered me, Mr Sinclair but there wasn't much I could do about it,' Susan retorted, opening a packet of biscuits, flinging them onto a plate so half spilled out onto the wooden table. 'The more you tell a teenager not to do something, the more they're going to do it.'

Katie managed a faint smile. She herself had been quite a rebel as a teenager, yet probably not to the extent of Allyson Carter.

'You have kids?' Susan Carter asked of James, who briefly hesitated.

'Yes, a son.'

'How old?'

'A few months.'

'Yes, well he's far too young to give you any grief but mark my words he will when he's older. Now I must soldier on with the ironing. I'm sure you will get back in touch when you have any news of value. Thanks for dropping by.'

Taking the hint, James and Katie stood up to leave. 'If you remember anything of importance please get in touch,' James remarked. 'Even small details can provide crucial evidence.'

'Goodbye.' Susan Carter ushered them towards the door, closing it almost before the visitors had stepped out over the threshold.

'She's hiding something,' James concluded, heading back down the driveway.

'Do you think?' Katie opened the passenger side door, slipping inside. 'She's certainly a bit odd.'

****

The Late Gothic architecture of the fourteenth-century Church of Saint Pancreas loomed in front of the Land Rover as James warily piloted it through the small picture-postcard village of Widecombe-in-the Moor. Gaining the moniker "Cathedral of the Moors" due to its 120-foot tower crafted from locally quarried stone, the church over hundreds of years had benefited from continual enlargement and maintenance, funded by proceeds from the tin mining trade.

Narrowly avoiding being sideswiped by a tourist bus, James parked the battered 4WD near the village green, strolling across the springy grass to the main entrance of the imposing building. Some effort was required to open the great wooden door which creaked and groaned.

Inside a cold draft engulfed him as his eyes adjusted to the dim light. The church appeared deserted.

'Is anyone here?' he called out, his voice echoing through the ancient edifice.

'Be with you in a mo,' a male voice called out, from near the pulpit. 'I'm just finishing preparations for Sunday's service.'

After a few seconds, a tall sprightly figure, recognisable as a man of the cloth, materialised out of the semi-darkness, striding purposefully up the centre aisle.

'I hope I'm not interrupting,' James said, offering the Vicar his hand to shake.

'Not at all my man, everyone is welcome into God's house. Is this your first visit to St Pancreas?'

James nodded.

'Then allow me to introduce this wonderful structure to you.' Reverend Carter beamed. 'Did you know the church was badly damaged in the Great Thunderstorm of 1638, apparently struck by lightning? At the time an afternoon service was taking place with over 300 worshipers. Four people were killed and around sixty injured. According to local legend, the village was visited by the Devil. Take a leaflet on your way out, there are so many interesting facts to be learned.'

'I might just do that.'

'This was not an easy place for burying people in the olden days,' Carter continued with gusto, pleased for the gift of a willing victim on which to practice his local knowledge. 'Can you imagine the strenuous task of carrying coffins up and down the steep outcrops that lie around these parts? What may also interest you is many small lanes close to Devon churches bear the name "Coffins Lane". This was the quickest and easiest route to get the bodies to the church. All fascinating stuff, now how can I help you today? Not in any trouble, are you?'

'Err, not exactly Reverend,' James articulated, producing his Moorlands ID. 'My name is James Sinclair. I'm a forensic scientist hoping to have a word with you about your missing daughter.'

'I see.' Reverend Carter's complexion paled slightly, momentarily lost for words as a surge of adrenalin shot through his arteries.

'Bovey Tracey, eh. Forensics? You're not the Police then?'

'Right, private consultants. We're contracted to help with the rash of recent homicides and disappearances.'

'Enchanting little town; I've been over there a few times to give the local vicar a hand.'

'Is there somewhere we can sit, which is a little more private?' James enquired. 'I expect on a fine day such as this one you have tourists dropping by to admire the church.'

'Yes, of course, forgive me for my manners,' Reverend Carter apologised. 'Come, let's head out the back and share some communal wine. A little tipple won't hurt, and I am sure it would meet with the benevolent Lord's approval.'

'This really is a beautiful church, very impressive,' James remarked, taking a seat in the ancient vestry, surrounded by antiquarian volumes and the pervasive smell of medieval oak.

'Indeed it is, I heartily concur with your astute observation. I was fortunate to get the temporary position of Vicar at St Pancreas. I often steal up here at night and sit for hours in the bell tower, watching the stars tracing their eternal paths through the heavens. There's something about Dartmoor, Mr Sinclair, that brings out the good and bad in many souls.'

'I don't know if you are aware, Mr Carter but the recent discovery of two bodies on the moors has stirred up interest in the disappearance of your daughter Allyson. At first, we thought one of the bodies might have been Allyson, but that was not the case.'

Reverend Carter sighed. 'To tell you the truth Sinclair; I was rather relieved to be told neither was my daughter. That still gives me a glimmer of hope Allyson may still be alive.'

'I would guess the past months have been very tough for you.'

'If it wasn't for the love of God, neither Susan nor I would have coped. There have been times I wanted to end it all, throw myself off the top of the church tower, but what would that achieve, nothing.'

'Were you and Allyson close, Mr Carter?'

'I like to think we were, but my wife may say otherwise. We did our best by both our children. We believed in offering them the best education money can buy, coupled with a positive start to life. I'm sure you're aware Allyson was a student at Abbey College, part of the St Oswald's Priory near Buckfast Abbey. The fees are steep, but you couldn't get a finer education. If you're truly seeking God, you'll find him, wandering around the Abbey. It has a tranquillity and beauty like no other place I've seen. Stop by sometime and see the great work they do there.'

'What else can you tell me about your daughter?' James watched Carter knocking back the altar wine.

'Allyson is a beautiful spirit,' the Vicar remarked. 'At times she can be direct, but underneath that tough exterior, she has a very kind nature. Not everyone would agree with me Mr Sinclair, nevertheless, I know my daughter. Whoever has taken her from us will be punished. I will see the evil bastards locked away for what they have done, may they rot in hell.' Anger etched his firm features; a steely resolve flashed across his grey eyes.

'So you're still convinced someone abducted your daughter?' James reaffirmed. 'Have you any idea who?'

The Reverend shook his head. 'No, I search for answers, but I find none. Go and talk with the Monks at Buckfast Abbey, Mr Sinclair. Brother Paul Tanner has his own beliefs but refuses to part with that knowledge. I even tried to bribe it out of him, but Brother Paul would not divulge anything, which sadly, I must respect him for.'

'Where exactly will I find Brother Paul?' James's interest kindled.

'Tending to his little friends, the bees of course,' Carter answered. 'He's head beekeeper, producing some of the best honey in the region. Quite a colony he's got going over there. You go pay the old guy a visit, he's full of interesting anecdotes.'

'Thank you, I may just do that. I appreciate you taking the time to talk with me today, Sir. I hope our current investigation can help solve your daughter's disappearance.'

'Oh, I'm sure it will, Mr Sinclair. You come across as an intelligent man, who will stop at nothing to discover the truth. I hope to see you again sometime. Remember, God's house is your house.'

Walking slowly out into the warm sunshine James felt a strange, almost spiritual calm slowly sweeping through his being. What normally mattered in life suddenly became irrelevant, as he made his way across the busy road, oblivious to the manic tourist traffic. He eased himself gently onto the grassy common, where within minutes he was in a deep, almost opium-like, induced slumber.

James's brain had finally cried enough, switching his metabolism into a state of suspended stasis. At last, his body succumbed and the one-million-year-old regenerative process inherent in all of us, that had been denied his neuron cells for the last eleven days, began in earnest.

Four hours later, Jim Sinclair was brought back to consciousness by a sudden drop in temperature when the sun dipped behind the church tower.

He lay there for at least twenty minutes, eyes still closed, motionless, revelling in the zen-like state within.

Sitting up, he gazed around to discover he was almost entirely alone in the village centre. The tourists had gone, save for a young girl nearby, on an old wooden swing.

He felt twenty years younger. Staring down at his chronograph, he couldn't believe the time. To his astonishment no one had attempted to call; no missed calls, no urgent messages – a miracle!

Rising cautiously to his feet, he checked jacket for wallet and walked slowly to the nearest pub. After devouring a half kilo medium-rare rump steak washed down with a pint of Guinness, he located the Landie, removed keys from under the seat and drove home at a 40-kph crawl across the high moor. Arriving at the duplex in Bovey Tracey just before 8pm, he collapsed into bed and slept dreamless for the next sixteen hours.

****

Waking at lunchtime the next day and being Tuesday, James left a brief message on Fiona's phone, making the decision to drive over to Buckfast Abbey in the hope of obtaining a few minutes with Brother Paul Tanner, the monk who claimed to be "harbouring a few secrets". He was also keen to enjoy time away from the office, deeming it not necessary to involve Parker and Co at this stage in any discussions, telling himself it was merely speculative following up, mixed with idle curiosity. Besides, he liked digging around alone unmolested, occasionally it bore fruit.

'I'm looking for a Brother Paul Tanner, do you know where I might find him?'

A plump, red-faced woman seemingly engrossed in unpacking a box of crucifixes behind the Abbey souvenir shop counter, looked up. 'This time of day, the herb garden around the back of the Abbey. Just keep following the path with the herbaceous borders and you'll get to a small summer house, Brother Paul will be around there, no matter what the weather brings.'

'Thank you.'

Following instructions, James headed in the direction of the greenhouse, passing visitors enjoying a day out. Buckfast Abbey was a rewarding destination to spend a good many hours, attracting sightseers from many parts. In a deeply troubled world, it provided a haven of solitude to reflect on many of lives' trials and tribulations. Even those with mixed religious views would come away having found a small piece of tranquillity and a modicum of spiritual strength.

The old Monk was easy to spot, going on the description supplied by Reverend Carter. Clothed in the mandatory, long black woollen habit of the Benedictine Order; oblivious to the attention he attracted he muttered away to himself, kneeling on the pathway lost in repotting a row of lavender on the edge of the herb garden.

'Brother Paul?' James enquired expectantly, coming to stand next to the Monk. The venerable friar turned slowly to look up quizzically at the visitor.

'Yes, you'll have to speak up if we're to have a conversation lad; I'm extremely hard of hearing. What did you say your name was? At nearly ninety-five I think I do all right though.'

'Jim Sinclair, sir. I've been visiting Reverend Carter at St Pancreas in Widecombe,' James proclaimed, kneeling down on one knee next to the friar. 'He suggested I drop by to see you; said you have many fascinating stories to tell.'

The wiry old friar turned back to the repotting. 'Ah yes, the Reverend Carter, he often comes by to spend time in the Abbey grounds and share a glass of port with me. His knowledge of local history is quite remarkable, especially considering he's not Devonian. How about you, Sir, are ye from around these parts? If you were, you would know all about witchery, demons and ghosts. Dartmoor has many a legend to tell young man, ancient secrets of gross peril. Although my days of fear are long gone, nowadays I focus on what brings me pleasure. I guess you'd know about the bees I keep here.'

'Bovey Tracey born and bred,' James remarked cheerfully, proud of his local heritage. 'My family has lived on Dartmoor for centuries.'

'I hardly need to tell you that in the twentieth century, thirty of our bee colonies were wiped out by a disease known as Acarine. All of the bees that died were of the British black bee variety. They were renowned for being hardy, but somewhat ill-tempered. Interestingly enough, the bees that did survive were all Italian.' The friar's discourse was cut short by a shallow cough, which saw him gasp momentarily for breath. 'The end result you see today from years of hard work, is the Buckfast Bee, a first-rate pollen gatherer and rather gentle. Remind me to get you some honey before you head home.'

'My grandfather used to attend the Abbey for Services on Holy Days and on Sundays for morning mass.'

'Then he would have walked in the Lord's footsteps,' Paul commented. 'By the fourteenth century, Buckfast was one of the wealthiest Abbeys in the South-West of England. The life here is one of prayer, work and study. Many a day you'll find us in the grounds seeking peace with the Almighty.'

James listened to the old man's history lesson, amazed at the coherent narrative and encyclopaedic recall for one of such advanced years.

'Brother Patrick currently takes care of the farm where we grow our vegetables and keep pigs and cattle. Drop into the shop and purchase some wine or perhaps a sacred item of precious metal, a medal of the Virgin Mary or scapulars crafted in real leather from Assisi. Brother Patrick will bless it for you. He is there most mornings chatting about his wares, there's not much he doesn't know about farming and religion.'

'I do remember coming here on school excursions,' broke in James. 'The Norman Abbey was razed to the ground during the Reformation wasn't it?'

'True, true my lad. Henry spared none of the monastic orders. The Saxons had an Abbey on this very site well before the invasion, then the Benedictines and finally the Cistercians.

You can read all about Buckfast Abbey, but I am happy to divulge a few interesting facts:

Above the high altar and stained-glass windows hangs the chandelier Corona Lucis. Before you leave today, I recommend you go take a look; quite remarkable.

Our lives at the Abbey are relaxed here but we work hard, lad. At twenty-five past five on weekdays, an hour later on Sundays, a bell rings and we leave our beds to gather in the abbey church for prayer. To work in God's name is a life of commitment and passion. Not for the faint-hearted. You need to be stoic to be ordained.'

'By any chance did you know Allyson Carter, the teenager who went missing on the moors a little over fifteen months ago?' James, seizing the chance to change the conversation, when Brother Paul finally came up for air. 'Her father, Reverend Carter says you still believe his daughter to be alive.'

Tanner put down his trowel, taking up unsteady residence on a nearby upturned pot. 'I only met Allyson on odd occasions. I used to teach History at Abbey College, but of course, that was a long time ago now, although mind you, I occasionally run beekeeping classes, that's where I encountered Allyson, she attended one of my lectures. I recall her being a high spirited, pretty young thing, bless her soul, but not without a few issues.'

'Mr Carter told me you have some interesting theories on what might have happened to his daughter,' James pressed.

'The Reverend said that, did he?' The old monk drew a deep breath, dabbing his brow on the back of an old gardening glove. 'Theories are all they are, young man. I look for all my answers from God, but God will never reveal answers. That would be mortal sacrilege in his eyes.'

Silence prevailed for several seconds before Brother Paul asked a question of his own. 'I hear you've found two other young women that went missing. Tell me, were they unrecognisable, had something happened to their faces?'

James was taken aback. 'If you know something about their disappearance Brother Paul, I urge you to tell me, you cannot suppress vital information in an ongoing investigation.'

'I only see what God wants me to see. The visions come and go, yet there is nothing which can really help you. Come, let the Parson have some Brandy and Baccy for the Clark.'

The old monk mumbled something illegible before beckoning James to follow him across the open lawns to the edge of a small wood and to an old potting shed cluttered with foldup chairs and old beekeeping equipment. Once inside, he half-filled two lead crystal brandy balloons from a dusty bottle of five-star VSOP and rummaged in his habit, producing an old crumpled cigarette.

'This is the life the Almighty intended for us,' he decreed, in a croaking voice, raising his glass high in the air, then emptying the contents in one gulp. 'No gain will ever come of us trying to drag up the past young man. You'd best let well alone boy. Leave the Powers of Darkness to their own devices.'

'If you do know something Brother Paul, you have an obligation to tell me?' James pushed once more. 'You won't suffer retribution for telling me what you know.'

'That's the thing, my son.' The old man sighed. 'I *don't* know anything. What I hear and see is all through the eyes of the Lord. Often at night, I wake in a cold sweat with images and voices all around. God is trying to tell me something, *but what*, I do not know.'

'Do you believe Allyson Carter to still be alive?'

'Oh, yes, she is very much alive. If she were dead her eternal spirit would be all around us... yet it isn't. Dear Allyson, is very much alive.'

****

'Next on the left, then left again and about 100 metres along,' instructed Ben Crispin, checking again the coloured graphics on the dash-mounted GPS.

Matt Tyler swung the unmarked police Jaguar saloon down the small South Kensington backstreet and brought it to a gentle stop to the chiming of the sat nav in a secluded cul de sac, in front of a row of Georgian terrace apartments.

'Yep, this is it, 43 Compton Mews. We can go right up. The guard was taken off this morning. Bruce Peters is allowed access after 8pm, so let's make it count.'

Mounting the stairs to the imposing front entrance two at a time, Matt extracted the code from his notebook and checked the list of residents above the keypad. Punching in the four digits, they waited for the clunk and pushed open the shiny, black Regency door. Entering a spacious, faintly lit, tastefully decorated main vestibule, Crispin pointed to the second apartment immediately on their left.

'You're the one with authority to be here,' Matt reminded the police officer, tossing the key to the Senior Detective. 'Wetherill hates Moorland Forensics with a passion, I've been reminded not to touch anything or remove anything without your permission. I'm surprised he even let me join you on this jaunt.'

Ben returned a smile, taking a step over the threshold, fingers searching for a light switch just inside the door. There was no need. Sensors detected their presence. Warm, seductive hi-tech lighting flooded the apartment, illuminating the hallway to a lavishly furnished living room, not out of place in Architectural Digest. 'Remember Matt old fellow; The DI has few friends, yet a multitude of crooked acquaintances. Wow, this place is quite impressive, there's some serious money in these antiques.'

Matt executed a swift sidestep as Ben nonchalantly waved around a valuable Art Nouveau Moorcroft vase, featuring a pomegranate design, vintage circa 1917, almost knocking it against a French Empire Revival side table.

'This computer looks like it has not been used in ages, but I'll take it anyway,' Matt conveyed to his colleague. 'You never know what hidden gems could be lurking on the hard drive; hopefully, I'll find something worth deciphering.'

Crispin was sceptical. 'Damn technology bores me to tears. You're welcome to rummage around on the old duck's computer. I expect all you'll find is a few ancient recipes, coupled with the latest patchwork quilt designs.'

'How old do you think Veronica Peters is?' Matt scolded. '*The old duck*, as you not so elegantly put it, must have seriously pissed someone off to have her head smashed in.'

'Nicely put,' Crispin conceded. 'Let's go, I want to check the flat above and find out if any of the immediate neighbours can fill us in on Veronica's habits. Funny her occupation didn't come up anywhere in hubby's records of the interview – I guess no one asked, or else it wasn't deemed important; it happens. Anyway, nothing much to be gained from hanging around here. The Met teams have already been through the place and taken items of interest, which no doubt includes a more modern PC.'

Ignoring Ben's comment, Matt followed him up a flight of stairs to the next level, checking the name on the intercom before pressing the buzzer. After a few seconds an elderly Sikh gentleman, recognisable by beard and turban, slowly opened the door.

'Sorry to disturb you, Mr Singh,' Matt began a little hesitantly, raising ID. 'I am not sure if you are aware of the recent death of Mrs Veronica Peters, she was living with her husband in flat 2 just below you.'

Singh cleared a congested throat. 'Yes, yes, dreadful state of affairs. I knew Veronica reasonably well. Come on in Mr…'

'Matthew Tyler and this is my colleague Senior Detective Ben Crispin, from the City of London Police.'

The two men followed Singh into a flat, similar to the one belonging to the Peters, taking up residence on a cane settee. It was the same layout, different furniture, a mix of Habitat and Indian provincial – a little more down-market.

'The funny thing is Mr Singh we know very little about Veronica Peters, her likes and dislikes, even her line of work,' Ben informed him.

The affable Sikh beamed. 'Please, call me Viram, I do hate formalities.'

'Viram it is,' Ben acknowledged. 'So what can you tell us about Veronica?'

'Veronica was a very private woman, mostly kept to herself the dear lady. Occasionally, she would drop up for a chat and bring a freshly baked apple pie when she was home. I hardly ever saw her husband and if I did it was only a nod. She travelled a lot, mostly on the Continent, sometimes away for weeks on end. I believe she was a fine art expert.'

'Did she mention who she worked for?'

'Ahh… I can't recall anything specific; I don't like to pry, you know. However, from what few things she did let slip; I got the distinct impression she dealt a lot with the German Federal Police… what do you think? Does that sound plausible?'

Matt and Ben exchanged glances.

'I understood she had affiliations with an art gallery, somewhere in the Borough of Kensington and Chelsea,'

Viram continued. 'Veronica may even have been the owner, again I can't be entirely sure of that.'

'Would you happen to know if Veronica rented office space in the local area or employed anybody.'

'No, I would have known if that were the case. Although at times she half-jokingly mentioned a John Constable in conversation. Could have been a confidant or love interest, I suppose.'

'Before the trip down to Devon, did you notice anything different in her behaviour?' Ben asked, not wanting to delve into Veronica's personal affairs.

The elderly Sikh gazed at the ceiling. 'Funny you mention that; yes, uneasy perhaps, fidgety possibly; but I merely interpreted this as excitement. Veronica was deeply religious, constantly searching for inner peace. She hinted at a meeting with someone of great spiritual values during the trip to the West Country, no name was mentioned of course.'

'Did this information get passed on to the Police?' Ben prompted, jotting down the details in a small notebook.

'Oh yes, indeed, a senior chap name of Rob or Ron Wetherhall, I think, took my call.'

Ben scoffed, quickly turning it into a cough. 'We appreciate your time today Sir, many thanks.'

'There was *one* thing before you go.'

Disappearing quickly into the study the Sikh returned with a sealed plastic courier packet. 'Veronica usually gets me to collect any mail or parcels. This came special delivery when they were in the South West.'

Back in the Jag, Crispin carefully opened the satchel, retrieving a formal brown envelope. He quickly scanned the contents and passed it to Tyler, who read aloud:

'Cohen, Milkin, Rabinowitz and Partners – Attorneys at Law

Avenue of the Americas,
New York City, New York
To: Ms Veronica Peters, Fine Arts International Search
Dear Ms Peters,

Thank you again for your efforts over the last eighteen months, which have resulted in the tracking down and finally recovery of the Cellini silver platter and the Rubens oil.

The Trustees of the Rothstein Estate and the family members are delighted that the pieces, missing since 1940, have at last returned to their rightful place.

In accordance with the terms of the arrangement please find enclosed, with their blessing, a cheque for $65,000, including agreed fee plus expenses.

Raymond Cohen
Senior Partner'

'Bloody fine art expert all right.' Matt whistled. 'I would suggest V. P. was also a professional agent, active in the recovery of lost and stolen artworks for victims of The Third Reich and Stalin.'

Both men stared at the raindrops forming on the windscreen.

'Okay, put two and two together and it sounds like our Veronica might have got too close to unearthing a few old watercolours. I suggest you make a start on going through Veronica's computer Matt my man. Hopefully, you'll unearth "a few hidden gems", that's if you can crack the password, which could take you weeks, months even.'

'Already done.' Matt laughed, giving Ben the "thumbs up". 'John Constable seems the obvious choice, wouldn't you agree?'

Dear Heavenly Father, sometimes a little power makes us do things we later regret. Help me to stay strong and do what is just and fair. They are starting to get close beloved Lord; help me find a way to silence them. I will once more have blood on my hands, but with your love and guidance, it is surely the right thing to do.

Teach me to forgive my own sins and show me the strength to bury the past.

May the Lord have mercy upon my soul.

Amen

Chapter Nine

James tore open the light brown envelope, allowing the contents to spill out onto the laboratory workbench. There were a few black and white photos all showing Lauren's husband in a compromising position with a well-endowed blonde. How authentic they were, was anyone's guess, as James well knew how Malcolm Frobisher and his team operated. It was highly likely they had employed a male porn model lookalike for the shots.

Pinned to the pictures was a photocopy of a signed Airway Bill document and Commercial Invoice, supposedly authorising a shipment described as coffee from Columbia, origin Medellin. The signature looked like that of Simon Greig, Lauren's husband.

For a brief moment, James felt a pang of guilt, before sliding back to reality. If underhand ways proved the only means to gain custody of Lauren's baby, so be it. Jason was his biological son, he had rights, Greig had none. Yet the officious left of the law would not see it in that light.

Alerted by the front door buzzer, James swiftly shovelled the contents back into the envelope, before pushing it out of view under the base of an electronic microbalance.

'You look bloody awful,' Fiona commented, walking in through the quarantine door, observing her brother rubbing both eyes and stifling a yawn. 'Get much sleep last night?'

'Not a lot, I have a few things weighing on my mind.'

'Care to share them with me?'

James shifted in his chair. 'I've been doing a fair bit of thinking lately, making decisions which could alter things around here over the coming months.'

'Is this serious, perhaps I'll bring in Katie, it all sounds rather ominous.'

James laughed. 'Yeah, why not, it does involve you both.'

'We're not selling up, are we?' Katie enquired, anxiety etched in her voice, James about to break his news.

'Nope, this is more a personal matter. I am claiming custody of my son. I see no point in him living with Lauren's husband, who is totally unrelated. I, as his natural father, feel it only right that he comes and lives with me.'

Both women stared at their brother, lost for words. Fiona eventually found her voice.

'Okay, so the baby is your son, but what happens next? Morally you can hardly contact Lauren's husband, admitting his wife was having an affair. The poor man has only recently buried his wife and now you want to take his son away from him. Think carefully about all this James, before you ruin so many lives.'

'He's my son for goodness sake,' James shot back. 'I have a right to get to know him.'

'Yes, but now is not the right time,' Fiona pressed. 'Let the dust settle first.'

'I for one, can't even envisage how you will manage to raise a child,' Katie chimed in. 'Running Moorland Forensics is a full-time job, when are you going to find time to be a proper father.'

James stood up to tower over his sisters, his annoyance coming to the surface. 'I'll sell up if I have to. You and Fi can buy my share of the business. I'm sure you can cope very nicely without me.'

'Now you're being ridiculous,' Fiona flared up. 'Besides James, it won't be easy to claim custody. Lauren's husband is a tough individual, he won't give up his son that easily.'

'My son,' James corrected his sister, his voice rising a notch. 'Jason is my son.'

'At least have time to think about things,' Katie counselled, trying to ease the tension in the room. 'Jason already has a loving father and is now growing up without a mother, why complicate things.'

'I won't let this drop; I plan to go for custody of Jason whether you or anyone likes it,' James fought back. 'I had hoped I would have your blessings and you would aide me with the court proceedings; clearly, I was wrong. Silly me, I deemed blood to be thicker than water; got that wrong, didn't I?'

****

'You could definitely do with cheering up,' Ben remarked, entering the Moorland office to find a downcast Katie, staring blankly into space. 'Fancy dinner at my place tonight. We can combine it with business to discuss Hayley Illbert-Tavistock if it will clear your conscious being alone with me in my one-bedroom rented apartment.'

Katie laughed. 'Dinner sounds great, what time and would you like me to bring anything?'

'Just your beautiful self, and be warned, I am a skilful cook and modest too.'

****

'So what's on the menu?' Katie enquired, sinking more comfortably into Ben's three-seater sofa in his tiny flat in Chagford, welcoming the opportunity to put recent woes behind her.

'The best Bolognese outside of Italy.' Ben smiled, busy chopping vegetables in the small galley kitchen, keeping a keen eye on his visitor, a lump forming in his throat as he realised, he was seriously falling for Katie Sinclair.

'Where did you learn to cook so well?'

'Well, if you must know I learnt from my daughter when she was only ten, she, of course, learnt from her mother.'

Katie looked surprised. 'I had no idea you had a daughter.'

Ben laughed. 'It's not something I talk about very often. I lost contact with Helena when she was finally adopted by a family in Taunton.'

'What about the child's mother, where is she?'

'Christina and I weren't very close; our relationship was nothing more than a casual fling. Christina never coped well with being a single mum, eventually, she returned to her immediate family in Andorra, our daughter was given up for adoption. As it goes, I was an overworked probationary constable, so the idea of me raising a young child wasn't even on the cards, in case you were wondering.'

Katie raised her hands in the air, mindful not to spill any red. 'Hey, I am not judging. My brother James is contemplating just that, raising a small child, whilst continuing a busy career.'

'It's possible, but not ideal,' Ben responded, reaching for an ovenproof dish. 'In fact, I've been trying to trace my daughter for the past few months, but so far I've not had any luck. Help yourself to the pinot. I'll join you in a minute. Shit.'

More loud expletives followed in rapid succession, Katie leapt from the couch to investigate.

'Nothing major,' Ben reassured her. 'Cut myself on the damn paring knife.'

'It's quite deep,' Katie remarked, holding his hand to take a look. 'Where's your first aid kit?'

'Top drawer, near the fridge.'

Katie retrieved the necessary equipment, putting pressure on the cut. 'One small wound and you bleed forever,' she grumbled, applying a pressure bandage. 'In future, you shouldn't be put in charge of knives. You could benefit from a woman taking care of you.'

'Marry me and we'll soon change all that.' Ben grinned, wrapping his unaffected hand around her waist. 'You can be a stay at home wife, cooking, cleaning and caring for our five children.'

Katie blushed.

'We can talk about this proposal later,' she scolded, finally able to apply a plaster. 'Now, if you're sure you can manage, keep chopping and I'll refill our glasses.'

****

'I don't suppose you know anything about this do you?' Fiona enquired of her brother, waving the local rag under his nose. 'Quite a front-page headline. And I quote;

Simon Greig, a lieutenant serving with the SAS based in Plymouth, is facing serious criminal charges for involvement in an illicit drugs importation scheme. It will be alleged by senior Customs officials that Greig was part of a ring attempting to bring a large quantity of high purity cocaine from Columbia into the UK through the Port of Southampton last November. If convicted, Greig could face a ten-year jail sentence.'

James leaned across the bench, quickly scanned the article and tossed the paper aside.

'Must I be responsible for everything Tom Markham chooses to print in his cheap newspaper?' James announced, feigning disinterest. 'Why not quiz Markham on this article, he wrote it, not me.'

'I plan to do just that,' Fiona retaliated, her temper flaring. 'I find it extremely odd at the precise time you lodge court papers to claim custody of your son, Simon Greig faces a lengthy jail sentence, very convenient if you ask me.'

'Purely a coincidence,' James said casually. 'Now, if you've finished blaming me for a life of wanton destruction, I must forge on with finalising this solvent extraction.'

Fiona stormed out of the laboratory, returning half an hour later, still spitting fire.

'So I spoke with Markham,' she enlightened James. 'Apparently, he received anonymous documentation indicating Simon Greig had a strong involvement with an overseas drug cartel. This evidence will be used in a court of law.'

'No surprises there then,' James mocked. 'What else did Markham tell you? Did my name come up in conversation?'

'No, but I also emailed Captain Travis Black, an old Uni buddy, fairly high up at Army in legal admin and did offer to undertake testing on the documents for fingerprints and physical evidence. Don't suppose I'd find yours on any of them would I James?'

'Nope, not mine,' James countered, with an air of smugness. 'The thing is dear sister; even if I were involved in this hair-brained scheme to frame 2nd Lieut. Simon Greig, do you think I would be stupid enough to leave my mark? I hate to disappoint, but no indication of my involvement will you find on any of those documents. However, feel free to test as much as you like, mind you it won't come cheap. As it's not work-related, you must pay for the equipment and time spent on all of this. The brilliant news is; I am happy to offer a discounted rate.'

Fiona shot her brother a scathing look, then marched out the door, slamming it firmly behind her. A gut feeling told her James was guilty as hell, yet how was she to prove it? Also, what benefit would it do anyway? Dragging up unwanted confessions wasn't going to score points or provide any benefits; it would only plunge them all into feud and misery. As much as Fiona wanted to find out the truth, she knew in her heart she couldn't throw her brother under a bus. On this occasion, she would have to live with it, but it didn't mean she liked the fact James was prepared to indulge in a fraudulent conspiracy for his own ends.

****

Katie reached for the telephone, wondering who could be calling at eleven o'clock at night. She loathed late-night callers, especially if they were trying to sell her something.

'Yes,' she snapped into the receiver.

'Is this Katie Sinclair?' The young woman sounded nervous.

'Yes, who's this?'

'My name's Annabelle Newton, I was Allyson Carter's best friend at school. We briefly met the other week when you called at the school asking questions about Ally.'

Katie flopped down onto the lounge, balancing the mobile to her ear, searching for paper and pen on the coffee table. 'How can I help you?'

'I was hoping we could meet up, somewhere private. I have information you might find interesting.'

'Why didn't you divulge this the first time we met?'

'I wasn't sure who I could trust,' Annabelle remarked. 'Please Miss Sinclair, this is important.'

'There's a small tearoom in the main high street of Bovey Tracey; *The Coffee Spoon,* I can meet you there tomorrow at ten o'clock.'

Annabelle ended the call without confirming the meeting, leaving Katie wondering if she would actually bother to turn up. Desperate for new leads, she scribbled down the details in her diary, knowing any new information could be valuable. Normally she would log this as an official meeting, but on this occasion, she decided not to.

****

Katie was on her second cup of premium Turkish blend black when Annabelle finally came through the door, her expression flustered. 'Sorry I'm late,' she apologised, taking a seat. 'I've only recently learned to drive and not too crash hot at parking yet.'

Katie managed a smile, noting the unintended pun. 'You're here, that's the main thing.'

She was struck by the girl's emaciated features, probably weighing in at around seven stone. When they first met at Abbey College, Annabelle was sporting a faded baggy jumper, covering up what now looked like the onset of Anorexia Nervosa. Her grey eyes were two sunken hollows, dull in contrast to Katie's bright sparkling blue ones. Chemically damaged hair hung limp and lifeless.

Trying to dismiss thoughts of concern, Katie watched Annabelle place a peppermint tea order with the waitress, then nervously rearrange the sugar bowl and other table items, until they all lined up in a neat row.

'I managed to get my hands on a copy of the original statement you gave when Allyson first went missing,' Katie began the conversation, hoping to ease some of Annabelle's nerves. 'Your story seems consistent with reports given by others at the time.'

Annabelle nodded. 'There was nothing to hide Miss Sinclair, the last time I saw Ally we were all heading over to Haytor Rock after classes to smoke weed. Before we got to the top of the Escarpment Ally chucked a sharp right along a rough bridle path to Heather Muse, the derelict property owned by old Bert Simms. Ally claimed to be meeting someone in the basement of the old property.'

'Did she say who she was meeting?' Katie asked, spellbound by this revelation.

'No, but she said we'd be amazed who it was.'

'Did you actually see Allyson enter the house?'

The conversation paused briefly, interrupted by the arrival of the tea order.

'Yep, that's when we all got scared and fled. One of the boys swears blind he saw a spooky face staring out across the moor from a top floor window. That was enough to frighten me. I ran all the way to the main road without stopping.'

'So what new information can you shed on Allyson's disappearance? Was she in trouble, an unwanted pregnancy perhaps?'

'Ask me no questions and I'll tell you no lies; famous smugglers poem by Rudyard Kipling, Miss Sinclair. Ally and I used that phrase when we had no intention of divulging secrets.'

'What if your secrets can help us discover what has happened to Allyson?' Katie urged. 'Perhaps Allyson is still alive, being held captive somewhere, has that thought ever occurred to you?'

Annabelle shrugged. 'I'd like time to think about it, Ally and I had a firm bond, I can't allow myself to waiver on assumptions. Besides, if Ally is alive, she would have reached out to me by now, we were best mates.'

'Not if she's in danger and can't make contact with the outside world,' Katie enlightened the young woman sitting opposite. 'Annabelle, I urge you to tell myself or the police if you know anything which might help us find out what happened to Allyson. Perhaps there's something Allyson might have mentioned before she disappeared that is only now starting to bounce back into your memory.'

'I'm sure it's all there for you to discover, you just haven't delved deep enough yet.' Annabelle stared directly into Katie's pale eyes. 'Keep searching and eventually, you'll uncover the truth, Ms Sinclair. What I can tell you is this: the ones dressed in robes have dark secrets, they cover up their sins before the eyes of God. If you want to find Allyson that's where she will be. She must have found out too much and we all know how they punish those who venture too far towards the dark nemesis.'

'Who are these people?' Katie urged.

'They were part of our lives nearly every day,' Annabelle acknowledged. 'You know who they are by recognising their footsteps. Their faces were often covered, as they made their way through the maze of stone corridors. Yet we knew each and every one of them Ms Sinclair. Some were pure and kind, others; well others, they were agents for the devil's work on earth. That's all I can tell you without betraying Ally, but I'm sure you'll work it out.'

****

'Fiona's gone to London to stay with Mike and Paula for a few days. I just dropped her at the station. Some cryptic stuff about a break to clear her head. Do you know what that's about?' Katie enquired of James when he entered the office the following morning.

'Haven't got a clue,' lied James, poker-faced, fiddling with the mini oven and avoiding eye contact with his sister.

'Maybe she wants to catch that West End musical she's been going on about.'

'What musical?' Katie questioned. 'That's news to me, anyway, she said we can use her car anytime.'

Before she could continue the interrogation, James's mobile rang, saving him from inevitable embarrassment.

'That was Will Parker,' James announced. I'm meeting him at the Carters place in forty-five minutes. I'll take up Fiona's offer of the TVR.'

****

'I've received a call from Will Parker,' James informed Nick, fiddling with the volume on the hands-free and shouting above the wind noise as he punished Fiona's flashy sportscar flat chat along the A38. 'The Carters have found a parcel on their doorstep with a note attached, claiming there's a small ceramic box inside containing strands of Allyson's hair. I'm heading over there now to catch up with Will. This could be the break we've been chasing.'

'Let's hope so, my guess someone's playing games, leading us on a merry goose chase as to what has really happened to Allyson Carter.'

Mrs Carter was visibly shaking when she opened the door to James just before 6pm. 'It must have been left late this afternoon,' she explained, handing over the small brown box. 'It wasn't there when I drove into Plymouth at lunchtime.'

James carefully unwrapped the brown paper wrapping, placing it into a clear plastic bag. He doubted there would be fingerprints but under the circumstances, they could leave nothing to chance. Even the best criminals made mistakes, becoming careless as they gained in confidence.

Inside were two small clumps of dark brown hair, which were spilt out onto a sheet of A4 paper.

'Do you think this could be locks of Allyson's hair?' Reverend Carter enquired, joining the small group in the sitting room. 'They certainly are the same colour.'

'We'll record them as official evidence and run some lab procedures,' James answered. 'The results will take a few days to come back. You also need to know that, even if this hair does belong to Allyson, there's no proof she's still alive.'

All this finally proved too much for Mrs Carter who broke into intermittent sobs. 'What are they trying to do to us.' She wailed. 'Why can't they just tell us what they have done with her?'

James eyeballed the crying woman in despair. Katie was more equipped to deal with distraught family members.

'As soon as I know anything, I will get in contact,' he remarked, beating a hasty retreat to his vehicle, leaving a hapless Will to deal with the histrionics.

By the time he drove in through the Moorlands Office courtyard security gate, James had already formulated in his mind the procedure. For insurance, he would split the hair sample between Moorlands and the Home Office contracted labs. Neither he nor Fiona had performed a hair DNA for a few years, and he needed the practice, besides it was healthy to test their technique and turnaround against the government boys' benchmark at every opportunity.

Back in the laboratory he systematically examined every hair under the stereomicroscope, being ultra-careful to employ rigorous handling methods and avoid any possible contamination. They were in luck, he identified and removed seven hair fibres still with the follicle attached. Reserving three for Moorlands, the other four were placed in a sterile container to be sent off to the Bristol labs. There was at least a 60% chance Moorlands could now successfully isolate, replicate and characterise the hair follicle DNA required for a match with Allyson Carter's.

Wasting no time, and with Fiona absent, James immediately started work.

First job, carefully remove the follicles from the hair strands together with any attached mitochondrial DNA, combine them in a small reaction phial, purify chemically and then extract the Nuclear DNA; the type required to perform a genetic match. Next, he added restriction nuclease enzymes to cut the DNA strands at 13 specific loci into fragments which contain the tandem repeat sections, the basis of the standard STR (or short tandem repeat) DNA profiling technique. Now put in train a rapid, simple and automated multiple replication process or PCR to dramatically increase the amount of DNA (up to a billion copies) in a process known as DNA amplification. With sufficient DNA repeat fragment material now available James ran a series of gel electrophoresis chromatograms to separate the DNA into its characteristic fragments by molecular weight.

After four days of careful, intense work, slotted in between other urgent laboratory jobs, he was able to visualise the DNA patterns with UV Laser light and record the electropherograms on a computer.

****

At 11am the next morning James parked the mud streaked TVR at Newton Abbot Station, directly opposite the entrance, just as the London Inter-City Service pulled in.

'I thought it was Katie picking me up, what are you doing here?' asked Fiona, throwing her bag onto the rear parcel shelf and climbing into the passenger seat.

'She's busy. How are the Westlakes?'

'Why do you want to know? You've never taken an interest in them before. They're not your friends.'

'You could at least have given me the heads up you planned a few days away,' James rebuked, readjusting his rear-view mirror and raising the driver's seat a notch. I've been going gangbusters in the lab for the last five days trying to get on top of your backlog lab stuff, coupled with some crucial DNA related to Allyson Carter.'

James's hope of a quick reconciliation had failed miserably.

Fiona ignored the remark staying silent for several minutes. 'Serves you right. I know; Katie rang me last night. You got a positive match on hair follicles to Allyson against her known DNA profile. She filled me in on the background.'

For the remainder of the thirty-minute return drive to the Bovey Tracey facility, the conversation was short, cryptic and decidedly glacial.

Back in the lab Fiona and Katie examined the Carter DNA electropherogram photographs, which James brought up on the overhead flat screen.

'Allyson's known DNA band profile using identical analytical methodology is on the left. It was on file at St

Thomas'. Can you believe they were doing a research project on kidney cancer patients DNA at the time of her operation over seven years ago? My contact says they still have her frozen tissue sections in a bank, what do you say; without any doubt a classic match with the follicle Nuclear DNA?'

Fiona nodded but didn't comment.

James continued, aware of the build-up of tension in the room. 'I sent some follicles to Bristol also as a check; could be weeks... I reckon they'll struggle with this one.'

'It's wonderful to have a match but it doesn't tell us much,' countered a still combative Fiona.

'If Allyson is still alive, perhaps there'll be letters to follow, demanding a ransom,' Katie suggested. 'I can then start building an accurate profile on the author or authors, which could help.'

'Perhaps.' James was dubious. 'It's like they want us to uncover vital clues, but they're not prepared to tell us what those clues are.'

'Given time they will,' Katie revealed. 'Bit by bit, piece by piece they part with knowledge, allowing us a chance to complete the puzzle, their way of testing our intellect.'

'Well, right now, I can do without the amateur dramatics, coupled with mind games.' James snorted. 'If Allyson is being held captive, they will undoubtedly eventually get bored and possibly resort to murder. Time is running out fast if we expect to find Allyson Carter alive.'

Our Father, who art in Heaven, hallowed be thy name. The walls are closing in. They are starting to discover the truth. I must be quicker with my actions, those who live must surely die. Once more I must have blood on my hands and take more lives. For this, I ask forgiveness.

Amen

Chapter Ten

'What can you tell me about Allyson Carter's medical history?' Katie inquired hopefully of Dr David Ashcroft over a coffee at a small teashop in the main street of Chudleigh. 'By the way, I called in to see your father at The Manors last week. He won the local bowls competition and was very pleased with himself, quite a bragger in fact.'

David laughed. 'He always did have that competitive spirit. Must we talk shop, Katie? I thought this was a relaxed social outing.'

'It is; however, I'm seeking confirmation Allyson had a diagnosis of Haemophilia. Can you give a small nod if I am correct? I know how precious your medical reputation is.'

Ashcroft smiled. 'Okay, you win. I confirm Allyson had Haemophilia but not the most common type. She is afflicted with type C, commonly found amongst Jews in Eastern Europe. Haemophilia C equally affects males and females. People of any age group can be affected.'

'How interesting, and can one presume one or both parents also had this type of Haemophilia, as they do say it's hereditary?'

David shook his head. 'No, that's what I found very odd when I made the initial diagnosis for Allyson, she would have been about eleven at the time. I tested both parents and neither had any trace of Haemophilia of any type.'

Katie's eyes opened with amazement. 'Sounds a trifle scandalous to me. Given your expert opinion on types of haemophilia, Dr Ashcroft, would I be correct in assuming Susan Carter and the amicable Reverend Carter are not Allyson's biological parents?'

'Without confirming and denying, which is clearly not my job Ms Sinclair, my advice to you is to undertake extensive research in the library and let me finish my coffee before it gets cold.'

'I'll take that as positive.' Katie smiled. 'How interesting, it would appear neither Susan Carter nor the Vicar are Allyson's biological parents. Not once have they mentioned this fact, I wonder why. What else can you tell me about Haemophilia C, I will then buy you another coffee, and if you're very lucky a scone to go with it, accompanied by jam and wait for it, *real Devonshire clotted cream!*'

Taking on a more serious demeanour, David leaned back in his chair. 'Haemophilia C is also known as Plasma Thromboplastin Antecedent (PTA) or Rosenthal Syndrome; a deficiency of Factor XI and is more problematic to manage than Haemophilia A or B. The inability to predict bleeding complicates treatment. Bleeding tends to occur more after surgery.'

'So it can be quite deadly?'

'Yes, if it isn't managed effectively.'

'Would Allyson be aware of how to manage this condition?'

'Most certainly. The advice given is to keep up to date with vaccinations, especially Hepatitis A virus and Hepatitis

B virus. She will also be aware of the unpredictable nature of her bleeding tendency.'

'If a person happened to know of Allyson's condition she could be in a lot of danger,' Katie surmised.

David nodded. 'That's true, but she'd have to be very unlucky for someone to know her medical history. Now, if that's all Ms Sinclair I would like to take you up on your offer of a Devonshire Cream Tea and if time permits, in your "oh so busy day", I know a great French restaurant in St Ives, renowned for the best seafood bouillabaisse in the country. What do you say to a leisurely drive into Cornwall, we can be there and back before midnight?'

****

'I'm still interested in that case you mentioned, the one about the young, rich journalist going missing back in 1986. Mind if I do a bit of spadework?' Ben Crispin announced, joining Katie for a ploughman's at the Frog and Toad. They had been spending a lot of time together over recent weeks, and Crispin had finally plucked up the courage to formally ask her out. At first, Katie was a bit reluctant, knowing there were other suitors in the wings keen to advance their friendship, yet there was something special about Ben, something mysterious that left her wanting more.

'It's really not my territory,' Katie answered, rubbing her fingers down the side of his left cheek. 'I've no objections, but if you're going to explore that case, I suggest you seek permission from DCI Parker first, but be prepared for a "No". He has a lot on at the moment and doesn't take too kindly to any form of interference.'

'I'll tread carefully. The DCI and I didn't exactly get off to an agreeable start, I'll be sure to sweet talk him. Let's call him now, you can check out the drinks menu.'

Ben reached for his phone, punching in the numbers. The conversation was brief, only a matter of seconds.

'Well that was easy.' Ben smiled triumphantly, ending the call and placing his phone back on the table. He's given me the green light to interview Lord Illbert-Tavistock, with the proviso I report back with anything worthwhile. Actually, it would be good if you'd come along. A person with local area knowledge could be very useful.'

'Yeah, why not.' Katie laughed. 'I vaguely know old Illbert-Tavistock, he may be more receptive to a familiar face.'

'My suggestion is we head over to the Manor house after we've eaten. Better stick to cokes, don't want to turn up smelling like a brewery.'

Katie laughed. She had fallen for Crispin in a big way. He had a rugged charm, which most women would find appealing.

'Also, have a look at this. Got it yesterday in Newton Abbot,' Ben started, pushing a glossy paperback across the table. 'It's in relation to the new documentary written by that Charles Whitely bloke you told me about, who put out the original book years ago about the death of Hayley Illbert-Tavistock.'

Katie, dumbfounded, picked up the thin volume and examined the cover.

'Contrary to what you suggested; Whitely isn't a candidate for the funny farm just yet,' Ben enlightened his companion. 'He only had the book released last month. Bloody interesting though, he proposes the theory Hayley's demise might be linked to the disappearance of Allyson Carter, what are your thoughts?'

'Might be something in it,' Katie responded, digesting this new information. 'We'll only know more by delving deeper into the mystery.'

****

Katie consulted her smartphone and typed in the details. Bringing up the required page she read aloud to Crispin, adjacent in the driver's seat.

'Tavistock Manor is a Classic early Georgian stately home set in 30 acres of woodland, parkland and sculptured gardens easily accessed within a leisurely 20-minute drive from the town centre of Ivybridge. Originally an impressive, fortified castle and moat constructed in the twelfth century by Baron Godfrey Lyon De Quincey, a distant relation of William the First, to establish domain over the still rebellious Wessex Anglo Saxons, it was put under siege and burnt to the ground by Cromwell's Army in 1648. The site lay desolate to well after the Restoration. Passing back to the original Catholic De Quincey family, a Georgian structure in the style of an Italian Antonio Palladio mansion, being the fashion of the day was built on the site including formal Louis XIV terraced gardens, similar to those at Versailles Palace. Although undocumented, in the late eighteenth century it is thought Capability Brown may have directed the major changes one sees today, adding classic landscape scenes featuring Roman and Greek summer houses and rotundas surrounding a small manmade lake. The title was changed to

Tavistock Manor in 1845 with the death of the last remaining De Quincey'.

'Fascinating,' Crispin responded cynically. 'A modest residence well out of reach of the average punter, that's for sure. Let's see what this Lord IT fella has to say for himself. Sit back and relax my lady, I'll have us pulling up outside this magnificent manor house in no time.'

Katie laughed, totally relaxed in Ben's company, driving through the Devon countryside, without a care in the world.

'I'm not sure his lordship is up to having visitors,' a valet of pygmy-like stature announced when Crispin informed him why they had called around, without a prior scheduled meeting. 'He's not been well, and often clams up when any mention of Hayley takes place, how about I take your names and contact details, then he can get in touch if he feels up to having a chat.'

'We won't press too much,' Katie said stepping in. 'Perhaps a few minutes would be permitted.'

'Well as long as you don't tire him out or upset him in any way,' the valet warned, giving in but still not convinced. 'I'll be keeping my eye on you.'

With the protocol agreed, he showed the visitors into an outrageously cavernous drawing room, decorated around the cornices and on the ceiling with painted Italian scenes featuring cherubs in classical landscapes. Bookshelves lined all four walls reaching up to the 20' high ceilings; stuffed with rows and rows of vintage volumes, mostly leather or Moroccan bound. Lord Illbert-Tavistock tucked into a wheelchair, a tartan patterned, woollen rug covering his knees stole an upwards glance, as his valet made the introductions.

'Fetch tea for my visitors,' he instructed. 'Tell Mrs Partridge to cut some of that fruitcake she made this morning.'

With the butler departed, he turned to Katie. 'I know you, don't I?'

Katie nodded. 'You were friends with my late grandfather, Richard Sinclair, he owned Waters Meet Farm, the other side of the escarpment.'

'That's right. Ricky Ticky Sinclair we called him.' He let out a splutter of laughter. 'Always on time, never late... Or was it Tricky Ricky, I can't recall.'

Katie warmed. That sounded just like her grandfather. He had a rebuke for anyone who turned up anywhere other than on time.

'We understand your daughter went missing whilst riding on the Moor?' Ben Crispin broke in, bored with general chatter.

'Hayley,' the old man mumbled faintly, eyes misting over. 'My beautiful Hayley.'

'Do you know what happened to Hayley?' Katie moved in closer to gently pat the old man's arm.

He shook his head. 'She vanished without a trace, my darling Hayley.'

A lump formed in her throat. So difficult for a father to lose a child. Even worse to not know what happened to them.

Illbert-Tavistock seemed to forget he had visitors and morbidly began quoting from Bunyan's "The Pilgrim's Progress". 'Though I walk through the valley of the shadow of death, I will fear no evil: for thou art with me; thy rod and thy staff they comfort me.'

Katie waited a few moments before asking another question. 'I understand you are a generous man Lord Illbert-

213

Tavistock, my late grandfather used to tell us how much you donate to charities each year.'

The old man grunted an agreement. 'Yes, I like to help others, most certainly our local churches who struggle for repairs and general upkeep. I bequeath a proportionate sum of money to the Abbey in Buckfastleigh twice a year, along with the nearby Priory. The Abbots and Brothers are true followers of God. I admire the work they do. You must pay a visit to old Brother Jeremy. He's the one who can tell you the truth behind many a dark tale.'

Illbert-Tavistock turned to face Katie, a glazed look on his face. 'Letters, there were many letters for a spy.'

'I'm sorry, I don't quite follow.'

'Knocks and footsteps around the house – whistles after dark. St Oswald's Priory was full of terrible demons. If you wake at midnight you see him rocking, his eyes burning into your soul.'

Ben Crispin stood up to move through the open patio doors, patently bored with the enigmatic conversation unfolding. Katie, on the other hand, true to her clinical calling, was fascinated by the old man's chatter, weighing up if he was confused or a little eccentric. Perhaps Brother Jeremy was likewise inflicted, neither able to tell truth from fiction, inventing obscure scenarios to occupy troubled minds.

'What else can you tell me about St Oswald's?' Katie probed, just when Mrs Partridge appeared with a tray of light refreshments.

As if coming back to the present, Lord Illbert-Tavistock seized Katie's left wrist twisting it forcefully until she cried out in pain. 'Find the body, you must find the body,' he wheezed.

Katie tried to wrestle from his firm grip to no avail.

'Help me,' he croaked. 'You must find where the body lies. Every night an angel sent by the Devil from deep in Hell's fiery catacombs appears before me and points the way. When I wake up those memories vanish, and I remember nothing.'

On hearing Katie's cry Crispin was back on the scene. 'The old fool's a crackpot. For the love of Jesus let's get out of here, there's nothing to be gained from talking to this imbecile.'

Katie waved for him to remain silent, urging Lord Illbert-Tavistock on, desperate to know more. 'Where do you think we will find Hayley?' She watched the old man closely, his eyes reddening and glazing over.

'Down where the river runs deep. Where the stones are cold from never seeing the sunlight.'

The old man started shaking from side to side, small sobs breaking through every few seconds.

'I think it's time to leave,' the valet declared, entering the room and fixing them an icy stare.

'We didn't mean to upset him,' Katie apologised. 'We had hoped to learn more about his daughter's disappearance.'

As they rose to leave, Illbert-Tavistock turned to Crispin. 'The answers lie with Henry Clemens,' he whispered. 'He's the one you want to find.'

****

Katie turned off the screen, yawned loudly and stretched back in the office chair, flexing tired limbs.

She picked up the dog-eared notebook and for the umpteenth time that morning, flicked through the pages, struggling to digest the few meaningful details she had scribbled down. After a marathon session relentlessly sifting through the data banks of the internet, the information gleaned was sparse and probably unreliable.

'That Clemens person lead, I can't find anything on him,' Katie announced, into the speaker on her tablet device. 'I'm going to have to get Matt's help on this one. He'll know where to look.'

'Seriously? You're joking, it's a load of old crock,' Ben retorted scathingly, picking up the phone, piloting the unmarked Jag across the Tamar Bridge into Plymouth. 'If you want my professional opinion; the old codger's nutty as that fruit cake he served up; and downright bloody scary.'

Katie smiled, thoughts of Ben on the other end of the line sending a short, sharp sexual tingle through her. 'Probably, but in my business, it is important to carefully dissect all types, before one dismisses them as crazy. In fact, I have a persistent hunch about this one that won't go away.'

'You got me, I'd never make it to first base as a shrink,' Ben chided. 'Don't have the patience for wacko minds. You'll be wasting your time my dear. I very much doubt this Henry Clemens ghost exists.'

'You could be right, but it's worth spending a short while investigating. I'm also going to pay this Brother Jeremy a visit at the Priory to find out if he really does know anything.'

'Best of British with that one and send through a report if you find things of interest. I'm hoping to contact Lana Gibbs, who works at the Star Head Office. I'd like to arrange a meeting. From what I've recently gleaned; Hayley worked alongside Lana's old man. She may be able to shed light on a few things.'

****

Matt strolled into the Moorland office desperately trying to conceal a grin. 'Nothing gets past Matt Tyler. Managed to stumble upon a couple of references to a Henry Clemens; risked a long shot and broke into some government immigration databases on the Continent, took me fucking ages and I almost got sprung. You owe me bigtime, Sinclair. Only a guesstimate understand, as there are at least a dozen candidates that fit the mould, there may be a very tenuous connection to a Henrich Clemminger who again, may have entered England under a false passport, possibly from Czechoslovakia or France, sometime in late 1971 or early 1972. Unfortunately, that's about it; I can't tell you anything more, then the trail dries up.'

'Splendid work,' Katie replied. 'I really do believe the church has links to all these abductions and possible murders. Why else would the Abbey and Priory keep cropping up in conversations?'

'You could be right,' Matt agreed. 'However, I don't think Buckfast Abbey has direct ties to any wrongdoings, nothing untoward goes on there, it's a beautiful place of worship, a sacred part of England. You know I get a distinct impression it's the Priory that holds the answers; it's got an aura, not of this world. I take a shortcut past that building every time I head back across the moors to my farmhouse. I don't know what it is, but the place gives me the creeps.'

Katie was intrigued by listening to Matt's uncharacteristic and somewhat surprising candour. She found it difficult to believe he was put off by an old building and what might lie behind the ancient stone walls.

'Any chance I can expect more stuff on this Heinrich person?'

'Unlikely. I anticipate no one knows anything more than that. However, give me a week, two max, I know some old contacts at HM Customs and Interpol now retired who may remember something cropping up from 1971,' Matt replied, ruefully inspecting an empty coffee cup. 'On another subject, let me shout dinner. 'It's been a while since we had a night out.'

Katie tried to look pleased, but in reality, she wasn't sure she wanted to be wined and dined by Matt, not anymore. She felt she would be betraying Ben if she so much as peered at another man.

****

'Day off?' James posed the question, noticing Ben entering the lab casually dressed in jeans and a light blue sweater. 'Probably rare in your line of work.'

'I actually do get some respite from chasing crims. Is Katie around?'

'You've just missed her, popped over to Lustleigh to take a look at a friend's new mare. I envisage her being about two hours. Help yourself to an espresso.'

James continued, typing at his computer, flexing muscles in the process and motioning towards the coffee machine.

'Any new forensic evidence on the case?' Ben was faking nonchalance.

'Nope, it will turn up, probably when we least expect it.'

'Katie has been filling me in on that old Hayley Illbert-Tavistock disappearance in the eighties, all seems very odd. The more I research the available files, the more convinced I am that there is a link between her disappearance and that of Allyson Carter.'

James looked up in surprise. 'Funny, that's exactly what Nick Shelby believes. His theory is; they have at some stage been at the same location, mostly arrived at from some recent DNA and physical evidence testing on material left over from the old Coronial investigation back in '87. Me, I'm a bit more cynical, DNA is not conclusive and there is major doubt hanging your hat on evidence samples held for so long.'

'Would Nick enlighten me on his findings?'

James closed the laptop and turned slowly to face Crispin. 'You won't get anything from him. Nick is a bit possessed by the Illbert-Tavistock case; I reckon it's an obsession. It was a cold case he was given to research when he first came down to Devon. He is unlikely to release any findings until he has a major breakthrough. Incidentally, speaking of Dr Shelby, could you do me a favour and pop over to his lab in Exeter and pick up an XRF Gun?'

'A what? Yeah sure, by the time I get back Katie will hopefully have returned, and we can go for a spot of lunch.'

James had unwittingly done him a favour, now could be the perfect opportunity to see what he could find out about Hayley's disappearance. An open invitation to Nick Shelby's lab was a heaven-sent opportunity.

****

Ben waited for Nick to disappear upstairs to the lab in search of the XRF analyser, then set about quickly searching his office. He knew what he was looking for but wasn't sure where to find it. The filing cabinets turned up nothing. He suspected that Nick prudently kept these files in a special place, away from prying eyes.

Ben tried the drawers to his desk – locked. Not one to give up easily, Ben hunted for the key, luckily locating it hanging on a piece of cord behind the wall clock. The clock seemed to tick louder; adrenalin started to flow. He tried the key in the lock where it easily turned, and the top drawer sprung open.

He scoured through the usual knickknacks; pens, calculators, a packet of condoms, a half-eaten Mars Bar, nothing exciting. The second and third drawers a raft of letters, lab reports, not what he coveted. The fourth and final drawer came up trumps.

With no time to lose, Ben quickly grabbed the dark blue file, heading straight for the photocopier.

'Won't keep you too long,' Nick's muffled voice broke through the silence from the top of the stairs.

'No worries,' Ben called back. 'Take your time.'

Ben pressed "copy" on the high-tech machine, and as the copies flew out, he swiftly placed the folded pieces of paper into his jacket pocket, pulse racing. Mission almost completed Nick's loud protestation suddenly reverberated through the office.

'What the bloody hell do you think you're doing?'

Startled, Ben turned around, his face crimson, the key still in the lock, the cord visible.

'Um, I lost my wallet, thought I might have dropped it in here,' Ben uttered, trying to sound matter of fact, but not succeeding.

'I hardly think you'd have lost it in the bottom drawer of my desk.' Nick's eyes stared into Ben's, clear disdain in his voice. 'Here's the XRF you wanted, sign here and then get out. When Jim has finished with it, get him to return it himself, I don't like sneaks, never have, never will.'

Crispin sheepishly retrieved the form Nick threw onto the desk, scribbled his signature, lifted the hand-held metals analyser and headed towards the door.

'By the way,' Nick called after him. 'That wallet you've misplaced, I'd fucking well try the back pocket of your jeans, where it's clearly visible, and next time you want to sneak around my office, try to think up a believable excuse.'

A long time ago I wanted to punish people. I am here to confess to all those bad things.

I killed in a fit of rage. She stood before me, begging for her life, yet I saw no reason for her to go on living.

I confirm her body is buried beneath a depth of despair. One day, I hope she will see sunlight and I can be forgiven for my sins.

Amen

Chapter Eleven

'Lana Gibbs, am I right?'

'Who wants to know?'

'Ben Crispin Senior Detective with the London Met.' Ben offered his right hand, and a broad, boyish grin. His natural good looks weren't wasted on Lana Gibbs, who scandalously enjoyed flirting with any member of the opposite sex, available or not.

'You'd better come into my parlour Ben. It's almost lunchtime, a good excuse to rescue a bottle of prosecco from the bar fridge.'

Ben followed Lana into the sanctum of her office, laying back on a deep leather lounge welcoming the glass of bubbly, placed in his hand. The stressful morning run-in with Dr Shelby had hit home, he didn't want to repeat that in a hurry.

'I take it this is a business call, not pleasure?' Lana teased, perching next to Ben, well within his territorial zone and crossing her legs seductively, so their bodies touched. An attractive woman, mid-forties, with a very elegant figure her cleavage was ample, visible in a tight-fitting, low-cut red chiffon dress. Lana was used to men falling at her feet and Ben Crispin instantly became an object of sexual desire.

'I was hoping you could enlighten me on the very last matter Hayley Illbert-Tavistock was assigned to, when at The Star. I believe it was around September 1986, shortly before she vanished into thin air.'

Lana reached across the office coffee table and topped up their glasses. 'What's in it for me?'

'What do you want?' Ben gave her a sly wink. 'Name your price.'

Lana leaned over, whispering lightly in his ear.

'I sensed you might say that.' He laughed, placing his hand on her knee. 'I'd be more than pleased to oblige but first, let's get down to business. I would like to know what Hayley was working on in her last days at the Star. Anything. Even the smallest detail.'

'It will be my pleasure.'

Lana disappeared, returning moments later with a red cardboard box. 'Everything you want is in here, you must return the lot to me by Friday, with everything intact. If Tom Markham gets wind of this, we'll both be in trouble.'

'It's a deal.' Ben downed a mouthful of the cheap sparkling and loosened his tie. 'So what do you know about Hayley, any juicy titbits?'

'I don't know much myself, she was at the paper well before my time here. All I can tell you is Hayley was trying to track down a guy name of Clemens or something like that, convinced he was fleeing from some nasty goings-on over the Channel, avoiding extradition by hiding out somewhere in Devon. She spent a fair deal of time at the old Priory, interviewing the Monks, delving into Clemens' past. Seems to me she stumbled onto something significant, result: some person or persons bumps her off. The body was never found;

a couple of the older journalists around here who knew her, claim the general conjecture at the time; she was buried within the Priory walls. No one would ever think to look there, or ever be granted permission. Can you imagine the police even contemplating smashing up a heritage building with no tangible evidence; the public outrage. Verdict: she vanishes without a trace.'

'Fascinating. What about the disappearance of Allyson Carter, any thoughts there?'

'Perhaps Allyson was following in Hayley's footsteps and she too met a similar demise, who knows. The box of documents and stuff may provide pointers, at least to the disappearance of Hayley. Now if we're done here, what about keeping your promise, unless you have acquired a conscious and have a gorgeous blonde waiting in the wings at home?'

A broad smile spread across his face. 'No, no one special. I am not tied to anyone, in particular. Why don't you slip into something more comfortable and let's get this party started?'

****

'Did you forget to switch your phone on yesterday? James mentioned you'd been around. I was expecting you to drop by and take me out to lunch.' Katie tried to keep her voice steady; inside she felt disappointed.

'So sorry, I must have switched it to "silent" by mistake,' Ben apologised, pulling her close for a warm embrace. 'It was an exhausting day, I was at home by 7pm, skipped dinner and in bed before nine.'

****

'Well, what do you know, I would say our acquaintance Mr Phil Price is in denial with regard to having no knowledge of Milton and Bailey Pharmaceuticals,' Matt decreed. 'Take a look at these.'

He pointed to copies of two invoices bearing Price's name and signature emanating silently from the printer on Fiona's desk. James picked them up, shaking his head in disbelief. 'How in Christ's name did you…'

'Not for you to concern yourself with a trivial matter of the fine details,' broke in Matt. 'Suffice to say that Price's email server is slightly deficient on security protection. Don't even think about telling anyone how you got them… and I mean anybody. Strictly between you and me old boy; I used a variation of the decryption program that our mates the Russians are using to hack into sensitive NATO military computers. I stumbled on it when working for the MOD on cracking the Iranian Nuclear Agency files, coincidentally, the Russians were doing the same to their supposed Middle East ally and inadvertently one of their geeks sent the program to me in error.'

'I haven't heard a thing you said.'

Matt chuckled. 'It's my insurance, or "fuck you" account, so to speak; just in case things go badly for me one day.'

'The lying rat,' James said in a voice of extreme annoyance as he quickly perused the documents and absorbed the contents. 'Any bets on what he's got to hide?'

Snatching the puffer jacket from the hook behind the door, he bolted out of the office with the invoices firmly in his hands, hell-bent on answers.

He didn't even bother introducing himself when he pushed open the doors at Price's upmarket surgery and clinic. Instead, much to the consternation of the duty receptionist, he headed straight down the corridor towards Price's office.

'You can't go in there I'm afraid. Mr Price is with a patient,' the practice nurse protested loudly, hurrying to keep up with James's long stride. 'You'll have to make an appointment.'

Ignoring the pleas, he barged into Price's room without knocking.

'What is the meaning of this?' Price fumed, James standing defiantly in the doorway, hands on hips.

'Drugs are the meaning of this,' James fired back, shoving a tax invoice under his nose. 'Now we can either do this in private or in front of your patient, the choice is yours.'

'I apologise for this inconvenience, Mrs O'Brien,' Price said turning to the female patient who was seated on a black leather couch, shaking his head and raising his bushy eyebrows. 'If you head back to the reception area Mrs O'Brien, Janet will reschedule an appointment for you, free of charge.'

The young woman, obviously flustered, did as she was told, stopping momentarily to glance towards James, throwing a look of disgust.

'Now what is the meaning of this?' Price demanded, no longer surprised, but angry.

'For someone who knows nothing about Milton and Bailey Pharmaceuticals I find it odd your name and signature are all over their stationary,' James fired back.

'Don't get all high and mighty with me,' Price retaliated. 'I distinctly remember you asking me if I had ever heard of a company called Milton Bailey, to which I replied with a firm "No". Milton Bailey and Milton and Bailey Pharmaceuticals are clearly different.'

James threw back his head. 'Clever, very clever, nice try Price, but we both know that's irrelevant. Now are you going to tell me what's going on, or is it necessary for me to involve the local crime squad?'

'Just a slight misunderstanding,' an embarrassed Price mumbled, still trying to fathom how Sinclair got hold of the invoices. 'I can explain.'

'Then start explaining.' James made himself comfortable on the leather couch, with no intentions of going anywhere until he got the answers he wanted.

'Private clinics in the area struggle to get hold of certain drugs, my background means I have the knowledge to manufacture these drugs and supply at a fairly low cost so the facilities that require these medicines can get them at a reasonable price.'

'Go on.'

'Once I have synthesised the drugs, I sell them and make a small profit margin. Quite simple really. Scarcity, red tape and cost are the major impediments. I'm sure you're familiar with what I'm trying to say.' He picked up a weighty copy of the MHRA guidelines and chucked it in James's direction. 'That's just one example of what the industry has to deal with.'

Price walked slowly to the door, checked it was locked, slatted the venetian blinds and returned to his seat. Pausing a few moments to gather composure he continued in a calmer, deliberate voice. 'True, I'm a qualified medico. However, my first job was as a research biochemist. I spent five years working on penicillin derivatives for a major Swiss drug outfit in Basel. Then I had a sea change and went back to Uni to get my M.D. Come on, you know how it is. The major pharmaceutical companies continue to rake in billions while the people who benefit from the drugs miss out.

So, naturally, I have the knowledge to manufacture these drugs at much lower costs and the facilities in need of these medicines get them; at a fair, reasonable price.'

'I'm listening.'

'M B are just a supplier of some of the precursor chemical compounds and intermediates required to make the end product.

Once the drugs are produced, in very small batches, mind you, I sell them and nett a small margin. I'm happy at the end of the day to provide the service.'

'Okay, in order to make these drugs I imagine you take short cuts by using inferior materials,' James conjectured.

Price flared up, his cool demeanour evaporating. 'What do you think I am? Some "crack-smoking junkie" churning out Meth in a backyard shed? I've got a PhD in Biochemistry Sinclair, that's the same as you, right, at least that's what it says on your card. My small manufacturing facility is just down the road in an industrial unit. I only have two technical staff, but you take your time and run whatever checks you like. My accreditation you'll find is all above board.'

'Yes, and in order to make money you would try to save on expenses.'

'All businesses are guilty of that,' Price confessed.

'What if the drugs you're making and selling are then mixed with other drugs, what would happen then?'

'I'm not sure I follow. All drugs are potentially dangerous with known side effects. I can't control what other medications people take with the therapeutics I supply.'

'I want a complete list of your customers,' James demanded.

'And if I refuse?'

'You'll wind up in more strife than you are in now. The Dept of Health and Social Care wouldn't look too kindly on your, shall we say, "unorthodox" practices, Good Samaritan or not.'

Price hesitated for a few moments, then moved over to his briefcase resting on a small side table. He flicked open the metal catch retrieving a printout of names and addresses. 'I want this list back when you're done,' he ordered.

'No guarantee,' James answered, moving towards the door. 'Oh, one last thing Price, I want samples of the drugs you've been producing in the last twelve months; plus the full chemical specifications. Moorlands has the latest analytical high-tech instrumentation that will tell me exactly what crap you've loaded into them.

I'll get authorisation and send around a police technician tomorrow to your facility. I'll fully brief him on what to look for.'

Price stared out the window, fighting to shut down the adrenalin flow from the verbal stoush.

'Till we meet again.' James smirked. 'Because we will Price, it's only a matter of time. Also, as a word of precaution; don't try a cover-up or erase any evidence. The police will be all over this once I pronounce my findings later this week. You may want to think of a sudden career change. They say dog walking is becoming quite a fashion, appealing to the young and old. It can also assist people in losing weight.'

James openly laughed, pointing to Price's beer gut, before making a hasty retreat.

****

'I want Price's surgery gone over from top to bottom,' DCI Parker informed James. 'And I want you to co-ordinate a thorough, combined forensic sweep with task force tech boys. Arrange it. If your theory is correct, Price is in deeper shit than we realised.'

'What exactly are you interested in?' James enquired. 'All the relevant drug information and representative samples Price has handed over. Is there something else?'

DCI Parker leaned heavily on the reception desk at CID, his eyes dark circles. 'I could be wrong on this one, and I hope to God I am, specifically, get the team to check for bloodstains, any evidence Rebecca and Nicola may have been in that surgery.'

'Surely you're not suggesting Price did away with his own daughter?' James enquired, mouth agape. 'I know he's involved in shady activities, but surely he's not a murderer.'

****

'What's going on with Crispin?' Nick Shelby shouted, barging in through Moorland's main door and confronting James dozing lightly behind a classic car magazine on the reception lounge.

'What's up, mate?' James eased up into a sitting position and hunted around for his glasses, noticing Nick's black mood. 'Had a bad day?'

'What do we really know about Ben Crispin?' Nick spat back through clenched teeth, now directing his anger at the girls preparing lunch in the kitchenette.

'He seems decent enough,' Fiona volunteered, mystified by their colleague's uncharacteristic outburst.

'I want you to do a profile on him, and I'd like it by the end of the week?' Nick demanded, pointing at Katie. 'Bill it to my expense budget, don't make this one official.'

'Ben's not a psychopath, junkie or low-life scum,' Katie retaliated. 'He's a well-credentialed cop partnering our current investigations, what's brought all this on Nick?'

'I found him snooping around my office, pretending he'd lost his wallet.' A modicum of calm had returned to Nick's voice.

'Maybe he did,' Katie interjected. 'Whenever we're out together he's often misplacing things. It's highly probable his wallet had gone astray, and he was desperate to try and locate it.'

'Not when it was visible in the back pocket of his jeans. No, the guy's an imposter with another agenda.'

'I really don't feel comfortable profiling him,' Katie spoke out, reaching for a fresh loaf of sourdough, forcefully cutting it into thick slices.

231

'Let your personal feelings slide on this one,' Nick bit back. 'You're the best profiler I know. I'm not accusing Ben of anything; I'd just like to know more about his make-up.'

Katie glanced over at James for guidance.

'It wouldn't hurt profiling him,' James concluded. 'It does seem funny he's been going through Nick's office stuff. Although I might be indirectly responsible.'

All eyes turned to James whilst he explained that he'd been filling Ben in on Nick's forensic testing on the Allyson Carter and Hayley Illbert-Tavistock cases, to try and establish a link.

'There you have it.' Katie beamed. 'All very innocent. Ben and I have been probing into Hayley's disappearance, he's just getting some background.'

'What, by going through my office?'

A crest-fallen expression spread across Katie's face. 'Okay, so maybe that wasn't a normal procedure. I'll do your profile Nick, under protest, but don't expect flashing lights or anything. Ben is a decent bloke, nothing threatening there, and next time you want some profiling done, I suggest you contact someone else as I have a right to a personal life.'

Katie snatched her coat off the lounge and marched out of the office, slamming the door so hard it bounced back open.

'She'll simmer down,' Fiona volunteered. 'She likes Ben a lot, you can't blame her for that.'

Nick sighed. 'The thing is Fiona, he lied about his reasons for getting involved in this case. He told everyone at Police HQ he shagged the Commander's wife at the station he worked at in London and was then sent to Devon as a form of reprimand. The truth is; the boss wasn't married, nor did he have a girlfriend, indicating Ben is a profound storyteller.

According to a reliable resource of mine; Ben Crispin demanded to be put on this case, what *I'd* like to know is *why?*'

****

The siblings stared at the mass of digital readouts and recorder charts spread haphazardly across the Moorlands laboratory bench. They were checked, rechecked and checked again. The cold facts were undeniable. It wasn't possible.

'You look like a bloody idiot,' mumbled Fiona.' What a waste of my time. There's no sign of anything unusual or any adulteration in any of these therapeutic drug samples of Price's. The Mass Spectra are clear, no funny peaks, no red flags. Nothing coming up on the databases.'

She picked up a random high-performance liquid chromatogram chart readout of a benzodiazepine sedative formulation, jabbing a finger at the clean, unambiguous Rf matches with a standard product and starting material. '2am. I'm stuffed for goodness sake. I'm going to bed. Don't dare call me, I'm not in tomorrow.'

So sure, so confident right up until the charts began spewing out. As reality dawned anxiety soared and cockiness ebbed. Completely deflated, James slumped in a lab stool and waited a few minutes mesmerised by the flashing lights on the control panel of the gas chromatograph. Noting the time, he switched on the desktop and composed a short, terse two-line email to Will Parker.

****

A visibly agitated Price sat at the table in the police interview room, nervously playing with the steel band on his vintage watch and stealing anxious glances at the door, waiting for his lawyer to emerge.

'You don't have to do this Phil,' the barrister instructed, pulling up a chair next to his client. 'Stick to the script. The less you say the better.'

'Shut up,' Price snapped. 'Of course I have to say something. My silence hasn't achieved anything thus far. I want to come clean and confess to the murder of my daughter and her friend Nicola. This torture has gone on long enough.'

'Here we go,' James muttered to Nick, watching expectantly behind a glass partition. 'Showtime.'

Parker breathed deeply. 'So what happened that day on the moor, Mr Price? It is important you tell us everything.'

Price looked Parker in the eye. 'I was rocked. I found out Rebecca had broken into the industrial unit and removed a batch of high potency tranquilisers from secure storage. She went on to threaten me, wildly claiming something about my lab venture being a cover for the manufacture of "designer narcotics". Rebecca threatened to shove it up on social media if I didn't hand over three hundred pounds each week. Can you believe it, my own daughter blackmailing me?'

'So you killed her?'

'Of course not, well that was not my intention. I phoned Beckie on her mobile, the second day she was away at camp. I explained we had to discuss things, sort a few things out. I arranged to meet at a disused quarry around midnight. It wasn't far from the school campsite, yet far enough away and out of earshot. When we met up, I became incensed, she brought Nicola, I wanted to talk to Beckie on her own.'

'What happened next?'

'We argued. Beckie refused to listen to reason, she started shouting manically and throwing stuff around. I knew I had to do something or risk losing everything, my home, my job, even my wife.'

'Go on.'

'Before the girls knew what was happening, I injected them with Midazolam. I only did it to teach them a lesson. I knew it would knock them out for a few hours. My plan was to take photos of the two of them in compromising positions and threaten to use that to blackmail them, to get even. With both girls slumped on the ground I panicked, hearing a noise from a nearby copse. I got scared and bolted, but I swear I didn't kill them. The amount of Midazolam in their system was no more than the equivalent of a couple of therapeutic doses.'

'So you headed home, leaving the girls, one of which was your own flesh and blood to a torturous death?'

Price put his hands over his face. 'I didn't know what was going to happen,' he pleaded. 'I had no idea. You must believe me.'

'Oh we do believe you,' Parker uttered, casually. 'How could you have known some psychopath was lurking about, ready to brutally rape and murder two incident schoolgirls? You may not have purposely killed these young women Phil, but you certainly played a part in their execution. My guess for your part in this crime is a lengthy prison sentence, wouldn't you agree?'

'Verballing my client won't work, Inspector. I'll have that struck from the record. And you can forget about any statement.'

Philip Price removed his hands, staring up at Parker. 'You cannot prove I was the one who injected the girls, nor the fact I was anywhere near the quarry.'

'Unfortunately, at this point of time you're right on that score,' Parker grudgingly agreed, glaring at both men across the table. 'Now get out of my sight.'

****

'What a bloody mess.' DCI Parker sighed heavily, collaring Nick and James outside the interview room. 'In a perverse way, I actually feel sorry for the poor bastard. He had no real intentions of harming either of the girls, yet his foolishness left open the opportunity for a mad man to come along and brutally kill those poor girls.'

'Yep, they happened to be in the wrong place at the wrong time,' James agreed. 'I only hope we eventually catch the prick who committed this crime. It's scary to think he's still out there somewhere.'

****

'Here's the profile on Crispin you requested.' Katie plonked the file in front of Nick, turning to head out the door.

'Want a drink?' Nick ventured.

Katie shook her head. 'Another time perhaps. I hope you find what you're looking for.'

'Katie, wait,' Nick pleaded. 'Come on, you must understand why I am doing this? In our line of work, more than most, it's vital to have the absolute trust of everyone we work with. It's within your normal scope of practice to conduct profiles on existing and new work colleagues, not uncommon for annual reviews.'

'Don't tell me how to do my job,' Katie rebuffed coldly. 'But here's the thing Nick; none of us is perfect, not even you.'

The chill of the fresh evening hit Katie as she walked to the Punto. She was livid, but not all her fury was directed at Nick. The truth of the matter was; she didn't like everything she'd written about Ben in the profile. Although definitely not a serial killer, there was more to Ben than he led them all to believe. He exhibited traits of being a pathological liar, and Katie was battling to come to terms with this revelation.

She requested he fill in a preliminary profile questionnaire, for her to use as a base for the report. At first, she'd expected him to be indignant at such a request, instead, he laughed it off, finding the whole business rather amusing. This in itself irritated Katie somewhat, she'd expected him to be defensive, not happy Nick Shelby was trying to undermine his authority.

Nick picked up the slim assessment, housed in a small manila file, hesitated, opened it and started reading:

This psychological profile has been put together by Katherine Sinclair (forensic psychologist) and conducted on subject Benjamin Arthur Crispin.

Ben exhibits signs of being a pathological liar; with the inability to consider the consequences of his actions.

Below are listed some personality traits the subject has a tendency to exhibit:

- *Impulsivity*
- *Deceptiveness*
- *Socially awkward, uncomfortable at times and isolated*
- *Low self-esteem*
- *Lack of empathy towards others*

When questioned Ben is reluctant to discuss his personal life in great depth and avoids answering certain questions. I was able to observe a distinct pattern to his body language.

Moving on to the "lie zone" it was easy to spot a change in facial expression and sentence structure. His tone changed dramatically, coupled with the cadence of his speech.

Conversation rapidly moved away from himself with a direct focus on other people.

The assessment form he completed clearly indicates Crispin suffers from an antisocial personality disorder, although this is by no means an official diagnosis.

On conclusion, Nick placed the report in his shoulder satchel, then proceeded to make a few important phone calls.

It is with great sadness Lord I am impacting so many lives. I want to feel their pain, but inside I am rejoicing.

Am I still to blame, or perhaps they inflicted this upon themselves?

Help me to understand what happens next.

Amen

Chapter Twelve

'So, you have what appears to be some sort of half-baked confession from Price admitting to drugging the two girls, but what I don't understand is why in blazes the killer committed the crime spontaneously,' Katie exclaimed. 'A person, yet to be identified by us, happens to stumble upon Phil Price dumping the girls near a disused quarry, when Price runs off, this person decides to commit rape and murder. Don't you find that a bit strange?'

'Psychopaths are not logical thinkers,' Fiona stated. 'For them, it's all part of the thrill.'

'Yes, I agree,' Katie acknowledged. 'But don't you find it a bit coincidental these young women were handed to this person on a plate, very convenient.'

'I would imagine that's how most psychos operate,' Fiona continued. 'They act at an opportune chance.'

'Of course, yet I still can't reconcile the facts how this person by some minute chance, happens upon the girls and has at hand the means available to commit the crime, then move them to another location. Our evidence proved the bodies were moved, their faces burnt, and both girls raped and tortured. Our killer must have been very lucky. With those odds, they should have bought a lottery ticket.'

'Interesting theory,' James broke in. 'Where exactly are you going with this Katie? You must have your own theory?'

'Indeed I do.' Katie smiled, holding her audience captive. 'The extensive outline I have thus far put together on our murderer indicates someone seeking revenge, settling old scores. Yes, they are capable of murdering in a frenzy, but not without meticulous planning.'

'So you are stating the killer was known to these two women,' James conjectured.

Katie reached for her coffee cup, shaking her head. 'Not necessarily. Our killer might not have known them, perhaps they reminded him of someone, or he may have merely killed because they were female, he might have wanted to seek revenge on all women.'

'Oh great.' James sighed. 'We're tracking a complete nut case, who happens to go around casually stalking their victims before murdering them, in which case, no one is safe.'

Katie grinned at her brother's annoyance. 'That's one theory; however, my profile of our killer leans towards a different dimension. I believe our killer was observing the girls for some time, waiting for the perfect opportunity. Consider this: Rebecca Price and Nicola Fletcher knew something about our killer, not to be confused with the fact they knew him, as this may not be the case. If our killer had a past, say a documented criminal record, there's every chance the girls found out about it, and our killer was obliged to do away with them, preventing his past catching up with him.'

'Go on,' Fiona urged, sucked in by the way this hypothesis was unfolding.

'There's not much more to tell,' Katie concluded. 'Let's do some more background work and find out what the girls were up to. My suggestion would be to head back to the School. The duo may have been working on a particular history or social assignment, encountering some dark secret, which happens to be linked to our killer, it's possible.'

'You're a genius,' James enthused, slapping his hands down loudly on the desk. 'It certainly makes perfect sense our killer didn't just happen to stumble upon the girls. Sadly for Price, he had no idea his irrational act would end up causing their untimely deaths.'

'Don't get too excited.' Katie looked around sheepishly at the others. 'I could be 100% wrong, but my profiles are normally pretty accurate, and our killer does seem to have acted in some form of rational way, not in a fit of anger.'

'So our killer could be linked directly to Abbey College?' Fiona grilled her sister. 'A teacher perhaps, or another student?'

'Yes, however, if we are studying a particular event or person then it's possibly linked to something in the past. As we already know the girls were participating in excursions visiting old war graves in churchyards, military museums and the like. Now, if we're done here, I'm dropping in for a quick chat with Brother Jeremy at the Priory, after that joining Ben for a cosy candlelit dinner for two, followed by a late-night movie.'

'You seem to be getting along famously with our Ben Crispin,' Fiona commented, with raised eyebrows. 'Seems pretty serious.'

'Let's just say, "watch this space".' Katie winked, donning her cardigan and heading out the door. Lately, she'd been doing a lot of thinking, coming to the conclusion she was starting to fall madly in love with the handsome Detective.

What did it matter if he had a past or if his profile didn't portray one of a saint? Everyone had flaws and for once Katie was fed up with a yearning for *Mr Perfect*. Ben was a decent enough chap, and as far as she was concerned, *he would do very nicely, thank you.*

****

'Beautiful day.'

'Indeed.' Katie sat next to the thin, frail monk, uncharacteristically dressed in street attire soaking up the late afternoon sun on the wrought iron bench. 'You must be Brother Jeremy; I've heard so much about you.'

'Don't listen to all them rumours miss, although I'm well past ninety now, I still can get around and make a contribution to Priory life and thank the Lord, that's one thing I know to be true.'

'What's your secret?' Katie prompted.

'Don't think I really have one.' He laughed, scratching his chin. 'I suppose the wholesome, unsullied country air in these parts keeps me lungs healthy, and a dram or two of Buckie brandy liqueur, well I certainly look forward to that every evening. Have done for the last forty years.'

'I've heard that stuff is pretty potent. Not for the less adventurous.'

'True, young lady true, Satan's brew some call it, but in moderation, it's a rewarding drop. Come on, I'll show you around our very own distillery. Not really legal, so we keep this little secret to ourselves. But first...'

He rose quickly to his feet, and shuffled off at a surprising pace, leading the way, waving for her to follow.

Katie, keen to indulge the old man and now anxious to learn more followed the venerable Brother into a high-pitched roof red brick building behind the chapel, down steep, cobbled steps and into an open, well-lit space set up with a bespoke distillation unit, filter press, holding vessels and a small hand-operated bottling line. The air, damp and refreshingly cool mixing with the pervasive heady aroma of herbaceous volatiles. To the right a heavy oak door, which he proceeded to unlock with a large master key retrieved from a glass case on the wall.

'These are not all Buckie wines,' Jeremy continued, turning on the light to reveal a cavernous cellar; the ancient Anglo-Saxon stone walls lined with rows of vintage wine, spirits and liqueur bottles covered in dust and mould. He deftly removed a bottle of Chateau Mouton Rothschild at random from a nearby rack, wiped the dust from the old label with a shirt sleeve, handing it to his visitor. 'For many years the Brothers have been amassing examples of the best classic vintages and spirits. St Oswald's has the best collection of Cognac Brandy I am told, some bottlings date back to Napoleonic times.'

'Wow. I'd guess a tidy sum, right?'

'Yes lass, the Priory of St Oswald's is the protector of many riches, including the magnificent art collection. Can I interest you in a small tasting?' added the brother in a conspiratorial voice, his eyes a mischievous sparkle. 'I keep a bottle or two handy, just in case visitors drop by.'

Katie hesitated, not sure it was the right time to be sampling an expensive, full-bodied Bordeaux or potent spirit.

'A tiny drop won't hurt,' Jeremy reassured, leading the way through another wooden door into a small tasting and records room, a pine table and six chairs at the centre.

'I was saddened to hear of Timothy Stanley's death Ms Sinclair, such a sad loss,' the old monk remarked, absorbed in opening a vintage French liqueur brandy and filling two small glasses.

'Not everyone would agree with you,' Katie remarked quietly, after considering his words. 'By all accounts, Timothy was a deeply troubled soul.'

'Even so, it's a terrible way for any of the Lord's children to go, being shot in such a way. I've known Tim since he was a young nipper, we got used to him hanging around the Abbey looking for odd jobs or helping out wherever, just out of generosity, almost like a member of the commune he was. I blame that wretched Mental Hospital for his demise. Professor Green pumped Tim with so many pills, the poor lad didn't know if he was coming or going. I tell you missy; Green was unashamedly experimenting with new drugs. God only knows what the side effects were. Before treatment, Tim was a normal well-balanced young man, never heard voices in his head, not one.'

Katie listened intently, straining to pick up all the softly spoken, sometimes incoherent words of Brother Jeremy's emotional story. Even though drugs were a necessary path for many mental health patients, she wasn't entirely dismissive of alternative treatments where possible. Since first encountering Green and his controversial retreat over the past few weeks, an unfavourable opinion was forming.

'Green treated him like a dog, wretched bastard. He suffered terribly under his supervision. Green should have copped the bullet.'

At this point the over-excited monk broke into a coughing fit, dropping his drink and falling against a barrel, waving Katie away when she offered support.

'The lad had no family to speak of, so the Head Council have agreed to a burial plot in the Priory grounds,' Jeremy advised, regaining composure. 'It's the least we can do.'

'You must have fascinating stories to tell about this place, being a member of the Priory for many years,' Katie prompted, anxious to steer the subject to a different path.

'That's true my dear, but you must understand we've all taken a strict vow of secrecy before God. To live and work here it is forbidden by Council decree, under the pain of original sin, to reveal the inner workings of the Priory... and of course not forgetting The Abbey, truly a place of grandeur and inspiration; yet the Priory is beautiful on the outside to be sure, but the inner sanctum provides little mortal comfort...' The barely audible words drifting slowly away into the dimly lit surrounds of the ancient cellar.

'Interesting choice of words,' Katie remarked, declining the monk's offer of a top-up.

Brother Jeremy caught hold of her arm. 'You be careful miss, there's evil afoot. If you wake at midnight and hear the horse's feet, don't go pulling back the blind, or looking in the street. He's here you know, not far from us, hidden somewhere in the Priory.'

'Who's here?' Katie quizzed, concerned Brother Jeremy was marginally senile.

'The Devil of course,' he wheezed. 'In the chapel, rocking in his old chair. Back and forth, all night long, you can smell the whisky on his breath.'

With unsettling images of *The Prince of Darkness* rocking in a squeaky chair sending a cold shiver up her spine, she jumped at the unexpected arrival of one of the Abbots.

'What nonsense has old Jeremy being sprouting now, mad fool,' he said, seeing Katie's pale face silhouetted against the bleak dank walls. 'Don't believe a word he tells you, lass.'

'Brother's just giving me some historical background on the Abbey and Old Priory.'

'Yes indeed, but he's not of sound mind anymore. He does appear lucid and knowledgeable at times, I must admit, but those of us close to our brother well know his mind is starting to play tricks.'

'I don't believe we've met.' Katie held out her hand. 'Katie Sinclair, forensic psychologist.'

The hand was accepted. 'Yes sorry, Head Abbot Maximilian; thankfully, there's little call for a psychologist around here. When we seek guidance we turn to the Almighty and the teachings of the Holy See to provide all the answers.'

'Brother Jeremy briefly mentioned your art collection. I'd be keen to see it at some stage. Art history is a passion of mine.'

Abbot Maximilian emitted a deep throaty laugh. 'I'm sorry to disappoint, but there is no art collection. That's Jeremy's mind playing tricks again. See there; he's all but forgotten you came to visit.'

Katie turned and looked across at the ancient monk, sitting on a wine barrel, staring down at his sandals tracing circles on the sawdust cellar floor, oblivious to anyone else in the room.

'Come,' Abbot Maximilian instructed, holding out his hand for her to accept. 'I'll show you out. I think we should leave our brother to rest.'

Katie allowed the Abbot to guide her towards the main entrance, but as soon as the coast was clear, she backtracked towards the Priory gift shop, not ready to head home just yet.

Browsing the small shop she picked up a couple of souvenirs, and ordered a take-away coffee, pondering the next move.

'Anything takes your fancy? Alex Trimble's my name, assistant gardener.'

She swung around encountering a young, fresh-faced lad in his early twenties. 'Katie Sinclair.'

'Pleased to meet you, Katie Sinclair. I can show you around if you like, how does a private guided tour sound, along with some interesting facts about this renowned structure thrown in?'

'Sure, why not.' Katie couldn't believe her good fortune. The young lad clearly infatuated by a pretty face, only too happy to spend some time in her company.

'The Priory is officially known as The Priory of St Oswald, of the Benedictine order,' Alex volunteered, guiding his charge to the back of the building. 'It is similar to the Norfolk one, founded in 1091 by Peter des Valoines, a nephew of William the Conqueror. St Oswald's was laid down in the twelfth century on the remains of an Anglo-Saxon long building on a site referenced in the ninth-century Anglo Saxon Chronicle and still boasts a church with cloisters and a fourteenth-century gatehouse. It was dedicated to Saint Mary, and you will see her statue in the main foyer. Up to your right, you will see the grand manor house of Abbey College, which undoubtedly you already know a bit about, as I am guessing you're a local with your West Country accent.'

He paused, dropping down on one knee to tie up a shoelace. 'The College caters for over two hundred students, offering day and term boarding options. The fees don't come cheap, but in return, the students receive a high level of formal and spiritual education, of course, most pupils moving on to Oxford, Cambridge and other top-rank institutions. Or the Holy Orders, naturally.

The Priory has no formal links to Buckfast Abbey, except for the fact our members enjoy spending time with the other Monks, often attending their services and other community events.'

'You certainly know your stuff,' Katie remarked. 'Do heritage buildings carry a particular fascination for you?'

'I'm doing a strand on medieval church history at Plymouth Uni, this is my weekend and holiday job, it helps with the fees.'

'What can you tell me about the cloisters and tombs? I've also heard rumours of hidden treasures, paintings to be precise.'

'Can't say I've heard of that one.' Alex blushed from the compliment. 'Not to say they don't exist. The Brothers are very secretive about certain things. There was some strange business doing the rounds five years ago, about the secret burial of a young woman, but every time I went anywhere near the subject, I was threatened with a clip round the ear, I've not been game to mention it for some time. Just a load of rumour-mongering I suppose. Just between you and me Ms Sinclair the Abbot has a Mr Hyde side to him, not exactly the image he likes to project to the outside world.'

'Did this woman have a name?' Katie followed her guide in through a side door.

Alex shook his head, turning to see the portal to the chapel opening. 'Sorry, I have to get back to the shop, outsiders aren't meant to be in this part of the Priory. Best you make a hasty retreat before we're both caught and escorted off the premises. I can't lose my job. Go that way.'

Katie made herself scarce taking the shortcut back to the car park through a well-worn gap in the hedge with no time to thank Alex for his hospitality.

****

'The thing that I find funny out of all this is why on earth Brother Jeremy would concoct such an obtuse thing as an "art collection" for God's sake?'

'The old guy must be as batty as the Abbot implied,' Fiona concluded, after half listening to her sister's long-winded discourse on bizarre encounters with the Priory friars. 'He's almost scored a ton. I'd say that's doing pretty well under the circumstances, but you have to allow for a bit of senility.'

'Ninety-five, I believe,' Katie responded.

'Didn't that young guy at the shop say the Priory dates back to the Norman Invasion?

'Yep.'

'Well, I dare say there's a good chance they have a few artworks or medieval artefacts lying about the place. If they have one of the best vintage collections of grog around, you can assume the collecting bug extends to other fields as well.'

'I suppose, like little known provincial medieval churches in Italy that have housed priceless paintings and murals by Pre-Renaissance Masters for hundreds of years.'

'You're the fine art expert in this family, don't ask me,' Fiona teased.

'I was just looking for suggestions.'

Fiona closed her laptop and ran hands through unruly, short brunette hair. 'Don't expect to find a bunch of lost Giottos or Botticellis gracing the walls of an underground vault. Wait, how about a piece of the original Cross. Better still "The Spear of Vienna something or other", surely, you've heard of that priceless religious artefact Adolf Hitler and Himmler were chasing. Gee whiz, if you got your hands on that sis, you could name your price, maybe start a Holy Crusade and kick start Europe.'

'Very fucking hilarious.'

'Seriously, best case scenario, how about a few eighteenth-century Russian or Greek Orthodox Icons by unknown craftsmen wrapped in a blanket and crammed in an old sea chest,' added Fiona, remaining determinedly poker-faced.

'I want to take a look at some other parts of the Abbey,' Katie continued, not letting up despite Fiona's blatant disinterest. 'The whole place fascinates with its history and pervasive sanctity. Too bad my brief tour this afternoon was cut short. I was hoping to at least get a look at one or two of the rumoured underground passages and secret ways. I can't help thinking if perhaps it's Buckfast Abbey that has the "art collection", Brother Jeremy may have got a bit muddled. Do you reckon the Abbey is where I should be seeking answers?'

'No, it's the Priory that fascinates me,' Fiona concluded. 'Even in the full light of day, the place gives off bad vibes. The Abbey is wonderful, I'll admit that, but if you want my opinion, that Priory is surrounded by an unnatural force.'

'Great Scot, sis, you're really into this spooky stuff, aren't you?' Katie mocked. 'What's interesting is that Brother Jeremy made similar comments. He mentioned it was the Priory holding all the secrets.'

'Then miraculously I share his notion. My senses tell me something sinister is going on over there.'

'A little less speculating on unworldly activities and more down to earth forensic evidence wouldn't go astray,' James remarked crisply, entering the confines of the lab munching on the last of a steak sandwich. 'I've had Bristol on my case all week, not to mention police liaison at Exeter wanting the DNA confirmations on that young guy they pulled out of the River Severn. I don't suppose you can have those to me by four this afternoon could you Fi?'

'Yes, boss, most certainly boss and please pardon me unless it's slipped your memory, I also have three Coroner's reports to complete by Thursday afternoon boss.'

'Make that five,' James directed. 'I'm granting myself a few days leave to attend an urgent matter, apologies for any inconvenience this may cause. However, as an equal partner in the business it's important you keep on top of the workload.'

Fiona shot her brother a scornful look. 'I'm already putting in ten-hour days,' she grumbled. 'I suppose another three or four won't hurt. Perhaps I can learn to sleep standing up.'

'Perhaps,' James spoke coldly, dismissive of his sister's sarcasm. 'Nick is around, should you require his assistance.'

'Fine.' Fiona turned her attention once more to weighing samples on the microbalance, learning over the years there was little to be gained from locking horns with her brother when in one of his "dictatorial" moods.

As soon as James left the lab Katie wasted no time interrogating her sister about his mood swings. 'What's up with him? He's been acting strange for a couple of weeks now.'

'Wouldn't have a clue. Perhaps he's still traumatised from having a gun shoved in his back and held captive by Fowler. That can't have been an easy time for anybody.'

'You could be right,' Katie acknowledged. 'I'd almost forgot that episode, it seems ages ago. Although I'm still convinced there is something else troubling him. We both know James when he gets into a pickle, his behaviour lapses into manic desperation, bordering on psychotic, and occasionally reason disappears out the window.'

'I hope you're wrong, if James has landed himself in trouble, we both know it won't be a trifling matter. Best we keep an eye on him and try to discover what's going on.'

'I agree, but we may not like what we find. James somehow manages to get a lot of people seriously offside when things don't go his way. I hope he's not planning something stupid in relation to seeking custody of Jason, now that would be foolish.'

Fiona confronted her sister. 'If he really goes too far this time, I for one am not prepared to come to the rescue. What's more, Katie, back me on this one. If it ends up just the two of us running Moorland Forensics, so be it. I'm getting sick and tired of James and his impulsive misadventures.'

****

'James. Many thanks for catching up today. Terribly sorry about the location! I've been meaning to get you this for the last few weeks but got called away urgently to a family crisis in Canada. Anyway, this is from the late Mal Frobisher, he wanted you to have it. As appointed Executor of his will, he left strict instructions for me to personally hand this to you, so here we are, even if I'm a bit late with the delivery, for which I sincerely apologise.'

Starting to shiver from the incessant, cold windblown drizzle on the side of the road, James shoved the package inside his puffer jacket. He had no intentions of opening it until he was by himself.

'I take it you're privy to the contents?' James enquired of Ethan Gray, raising his voice to be heard above the frantic motorway traffic.

'Of course, however, we never had this conversation. If you must make contact again there is a non-traceable mobile number. Everything outlined in the arrangement has already been set in motion. The ten thousand pounds must be paid in cash at the agreed day, time and place. It will not go well for you if the payment is delayed. Do I make myself clear?'

James nodded. 'Is it ironclad?'

Ethan let out a deep controlled laugh. 'Of course, nothing can go wrong, so long as you keep your mouth shut. Just ensure you fulfil your part of the contract. Now fuck off, before anyone sees us, let's hope there are no fixed security cameras along this stretch of the motorway.'

James hastily retreated to the warmth of the Citroen rental, driving away from the M4 layby, heading South. Gripping the steering wheel with clammy hands a sliver of doubt ebbed slowly into the back of his mind. It was patently clear what he was doing was wrong, yet what other choice was there?

Arriving back to the sanctuary of the living room in his small duplex at the bottom of Indio Road, James, hands shaking slightly, fixed a double vodka with tonic, then with trepidation removed the small package from his jacket pocket, carefully opening the contained letter with a Swiss Army knife. Casting the envelope on the floor he removed a folded sheet of expensive, cream coloured bond paper and slowly absorbed the note, hand-written by Malcolm Frobisher.

Dear James,

If you are reading this, then I must be in a position where it is not possible for me to meet or for us to be seen together in public. Otherwise, I would be relating this to you in person.

After our meeting and subsequent coming to terms on the sum payable I have devised and already implemented the following actions:

Lt Simon Greig will be depicted in explicit photos which will be anonymously delivered to selected media outlets. Co-currently, importation documentation implicating Greig with involvement in cocaine shipments from South America will find their way to the Office of the Minister responsible for Customs and Excise.

The subsequent fall out we have calculated will be more than sufficient to guarantee the end of Greig's career and destroy his ability to argue with credibility in a Civil Court of Law.

You will now be able to claim full custody of your son.
All the best,
Mal Frobisher
PS: I now urge you to destroy this note immediately.

Tasting the rise of bile in his throat James fought back against the urge to throw up, heading out the door and into the dark, inhospitable night, desperate for fresh air. The fine sleet stung his face as he headed across the road, crossing over into one of the neighbouring fields.

Nearing the fast-flowing Bovey stream James retrieved his grandfather's Dupont lighter, setting fire to the parchment, watching it flare and eventually fizzle into ash. There was no going back, he had now played a major part in crucifying Simon Greig. He had to forego any moral compass and concentrate on the future, a future with his son.

Dear Lord, did I play a part in their deaths? I have been told I did.

Is it wrong to fight for what I believe in, to want more than others? One day I hope to be forgiven for all my sins.

Those who do not seek solace in prayer are the ones to be punished, do they really feel they are beyond suspicion and doubt? In the eyes of God, everyone must be forgiven. In my eyes, they must all be punished, and I strongly feel it is my job to do that. Those who sin must burn in hell's eternal fires.

Lord, help me to end the lives of those who are troubled, for all our sakes.

Amen

Chapter Thirteen

'I must speak to you, Ms Sinclair. Can you come over today?' Katie detected an unnerving urgency in Brother Jeremy's high pitched, faltering voice. Throwing off the bed covers and groping in the semi-darkness on the bedside table for her watch, she noted it was still early not yet 8am.

'Where are you?' she mumbled.

'At the Priory. You will come, won't you?'

'Yes, that's fine. I can visit after lunch. What do you want to see me about?'

'I can't tell you any more than this over the phone, in case someone is listening in, but you have a right to know where the body has been placed, I feel obliged to show you before something happens to me. I'll be waiting for you in the old scullery.'

About to ask further questions, the phone went silent.

Driving over to the Priory early in the afternoon, the words Brother Jeremy had spoken kept churning over in her mind; 'She had a right to know where the body had been placed.' *What body was he talking about?* Passing the Abbey and rounding the corner towards the ancient Priory nearby, nervous anticipation mixed with feelings of guilt grew. *Should I have informed someone of the meeting?* If James had been around, he would have accompanied her, or better still Ben could have been involved. On the other hand, if Brother Jeremy *was* borderline insanity, as she was led to believe, why tell anyone, she'd only be made to look foolish, even worse gullible.

Katie parked the Punto in a near-vacant gravel car park, scanning the surrounds for someone to ask directions. She recognised the Abbot in the garb distinctive of the higher rank, standing near the Chapel entrance deep in conversation with two other friars, Maximillian breaking off the discussion, turning around as she approached across the immaculate, manicured lawns of the quadrangle.

'I'm here to visit Brother Jeremy. He's told me to meet him in the old scullery.'

The Abbot offered a quiet prayer and made the Sign of the Cross. 'It's Ms Sinclair, isn't it? Sadly, young lady Brother Jeremy had a fatal accident, a nasty fall down a flight of steps, on his way to the chapel. He hit his head, there was nothing anyone could do. Our brother thankfully would have suffered very little.'

Uncomprehending, Katie digested this information in stunned silence. She'd only been speaking with Brother Jeremy less than five hours ago.

'He sounded distressed when we spoke on the phone this morning,' Katie blurted out. 'Have you any idea why that might have been the case?'

The Abbot declined an answer. 'If you leave me your number, I will contact you with the funeral information. I'm sorry your journey here today has been a wasted one. I have other pressing pastoral matters to attend to as the spiritual head of Abbey College. Good Day.'

The Abbot turned away, resuming his conversation with the two friars, leaving Katie no recourse but to walk slowly back to the car park in stunned silence.

****

'At ninety-five or something there's nothing to be gained conducting an autopsy,' James said calculating. 'It would also be highly problematical determining if he fell or was pushed, presumably there were no eyewitnesses. Then a further complication would be establishing if the push was deliberate or accidental. You'll just have to move on from this one Katie, and hope Brother Jeremy is now in a nicer place.'

'I know he was pushed. For some reason, Brother Jeremy was silenced and removed from the scene.'

'I'd be very careful promoting that hypothesis publicly,' James warned his sister. 'Speak to DCI Parker if you have concerns.'

'Oh, don't you worry, I plan on doing just that,' Katie retorted confidently. 'The old boy, even though he's assumed generally to be a crackpot, was about to pass something on to me when he conveniently came a cropper, that's too coincidental.'

'Go carefully,' James warned. 'If there was a conspiracy to do away with Brother Jeremy, you could suddenly find yourself not the flavour of the month.'

Katie bit her lip. 'If the old guy was done away with, we have a duty to find the culprit.'

'Sadly, we don't,' James reminded her. 'We're forensics, not the police. I can call Nick and find out if there is any likelihood of an autopsy, but from what you tell me I very much doubt it. An elderly man accidentally falling down a flight of stairs, with no other evidence to the contrary, won't warrant much interest.'

****

Nick viewed the body of Brother Jeremy dressed in a white undertunic, lying in an open coffin in the small Priory chapel in front of the altar.

'Come on Nick, what do you think, any possibility he didn't fall accidentally?' Katie ventured hopefully, shielding her eyes from the warm, diffused sunlight filtering through the medieval, stained-glass window overhead.

'Too soon to tell,' Nick replied, studying the old monk's face, eyes closed, seemingly at peace with the Almighty. 'Might be able to come up with a probable cause of death, but it will be mainly guesswork, and technically I don't think either of us should really be here, could stir up a hornet's nest. And if you really want my...'

'Ah there you are,' Maximillian exclaimed, rushing up to Nick cutting him short in mid-sentence and catching hold of his hand. 'I'm glad I found you. We appreciate you both dropping by to show your respects and cast your expert eyes over our dear departed brother, but I have been formally advised an autopsy won't be necessary. The Priory is happy to welcome Brother Jeremy into its garden of paradise, realising he was of advanced years and surely now deserves to rest. All those, I am certain, wonderful little tests you conduct will not bring him back, but we thank you for your support.'

'Hey, hang on there a minute,' Katie interjected, throwing restraint out the window. 'This could be a homicide investigation.'

'I am sorry, but I feel there has been a terrible mistake, a gross misunderstanding,' the Abbot pronounced. 'Poor Brother Jeremy lost his footing and fell. You must not read anymore into it my dear. Now if that's all, I'll show you out, so we can take care of our dear brother. We have scheduled prayers to start the next hour, which will go well into the night and we are due to dress the body in a special garment. Once again, thank you for coming.'

'Nick do something,' Katie demanded, glaring at the Abbot with disdain. 'This is a cover-up.'

Nick put a reassuring arm around Katie. 'If this is the Abbot's wishes, we can hardly intervene Katie, I assume our Brother has the paperwork, releasing the body to his care.'

Nick turned to Maximillian expectantly.

'Ah, yes of course Dr Shelby. Right here, inside my habit. I was afraid of misplacing them.'

Nick seized the documents and flicked quickly through them. After a few minutes he addressed The Abbot. 'All appears to be in order. We'll be off then.'

Katie was furious. 'Are you for real? Brother Jeremy was murdered. He wanted to pass information of vital importance on to me, we had arranged a meeting. There is a conspiracy going on here and I want to know what it is.'

Nick seized Katie's arm, leading her towards the car. 'Not now,' he hissed. 'If something sinister is going on around here it won't help if you announce it to the world. The Home Office documentation unequivocally states we are not to conduct an autopsy and the cause of death decreed by the

Coroner is accidental. Yeah, I know. I have the authority in extreme circumstances to have the Coroner findings overruled or re-examined but it's not in my or anybody's interest to take on the Coroner. Politically it could end up costing me my job. Now let's get out of this place before the shit hits the fan!'

****

For most of the night, Katie lay awake staring at the dappled shadows moving on the bedroom ceiling, rising several times to brew a cuppa and devour a full packet of chocolate biscuits. Something she invariably did when unresolved questions filled her head.

She felt compelled to return to the Priory without delay and seek answers. Being Sunday, there would be the usual Morning Prayer service at eleven. This would be the perfect opportunity, arrive early and with luck find a brother with his guard down, willing to talk.

****

'Brother Maximillian, I was hoping to have a few words with you, if you could spare a few minutes of your time.' Katie hurried down the old paved stone pathway, catching the Abbot about to enter the chapel, his black Benedictine habit flowing in the strong breeze.

'My dear child, you can't keep away from our little sanctuary can you,' the Abbot spoke brusquely; there was no mistaking an air of cynicism in his dark voice. 'Perhaps you've chosen the wrong vocation, have you ever considered taking the vows of poverty and chastity of our fellow sisters?'

'Were there any witnesses to Brother Jeremy's fall?' Katie struggling to keep up with the Abbot's long gait, ignored the flippant remark and immediately upped the ante. 'Are you 100% sure it was an accident?'

The Abbot stopped in his tracks, removed the hood back from his face, looking her in the eyes. 'God the Father in Heaven had decreed it was time to be reunited with his dear brother, you must leave it at that my dear, and not try to interfere with the will of the Almighty.'

'There's the matter of a hidden body. Brother Jeremy was most anxious to let me know where one was buried.'

'Many souls of nobility and the faith are buried inside the chapel; our Monks, of course, are laid to rest in the Cloisters. I expect he was referring to one of them. Please remember child; Brother Jeremy was a confused old man, many a time he spoke in riddles. He was one not to be taken seriously.'

'Brother Jeremy mentioned having Timothy Stanley buried within the Priory grounds. I presume the Council will no longer agree to that?' Katie challenged.

'I have no reason to object, Ms Sinclair. I do not want to go against the wishes of the venerable Brother, who was also a dear friend and faithful servant of the Lord.'

Katie was taken aback by this small act of kindness. Previously the Abbot had not offered up a single good word on the subject of Timothy Stanley. Odd he was now adopting a different stance.

'I must now bid you a good day,' the Abbot informed her, as they reached the entrance to the Chapel. 'On this special Sabbath, our prayers are for the brotherhood only. God bless you, my child.'

The Abbot reached out to gently touch Katie on the head, then entered the Chapel, quietly closing the door behind. The calming, melismatic song filled the ancient structure, the monks rising in unison to a ninth-century Gregorian chant began their morning of worship.

****

This was not at all panning out as hoped. Katie was within an ace of admitting defeat, there were other work matters requiring urgent attention. She suspected James and Fiona had already discussed pulling the plug. Rather than turning right at the intersection and towards Totnes, Katie headed out onto Dartmoor. She hadn't spoken with Matt in some time, a loyal friend was needed to confide in, someone who would listen, impartial and non-judgmental.

When Katie reached Matt Tyler's old farmhouse near Cadover Bridge, she eventually tracked him down encamped in the summerhouse, cosseted in an old office swivel chair behind a computer screen, deciphering codes. A small, noisy fan heater fought valiantly to maintain warmth in the dank, makeshift office. He smiled. 'Hello stranger, what brings you all the way out here? Must be something important.'

'What do you do Matt when you earnestly believe someone to be telling the truth, but others swear that person is certifiable?'

'I'd tackle that person for proof.' Matt lit up a cheroot, reaching for a half-empty bottle of Rosé. 'Produce hard evidence to corroborate their story.'

'What if that person is no longer with us?'

'Well, I guess that complicates things a tad. What's this all about anyway? That frown doesn't become you.'

Katie blushed, rubbing her forehead and declining a drink. 'I paid a visit to an old Monk only the other day, over at St Oswald's Priory, you know it, near Buckfast Abbey. He was adamant there is a cache of artworks, paintings and the like hidden at the Priory; he also tells me in confidence a body is buried in the Cloisters, but that's all I know. Before I get any closer to the truth this Brother Jeremy mysteriously falls down a flight of stairs, the end result; a fractured skull. Bloody hell, the whole business has really shaken me. My instinctive feeling says it was no accident. I'm certain he was being silenced.'

'Well that's interesting, old paintings you say.'

'Yes, too damn bad I didn't get to be shown their location.'

Matt drained his glass, leaning back in the chair, a wry smile gradually spreading across his face. 'Ah, actually, there could be some credence in the old man's tale. In fact, it's slowly coming together.'

Katie studied Matt's face. 'You've lost me, care to elaborate.'

'I've been steadily going through the encrypted documents and other bits on the hard drive of the computer belonging to Veronica Peters, the one I confiscated from the Peters' London flat. At first, just the usual, pretty standard stuff, also a lot of classified email traffic from the German Feds, origin a special unit in Bonn I must admit I've never heard of before; that's no surprise as we already know she was doing some work with them.'

'That's right. I remember the Sikh guy telling you that.'

'Viram.'

'That's it.'

'However, the best part is a very interesting file named "Operation Albrecht Dürer", which contains a list of paintings and other artworks "appropriated" by the Reichstag from certain occupied countries early in the War years and still on the "missing" file. And from my interpretation of the correspondence, Veronica had accumulated credible intelligence indicating some of this loot, in particular Old Master paintings and drawings, mostly Dutch and Italian, eventually ended up in the South West. According to iPad phone records and texts, she'd arranged to meet a "Jeremy Richards", who supposedly had a few leads on the paintings' whereabouts.'

Matt punched a few keys on the desktop, brought up a document and turned the screen towards Katie.

Katie caught hold of Matt's right arm. 'Jeremy Richards, could that be Brother Jeremy? He's the old guy I was telling you about, the Monk who fell to his death.'

'Quite likely,' Matt acknowledged, turning back to the computer screen. 'I've still got more files to sort through, but just might be we're on the right track.'

Katie's face lit up. 'Marvellous, what a find. If we can discover where these paintings are stashed it may lead us to Veronica's killer, and also find the body Brother Jeremy was talking about.'

'Hey, hang on,' Matt warned, swivelling back to face an excited Katie. 'Do not go around playing Miss Marple. Please put Crispin and Parker in the picture, we've done our bit. The cops will take it from here on. Promise me you will at least do that before you go snooping around any Abbey or Priory.'

'Okay, I'll see what I can do. I'm glad I called around.'

'Not staying for a drink?' Matt detected reluctance in her voice.

'Nope, think I'll treat myself to a quiet night.'

Matt walked her back to the Punto. 'Now promise me, Katherine, you'll not do anything stupid. I know what you're like when seeking answers. Veronica Peters was brutally murdered, I wouldn't want you to be the next victim.'

'Yep, I promise.' Katie deliberately avoided eye contact. As much as she appreciated Matt's concern and pragmatism, she could not guarantee to keep the promise. If she happened to come across something important, it was imperative to chase that lead, always believing in the hand of fate and that in life things happened for a reason.

Katie drove through the farmhouse gates waving a cheery departure to Matt. Crossing over the bleak open moors into a darkening sky and late afternoon rain squall, her mind flashed back to Brother Jeremy's fatalistic words. Desperate to find out what he was trying to tell her, Katie had no immediate intentions to heed any warnings. She craved some sort of justice for the old man.

****

Navigating along the narrow country lanes towards Buckfast, Katie wound down the window to ward off drowsiness and catch the strains of an early Tudor oratorio, most probably Tallis, drifting up the valley from the Abbey Cathedral and out across the open moorland. Earlier afternoon storms had abated, moving inland, the unseasonal humidity of the day gone, the night cool and inviting, the familiar country smells invigorating, lifting her spirits.

Swinging a sharp left at the crossroads, before heading along a small narrow B road for the second time that day, Katie drove towards Abbey College and the Priory, the Abbot's persistent telephone calls from earlier, repeating in her head. 'I have some documents Brother Jeremey wanted me to give to you. Can you come to the Priory tonight after Benediction?'

Her plans for the evening were in disarray. Wrung out from the confrontation earlier in the day and the stressful drive back to Bovey Tracey through a monsoonal downpour, she was relaxing in a hot bath with a large glass of port when the mobile rang, On the fourth call she yielded and picked it up.

The Abbot was insistent. *No, they couldn't be dropped in the mail. They were too valuable to risk that. It was a special affirmation in our departed brother's will that you receive them personally.*

A darkened Priory greeted Katie driving in through the gates just after 9pm, further up the driveway one or two lights were still burning in the College dormitories, boarders most likely. Judiciously she left the Punto under the only light in an otherwise deserted car park, well aware of the fact the moon had disappeared behind scudding clouds, and this was alien territory. What did The Abbot say? *'I'll leave the side door open to the vestry, down the path from the car park, just after the statue of St Benedict in the Chapel rose garden.'*

It was a situation she vowed never to repeat. Dark memories of the last time being alone at night; fearful thoughts flooded her consciousness.

The indistinct shapes of trees and buildings morphed into unworldly beings and ghosts, but she hastened on down the ancient stone paving, breathing a sigh of relief when the small rounded oak door materialised in the torchlight.

She briefly flirted with alerting Matt or Ben to her late-night foray but dismissed it as childish and petty.

Closing the heavy gothic door behind she entered the sacred place, quickly donning a silk scarf and crossing herself with holy water from a font, almost by reflex in the devote Catholic ritual as her mother had done and her grandmother before. A bank of candles to the left of the altar faintly illuminated the void, their hypnotic flames wavering gently in an almost imperceptible draught. The invasive, pungency of ceremonial incenses left over from the earlier Benediction stung her senses. She called once or twice, to no avail, then sat down on a pew near the altar waiting patiently. A number of times she glanced at her watch, frustrated as it was nearing half-past nine and the Abbot had not yet materialised. Getting anxious and yearning for the haven of the Punto Katie heard someone bustling down the aisle.

'Ah there you are.' The Abbot rushed up, his flushed, gaunt, ruddy features clearly discernible in the eerie half-light. 'Sorry I'm late; I was unavoidably detained.'

'I couldn't miss the Monks at song as I drove past Buckfast Abbey gates.' Katie rose to her feet. 'Such a heavenly sound.'

'Yes, I do love the sacred choral works of the Tudor composers, I believe that was Thomas Tallis, however, William Byrd is my favourite. You know we can all be harmonious at times.' Abbot Maximilian smiled. 'Now, I've already kept you way too long, if you care to follow, we'll get those documents I promised.'

The Abbot marched off back along the aisle, forcing Katie to keep pace. Down a set of steep, stone circular steps at the rear of the chapel and through a series of narrow, twisting corridors, dimly lit by candles in sconces, they arrived at a wide, iron-barred gate; pushing it open, the Abbot searched for a light switch on the wall.

'That's funny,' he announced when the light failed to come on. 'Must be a blown bulb, not to worry I have some candles in my office. Please wait here while I get them. Thankfully, my sanctuary is just along the next corridor.'

Katie waited in the sparse anteroom, her latent sixth sense promoting an uneasy, watchful silence. She snuggled into her all-weather jacket for warmth. She searched her handbag, checking the iPhone for messages, ensuring it was active.

Within an instant of doing so, an unexpected sound fractured the calm, triggering a primaeval adrenalin response, a ghostly creaking noise originating from the far corner of the room. Katie let out a muffled cry, training her eyes towards the sound, witnessing an old rustic country chair moving back and forth, bathed in a shaft of moonlight from a window slit above her head.

She fumbled in her jacket pocket for the led torch, hands shaking, managing to flick it on, providing momentary security in the underground cavern. 'Jesus Christ, who's there?' she called out, in barely more than a whisper, probing the darkness with her trusty light. Brother Jeremy's prophetic visions flooded back. The chair kept creaking, but no voice came from her pleas. Katie unable to move, found terror had paralysed her, witnessing in horror the chair rocking backwards and forwards. Then without warning, a tall, wraith-like male figure in brown robes, hands hidden in the long sleeves, eased himself up from the chair to walk towards the door, turning momentarily to look in her direction.

'Who are you?' Katie called out, impossible to discern facial features, the dark hood pulled down over the eyes.

The robed figure remained silent, melting away into the darkened passageway, leaving Katie to stare after him. Her heart was beating loudly in her chest, her pulse spontaneously skipping a beat.

'Sorry I was so long,' Abbot Maximilian apologised, returning to the room only a matter of seconds later, carrying a candle. 'Are you all right my dear? You look pale.'

If the Abbot had seen the Monk, he did not let on.

'There was someone here,' Katie enunciated slowly. 'A monk, who sat rocking in the chair.'

'So he did come to visit.' Abbot Maximilian's eyes lit up. 'I'd forgotten he might drop by; you must have been terrified. I am so sorry my dear, I should have warned you.'

'Who came to visit? Who was it?' Katie demanded, annoyed at the Abbot's calm indifference.

'The ghost of Henry Clemens; on nights when the Devil starts to pray, he comes. I am sure he is here to bid farewell to Brother Jeremy.'

'It wasn't a bloody apparition,' Katie insisted, colour flooding back into her cheeks, releasing a burst of anger.

'Poor girl, you are shaking, let me get you out of here,' Abbot Maximilian instructed, gently coaxing Katie along another narrow passageway. 'I'll get brandy.'

'I didn't see a ghost,' Katie insisted defiantly, as they entered the main part of the Priory.

'We always feel the presence of tortured souls. God's house is sporadically visited by the forces of evil; often one's

271

mind can conjure up disturbing visions. For over a thousand years our brethren have waged a never-ending fight against the relentless armies of Satan and the Conspiracy of Souls. It is now we feel the battle is one we are losing, and Heaven is under final siege. Every day in the Priory, almost without fail, the brothers confront Hell's dark angels, emboldened as His strength grows. Alas, today I fear our Holy Mother Church and the very foundations of our Western civilisation are facing their greatest challenge at any time in history, under attack on all fronts from the insidious march of amorality and conformity cult ideology, spread by Structural Post Marxism propaganda and the atheism of the new technologists. The assault on our beloved institutions and society is unprecedented. Sadly, Rome at its highest level and even Our Holy Father is capitulating to the baying mob.'

'There was someone in that chair,' Katie implored unhearing. 'A real human being.'

'Please excuse the preaching. I'll see to that drink.' The Abbot moved to a Victorian dresser filling two small glasses from a crystal decanter, handing one to Katie who accepted it with shaking hands, before sinking heavily into a chair. Maybe her mind had been playing tricks, imagining seeing and hearing a phantom friar rocking in the chair. Sleep deprivation was a known contributor, leashing havoc on mind and body. Yet the Abbot had mentioned 'he' might visit. She was anxious and confused.

'These are the documents Brother Jeremy wanted you to have,' the Abbot informed, handing over a grimy, dog-eared folder, bound together by a piece of cord. Katie gratefully accepted the sheaves of paper, dropping them into her shoulder bag.

'We always try to present a worldly welcoming picture for the wider public, of course with our pastoral commitment to the College and such. But the Priory does have its darker side,' Abbot Maximilian explained, watching Katie with interest. 'I guess we brothers are used to souls coming and going from the spiritual world. For outsiders, it's more confronting, and I do understand, alarming.'

Katie sat quietly, relishing the warm brandy, which seared the back of her throat. 'I expect you're right,' she agreed at last. 'Thank you for the papers, I really should be heading off.'

'I shall walk you to your car, are you sure you will be okay to drive? You've had a nasty shock.'

'Yes, I feel much better now, thank you,' Katie replied truthfully, eager to leave the confines of the Priory behind.

Abbot Maximilian bid his visitor a safe trip home, striding briskly away across the wide lawns to the communal sleeping quarters in the South Wing of the building. She stood under the car park light for several minutes, checking her iPhone, gladly embracing the breeze coursing in off the Atlantic and up the escarpment, cooling a flushed complexion and easing an agitated temperament.

Manoeuvring out of the car park towards the main Priory gates something snared her attention in the rear vision mirror. She tried to make out what it was, gently applying the brakes. The sparse, shadowy figure of a monk standing near the entrance framed in the moonlight, taking her by surprise, dressed in the same dark robes as before, facial features part masked behind the hood. It was then he started waving in a half salute, the corner of his mouth rising in a sardonic smile. Not waiting to find out if he was real or a figment of her imagination Katie floored the little Punto through the Priory gates in the direction of the A38, towards North Bovey. Reluctantly, she found herself agreeing with Fiona and Matt; there was something tangibly sinister about the Priory, but she couldn't put her finger on it. A stark contrast to Buckfast Abbey. The Priory projected an air of malevolence, eerily cold and distant.

Today I stood by the Priory gates and waved to a lovely visitor. I scared her Lord, yet I don't think I meant to cause alarm.

I sat rocking in my chair, for comfort more than anything, to protect the bodies. To be there in case they ever wake up.

Dear Lord, forgive me.
Amen

Chapter Fourteen

'Where did these come from?' James inquired, removing the old folder from its plastic sleeve, and opening it carefully under a magnifying light on the laboratory examination table.

'Well, actually I got them from the Head Abbot Maximillian at the Priory yesterday. Handed them over to me, personally. According to him, Brother Jeremy specifically insisted I take ownership,' Katie answered. 'It was the only major item in his last will. They were found in his room on his desk with last requests and an attached note, dated the day he died.'

'Any idea what we're looking at?

'Not a clue. Not the slightest indication from either old Jeremy or Maximillian. Just put it in a plastic cover last night, haven't even looked at the contents.'

'Okay.'

Katie pulled up a stool and moved in closer to observe as James, donning disposable gloves, methodically and quickly flicked through the yellowed and torn contents with tweezers, occasionally shaking his head and mumbling to himself.

'Very interesting stuff. Can I borrow them to take a closer look?'

'Sure. What do you think?'

'Let's see. A mixture of handwritten notes, signed statements, a couple of official-looking documents, plus some old newspaper cuttings and original wartime photos. Most in English and German and I think some Latvian or Russian, can't tell, but all to do with the same subject.'

'Which is?

'Don't know. I'll take them home on the weekend and spend some time on the internet.'

'James, do you believe in ghosts?'

'I'm not sure I have any firm beliefs,' he replied casually, placing reading glasses on the bench. 'What's brought all this on? Seen a few lately?'

Katie explained about her meeting with the Abbot and what she had witnessed last night, bringing James up to speed on Matt's discovery in connection to Veronica Peters, and why they surmised Brother Jeremy was murdered.

'It's not like Matt to keep vital information from a current investigation.'

'He hadn't quite finished going through Veronica's hard drive files,' Katie added, quickly detecting her brother's bruised ego. 'Come on, you know Matt won't divulge information until all the facts are in. Anyway, I'm telling you now.'

'Even so, as equal partners in Moorlands, we all have a right to know what's going on.' James's mood was still muted. 'Currently, we have a morgue full of bodies and no one responsible for any of them. If anyone has new information, it's critical I know asap. Also, it's not in your job description to go on risky, solo midnight jaunts, playing the role of a covert operative in a B grade movie.'

Hi Katie,

Got thinking after you dropped by the other day. Your insistence to keep digging at the Priory (and generally making a nuisance of yourself) got me a little concerned for your safety, especially what we picked up about Brother Jeremy, etc. Therefore, I spent a few hours on the web and a bit of ringing around, researching the Priory, more particularly Head Honcho Max who became my primary worry. See attached. Make your own conclusions but I'm a lot more relaxed now.

(Big Warning* – Keep this stuff to yourself and delete this email when read. Had to access a secure Vatican file for some of this!)

P.S. Also attached my latest invoices for MFC to endorse and send off to Bristol. Please expedite, the Mustang is in the garage!

Also, can you chase H.O. for my last batch, which remain outstanding – I have to eat.

Take care,
Matt

Smiling inwardly, Katie downloaded the attachment and brought up the cryptic summary:

Subject: Abbot Maximillian. Christened David Maxwell Wise
Born 15 June 1942, Long Island NY to British Parents: Percival and Doris Wise. Therefore holds dual nationality.

After War attended upmarket private Catholic boys college in Dorset, scoring max in A levels. Followed by Notre Dame Uni in the States, graduating First Class Honours in Physics, top in the Year.

Surprise, surprise, immediately enrols in PhD Cambridge (the UK not the US), reading Modern Theology graduating 1966 and spends next three years in Rome at the Seminary reserved for fast-tracking of Vatican's finest and brightest.

Until 1975 is shuffled around various overseas postings as Vatican rep, mostly Third World (the usual pathway to the Church upper echelons).

Get this: General opinion is; for the better part of the eighties he was a major influence on Church policy in Rome and had the ear of at least two Popes.

But then, he suddenly turns up in 1987 as No. 2 to the Head Abbot, running a small private school at a back-water Priory in the South West of England! Generally believed a "progressive" Jesuit bloc, which wields inordinate control behind the scenes at St Peter's, knifed Max in the back, partly due to his growing influence, but mainly because of his well-known, impeccable moral standards and steadfast advocacy for maintaining the old Church traditions. The feedback I get unequivocally; he is "The Good Guy". Can't find anyone with a bad word and no skeletons!

Cheers x

****

'What's the bloody urgency?' DCI Parker demanded, clasping a pint of Guinness and walking over to join the others in the beer garden at The Royal Sovereign in Totnes.

'Don't know,' they echoed in unison, moving up to make room on the bench for the portly, sweaty DCI.

'Crispin suggested meeting here for an informal case catch up, busting with some news. Better be good, got to be back at Bovey for an International Forensic Accreditation certification at 2pm,' a concerned James exclaimed, snatching a look at his watch every thirty seconds.

'Sorry Guys. Won't be a sec,' came the call from the car park. They turned to see Crispin on his phone, exiting an unmarked KIA saloon and waving in their direction.

'Did you get my lemon squash?' the senior detective questioned breathlessly, taking up residence next to Katie. Receiving blank looks and sensing irritation all around, he didn't wait for a reply.

'I managed to catch up with the Star chief editor, Lana Gibbs,' Crispin explained, sounding excited. 'Following my instructions, she recently uncovered articles written about Hayley Illbert-Tavistock in the short time after she vanished. Anyway, according to accounts, young Hayley was running requests for information to a number of UK and European agencies on persons who might have turned up in the British Isles after the War, specifically those implicated in war crimes. Now, according to my research, Hayley believed there was a Clemens bloke living in Devon around the time of her disappearance and had arranged to meet up. I bet my last fiver, he's the one who killed her.'

'The Clemens phantom again.' Matt exchanged knowing glances with Katie. 'Yesterday we interrogated the hard-drive of Veronica Peters' computer, coincidentally there was a brief mention in a highly confidential email, origin the German Feds in Berlin of a Henry "Clemence" being implicated in artworks confiscated by The Third Reich. My guess is; she had an appointment with a person who had knowledge of this, but before the official meeting was held, whammo, she's terminated.'

'For what it's worth, I believe Brother Jeremy had the inside knowledge on this character and was about to spill the beans, as they say. It might also tie in with the documents James is currently looking at, given to us by the Head Abbot at the Priory,' Katie added. 'So what happens next?'

'I honestly don't know,' James uttered. 'What's your opinion, Parker? In truth, we are a bit lost with forensics on this one, without any strong suspects and no concrete motives I don't know where to go. The one interesting fact being our bodies were discovered within a five-mile radius of each other. Apart from Hayley of course, who has never been found and maybe living a life somewhere else, under an adopted identity.'

'That's assuming the deaths of Nicola Fletcher and Rebecca Price are linked in with all of this,' Fiona interrupted. 'So far we have no real proof.'

'I'm dropping over to Abbey College this afternoon,' Katie advised. 'If there is a link, let's assemble what it is. I think it's worth the effort to follow up this Clemens lead and where he could be hiding. Sounds to me he's our likely person of interest.'

'What? Hold on a minute. Assuming he's still alive,' Nick added, shaking his head in disbelief. 'If you do the basic arithmetic, Clemens could well be deceased or barely alive in a nursing home. Just decided I would throw that spanner in the works; we have a possible murderer, who is almost certainly long-gone, interesting concept! I can't say I've come across that one before unless you believe in ghosts. Or senile serial killers?'

****

'I do apologise for keeping you waiting, Ms Sinclair. It's coming up to examination time, so things naturally are a bit hectic around the place.'

'Yes, I understand, sorry for the unplanned intrusion, my meeting won't take long,' Katie apologised, accepting a seat and placing a card on Larry Miller's office desk. 'As you're aware Mr Miller, I am a forensic psychologist attached to the official investigation team looking into the homicides of Rebecca Price and Nicola Fletcher. Certain information has come into our possession, in the last few days, that leads us to believe the excursion the girls were on when they disappeared, may have had something to do with their murders.'

'Nasty business. Everybody at the school, pupils and teachers alike are still struggling to come to terms with the tragic events. Anything I can do, please ask.'

'Can you shed any light on what projects Rebecca and Nicola were working on, shortly before their disappearances.'

Larry Miller turned to his desktop computer screen, pulling up specific subject schedules by class and by pupil. 'The only one I can see here is a history assignment set by our holy ordained Abbot Maximillian and supervised by Head of History, Dr Lewis Lansky; something about a little-known

Nazi war criminal name of Henry Clemens. Quite a sinister chap by all accounts.'

Katie tried to keep her face void of expression. 'I don't suppose Allyson Carter was also working on the identical project.'

Principal Miller once more brought up the relevant details on the file. 'As a matter of fact, she was,' he declared, turning slowly back to face his visitor. 'Surely you're not suggesting this Clemens fellow is linked to any of these girls. I very much doubt he would still be alive. If he is, he'd be pushing the century mark.'

'Yes, I'm sure you're right. This case has not been without complications Mr Miller, it remains a real mystery why these girls were attacked and killed. If we can find a common link, it may lead to a breakthrough.'

'Life was not meant to be easy,' Larry Miller stated softy. 'I keep reminding all our students to "never give up" and I suggest you do the same. Instinct is a powerful thing Ms Sinclair. Perhaps your feelings have credence; the trouble is; you may be viewing things from the wrong angle. Heed this advice; take a step back and then things will start to fall into place.'

Katie drove back to the Lab, deflated and discouraged, resigned to the hard reality the "phantom-like" Clemens was not directly involved with the death of Veronica Peters, Nicola or Rebecca. She reflected on what had been achieved so far, which in her summations, unfortunately, amounted to very little.

Okay, say he did have a hand in killing Hayley Illbert-Tavistock, thirty or so years ago, clearly the man is long gone, so what was the point in pursuing that one. James was right. Without a corpse, a physical trail or eyewitness testimony, there was no evidence Hayley was murdered. Adding Allyson to the equation; there had also been nobody unearthed, hence no evidence of a common assassin. The team were only working on assumptions, speculation.

Katie stretched out on the office lounge, her psychological mind in overdrive. There had to be an indisputable connection somewhere. Perhaps Larry Miller was right; if she stepped back, things would start making sense.

****

'Your sister is very stubborn.' There was obvious annoyance in Parker's tone. 'How she thinks trekking across Europe will miraculously uncover clues to the current investigation, is beyond me.'

'Yes, Katie can be very wilful at times,' James agreed, smothering a grin. 'Although I'm not opposed to her taking a short break away from the office, we're all equal partners here. If there's a convincing argument; we do what we like within reason, and throw in the pressure around here lately, I may also be a contributing factor. By the way, do you have contacts over there, in case she requires support or gets into a bit of strife?'

'Way ahead of you. An old colleague of mine Commander Roscoe Telfer is on active long-term secondment to the German BND out of Munich. Some sensitive joint task force intelligence operation to do with the Turks, believe it or not – by the way, keep that to yourself... Just happens he's on a short rec leave and is not fussed to do something different for a few days. I've already given him the heads up and put Katie in contact.'

'Thanks. I worry about her doing it alone. My sister often rushes headlong into things, without weighing up the consequences.'

'Why she keeps on about this Clemens, I have no idea,' Parker continued. 'Those old documents handed over by the Abbot should be torched, utter nonsense if you want my honest opinion, and everything else we have thus far discovered about Clemens is merely hearsay, coupled with old newspaper articles, which won't help in catching our killer. It is also paramount I keep Katie's little jaunt a secret from the DCC, who is threatening to redirect police resources if we fail to come up with any tangible evidence. The rumour circulating in CID is the case will be put on permanent hold. There is mounting public disquiet we've been unable to charge anyone with these murders. If it gets around H.Q we have contracted people jaunting across Europe on a flight of fantasy, all hell will break loose.'

James refrained from comment. The way the investigation was shaping up, getting on board the plane to Munich alongside his sister was looking like an attractive option, thereby escaping an updated task force press release scheduled for two days' time. James detested speculation, what he wanted was legitimate forensic evidence, which brought a felon to justice. So far, there wasn't much to go on and dare he say it, he was getting a bit bored.

****

The moment she finished the call Katie logged on to her favourite site and booked a seat on the next day's flight to Munich, departing Gatwick at 12:20 pm.

It wasn't much, but it offered a glimmer of hope, a one in a thousand chance. Deep down inside something kept niggling, the single-minded doggedness driving everyone around her insane, the innate intellect saying she was right, egging her onwards. Katie devoutly believed the solution lay with unravelling Henry Clemens past; and Roscoe Telfer had just delivered that chance, arranging to meet up when she landed in Munich.

****

Katie was up and away early the next morning, just scrambling on board the commuter London service from Newton Abbot with two minutes to spare. At Victoria Station, she cooled heels for twenty minutes, finally connecting with the express for Gatwick. Bag checked in, boarding pass in hand and checking her watch indicated forty-five minutes before boarding. She'd missed the snack trolley on the train, falling quickly into a deep, undisturbed slumber for most of the trip. A bad move. Suffering from a severe sugar drop and a growing migraine, she craved a strong coffee and a big breakfast.

The airport's main café was full and abuzz with frantic activity, forcing Katie to squeeze in next to a young Italian couple, who were arguing emotionally about some trivial matter, the raised voices attracting stares from other diners. Keen to exit the scene as swiftly as possible, Katie rushed her meal, and after devouring the last mouthful she headed to the newsagents to pick up something to read and check final messages on her phone.

Finally, she was able to relax, settling into a window seat, revelling in the fact she had made good her escape from Bovey Tracey, enjoying her first decent break away from the office in eighteen months, experiencing no pangs of guilt. There still remained a fondness in her heart for Germany, gained from several trips both business and pleasure, since being let off the leash as a teenager. The urban sprawl of Bavaria spread out below, as the flight descended on the glide path into Munich, reviving memories of Katie's last visit; a three-day seminar in Hanover, unimaginatively titled "Forensic Aspects and Procedures for the Clinical Psychologist".

Quickly clearing customs, Katie hurried out in search of the information desk, where she'd arranged to meet Telfer. Embarrassingly, she sighted the Commander at the arrivals hall holding a piece of cardboard close to his chest with her name in large black letters, trying to be as inconspicuous as possible. Not as she imagined, more Jason Statham than Lewis, hair shaved to disguise premature baldness About 5′ 8″, compact in stature, lightly tanned features, but she sensed powerfully built under the suit. Alert, probing brown eyes constantly scanning the crowd and surrounds, but retaining a warmth, instantly putting his guest at ease. He ditched the sign, shaking Katie's hand with a vice-like grip and reached for her overnight bag. 'Pleasant flight?' he enquired, leading the way to the terminal exit. By the effortless gait, like a tiger cat on the prowl, Katie guessed a previous career soldier background. By how he spoke, always in command, the consummate professional. An FN 5-7 semi-automatic secreted somewhere on his person backed up the self-assuredness. It was comforting to be in safe hands.

'Yes, it's not the short trips, it's the long hauls I loathe,' Katie answered politely, watching Roscoe swing the bag into the boot of an intimidating, flashy, red Mercedes AMG Coupe.

'Nice car.'

'Don't get used to it.' He smiled, opening the passenger door, and jumping in the driver's seat. 'Stands out like a nudist at a Windsor garden party. Afraid we're going to have to drop this beast off at home on the way through, then pick up something more "appropriate". Anyway, welcome to Bavaria. We'll be heading straight down to Füssen, so you can get checked into the guest house. You'll like it, a favourite of ours in the ski season, old-worldly, but has everything. Should only take an hour and a half; if we don't encounter traffic. Your first visit to Southern Germany?'

'Yes.'

'It's the best part if you want my opinion, comparatively unspoiled to the rest of Germany.'

'Been over here long?'

'Actually, I've been stationed in Munich nearly three years now, prior to that I was with GSG9 Operations H.Q. in Bonn, and of course, Plymouth before that, where I had the privilege of working with Will Parker.'

'Do you miss Devon?' Katie probed, gripping the overhead grab handle, as he executed a sharp left turn out of the terminal car park and accelerated violently, slotting into the high-speed conveyor belt known as the Autobahn.

'Yeah, to some extent, but I've settled here quite nicely. Although, I do miss the English soccer, in particular watching

Plymouth Argyle play at Home Park. My son and I would turn up for a match, regardless of the weather.'

The Merc swapped for a small, ubiquitous rental, Katie sat back, luxuriating in the journey through the Bavarian countryside, the lush undulating landscape a total contrast to rolling Devon hills, framed by mountains to the South, the highest Alps topped by a smattering of snow.

'Füssen is only five kilometres from Austria,' Roscoe announced. 'There's lots of things to see down here. Before you return to England, you must visit Neuschwanstein Castle, which literally translates as New Swan Stone. The castle is a nineteenth-century Romanesque Revival palace, built on a rugged hill above the village of Hohenschwangau, a short drive out of Füssen. King Ludwig commissioned the place as a retreat and in honour of his brilliant friend and composer Richard Wagner. Ludwig actually financed construction from his personal wealth and extensive borrowings, never once using Bavarian public funds.'

'Yes, seen many photographs of Neuschwanstein. It's definitely on my "bucket list".'

On arrival at the boutique guest haus, cum hotel, Katie collapsed on the bed, vegging out checking the local TV streaming service, then appreciated a lengthy shower, before changing for dinner. The plan was to meet Roscoe and his wife in the Foyer, just before seven, then take a short stroll through the town to a restaurant and Wine Keller, situated by the side of Lake Forggensee.

'This is my wife Anita,' Roscoe said, smiling warmly as they all met up in the hotel bar for a pre-dinner aperitif. Anita was friendly enough, and her English near impeccable, gained from having lived with Telfer in the UK for many years.

Immaculately dressed in a blue Bavarian folk-style dress, her hair was neatly rolled in a tight bun, held in place by a diamond-encrusted clip. Katie soon learnt she was born in Munich, descendent from a wealthy aristocratic family of the local nobility.

Entering the Keller down a flight of steps, the trio was greeted by a noisy eclectic throng of local and tourist clientele, urged along by an over-amplified four-piece um-pah band dressed in traditional alpine costume on a makeshift stage, belting out the usual lively German renditions. The atmosphere energetic and friendly and addictive.

'I hope I'm not putting you to any trouble with my visit,' Katie said, raising her voice to be heard over the music.

Anita laughed. 'Not at all, I've been begging Roscoe to take time off for ages, so this is a welcome break. I have family living in Oberammergau, not too far from Füssen, so we plan to turn your stay into a mini holiday.'

'I'm pleased to hear it.' Katie smiled. 'It is so easy in the modern-day working environment to constantly worry about job security and never have a proper break.'

'I understand you are based near Buckfast Abbey,' Anita remarked. 'I suggest you visit the Museum of St Mang's Abbey, whilst you are here. They showcase our local violin and lute making industry, which I'm sure you'll find interesting. It would be fascinating for you to compare the two places; St Mang's was a former Benedictine Monastery.'

Katie nodded, as the waitress came over to take their order, and with Anita's guidance, they ordered traditional Bavarian fare.

Having spent a year as an exchange student in Germany, during her youth, Katie was more than proficient in the language, so Anita encouraged her to practice throughout the evening. 'You'll be required to use it over the coming days,' Anita advised. 'Not many Bavarians speak English unless they were taught at school. The older generation prefers visitors to learn German, having said that; to complicate matters, we Bavarians do talk a lot of slang, comprising a local dialect.'

'I picked up on that,' Katie acknowledged. 'I'll do my best but can't guarantee I won't slip up occasionally.'

'Now, I've put a couple of my intelligence analysts to work, trawling through archive databases,' Roscoe said, finally broaching the subject of business when Anita vanished to the restroom. 'Your person of interest; this Heinrich Clemminger fellow, popped up a couple of times in old Civil Records. We tentatively agree there could be links to the person known to you as Henry Clemens.'

Katie listened, with intent.

'Couldn't get viable leads on any next of kin who may have lived in or around this region before the War,' the Commander went on, pulling his chair closer and dropping his voice. 'Yet, I did turn up a few details on the family concern that employed him. We're talking well after the War actually, name of Linder. They still have the business, operating at the same location near the town of Pfronten, not far from here. I can take you there first thing tomorrow morning.'

'Will they be willing to talk?' Katie noting Anita walking back to the table, twigging that Roscoe wasn't keen to talk shop around his wife.

'Can't answer that I'm afraid, but it's worth a try. You have to start somewhere. Now, what do you like on the dessert board?'

Katie glanced up at the lightly snow-capped Allgäu Alps in the near distance, resembling mythical giants from an ancient Norse legend surrounding the old town. Instinctively zipping up her all-weather jacket she threaded her way through the narrow, winding Medieval streets, the buildings amazingly preserved and untouched by the ravages of conflict or urban renewal. *Makes sense*, she thought. *Nothing down here to bomb.*

Picking out a small café overlooking the River Lech, she ordered a typical German breakfast; pastries, creamy rich coffee and a selection of cold meats, allowing the chance to catch up on diary notes and peruse the tourist brochures, before meeting Telfer at nine.

Consulting her smartphone she noted the village they were heading to was 853 metres above sea level, sitting just on the Northern edge of the Austrian border.

'Excellent, you're on time,' Telfer announced, pushing open the passenger door of the rental Opel hatch for Katie to slide in. 'It's only a fifteen-minute drive out of town. I know the cattle get moved into the pastures around eleven; gives you a pretty good window; most folks are already up and about.'

Katie was impressed.

Roscoe was a stickler for detail and meticulous preparation; having learnt early from hard lessons of experience. He lived and worked on the principle "do it right the first time", an asset to his time with the Devon and Cornwall Constabulary. The Bundestag was now lucky to have the Commander on their payroll.

Within a short space of time, the Opel pulled over to the side of the road in the small, picture-postcard village of Pfronten. 'Just follow the small track up to the main house. I'll wait here; remember, keep it light-hearted. These people get a bit funny if too many strangers drop by and they'll clam up. They're distrustful of outsiders. Good hunting.'

Katie stepped out of the car, flinging the small backpack over her shoulder. Casual attire was the order of the day. Again she quickly checked hair and appearance in the car window. She had hoped Roscoe would come along but understood his desire to remain in the car.

'Typical Bavarian architecture,' she mused, as the residence came into view; a cream coloured structure on three levels, each featuring a narrow balcony abundantly decorated with hanging pots, overflowing with arrays of colourful flowers. Behind the house, a couple of small trucks and a tractor were parked outside sheds and storage facilities, plainly visible. The sound of voices cajoling uncooperative dairy cows wafted on the breeze, mixing with bells, resounded through a lingering morning mist.

Long green pastures stretched up the hillside toward the snowline; for all intents and purposes the property was a working farm and dairy.

Katie spotted an elderly woman manhandling an antique rug on a paved terrace, accompanied by a small excited schnauzer, snapping at her ankles.

'Sprechen sie Englisch?' (Do you speak English?) Katie enquired, somewhat wary of the dog, which growled as she approached. She knew the German for Bissiger Hund was Biting Dog but remained confident this didn't relate to the ankle sized pooch, running around in circles.

'Ich spreche ein bisschen Englisch.' (I speak a little bit of English.) came the hesitant reply. 'Ich lernte nach dem Krieg, als ich Krankenschwester war.' (I learnt after the war, when I was a nurse.)

'I wonder if you can assist me. I'm looking for a Herr Heinrich Clemminger, or perhaps you might know him as Henry Clemens?'

'There is no Heinrich or Henry here,' the old woman answered, surprisingly demonstrating a reasonable command of English.

'But you know who he is?' Katie slipped the photograph provided by Roscoe out of her phone wallet and showed it to the woman, keenly watching to see if her eyes betrayed emotion.

'The man you seek has not lived in Germany for many years,' the woman grumbled, without a glance at the black and white image. Surrounded by a cloud of dust she continued to vigorously attack the worn rug.

'Do you know where he went?'

Frau Linder gazed quizzically at the young blonde.

'And to whom should I be telling such secrets?'

How stupid of me, mused Katie. *I wasn't ready for that one. Let's s try this.*

'I am sorry, my name is Katie Sinclair, my legal firm in England is trying to track down beneficiaries of a recently discovered will, of a certain Henry Clemens.'

The woman appeared perplexed, so Katie tried again, this time in German. 'Es bleibt Geld in einem Testament.' (There is money left in a will.)

'In that case, I suppose it can do nobody any harm,' the old woman finally ventured, after a few awkward moments interrogating Katie's eyes.

'That was a long time ago fraulein. I am old and my Gedächtnis (memory) is very poor, but Heinrich would also be an old man now, he is probably no longer alive. He was indeed some years older than me. So ein weltiger und starker Mann.' (Such a worldly and strong man.)

'So then, he worked for your family?'

'Ah yes, Heinrich was originally from around these parts. It was only natural to give him work after he returned from the War.

I can tell you; Germany was a shattered nation. We had to give our young men hope and the chance for a future after the things they had done and seen, they were dreadful times.

My husband put him to work making cheese. He knew a lot about it. He was very upstanding with the men. They respected him; I recall. Heinrich was well suited to our business.'

The old woman's voice became croaky and faltered. She put down the rug and placed both hands on hips, lifting up her eyes earnestly towards the young woman standing before her. 'I was sad to see him leave, although my son Gunter never liked him so much.'

Her face softened, memories flooding back. Katie detected an ancient hint of affection in her voice. 'It was all very sudden my fraulein. He just disappeared one night, without telling a soul. We were all shocked.'

'Can you remember where he went?'

'I do believe he went across the border, maybe Innsbruck or Italy even. My son might know, wait here, I'll see if I can find him in the milking sheds.'

Katie sat herself down on an old wooden crate, waiting for the woman's son to appear. Thankfully, the schnauzer had scooted off with the old lady, granting Katie instant peace.

Presently a stocky, thick-set individual of middle age appearance materialised from around the side of the house, wearing a full length, dirt-stained, brown leather apron and rubber gumboots, wiping his hands on a soiled hand towel which projected from a rear pocket.

'What do you want to know about Heinrich?' He cast wary eyes over the visitor as he approached, his English clear and precise. 'We haven't heard from him for many years. Heinrich was bad blood, with any luck he is now residing with the Devil, he was a wicked man.'

'Why was that?' Katie probed.

'You know anything about the Schutzstaffel?' Gunter ventured, lowering his voice and watching his mother return inside, before producing a pipe from inside his coat, tucking a small wad of tobacco into the meerschaum bowl.

'A little.'

'I tell you something fraulein, you should go look up names of the SS and you will discover everything there is to know about Heinrich Clemminger. Do you know the meaning of Clemminger?'

Katie shook her head.

'It means kind-hearted, yet Heinrich was not kind-hearted. He was the right-hand man of the "Butcher of Riga"; he shot many Russian prisoners and then rounded up the Jews.'

295

Katie's brain spun wildly, rocked by this revelation. How in God's name did Brother Jeremy happen to come into possession of documents possibly belonging to Clemens, who she now suspected may indeed be Clemminger? She very much doubted they were friends. The Monk struck her as a gentle, kind individual, his make-up certainly not indicating a tendency to buddy up with a possible mass murderer.

The old woman's son continued with his story, in no hurry to return to the hard labouring on the farm. 'Heinrich used to have a saying *Ich habe immer recht,*' he informed her. 'The English translation is *I am always right.*'

'And was he?'

The man snorted indignantly. 'Heinrich didn't let anything get the better of him, he saw himself as God-like, indestructible.'

'Did you have any communications with him after he disappeared?'

'Not me personally. I despised him.' A scowl appeared on Gunter's weather-beaten features, his voice reduced to a whisper. 'When he left, it almost destroyed my mother. I speculated there was something more than friendship between them. A number of times he sent short, passionate letters to her which I intercepted and never let her see.'

'Can you tell me where he ended up.'

'I put the clues together and did a bit of my own private investigation work,' Gunter continued, the scowl now turning into a self-congratulatory smirk.

Katie urged him on.

'Zurich. Manager of a profitable cheese factory; I am sure of that, married as well. I checked the marriage records. That was in 1968. After that, I know nothing, except...'

'Except what?' Katie pushed.

'In 1972, he was no longer in Zurich. Yet, his wife was still in residence and there was a son. Birth records.'

'Do you think he was caught?'

'It would have been in the news. Captured ex-Nazi and SS criminals were big headlines in the sixties and seventies. You know fraulein, like Eichmann and others.'

'Perhaps he was secretly executed by the Mossad,' ventured Katie.

'For a young person, your knowledge of worldly things is very good.' Gunter smiled, beginning to warm to the visitor. 'I hope and pray for the latter. But I suspect he eluded capture and died an old man somewhere, forgotten and still defiant.'

'Assuming he survived, he would have changed his name?' Katie predicted.

'Yes of course. He would have spent the rest of his life in exile, running from the authorities, forever looking over his shoulder. Europe would have been "too hot", as you English say. Maybe Paraguay or Bolivia or the like, where the Odessa Organisation helped many SS to resettle.'

'If I really wanted to find out what had happened to Clemminger, where would I start to look?' Katie was on a roll, desperate for further details.

'I think you would be best to go to Switzerland and pick up the threads there. I'm not saying it will be easy though. Heinrich would know how to cover his tracks. Maybe start with his wife and son.'

'Thank you for all your help.'

'You are most welcome but be careful fraulein. I am almost certain his progeny would have followed in his footsteps; bad blood continues down the line.'

Katie hurried back down the dirt track to Roscoe Telfer, waiting patiently in the Opel, half-awake, the seat reclined, listening to the local radio station.

Driving back to Füssen, Katie blurted out the crux of her conversation with Gunter Linder, trying not to sound over-enthusiastic.

'Take it easy,' Roscoe pleaded, raising his hand as he braked suddenly for a herd of cows meandering onto the road. Digesting the revelations he turned to his passenger when the road was clear.

'Okay, yes I concur the next step would be to head to Zurich. First, however, before we go off half-cocked, let me do a bit of digging around to see what I can turn up. You'll enjoy the drive along the border and I'm happy to be your Chauffer. Beats a stuffy plane any day. I must say, a good job to obtain that much information after only one meeting, well done. Give me a day or two, I'll email someone I know in the Swiss Intelligence; in the meantime have a break and take it easy, you can be a tourist and have a look at the stuff around Füssen... The Butcher of Riga, eh. Oh, by the way, I could use someone like you over here. If you ever get sick of forensics and want a change of scenery.'

****

The frantic, languid days of summer were now well past, and Katie strode out from the Guest House invigorated by a stiff, chilling breeze rolling down from the Austrian peaks. The first snow of autumn was coming, that undeniable sniff in the air. Ideal, a chance to see the sights, without the long queues and rude, loud mouthed tourists. The cell phone wielding hordes had miraculously disappeared.

The day before she spent almost entirely in the hotel, sleeping in an opium-like coma for most of the day, only venturing out after dinner to sample gelato at a small, intimate ice cream parlour. She stayed up late imbibing liqueur coffee in the lounge, relaxing with other tourists in front of a log fire. Alone. when the other guests had retired Katie's mind cleared. Doubt and old insecurities rose up to invade the space. Maybe it was all lies, a fraud, a toxic mix of hate and confused memories from decades past. Was she just wasting time chasing long-dead ghosts?

****

The young female guide mounted the steps in front of the small crowd gathered on the castle forecourt and raised her hands for quiet. She waved them forward and spoke loudly:

'Seven weeks after the death of King Ludwig II in 1886, Neuschwanstein was opened to the public and to this day remains one of the most visited of all the palaces and castles in Europe.'

Popular with Walt Disney of course, but also with Hermann Goering and the Reichstag, Katie chuckled inwardly, no doubt not something the castle guides and pamphlets were keen to elaborate on.

Standing inside the imposing main entrance she pictured in her mind the scene in May 1945, confronting GIs staring open-mouthed at the eclectic horde of European art treasure jammed into its cavernous halls and rooms.

****

Roscoe Telfer punted the small hatch through the Bavarian back roads, across the so-called *Austrian border* for a brief ten minutes, and to the amazement of Anita and Katie, ignoring attempts by two brown uniformed Austrian police to flag the car down before the Swiss border.

'Trying to scam "toll fees" out of naïve tourists in campers and rentals,' intimated Roscoe, accelerating into the tunnel and through to Switzerland on the other side. 'Stop us and I'll make sure those bozos are out on the street without a job before the end of next week.'

For the rest of the three-hour trip, Anita and Katie lounged in the backseat drinking in the spectacular scenery, Germany to the right, Swiss Alps on the left. Arriving in Zurich, early evening, the trio checked into a pre-booked boutique hotel in the centre of the city and whilst the women rested before dinner the Commander put in a follow-up call to his contacts at the Swiss Police.

'There are three large cheese factories on the outskirts of the City,' Roscoe informed Katie the next morning, over a light breakfast at a small, busy patisserie off the Bahnhofstrasse. 'Two we can rule out on the basis they are fairly new and multi-national outfits. The other one, an "Ernst Tellerone et Fils", in the same family for four generations, making dairy products on the site since the First World War.'

He picked up his mobile and dialled a pre-programmed number. 'The local boys know their stuff. They're pretty sure this is the best bet.'

He was put straight through by reception, conducting the entire phone call in rapid-fire German, enabling Katie to catch only snippets of the conversation.

'We're in luck. No problem for us to drop around,' Roscoe concluded. 'I get the impression the management knew we might be calling. They've been "asked" to be accommodating. Only twenty minutes the other side of town, across the river.'

Roscoe dropped one hundred Swiss francs onto the table and pushed back the chair. 'We'll drop Anita in the shopping district and pick her up later at the hotel.'

By ten-thirty, the duo was signing the visitor's book at the front office of Ernst Tellerone et Fils SA. The front building still retained its twenties Art Deco façade and vintage feel but concealed a state-of-the-art cheese and yoghurt factory on four acres. Almost immediately, a well-groomed, statuesque brunette appeared from behind a glass partitioning and exchanged a few words in broken English.

'They were expecting us apparently but are a bit mystified as to what we want,' Roscoe remarked to Katie.

'Oben, dritte Tür auf der rechten Seite,' (upstairs, third door on the right) the woman clarified, pointing to a wide staircase, and producing two visitors badges.

'We've been given a chance to speak with the company owner Boris Boumann,' Roscoe whispered. 'He retired a few years ago now as the MD but hangs around most days, ensuring things at the factory go smoothly; obviously doesn't quite trust his son with the running of the show.'

Pushing open the door at the top of the stairs they entered a large open plan office space. A modern processing facility lined with stainless steels tanks tended by workers in white coats and shower caps was clearly discernible on the other side of the glass. 'That's his son over there, I recognise him from an internet search I did last night in bed.'

Katie smiled at Boris junior, who in her estimation seemed more than capable of running the dairy factory. At well over six foot, with a commanding presence and going by the plethora of awards lining his office, the son possessed a natural flair for the business – there didn't appear much for his father to be worried about. The son waved them in and indicated to a large office on the opposite side, where an elderly gentleman leaned over a desk peering at a computer screen. Valuable antiquarian and folk examples of ancient Swiss cheese-making equipment filled the room and occupied pride of place on the desk.

'Herzlich willkommen.' (Welcome.)

'Guten Morgen Herr Boumann, mein Name ist Roscoe Telfer. Sprechen Sie Englisch?' (Good morning Mr Boumann, my name is Roscoe Telfer. Do you speak English?)

'Ich cann kein English Sprechen, was willst du?' (I do not speak English, what do you want?)

Roscoe introduced Katie and went on to elaborate in German, hoping Herr Boumann would co-operate with his requests. With a condescending nod, a sprightly Boris Boumann led them to a spacious meeting room where all three took up residence around a board table. A young woman brought out three small double espressos as thick as treacle and departed leaving a jug of water and glasses.

Katie listened patiently to the lightning-like and heavily accented conversation, straining to pick out recognisable words and phrases in so-called Swiss German. After twenty minutes, Telfer stood up, bowed and shook Boris' hand warmly, thanking him in German and English.

'Useful?' Katie enquired, as they walked out into the warm sunshine.

'Oh yes, very. You struck it lucky, girl. Boris remembers Clemminger, who back then was about fifty. He appeared out of the blue one day; having recently married a local Swiss girl Ailsa, and desperate for work. He liked his outgoing personality, putting him on as assistant senior cheesemaker. Clemens or Clemminger was a hard worker and liked by his colleagues and peers. He remained in his employ here for almost four years, before just upping and leaving without saying goodbye. According to Boris, your man abandoned his wife and child, and no one knew what happened to him.'

'Okay, we've hit a brick wall.' She sighed. 'What next?'

'Sorry, can't really help much from here on in. I can check if anything else has surfaced, but I've got to get the wife back to Germany this evening. I'll call you if something interesting comes to hand. There was one other thing; As we were leaving, Boris turned to me and said, "Seien Sie vorsichtig, Sie können bereuen, was Sie entdecken"; that's "be careful, you may regret what you discover". Be mindful of this investigation, Katie, tread carefully as you could be heading down an unknown path, towards danger.'

****

That evening, as Katie killed time at a Zurich Airport bar waiting to board the delayed flight home, Roscoe phoned, mild excitement evident.

'Now, this you may find interesting; according to a couple of reliable sources, our man turned to religion sometime after the war ended. He spent a few years at a Monastery in Florence (Certosa di Firenze or Certosa del Galluzzo), which is situated on a hillside south of Florence. Looks like he was here in the early sixties.'

Katie switched to the soft speaker and waited impatiently for Roscoe to draw breath.

'Niccolò Acciaioli, one of the most powerful Florentine citizens of fourteenth-century Italy, built it in 1341, not only as a religious centre but also for the education of the young,' continued Roscoe, providing a bit of background history. 'In 1958, a small group of Cistercian friars replaced the Carthusian monks as the inhabitants of the Certosa. Today they are largely self-supporting and maintain their old traditions, you know, like the distillation of herb liqueurs, manufacture of handmade religious articles. That sort of stuff.'

'Right.'

'After making a few phone calls and sending emails to tie up some loose ends, I received a return call from an old parish priest, now residing in a Siena infirmary. Got his name here somewhere…'

Katie could make out Roscoe thumbing noisily through the pages of his notebook.

'Here it is… a Monsignor Umberto Angelucci, I think that's it. Worked for Rome as a liaison priest in the sixties. Part of his day to day duties being to visit the friars at Certosa and ensure they received mainstream guidance, confessionals

304

and such. I understand that he was also an undercover operative reporting to the highest echelons in St Peters. Sort of a Vatican spy keeping a weather eye on some of the more obscure orders.'

'Go on, I'm listening.'

'How lucky is this; he remembers Heinrich well, got to be on casual speaking terms. Now, he claims overhearing conversations between Heinrich and a third party, discussing Buckfast Abbey and the unrelated Priory of St Oswald. and for some reason, it stuck in his memory. One of those bizarre things, I suppose.'

Roscoe sensed Katie's interest skyrocketing.

'Probably pure speculation but given your current investigation and the belief your target fled to England, I'd say there's a slim chance he eventually made his way to the Abbey or the Priory.'

Heavenly Father, the walls are once more closing in. I sense I can no longer run and hide, yet I do not want to be forgiven for my sins.

I am hungry for more deaths to occur. Those who get close to discovering the truth must be punished.

Amen

Chapter Fifteen

Katie watched the fine bubbles rising from the bottom of the glass of German Brut and tried to make sense of the information overload muddling her brain. There was something missing, a link to tie up all the relevant or perhaps useless facts. A lot of sketchy and probably hearsay detail had emerged in the last weeks about Clemminger and Clemens, but who in fact was this man, a real enigma presented itself. She still had no idea who they were chasing. Then the penny dropped.

She scrutinised the overhead flight departures screen, checking the immediate schedules. Excellent, there was still time. Quickly throwing down the half glass of bubbly with a handful of beer nuts, she gathered up bag and satchel and headed back down the escalator searching for the Swissair booking desk.

She always wanted to order breakfast in a Viennese Art Nouveau coffee haus.

****

The Bahnhofstrasse, Zurich – Sometime in Late 1971

Heinrich Clemminger shifted uneasily in his seat and peered anxiously through the sleet covered windscreen of the company charcoal grey Simca sedan. He glanced at the luminous hands of the new EDOX automatic, a birthday present from his wife and for the fifth time that evening asked the question; *what am I doing here? Twenty minutes late. I'll give it another ten.*

He had been in two minds most of the day and wasn't going to turn up. His wife was suspicious of the half-baked pretence proffered. He had sacrificed a favourite TV show and the log fire warmth of the living room to make the meeting.

'Be there early and wait for my signal,' was the command.

Definitely, unsettling behaviour. Uncharacteristic of Christian. Not the usual pragmatic, measured words and dogmatic rigmarole expected from an ex Colonel in the SS. Then, those unexpected short, cryptic hastily scribbled messages dropped into his office at the cheese plant.

As the cold bit, he switched on the engine and ran the heater again for another five minutes. His mind drifted. He raised the collar of his duffel coat and cursed softly.

There had been no contact for three years. Last communication was the trail had gone cold and the bureaux were pursuing other targets. What could be the problem? Numerous possibilities were vetted, none were logical. No way, after so many years.

Bullshit I reckon, probably just wants to catch up for a Schnapps and reminisce.

'Bobbo, wake up, turn off the engine.'

Startled, Heinrich snapped back to consciousness, staring uncomprehendingly at his old C.O. banging loudly on the side window. 'You were asleep, you missed my signal old man.'

The next ten minutes changed his life forever; he couldn't believe what he was hearing as Christian unleashed. He broke into a cold sweat and rapid heartbeat, he felt palpable fear the first time in thirty-five years.

'Our people inside the Mossad and in Bonn alerted me just in time. They have picked up your trail again and as of ten yesterday morning, their people were in Zurich running down final leads. I'm on the list as well. It's become a race between the Zionists and the Feds to see who nabs us first. The Jews are desperate to add you to Eichmann's scalp. We think your mail has been intercepted and maybe your phone tapped.'

That was a possibility; there had been strange clicks on his phone for a few weeks.

Christian grabbed his old comrade's arm, the words delivered with an icy, grim determination and foreboding. 'Now hear me. Get a grip of yourself. We had been warned months ago this could happen and have made some arrangements. You must do what we tell you for the good of yourself and those of us left. There is no other course of action.'

Heinrich listened, absorbing every detail, becoming more incredulous by the second. When finished, Christian got out and closed the door, looking back in through the window with parting optimism:

'Okay, my good friend. Best of luck, and auf wiedersehen. We'll have a beer on the Avenida Corrientes six months from now. Don't be late.'

****

The following morning, a Tuesday, Heinrich Clemminger kissed his wife and young son goodbye as usual, like on any other day in the last three years, and instead of driving to the cheese factory on the outskirts of Zurich, where he normally commenced work at eight o'clock, drove to the city financial district depositing the Simca at an underground parking lot for long term patrons. Removing all incriminating evidence from the Simca he gathered up a small leather overnight bag off the passenger seat, before locking the car. On the way-out Heinrich dropped the keys and unwanted papers into a waste bin and walked the two blocks to the CommerceZ Bank of Credit on the Paradeplatz.

Striding up to the reception counter he presented a letter of authority and driver's licence to a short, dumpy, bespectacled female teller, entrenched behind a metal grille. Fifteen minutes passed. With anxiety levels escalating Heinrich was, at last, ushered through a set of large metal doors and shown to the small desk of the private accounts manager where he signed a formal consent and withdrawal forms. Another twenty minutes, the air was warm and humid, it was getting hard to breathe, something was amiss, it was taking too long. He tried not to look up at the CCTV camera. The minutes ticked by slowly on his EDOX.

That was it, the game over. The police would be around the corner…

'Herr Clemminger come this way, please. In through the Vault. Box number 4387. Take your time, press the button when you're done and don't forget the key.'

Heinrich bumbled around the cavernous vaults for several minutes trying to avoid attention, waiting for his metabolism to return to normal. Locating the correct metal box, he withdrew it from the wall, taking it to a small bench. Here he opened it with the key provided and spilled out the weighty contents slowly and deliberately. It was all there exactly as Christian predicted: two passports, together with a Lufthansa Airlines one-way ticket for lunchtime via Madrid, direct to Buenos Aires; and letters of introduction in English and Spanish. He counted ten thousand dollars in wads of large denomination US Dollar notes in two envelopes, and six 1 Kilo 9999 Fine Gold Investment bars stamped with the "Credit Suisse" and "Johnson Matthey" London Bullion Market refiner marks. As well, an old friend in a thick brown envelope – a Walther P38, 9 mm Parabellum, complete with a spare 8 round box magazine; the standard equipment sidearm of the Wehrmacht. He placed the contents into the overnight bag and remained pondering the last item for several moments; two small capsules containing a white powder smelling faintly of bitter almonds. 'No, that's not me,' he decided, with a mind now crystal clear and razor-sharp; leaving them in the box which was closed, locked and returned to its slot.

Walking out into a crisp but sunny Zurich morning Heinrich breathed a long sigh of extreme relief, resolutely resigned to his new existence. The tantalising aroma of fresh coffee and croissants drifted from nearby street-side cafes; *I will wait till the Airport.*

He walked to the nearest taxi rank. Sitting in the rear of the cab he could at last coolly and logically digest the events of the last day. The same inescapable conclusion, however, kept coming back; this was all bizarre. If everybody has fled to South America, they will all be rounded up eventually. He pictured himself swinging from the end of a rope in the courtyard of a maximum-security Tel Aviv military prison. There had to be another viable alternative. He redirected the cabbie to drop off at the Central Bus Station and enquired at one of the tourist sales desks.

After half an hour of deliberation, he purchased a ticket on the 2pm coach to Paris with an immediate on connection through to Cherbourg… He finally knew where he was going.

****

Near Vire, Normandy – The 2nd SS Panzer Division Das Reich –
4 August 1944

SS Obersturmbannführer Claus Bobich raised the hatch on the lead "late type" Tiger Mark I and trained his yellow binoculars at the black smoke rising from the village five hundred metres away.

The three 57 tonne behemoths lay in wait, cleverly concealed from the ground behind a three-metre hedgerow. From the air and the ever-present threat of prowling Allied aircraft with camouflage nets.

Slowly and quietly he pressed the button on his headset and transmitted orders to the four-man crew and the commanders of the other two tanks.

'Easy men, relax. I can hear them, but nothing yet.'

M4s by the distinctive growl of the American V8 engines, he conjectured. *We've got plenty of time.*

It had been three years, but still felt like yesterday when he stood in the forest clearing, only a few kilometres outside Riga. Twelve months ago, since his beloved Das Reich battled valiantly against the overwhelming hordes of Russian armour and predatory Shturmoviks at Kursk. Yes, the retreat from Kharkov forever burnt into his psyche, where he earned the Oak Leaves to his Knight's Cross by flaming ten T-34s but also leaving him with a fragment of 37 mm cannon shell embedded in the left lung. It felt fantastic to be back in a Tiger after a year of rehabilitation and a brush with death.

But it was the last three months he treasured most, learning what it means to be human again with his family in the lush pastures of Southern Bavaria. Near the bridge where the river flows fast under the medieval fortress town; with the gleaming blue turrets of the fairy tale castle thrusting out from the alpine forest above.

'Herr Major, Herr Major. Achtung,' the excited cry crackled through the radio.

Shaken from his hedonistic slumber Bobich glanced across at Willy gesticulating wildly from the turret of the Tiger, 20 metres away.

'I count at least six Shermans, escorting maybe six platoons.'

Bobich wiped his forehead against the black sleeve of his tank uniform, bringing the glasses to bear on the road ahead. His vision slowly cleared, the sight of enemy armour raising the hairs on the back of his neck.

The familiar, stubby, top heavy form of seven American M4 Sherman tanks in line astern three hundred metres away, now easily identifiable by the white stars on their turrets.

'I'll take the lead tank first,' Bobich announced, in a voice devoid of emotion, to the other two commanders.

'Willy, the last one is yours. Michael, hit anyone when you get a fix. Fire when ready, Eric,' Bobich shouted down to the gunner, now bringing his sight crosshairs to bear.

Instinctively, each crewmember covered their ears with their hands, as the fearsome 88 mm cannon recoiled, shaking the Tiger and sending an armour piercing shell screaming at twice the speed of sound toward the advancing column.

The lead Sherman disappeared in a blinding flash, the men inside despatched to eternity, not even hearing the sound of the projectile. In a heartbeat the tank bringing up the rear lost its turret as the white-hot copper stream of a Rheinmetall shaped charge, scything through the armour plate like a hot knife through butter, ignited ammunition, incinerating the interior and its hapless crew.

The remaining tanks now trapped hopelessly between the hedgerows on the narrow road, manoeuvred wildly in a desperate, frantic attempt at escape but were mercilessly picked off one by one by the powerful Tigers.

Bobich stole a minute to survey the scene of devastation in the distance, waiting for the adrenalin ride to subside.

Then experience kicked in. The cover was blown. It was time to leave.

He barked orders to the other Tigers. 'We will be sitting ducks now. You're on your own. Meet back at the rear. Refuel and scrounge around for any ammo you can find. Good Luck.'

'Let's go, let's go, start her up, start her up,' he continued to scream.

The crew responded as they had done a hundred times before, coaxing the recalcitrant Maybach engine into life and reversing the unwieldy Tiger, spewing clouds of black unburnt gasoline, crashing backwards through the hedgerow in a series of wild jerking movements.

Five kilometres back to safety. Bobich swore on his mother's grave hoping, hoping.

The Tiger he kept to a crawl, utilising every available cover; bushes, hedgerows, trees, walls, burnt-out vehicles, farmhouses.

An hour later and within sight of the rear supply dump, the cry he was dreading came from Max, manning the hastily turret-mounted MG42. 'Fighter bombers Claus. We're spotted. Fuck.'

With no other option, Bobich ordered full revs.

The Tiger leapt forward like an angry bull breaking cover from behind the field wall and out onto the open road in a cloud of dust. He craned his neck, frantically scanning the sky to the West, just under the low cloud bank to where his anxious gunner pointed. Blood ran cold through his veins, bringing binoculars to bear on the two blunt-nosed aircraft, with the characteristic chin radiators. Unmistakably RAF Typhoons, wearing highly visible black and white D-Day stripes, the Allies supreme tank buster.

The pilot of the lead Typhoon broke off the circling "cab rank" pattern and pushed the throttle forward, urging all 24 cylinders of the Napier Sabre to maximum war rating. Diving sharply to port, he levelled the aircraft off at five hundred feet and flicked the safety on the control stick.

Catching the lumbering Tiger in the field of the electronic sight, he pressed the red button unleashing with an ear-shattering crescendo, all eight of the 60 lb armour piercing rockets, packing an explosive punch equivalent to the broadside from a heavy cruiser...

For many years after, Claus Bobich didn't remember much of the events on that fateful summer day in France in August 1944. He recalled being blown backwards off the tank in slow motion, watching dear Max, heroically pumping lead at the rate of 1000 rpm at the departing Typhoon, then a ghostly vision of Heinrich Himmler placing the Oak Leaves around his neck.

As the light fades, Bobich sees his father walking slowly towards him from the milk shed, arms outstretched, smiling, ever forgiving. Then the grey mist closed in.

****

'You are pretty certain this Heinrich Clemminger was on the run from something on the Continent and hiding out in England?' DCI Parker confirmed, greeting Katie at Exeter airport, disembarking the morning commuter flight from Gatwick.

'He had to have been.'

'Any idea where he might have ended up?' DCI Parker enquired, ordering two take away coffees from a nearby stand.

'I have a hunch it might have been at the Priory,' Katie replied, in a hushed voice. 'After all, it would make perfect sense as to why Brother Jeremy had detailed documents supposedly about Clemens in his possession.'

'Can't understand the necessity to dig into Clemens' past,' Parker remarked, ushering her towards the Skoda parked in the emergency vehicle zone outside the Terminal. 'The man is probably dead, if not he'll be about one hundred. He's hardly the person who killed Rebecca and Nicola. Regardless if alive.'

'Yes, yes, I know.' Katie wished she had something more concrete to offer the DCI from her trip abroad. 'My gut feeling says there's a connection somewhere.'

'Let's hope you're right. A detailed status report is due on the Commander's desk by 5pm Friday and so far, we have nothing to show. I've practically exhausted all the leads from our end, a big fat zero.'

'I'll do more delving into Clemens' history.' Katie tried not to look despondent. 'Actually, I was hoping you would allow me access to some CID records, in particular going back to 1986 when Hayley Illbert-Tavistock went missing.'

'Give me what you've got anyway, even if it's irrelevant and I'll stick it in the report. In the meantime let me see what I can do. Envisage no problem getting you access but only for one week, then if we're not nearer solving this crime Katie, step away. I will be copping a lot of heat from above if they conclude I've been throwing away taxpayers money.'

****

'Have you ever heard of a Heinrich Clemminger?' Katie ventured, observing the Abbot stack Epistles into a small wooden trolley following Sunday mass.

'Can't say it rings a bell. *Should* I know of him?'

Katie shrugged. 'I don't know.'

'I sincerely hope it has nothing to do with this manic infatuation with dear Jeremy's death, Ms Sinclair, any concern you had by now, must surely have been put to rest. Does it pertain to something you found in the Brother's documents?'

'Well, no, not at this time anyway. More in relation to the current multiple Dartmoor murders probe. The name keeps coming up in my research linking it to St Oswald's, and so I naturally assumed you might have encountered it.'

'He doesn't sound very English; perhaps he visited the Priory whilst on holiday in Devon. It's not uncommon for overseas visitors to drop in for a little soul searching.'

'Yes, that sounds plausible, although if he *were* to want to remain incognito over a period of time the Priory would be the ideal place to lie low.'

'God's house is not a retreat for wayward strays,' Maximilian responded, slamming a weighty leather-bound book hard onto a shelf, causing other volumes to jolt violently. 'I can assure you young lady; I know what goes on behind these closed walls, and there is no one hiding in the woodwork. I've been the Abbot here for almost thirty years and I would have remembered coming across this person.'

'What if this person was masquerading as someone else?' Katie pushed. 'Please, look at this photo of Clemminger, which in all probability is an alias, have you ever seen this man?'

The Abbott threw a cursory look at the photo.

'This was taken back in 1958,' Katie added.

Maximilian laughed. 'If he were still alive, he'd be no youngster, that's for sure. Why don't you direct your investigation to the old people's retirement village down the

317

road? Ha, he could well be one of the oldest persons alive in Britain, how grand would that be?'

More sardonic laughter sounded through the chapel, a couple lighting candles near the altar turned in their direction.

'Take another look,' Katie urged, perhaps there is some recognition.'

Reluctantly, Maximilian cast his eyes once more at the photograph. This time the smile faded from his face.

'What is it?' Katie urged, catching his eyes narrow, as a brief look of horror engulfed them.

'No, it's nothing,' he spoke curtly, pushing the old image away. 'This really is a waste of my time. If you would please excuse me, I must get on, I am in charge of beekeeping today over at the Abbey, a duty I often take on when one of my brethren is on yearly Retreat. Perhaps we can talk another day when time is not of the essence.'

'Yes, of course.'

Once more Katie secured procession of the photograph, watching Maximilian stride purposefully away towards the Vestry. Something had unsettled the old man and Katie was anxious to know what it was.

'The Abbot knows who you are,' Katie spoke aloud, staring down at the photograph. 'Who are you Heinrich Clemminger and where are you now?'

****

'Tom, can we meet for coffee, say after lunch if you're free?' Katie was being casual, even pleasant, although the latter took some effort.

Tom Markham's chuckle sounded down the other end of the phone. 'Are you serious Katie? Surely we're not becoming friends all of a sudden.'

Katie tried to sound aloof. 'Just because we don't always see eye to eye, that doesn't mean we have to remain sworn enemies.'

'Okay, spit it out Katie, what do you want from me this time?' Markham chided, tossing the Mirror Racing Guide on the desk.

Katie lowered her voice. 'Give me as much information you can lay your hands on pertaining to Hayley Illbert-Tavistock. I understand she was a junior journalist on the Star when she vanished in 1986. In particular, what her articles were about and if they possibly had any bearing on her disappearance.'

'Before my time sweetie, I didn't cover that story. Besides, surely the cops at the time would have gone through all that stuff, trying to establish a link. Sorry, can't help you with this one, I'm afraid. Now if that's all I must press on, got my money riding on Picadillo, a two-year-old filly debuting at Newton Abbot this afternoon.'

'Oh no you don't,' Katie fought back. 'I know you can get me the information. You have to help me.'

'Some other time, I have to run,' Tom retorted, dispassionately. 'Cheers for now.'

He hung up before Katie could squeeze in another word.

Slamming down the phone Katie pondered her next move. Okay, if Tom wanted to play rough, she would match him at his pathetic game.

Today oh Lord I gave my captor food and water because that's the magnanimous being I am. She knows who I am, but she won't speak. For that, I am a little sad.

Why did it have to come to this, oh Lord? I never wanted any of this to happen, but what choice did I have, my raison d'etre on this earth is to protect the past.

Amen

Chapter Sixteen

Marching in through the glass doors of *The Star Newspaper*, Katie spied Tom's tall, hunched form, leaning on the front reception desk, drooling over a young receptionist, who happened to be buxom and blonde.

'What do you want now?' Markham scowled; eyeing Katie framed in the doorway. 'I've already told you I'm busy.'

'Yes, I can see that,' Katie retorted, a note of sarcasm in her voice. 'I only dropped by to inform you that Moorland Forensics are scheduling spot, random drug testing on all nine horses running in the third at two o'clock today. It's well within the requirements of our current contract with the British Horseracing Authority governing body. Even if we don't find anything, I'm certain your bookie mates and the trainers undoubtedly, will be most anxious to make enquiries as to why the tests were carried out, and hey presto, your name might happen to pop into the conversation. Well, I must be off but believe it only fair to give you the heads up.'

Tom stepped forward, coaxing Katie back through the door with a friendly hand gesture. 'Okay, you win this time. I can spare you half an hour. Meet me at the Café Zanzibar near the train station at one and I'll have all the information you're after.'

'You're an amazing man, Tom. Despite what others say, I know you have the makings of a real saint.'

Tom snorted in disgust as he headed back to his private office, leaving a satisfied Katie to meander around the shops for the next hour before making her way to the rendezvous.

'What do you have for me? I know you won't disappoint.'

Markham now in casual attire, drinking noisily from a large bowl of latte, looked up when Katie entered. Etiquette clearly not one of Tom's strong points.

'Firstly, let's be clear on this, your questionable tactics are wearing a bit thin,' Markham responded, watching Katie pull out a chair and slide into it. 'Your standards are slipping Katie; I'd be careful if I were you.'

She beamed, unfazed by Tom's idle threats. 'I'll take that as a compliment, blatant bullying doesn't go down too well with me. I'd also like to remind you how ruthless you can be at times, so tit for tat I'd say we're even in those stakes. Now, if you've finished the lecture, can we get down to the nitty-gritty. It would be a shame for you to miss that donkey race.'

'I don't know why you want any of this ancient crap, it's hardly front-page news.' Markham snorted, attacking a chocolate croissant. 'Hayley Illbert-Tavistock was a mediocre journalist, not really suited to the deadlines and cut and thrust of 24/7 news reporting. She would have been more at home churning out history documentaries or boring essays for one of those specialist magazines, not a tabloid newspaper.

All I've unearthed is a crummy little story about Jewish exterminations in WWII. For some reason, she held special interest in a guy called Heinrich Clemminger, whoever he might be, kept some kind of folder on this bloke, newspaper clippings and other stuff.'

Katie looked down at her coffee, adding two teaspoons of sugar to disguise a look of surprise. Tom unwittingly divulging valuable detail.

'Can I borrow the "stuff"?' Katie asked faking nonchalance, not for one moment wanting to alert the Star's owner.

'I suppose it won't hurt. If you come across something of interest, I must be the first to know.'

'Oh of course,' she lied, trying to sound convincing, not quite able to make eye contact across the table.

If anything of interest did surface, Tom Markham would be the last person to know.

'By the way,' Tom added. 'What's with that Ben Crispin joker? He came snooping around the other day acting super friendly with my chief editor if you know what I mean.'

Katie knew when Tom was lying and now was not one of those episodes.

'Oh yeah,' Tom continued. 'It was obvious to even "Blind Freddy" there was some serious flirting happening; I think our Lana might have got herself a new "fuck buddy". When she returned to the main office, just before 6pm, she looked satisfied, get my drift.'

It was all Katie could do to stop exploding. She trusted Ben, surely there had to be some mistake, probably all a misunderstanding. Most likely Lana had tried to latch on to Ben, but when he explained he already had a girlfriend, she backed off.

Katie pushed Ben to the back of her mind, refocusing and directing a few more work-related questions. 'I understand, after Ben's meeting with Lana Gibbs, he managed to discover interesting facts about Hayley and her research. However, I felt *you,* in your capacity as a top rank investigative journalist, might also be au fait with some of the finer details.'

'I guess it won't hurt parting with a bit more knowledge,' Tom declared, oblivious to the sarcasm. 'Hayley was definitely on to something; I'm convinced of that. A few years ago, I stumbled across a confidential file Hayley had squirrelled away in our archive department. Being twenty-five years or so, after all the hoo-hah, I saw no urgency to pass it over to the police, perhaps on reflection, I was wrong. Anyway, you can have a lend. If anybody asks, I never gave you anything. Even Lana's not privy to the file's existence, and it's to remain that way, do you understand?'

Katie crossed her heart. 'Absolutely.'

Tom disappeared, finally returning to the café fifteen minutes later with a thick leather folder. 'Go easy with this,' he instructed, handing it across. 'I want it back first thing Monday morning, still intact.'

Katie nodded. 'Thanks, I really appreciate this.'

****

Alone, in the back of the laboratory instrument room with the others absent, Katie settled down on a bench stool behind the gas cylinders, a place where she often hid out to escape the office turmoil and started to sift methodically through the file Hayley had put together on Henry. It was immediately clear by the copious handwritten notes and plethora of photocopied material, a good deal of time, effort and meticulous research was expended researching this man. It came to light Hayley even squeezed in a quick seven-day round tour trip by bus to Austria and places in Switzerland, notably Zurich, similar in some respects to her own recent excursion. Most of the detail contained, related to Clemens' life and activities after arriving in the UK early seventies. The young reporter's efforts to uncover anything on his origins and earlier life abroad were mostly in vain. The visit to Europe resulted in little of any substance; probably she lacked the nouse or contacts or both, to dig in the right places.

However, the next piece of news was a revelation, making Katie sit up and take notice; according to Hayley's barely legible hand-writing and cryptic notations, she became aware Henry Clemens had a son, who had spent his youth as a student at Abbey College. Katie's sharp mathematic brain indicated the son could now be late forties early fifties, extrapolating from what she and Roscoe had uncovered in Zurich on Clemminger. What's more, Hayley was convinced the son was still residing in Devon, close to the Priory.

It was too premature to speculate and draw solid conclusions, but could it be that Clemens' son had inherited some of his father's traits? Was it in the realms of possibility for a man to kill and torture so many people and pass those genes on to his only son? From case studies and real-life examples encountered in the last ten years, she conjectured it was quite plausible, despite overwhelming support in the literature for environment, being the chief driver of human behaviour.

Pushing the file into a bottom drawer back in the office, Katie about to call it a day and close up early, noticed a letter sitting atop the in tray:

Katherine Sinclair, followed by the Moorland address, it said on the envelope in bold lettering and had evidently been posted, with a small local postage stamp in the far-right corner. She prised open the envelope, retrieving the note inside. It was several moments before fatigued eyes focused on the short, enigmatic sentences, a long week and exhaustion were taking over. At the earliest opportunity, Katie would petition the others for a much-needed holiday.

She read the handwritten words out loud, again and again:

Silence still prevails; they come and go, the figures in dark habits. In the shadows, I hide, fearful their secrets will mean a slow and tempestuous death for all.

Yours,
Allyson Carter

Several minutes passed before the words sunk in; was Allyson Carter sending Katie a message, imploring someone to come forward and set her free? Instantly Katie dismissed the thought. James had obtained a sample of the girl's handwriting and it certainly didn't match the note she now held in her hands.

With Fiona and James under extreme pressure, Katie was reluctant to add to their burden by showing them a letter she knew very little about, instead, she decided to chat with Ben. She sought him out at his rented bedsitter accommodation in Chagford, feet up on the coffee table relaxing in an easy chair with a beer, engrossed in the final overs of the test cricket.

For the time being, she had no intentions of raising the subject of Lana Gibbs, that could wait for a more appropriate time.

****

Crispin inspected the mystery note and listened intently to Katie's concerns. 'I'm glad you brought it to my attention. In light of this new development, I'll pass your assumptions onto the guys at task force immediately. If this is a reasonable indication Allyson Carter is still alive, we might be able to get a search underway.'

'Yes, but, where is she? All I have to go on is this gut feeling. The handwriting does not match the sample given to us by Allyson's father, which means the police will automatically dismiss my conclusions as paranoia.'

'That is a distinct possibility,' Ben concurred, putting down the beer and searching for the remote. 'I guess you've already picked up on the negative vibes coming out of CID. The boys at Command level are ready to deactivate the task force and divert resources elsewhere if a concrete lead doesn't surface soon, although there must be something leading you to believe Allyson is still alive.

Just suppose Allyson did pen the note. Perhaps she has the skill to disguise her normal handwriting, it's possible, anything's possible.'

Katie laughed. 'Yes, but highly unlikely. Besides, it does beggar belief she has access to pen and paper, and even more puzzling, how she can post letters. She can't be in that much danger if she can access a post box. It's damn ridiculous. I think we'll let it go.'

'Has it not occurred to you someone might have forced Allyson to write the letter, posting it on her behalf.'

'Or, it might be someone wanting us to believe she is still alive and signing Allyson's name at the bottom for a joke.'

Ben leaned forward in his chair. 'Pretty bizarre joke. No, I think it actually came from Allyson. Seriously, Katie, she must be in extreme danger.'

Katie's eyes widened; Ben sounded genuinely concerned for the missing girl. 'Then you'll help me?'

'Of course, but for now, we keep this to ourselves. It will be easier for us to do our own investigating, without added complications. Time is probably running out.'

'Is it wise to give Will the heads up? At least to show them the note and what our theory is.'

Ben shook his head. 'Not just yet, let's see what we can uncover first. Be a sweetie and get me another beer, I have a quick phone call to make.'

Katie dutifully obliged, as Ben disappeared out on to the back veranda, closing the door lightly behind him, to make the call in private.

'It's me, Ben. Katie Sinclair at Moorlands is in receipt of the same info as me and believes Allyson is still very much alive. I can't stop her from uncovering the truth. My main concern is the immediate danger I've put her in. Whatever happens, keep an eye on her, shield her from any danger. Me, I'm tough, I don't expect to get out of this in one piece. Katie is a totally different proposition. She's innocent and deserves protecting.'

The reply from the other end of the line was swift. 'For the love of God, I will do my best, but eventually, the past will entwine with the present.'

Our Father who art in Heaven, show me the light from all this darkness.

Amen

Chapter Seventeen

Katie sat on a bench in the rear courtyard, reading over Allyson's second letter, until her vision blurred. It was one sentence, which kept puzzling; *Saint Mary will guide you to me.*

The letter arrived the following morning going almost unnoticed, hidden under a pile of paperwork, only surfacing when Katie started digging for an old petrol receipt. She reminisced on her visits to the Old Priory, her brain systematically sifting through the material she'd read about the Abbey; finally, things began to make sense.

Fumbling for her phone, Katie punched in the numbers for Ben.

'She's in the Priory, I'm sure of it,' Katie blurted out breathlessly. 'Allyson is in the Priory; we have to find her. The anteroom holds the key. It's the logical place.'

'Then that's where we begin our search,' Ben instructed, sounding excited. 'Stay put, I'll pick you up in half an hour.'

Katie waited anxiously outside the Moorland gates for Ben to arrive. As the unmarked, white Kia saloon pulled up alongside, she raced to get into the passenger seat.

'Now, keep close to me at all times Katie. I can't risk anything happening to you.' He planted a quick kiss on her lips, before hustling the car down the lane, ignoring an irate pedestrian and out onto the main road. 'So how did you work out Allyson's whereabouts?'

'I kept mulling over her letters and the sentence, "Saint Mary will guide you to me." I remember reading and hearing about the Priory being dedicated to Saint Mary. Also, Alex Trimble mentioned it when he gave me a guided tour the other day. After that, everything logically fell into place.'

****

By the time they reached the Priory, the sun had already sunk below the horizon, the remains of a radiant red and violet Autumn sky were rapidly yielding to the onset of night. Ben judiciously parked the ubiquitous police pool saloon in a grove of poplars, a short distance from the main entrance, mindful not to betray their presence. If confronted by an overzealous staffer or Monk and questioned as to their intent, they would be in a tricky and potentially embarrassing situation. The Abbot had already filed a string of complaints to the Home Office, thus ensuring for the foreseeable future police only conducted visits and meetings under strict guidelines, insisting they formally provide at least twenty-four hours' notice.

Entering through the unlocked side gate and keeping to the shadows in the fading light they crossed over the quadrangle, nodding to a trio of passing friars heading to dinner who returned the greeting and hurried on.

Katie led Ben down the stone path past the rose garden, the route she went when previously meeting the Abbot and in through the side door to the Chapel. Avoiding two senior male pupils fervently reciting the Rosary in a front pew, they carefully negotiated the steps at the rear of the chapel and down into the eerie passageways, Katie retracing the way she remembered, eventually encountering the iron-barred gate and the darkened anteroom housing the rocking chair.

Her heart raced, her mind shifted to stark images of the Monk rocking back and forth, rising to his feet and disappearing into the night. There was nothing comforting about that thought, she longed to get out of the place.

'Allyson could be anywhere,' Ben grumbled, casting a look around the uninviting space. 'Should we try looking...'

'What's that?' Katie broke in, the led beam illuminating a far corner, revealing a small bookcase lining one wall.

'It has obviously been put there for a reason.' Ben strolled over to take a closer look. He pulled off one row of books, haphazardly throwing them on the floor, creating a cloud of aspergillus spores thrown up in the torchlight. He knelt on the damp stone floor to take a closer look, handkerchief over mouth. 'I can make out what looks like a small room beyond this shelf. There must be a button or lever that slides open a panel to allow access.'

Pushing the bookcase to one side Katie accidentally activated a switch under the shelf, causing a man-size panel in the wall to move slowly away on runners, exposing the room behind.

'Nice work.' Ben clapped her on the arm, his phone torch probing the confines of a cramped, dark, galley like space. It was Katie's sharp eyes which eventually rested on a figure slumped in the farthest corner.

'Ben, she's over here, hurry.'

Ben moved fast to where Katie knelt beside the frame of a young woman curled up on the floor, her breathing laboured. Her wrists and ankles were bound by thick rope, cutting deep into the flesh.

'She's been heavily sedated. We have to get her out of here, as swiftly as possible.' Katie instructed.

'Wait here, I spotted a rusty bread knife on the ground outside in the passageway. I'll fetch it to cut the ties.'

As Ben hurried back down the tunnel Allyson slowly raised her head, managing a few broken words. 'Help,' she pleaded. 'Evil past, help. He's a murderer.'

'Who,' Katie demanded. 'Tell me who he is.'

'Don't be fooled by what you see, he is evil. Please help me.'

'Tell me his name, I must know who he is.'

'One is pure, the other is evil.' Allyson was struggling for breath.

Katie embraced her. 'You're going to be okay; you will be out of here soon, I promise.'

After freeing her limbs, Katie and Ben attempted to lift Allyson to her feet, a near-impossible feat in the low narrow space, as she flopped like a rag doll. Ben eventually hoisted her up over his shoulders, and half crouching squeezed out into the anteroom.

With no firm direction, Ben struck out along the dank passageway, trying to recall the tortuous route back to the chapel or hoping to fortuitously stumble on an exit, Katie following blindly.

After a frustrating few minutes, Ben stopped and put up a warning sign. 'Katie, lookout, someone's coming along the passageway,' he said, his voice just a whisper. 'You must hide.'

'Shit.' Katie stopped abruptly, instantaneously wrenching her ankle on a sunken paving stone and crying out in pain, her led pocket light bouncing on the ground with a sharp crack. Ben somehow managed to shove Katie into an alcove, before making a hasty retreat back down the passageway, still balancing Allyson over his shoulder.

****

Katie's adrenaline secretions shot into overdrive as she waited for Ben to come back and rescue her. She was cold and frightened, trying to stave off an asthma attack hiding behind a mould-streaked, crimson curtain, hardly daring to breathe. What insanity had prompted her to go on this jaunt? She wasn't meant to be here. A bloody stupid move. More bad news, her phone registered no mobile coverage and insufficient battery for the light.

Checking her watch she soon realised Ben wasn't coming back; it was imperative she find her own way out of the underground maze. The dimly lit passages gave little comfort as she felt her way along the cold, sparsely lit walls, frantically trying to remember which direction they had previously trodden.

After what seemed like an eternity, she thanked God, spotting a shaft of light cutting into the gloom from a small dormitory room. She must be in the Priory living quarters. Inside a wood crucifix hung on one wall, a picture of the Virgin Mary on another; a hurricane kerosene lamp burned in a corner, offering a modicum of comfort in the musty space.

On a small bedside table, there was an old red diary, its pages stained and tattered.

Katie reached out for the book, almost within her grasp when she buckled under the force of a karate chop to the neck; her last memory falling to the floor, impacting the stone slab with a sickening thud.

Her throat dry and gravelly, a pounding contusion on her forehead, Katie slowly emerged from the whirling fog of unconsciousness taking in the surrounds, briefly focusing on the all too familiar rocking chair; on the desk a pitcher of water and chipped glass.

Overcome by thirst, she stretched up for the water. After several efforts the glass became half full as she slumped back down swallowing the ice-cold liquid, barely slaking her thirst. Visions of Ben manhandling her into the alcove and disappearing back down a passageway were her last recall. How she came to be isolated and incapacitated in the small underground bedroom, Katie had no idea. Her body refused to obey commands. She fought valiantly to stay awake, but her mind closed, and she collapsed back on to the cold floor.

They are now close to the truth; urgent action is required.

Heavenly Father, for what I am about to do, please forgive me.

Amen

Chapter Eighteen

Katie woke to a crippling migraine and nausea, unsure if it was day or night. She knew she'd been drugged with a powerful sedative, sending her in and out of consciousness.

She forced her eyes open, her lids still heavy, her watch showed a little after five: She had been in the same room, somewhere beneath the Priory, for several hours.

The sound of approaching footsteps echoing in the passageway alerted her senses, was it Ben coming to her rescue? Surely.

Her mouth dry like a stone stifled her cries until the person was kneeling down beside her. Gazing up, she didn't recognise the man in clerical collar before her.

'My dear girl, what on earth are you doing here?' he asked, concern in his voice. 'These ancient tunnels are a maze of despair. Come, let me lead you back into God's sunlight. This place is not for the faint-hearted.'

Thankfully, Katie accepted the hand he was holding out to her.

'Who are you?' she ventured at last, as she staggered with his support, through winding passages.

'Reverend Samuel Carter is my name. I'm the Vicar of St Pancras in Widecombe. Strange I know, but I lecture the students here at the College a few times a week on Pre-Norman History; you could almost say this is my second home. What is going on dear child, are you in danger?'

'I didn't come here alone. I have friends still inside; you must help them.'

'Yes, of course. Wait here. I will see what I can do.'

'No, please, don't leave me.'

He ignored her pleas, charging off back through the myriad of tunnels, returning minutes later, fear in his eyes.

'A fire has broken out in one of the wine cellars. It is too dangerous for me to go back inside,' he warned. 'We've got to get up to the surface as quickly as possible.'

Katie's eyes widened. 'There are two people I was with; I think they may be still in the tunnels. We have to raise a search.'

'There is no time,' Carter informed. 'We will soon be overcome by smoke, we must hurry.'

****

Fiona sat down beside her sister, the look on her face said it all.

'I'm so sorry,' she muttered. 'The police are almost positive Ben perished in the fire; he hasn't been accounted for. There was nothing anyone could do. It was too old, too much ancient oak. It caught hold quickly and burnt through a large section of the East Wing of the Priory, the fire was too fierce.'

Katie openly wept, no longer able to contain her grief. She loved Ben, they had planned to marry, now her whole world had been turned upside down.

****

The last few days passed in a blur. Katie hadn't wanted to talk to anyone, she'd barely eaten or drank; crying herself to sleep at night, hoping to numb the pain.

She woke on Saturday morning, wondering what the future held without Ben. Her life empty.

Katie rode over to St Pancreas in Widecombe, opting for a long-overdue workout on her Connemara, rather than taking the Fiat. There were many things that troubled her, many questions, few answers. In her heart, she believed the Reverend Carter would be sympathetic. Not only a man of God, but he also happened to be Allyson's father. There was a good chance if anyone could assist in this time of grief, it would be him.

Katie tethered a tired and thirsty Polo Mint to a gnarled grapevine in the church grounds near a welcome trough. Finding the door slightly ajar she hesitated a moment, not sure this was a good move, then entered the ancient space to her surprise encountering the Vicar near the front of the church a world away polishing the stops and buttons on the organ.

'I'm sorry, I didn't mean to disturb you.'

The Vicar looked up from his cleaning, smiling warmly. 'Come on in child, you are most welcome. You just caught me, I'm about to finish up, Mrs Maddox the sexton is due any moment to lock up.'

'How are you managing?' Katie inquired, voice shaky, betraying the effects of delayed shock and sleepless nights.

'God is shining a light of hope and I keep the faith,' came his reply.

Silence prevailed for a long time before Katie found her voice again.

'Do you ever get lonely spending days here by yourself?' She moved quietly into one of the long wooden pews, soaking up the solitude and the fragrant, calming aroma of freshly cut flowers.

He came to sit next to her. 'Not at all, you see I'm never alone. God is continuously by my side. Well, Mrs Maddox does hang around, checking up on me I suppose. And tourists and such drop in for a chat, of course.'

'Have you been here long, I mean at the parish? I ride past sometimes on my Irish pony. Wasn't there another vicar here before? I vaguely remember reading about him in the Village Voice.'

'I am filling in whilst the cherished Reverend Galton is taking a sabbatical,' Carter said obligingly. 'We moved to the West Country a few years ago. Sadly, upon arrival in this beautiful county, we have been plagued by persistent tragedy.' Carter picked up a prayer book, turning it slowly in his hands.

A lump stuck in Katie's throat. 'Yes, I'm sorry. Even with your daughter still missing you still maintain your faith in God.'

'Yes indeed, but sadly Ms Sinclair you and I both know the police believe Allyson died in the fire, it is only a matter of time before the forensic team has confirmation. Once that determination has been made, my wife and I can finally lay our gorgeous child to rest.'

'They say a kerosene lamp may have been the cause, we are still waiting on forensic results,' Katie enlightened him, not sure if this would offer any comfort.

He declined a response, instead, holding out his hand, which she graciously accepted. 'Enough woes. Come, I want to show you something.'

He led her to the back of the church and out through to the vestry. Opening a small ornamental pine casket he retrieved a withered daisy and a withered buttercup, placing them in her hand.

'Remember what life is about Ms Sinclair; Daisies are our silver, Buttercups our gold, this is all the treasure we can have or hold. Now go and embrace the day, life is for living, not for mourning the dead.'

****

Moorland Forensics Facility, Laboratory Instrument Room, Bovey
Tracey – Three Weeks Later

'Will Parker and most of the guys are betting the charred remains are Allyson. There wasn't much left, although the usual pugilistic position was only just discernible. The heat must have been bloody unbelievable. They're saying well over 1500 degrees C because some medieval iron artefacts in the affected Wing melted into pools. That's the temperature of a blast furnace, no wonder only a few bone fragments and some teeth were left,' James advised the team, after returning from an all-day briefing in Exeter.

'Holy hell. Cremation temperature is only 1000 degrees,' mumbled Fiona.

'Yeah, the boys said a beam also fell on the body, crushing any remaining bone. They were astonishingly lucky to recover a sliver of unaffected connective tissue, just enough for DNA extraction and PCR replication without foreign contamination. I've got to say that things are a lot easier these days thanks to victim identification techniques and procedures developed in the wake of 9/11 and other jihadi terrorist atrocities such as the Bali Bombing.

Bristol is working with police pyrotechnicians to determine the cause; top of the list; an electrical short or accelerant, most likely...'

His sentence was cut short as Nick waltzed into the office, letting himself in through the rear entrance off the courtyard, joining the conversation, a tray of takeaway cappuccinos in hand.

'Sit down for this one,' Nick directed his colleagues. 'After repeat DNA testing confirmed by two independent labs, we can confirm only one person died in the fire; Sen Det Ben Crispin, what's more, forensic anthropologists have identified a remaining piece of pelvic bone as male...'

'What? But I don't understand,' James interrupted. 'The preliminary tests I conducted looked like a match to Allyson.'

'Well, they would, considering Allyson is almost without any doubt Crispin's biological daughter,' Nick uttered with confidence.

Everyone stared in surprise, speechless.

'She can't be,' Katie responded. 'That's not possible, why didn't Ben tell me?'

'That my dear I can't answer,' Nick continued. 'However, I am one hundred percent satisfied with the test results. Allyson and Ben share similar but not identical DNA. We'll be contacting Allyson's mother Christina in Andorra to arrange DNA swabs and put it to rest.'

This news was too much for Katie, who pushed back her chair to make a hasty exit. It only went to show the man she planned to marry and spend the rest of her life with was a man she hardly knew; her profiling had been accurate after all.

James put a reassuring arm on her shoulder, encouraging her to sit down. 'If Allyson is still alive, it's imperative we try and find her. Katie, you may be the one person she will talk to and if we can get her to testify for the Crown, the person who committed all these crimes will be brought to justice. Surely you at least owe that to Ben.'

Katie stared up at her brother, her mind in overdrive. 'Yes, but where would we begin to look? Besides, even if we do locate Allyson, there is no guarantee she will even talk to me or anyone for that matter. She could be traumatised beyond recovery.'

'Yes, but it's worth a decent go,' Nick remarked, dropping a folder back into his briefcase. 'I would also like our findings kept under wraps. The Vicar and his wife have raised Allyson for many years, we don't have to notify them one of our investigating officers happens to be Allyson's biological father. The news might tip them over the edge.'

'What now?' James asked, wondering if he was in the middle of a bad dream.

'It's up to DCI Parker on where they want to go on this, but my recommendation would be to start looking for Allyson. I still require final clarification, but do I believe the fire at the Priory was started by an electrical fault? No, I do not. Reconstruction of events at the source so far; indicates someone emptied a can of mineral turps near an old wooden stairwell and dropped a hurricane kerosene lamp on it.'

Nick halted; his voice subdued. 'Somewhere out there is a killer who will stop at nothing until everything and everyone getting in their way is destroyed. Oh and... the Commander has approved more resources for the task force.'

****

'I reckoned on finding you here,' Matt said gently, joining Katie leaning on the bridge railing, staring mesmerised at the fast running steam as it gurgled its way towards Tavistock. 'Gee, you look like you've been through a wringer.'

'I couldn't sleep.'

'Thought as much. Look, Katie, there's something important you ought to know; Ben Crispin is not a murderer. I think you already sort of knew that anyway. I've completed a thorough background research on Ben down at CID records with a task force constable; the upshot being he was basically a decent bloke.'

'He lied,' Katie whispered, unable to prevent her eyes misting over behind her sunglasses. 'The man held onto secrets; he was deliberately deceitful.'

'Hardly, he just didn't opt to tell you he was Allyson's father,' Matt concluded. 'I'm certain he'd have enlightened you in time, but the overriding motive must have been to protect his daughter, surely you can see the logic in that. You're a psychologist and aware people keep family secrets and intimate facts from others especially those they like, for any number of reasons, it's human nature; I've done it myself.'

Katie wanted to believe Crispin was a good man but doubt lingered.

'Almost assuredly he came to Devon for the sole purpose of finding his daughter,' Matt soldiered on. 'You can't blame him for wanting to keep things under wraps, especially if telling the truth would put Allyson in greater danger. Undoubtedly, he was protecting someone he loves. His act should be commended, not condoned. Please be subjective about this Katie, put your feelings behind you and start acting like a professional.'

Katie threw a wayward stick into the rapids, watching it float away downstream. Perhaps Matt was right. No amount of anger would bring Ben back, she ought to try and locate his daughter, she owed him that much.

'Will you be attending Ben's funeral?' Matt kept his eyes fixed on her face.

'No, after all, I hardly knew the man,' came her blunt reply, picking up another stick and throwing it with gusto into the water. 'I'm sure there'll be others to give him a decent send-off.'

****

'Something troubling you?' Fiona looked across at her sister seated at the desk opposite disinterestedly flicking through the internet on her laptop. Normally Katie was one for idle chit chat throughout the day but this morning she'd barely spoken, a tray of urgent reports untouched. Two weeks had passed since Ben's funeral, and Katie had hardly mentioned his name, even in line with their investigation. 'Fancy a takeaway pizza?'

'Yeah, maybe. Fi, I vaguely recall Allyson speaking to me in the underground tunnels. Okay, I did receive a knock to the head, but I'm convinced we had a brief conversation, and it wasn't purely imaginary. She was trying to warn me of someone.'

'It may take time for you to remember what happened. You can't push these things.'

'Yes, I know but it is so frustrating. The visions are getting stronger if only the words would come back.'

****

'Back again.' The Vicar smiled, watching Katie walk slowly down the aisle to where he stood by the Baptismal font.

'When you rescued me from the fire, did you see anyone else there, apart from Ben Crispin?' Katie asked, skipping any small talk. 'This may sound silly, but I believe I saw Allyson before she died. No, correction, I know I saw Allyson and she spoke to me.'

He reached out placing a hand firmly on Katie's arm. 'It is not uncommon for people to see those who have passed to the other side,' he explained. 'Our Lord allows that to happen, from time to time. As a devout member of the Roman Catholic Church, I know you will accept it.'

'Yes, but the forensic tests have proven Allyson didn't perish in the fire,' Katie protested. 'This means she could still be alive.'

'If only I believed that were true.' Clutching Katie's hand, the Vicar gave it a reassuring squeeze. 'I thank you and your entire family for keeping the faith, Ms Sinclair, but we must finally put the past behind us. Allyson is now with the Lord and he will take care of her spirit. If one day we find her body I will ensure she gets a proper burial. Until that eventuality; it is best for all of us that she rests in peace, comforted by her maker.'

'No, you're wrong,' Katie insisted. 'I can show you convincing test results. Your daughter is very much alive, and I sense nearby.'

****

'Matt, I have a hypothetical question. If you were a serial killer, how would you go about your everyday life faking a normal existence, coping with the knowledge of what you have done?'

'I don't know if I can answer that,' Matt pondered, dishing up some bacon rashers and placing them onto the table. 'I guess it would depend on what sort of life I lead, simple or complex.'

'Go on.' Katie sat down reaching for the sauce bottle.

'Well, if I were a bus driver say, I'd probably go off the deep end every five minutes, being confronted by people I'd probably want to run over. On the other hand; if my life was less chaotic and ordered, a gardener or carpenter, maybe a writer... I suppose what I'm trying to say is; if a killer leads a quiet or low-profile life they can commit the crime and then slip back into a peaceful existence, going under the radar until they decide to kill again. It's all about feeling in control.'

'Um.'

'Where exactly is this heading, Katie?'

'I'm trying to construct an in-depth analysis on our felon. To this point, all my research indicates our killer is composed, they never get flustered or angry. How is it a human being is capable of such obscene crimes, yet remains calm on the inside, I don't get it.'

Matt laughed, cracking a couple of eggs on the BBQ. 'You're a clinical psychologist; worked with some of the best shrinks around, surely you have come across this stereotype before.'

'Yes, and would you believe I keep coming up with the characteristics of someone bordering angelic.'

'Then, there's your answer,' Matt concluded. 'Start looking for an individual with those traits and you might hit the jackpot.'

Katie smiled ruefully, sticking her fork into another piece of bacon. 'Sadly, Matt my love, the perfect person doesn't exist. I'll be searching for someone almost Godlike. Wish me luck on this one.'

****

Katie woke in a cold sweat, still feeling the heat of the fire and staring at the flicker of desperation in Ben's eyes; the smell of burning flesh seeping into her nostrils until she almost felt the flames starting to consume her entire body. Her legs started shaking, her breathing became rapid, panic set in.

Reaching for the desk lamp, she flicked the switch, comforting circles forming on the ceiling. Her palms were clammy, she clenched them together, wondering when this eternity of a nightmare would end. The bedside alarm clock indicated a quarter to one in the morning. She only went to bed just before midnight.

Acknowledging sleep was out of the question, Katie donned dressing gown, made her way down to the kitchen, opened the fridge and poured a glass of water. She toyed with the glass in her hand, taking the occasional sip; the water so cool, fresh and pure, uncontaminated, free from anything bad or evil. Her mind drifted, her grip loosened, the glass finally slipping out of her hands, smashing to the ground, fragmenting into a thousand pieces across the slate floor. Suddenly things sharpened to crystal clarity. She knew exactly what she was searching for.

I enjoy rocking in my chair. It gives me comfort. I drink a little wine and sing softly to myself:

Five and twenty ponies.
Trotting through the dark –
Brandy for the Parson,
'Baccy for the Clerk;
Laces for a lady, letters for a spy,
And watch the wall, my darling, while the Gentlemen go by!

Amen

Chapter Nineteen

The Abbot greeted Katie outside the Chapel entrance, a troubled expression on his face. 'What are you doing here,' he warned, pulling her into the cool interior and forcefully closing the door behind. 'It's not safe. It's vital you leave before you are seen.'

'Why are you covering for him?' She seethed, her anger surfacing. 'You are not meant to protect those who have committed sins against society.'

'I calculated it would not be long before you put two and two together and come searching for me.' The Abbot's face showed little emotion. 'I cannot control people who seek vengeful retaliation for what they believe is morally right.'

'You knew them to be inhuman, you had the power to stop them taking innocent lives, yet instead, you chose to protect them.'

The Abbot remained standing at the rear of the darkened Chapel indicating for Katie to sit down. 'You are wrong child, God is the one protecting them, not me. It was not my place to get involved. Eventually, I knew the will of God would prevail.'

Katie perched on the end of the pew below where a single candle burned fitfully under the 12th Station of the Cross.

Was the Abbot a true believer or just an actor playing a part, without really committing?

After a few minutes, the Abbot inhaled a deep breath. 'You want to know about him, don't you? You are here to learn about Henry?'

Katie merely nodded, waiting for the Abbot to explain.

'He was a good man, Abbot Henry. He had changed. I saw the good in him and believed he deserved a second chance. I loved him like an older brother. I benefited greatly from his wisdom and guidance. He imparted so much knowledge and showed extreme kindness to others. That is a man who repented, the past was left behind. He ran the Priory with passion and compassion. He embraced his new life, gave so much, yet requested nothing in return.'

'He was a murderer,' Katie shot back. 'He killed Russian POWs; he was implicated in slaughtering hundreds of innocents. No one who does that can be classed as good.'

'Ah, but you are wrong my dear, you will see that when you reach for the love of God.'

Katie felt her breath catching in her throat. Her sixth sense instinctively said; get up and leave, get out, but she craved more, she had to let him finish his story.

'I shielded Henry Clemens from the world, that's all I did. Behind the Priory wall, Brother Henry became a reborn human being, one to look up to. He was a great man and a model father. I loved him and his son, as I would my own.'

'You knew his son?'

'Yes, he grew up here at the Priory. His whole life was devoted to God. Now, you can't tell me that is wrong. At the start of each day, before sunrise, almost without fail he visited the Chapel and knelt next to his father's grave. I reminded him how wonderful his father was, how Brother Henry ran this Priory with such devotion and how he would have been proud of his boy. Their bond was special.'

'Did he know of the things his father did in the War?'

'Why, of course, but life is all about forgiveness. I also know what lengths he would go to, to protect his father's impeccable name. We had many discussions on life, faith and morals. It was important for him to be reminded of the inherently good instincts of his father, he didn't want the past being dragged into the present or the future.'

'Would Clemens' son kill if it meant guarding his father's honour and keeping the past hidden?'

'Perhaps, but if that is the case, we can't be the one to judge. We must turn a blind eye and let God be judge and jury.'

'Some will see what you have done as perverting the cause of justice. In my eyes you are just as much to blame, you hide behind the habit of your Order, using it as a bulwark from which to condone evil.'

The defiant reply echoed through the ancient structure. 'No, I will not take the blame for what he has done, for what either of them has done. Now go, find forgiveness, before hell's rhetoric consumes your very soul.'

Katie shot one more question back at Maximillian as she walked to the side door. 'Where will I find Clemens' son?'

'That I have already told you, my dear. His life is devoted to God, I imagine you will find him at home, in God's house.'

****

351

James picked up the laboratory phone, switched it to loudspeaker and summoned Fiona by intercom from the office.

'James, Fiona, I think I may have identified our sociopath,' Katie's breathless excited voice rang through hyperspace. 'What's the chance of Nick petitioning the Home Office to dig up a body in a sanctified tomb in the Priory?'

'Depends, what's this all about?' James replied, shaking his head slowly at Fiona.

'I have my theory, but we need conclusive DNA, or anatomical confirmation if decomposition is advanced.'

'Half-baked hypotheses won't get us permission for a major exhumation,' Fiona informed her sister. 'Detail the facts your idea is based on and come up with credible supporting evidence.'

'No problem. Get Parker on the line and I'll fill you in on everything,' Katie responded.

Fiona hesitated, before picking up her mobile. 'Katie, before I make this call, there's something we have to tell you; Allyson Carter was found deceased by the entrance of the Priory this morning. Indications are she threw herself off the top of the building. Death would have been instantaneous.'

I now await my fate, dear Lord.

Forgive them all for their sins. I am the one who is worthy of your love, not the ones who dig up the past.

Amen

Chapter Twenty

'This is preposterous.' The Abbot was pacing up and down amongst the burial sites and raised tombs, his fists clenched. 'Bodies are to remain undisturbed in God's care, not resurrected for obscene scientific experiments. The world has gone mad.'

James and Nick ignored his remarks, entering the crypt followed by two SOCOs manhandling a collapsible tent, and floodlights in preparation for the exhumation.

'Who or what are you looking for?' the Abbot finally questioned, curiosity taking over.

'Heinrich Clemminger, known to most as Henry Clemens,' Nick enlightened, moving the Abbot firmly out the way, spotting DCI Parker and a uniformed constable entering the precincts. 'Now if you don't mind, an audience is not required. Goodnight Abbot, I hope you have a peaceful sleep.'

Abbot Maximillian shot Nick a scathing look, crossing himself as he strode away down the side corridor.

'He's in a hurry,' a male voice broke in, joining the men standing in the crypt. 'You boys haven't aged much from the time I saw you last, although the waistlines certainly have.' The remark was directed squarely at Nick and James.

Nick slapped Justin Osbourne on the back. 'Nice to see you too, Ozzy. I'd surmise you were the only one available at such short notice, beggars can't be choosers. Couldn't resist the chance to get away from the paper-shuffling up at Home Office Central admin, eh?'

Justin received this with total humour. 'Looks that way, Nicky, old boy. Ah, here comes Chapman now, he's the designated Environmental Officer. His job is to ensure we follow all health regulations when handling the corpse.'

Chapman was small-framed, about five foot seven, with a demeanour that immediately alienated. He came marching up, head high, chin in, eyes fixed straight ahead. A supreme example of bureaucratic political correctness and officiousness he was universally hated by the forensic rank and file throughout the UK Police Forces. 'Morning gentleman, I'm sure everybody is aware we have forty-eight hours before the body's to be reburied.

I have sighted the licence for this exhumation, am satisfied everyone is kitted out in suitable garb, including gloves and masks. You can now proceed.'

The careful task of exhuming the body of Heinrich Clemminger began.

The last resting place of Henry Clemens was located by Nick in the far corner of the crypt. Discovered when he tripped over it searching next to a large imposing, extravagantly embellished stone sarcophagus of a Norman baron who died around 1187 AD at the Siege of Jerusalem in the Second Crusade.

The tomb was inconspicuous, about six inches above the ground of plain pink marble, permanently sealed with a cemented concrete slab.

The only markings; a small engraved cross and the inscription: *"Brother Henry Clemens. Redeemed in the Eyes of the Lord."*

Curtis Chapman, despite the handicap of severe personality deficiencies, was efficient and precise in his work, ensuring the team conformed to all strict detail guidelines.

An hour into the operation the team finally removed the lid covering the coffin, using a portable mini jackhammer.

'Shit, we're hit a snag,' Nick exclaimed, peering into the casket. 'There appears to be another body dumped on top of Clemminger, what the fuck.'

Osbourne stepped forward, raising his right hand. 'By law, the procedure has to be put on hold.'

'No way,' Nick scoffed.

Osbourne was adamant. 'Like I advised Dr Shelby, paragraph six, section three of the Regulations stipulates…'

'By law, we need to discover who this other person is,' DCI Parker interrupted. 'This is my case Osbourne and I say we continue; do you understand what I'm saying?'

'And I say…'

'Gentlemen, may I remind you we only have forty-eight hours.' Chapman was watching on, periodically glancing at his watch. 'I suggest we get on with it and argue the point later.'

Finally, with both bodies removed from the tomb, the team wheeled them out of the Chapel in body bags on trollies for transport to the lab. The Abbot cursed softly as he surveyed them loading the bodies into the attendant police forensic van.

'You will waste in Purgatory for what you've done,' Maximillian fired at the group, his fury echoing around the quadrangle in the still night. 'Everyone has a right to a peaceful death, even Henry Clemens.'

'Friend of yours was he?' Nick retaliated. 'Perhaps in future, you can choose your friends more carefully, Abbot.'

****

Back in the cool, sterile confines of the Exeter Forensic Centre, Nick, James, and Fiona set about examining the semi-decomposed remains of both bodies in the Annex Laboratory. A team of specialist pathologists and technical experts had been assembled by Will Parker and bussed down from London at the last moment to assist with the task. He hovered nervously in the background, the smell of death and decay not his thing.

'That's definitely a female, possibly early thirties,' Nick remarked, examining the first body after removing a yellowed, decaying shroud. 'I have my suspicions this might be Hayley Illbert-Tavistock, but conclusive tests will determine this.'

Fiona reached for a clipboard to jot down additional observations. 'We'll be able to pin down the age of both corpses by studying the pelvis and general dental condition. Ah, now have look at this, our male body appears to have an old knee injury with heavily calcified metal fragments around the cartilage.'

Fiona directed light on to the area of interest, exposing the atrophied tissue with a probe and forceps for the assembled entourage who craned forward.

'You can see where he was patched up, a poor job, obviously rushed,' Fiona continued. 'Another interesting thing, see here; that may be a large twisted piece of shrapnel embedded in what remains of the left lung. I'd say this chap was blown up and cleverly put back together. What do you make of this James?'

James pushed in to take a closer look at Fiona's discovery. 'Well, I'm blessed, surely this can't be.'

'Can't be what?' Nick probed.

'I've been spending a lot of time researching the photos and old Wehrmacht documents contained in Friar Jeremy's folder. If I'm not mistaken these injuries match those sustained by a highly decorated officer who served with the SS. The Panzer Division Das Reich in particular.'

Nick ushered James to one side, out of group earshot, as Fiona continued with her masterclass to the assembled. 'What! How sure are you of that?'

'I'll bet one hundred notes my friend, the fragment of shrapnel in the left lung is a piece of armour-piercing shell from a 37 mm Nudelman-Suranov cannon used by the Russians in WW2, almost certainly fired by an Ilyushin Il-2 antitank ground attack aircraft. Wow, this is remarkable.'

'So this isn't Henrich Clemminger, aka Henry Clemens?' Nick quizzed, staring incredulously at James.

'Oh, I expect it is,' James replied casually. 'However, I also have a feeling his real name is one Major Claus Bobich. I can arrange for instrumental analysis on the metal shards. I'm confident I can match to databases and liaise with overseas curatorial labs and hopefully get the additional evidence.

I have to tell you that Katie has been keeping secret some aspects of her recent trip, which she only confided in me. Before leaving Zurich to return home she diverted to the Wiesenthal Institute in Vienna.'

'Bloody cunning vixen. She didn't put that in her intel report,' interjected an annoyed Parker, eavesdropping on the conversation behind Nick.

'Anyway, I think she dispensed her charm,' James continued. 'They gave her unlimited access to confidential files on Nazi SS criminals still unaccounted for. She brought back detailed case info on five persons whose profile could have matched Heinrich Clemminger; age, appearance, place of birth, early years etc. Bobich is one of them. More importantly, old Wehrmacht records had plenty of detail on Bobich's hospitalisation and repatriation. After all, he was a war hero, idolised by the German nation.'

****

'Let's get out of here.' Nick stretched his back muscles as the semi-decomposed bodies were placed in temporary freezers. It had been an arduous task, he longed for rest. Removing his mask, he tossed it into a pedal bin before addressing Justin Osbourne. 'Ozzy, we'll leave you and Chapman to return our mystery man to the crypt. Good night gentleman, or should I say "good morning"; it's nearly six o'clock and the sun is already on the rise.'

****

Moorland Forensic Consultants – Bovey Tracey – 10 days later

'Veronica Peters knew all about the horde of Nazi artworks. They were part of a special "collection" assembled to a specific order list put together by Goering and missing since 1945; that's why she made the pilgrimage to Devon,' Parker informed the team congratulating themselves on a job well done. No one was in the mood for an early night, so they sat around in the Moorland office well into the early hours, drinking copious amounts of strong coffee with the occasional dash of Drambuie, and tucking into takeaway pizza. 'She had arranged to meet up with Brother Jeremy at the Priory and together their intentions were to expose the artworks and have those responsible brought to justice.'

James took up the commentary. 'It's not clear at this stage why the cache ended up here in St Oswald's Priory. Odessa may have been "salting" them away to guarantee a source of capital for future funding of their escape organisation activities. The task force investigations will be ongoing, Max might know something, but I doubt it. I suspect it went to the grave with Clemens. What do you think, sis? You've had a good look at the artworks with an expert from the Tate. It was a godsend you discovering the stash in the concealed panel room under the Priory, a miracle they were unscathed in the fire.'

'When the news is released, the art world will go crazy,' Katie replied. 'Could be the story of the year. The standouts; a Van Dyck portrait and a couple of unrelated preliminary sketches, a Van Eyck oil presumed destroyed in a thousand bomber raid in 1943, not to mention an evocative and intimate Vermeer interior and four Rembrandt drawings from various Dutch museums. My favourites; what looks like an Albrecht Dürer drawing of a hare from a now-defunct private Jewish collection and a Piero della Francesca oil of the Madonna thought lost forever. The value, hundreds of millions...'

'Unfortunately for his sake, Jeremy must have inadvertently informed Reverend Carter of these findings,' James continued, 'who in turn felt compelled to do away with Veronica and Jeremy. He wanted to silence them both, in case they discovered the truth behind his father's past; he couldn't risk having the links to the SS exposed.

He also made sure Hayley, Rebecca and Nicola met a similar fate to keep these secrets under wraps. If his connection to Henry Clemens were revealed he would lose all respect and most likely be subjected to acts of revenge, probably fatal.'

'What about Allyson?' Fiona raised. 'Why did she evade his wrath?'

'One can only assume he wasn't up to finishing off his own adoptive daughter,' Katie explained. 'It was easier to keep her held captive in the Priory, presumably to keep her out of harm's way, but still very much alive. The Priory was the last place anyone would think to look.'

'How does our old friend Abbot Maximilian fit into the equation?' This question came from Matt. 'Was he involved in any of these murders?'

James answered, 'No, his only crime was helping to preserve the paintings.'

'Not forgetting his long-time friendship with Henry Clemens,' Nick concluded. 'I'm convinced he helped nurture that wretched man, keeping him safe in his new life at the Priory. That in itself is a serious crime; aiding and abetting a known criminal.'

'Although Max won't see it like that.' Katie sighed. 'He'll say everything he did was under God's watchful eye. He'll even deny knowing anything about Henry's past, and what proof does anyone have to say differently.'

'What about our SS Major Claus Bobich, what did you get from Wiesenthal?' Nick questioned.

'Plenty.'

Katie flicked open her notebook and out loud read the paragraphs:

Born Claus Wolfgang Bobich in Southern Bavaria in 1918 he spent his youth involved in dairy farming and cheese making. Too old for the Hitler Youth he enlisted straight into the SS in 1938 just in time for the invasion of Czechoslovakia. By 1941 he had risen to the rank of Obersturmführer (Lieutenant) and was attached to an SS Death Squad early into Operation Barbarossa, the invasion of Russia in May 1941. During the blitzkrieg through Latvia in early July 1941, he supervised the execution of 50 Russian Officers in a mass shooting and burial near Riga.

He then came to the attention of SS-Obergruppenführer Friedrich Jeckeln and later Eduard Roschmann the notorious "Butcher of Riga" who was assigned the job of liquidating most of Latvia's 80,000 Jews. At the end of the War, he lay low in Austria for a few years to avoid arrest and changed his name to Clemminger... the rest we pretty well know most of.'

'Which reminds me,' butted in James, turning to the desktop and bringing up a mass of tabular data on the overhead slave monitor. 'I contacted Yuri Kutsenov, Deputy Head Curator at the Central Air Force Museum, in Moscow Oblast. Besides being a first-rate chemist he's also a good buddy. It was no trouble for them to run a full AES and XRF analysis on WW2 vintage high velocity, anti-tank 23 mm and 37 mm cannon shells held in their collections.

Their comprehensive elemental analyses of the hardened steel alloy casing are on the right. Note the high Tungsten content of course, but also very high Chromium and Tellurium for the 37 mm case. Moorland Forensic outsourced ICP/MS analytical results on the shrapnel fragment Fiona found in the lung remains, is on the left screen. Look for yourself, a pretty good match for ten most common elements. High Beryllium, most unusual.

Haven't had a chance to check the metal fragments in Clemen's knee but I sent a sample off to BAE Systems and on initial inspection, they reckon it's from a 20 mm cannon shell, RAF War Office Order, vintage 1944.'

'So do we know if Henry Clemens was in fact, Claus Bobich?' DCI Parker enquired.

'Without any doubt,' Nick concluded. 'Jim's one hundred quid is safe.'

Matt reached for an unopened bottle of Spanish Cuvee and drew heavily on a cheroot. 'One thing's for certain, old Simon Wiesenthal will rest easy in his grave tonight.

Right-hand man to The Butcher of Riga, eh.'

****

'I'd like a word with the Vicar before you take him away,' Katie informed DCI Parker, who had stepped forward with a set of handcuffs.

He looked sceptical, finally giving a brief nod.

'You must have killed Hayley, concealed the body, then three years later, after your father died, dumped the corpse on top of his and resealed the tomb. Not an easy feat. Why did you murder those young girls? I've tried to work it out, but so far nothing makes much sense.'

'Occasionally, we do things in life we later regret, when that happens, we turn to God.' His face held a blank expression.

'To seek repentance?'

'In a way, but understand I was left with little choice. My father led a troubled life, no good would come of dragging up such evil, I was compelled to silence those who dared to reveal the truth.'

'You killed innocent people,' Katie said fuming.

'Ah, but they weren't innocent, they wanted to resurrect the past and that in itself is a sin. All I did was protect the souls of the dead, allowing them to rest in eternal peace.'

'No one will forgive you for what you have done.'

Laughter resounded eerily through the church. 'Evil lies within us all dear girl. The very anagram of live is evil. Therefore; are we all evil to live or do we all live for evil?'

Heavenly Father, I am now to be punished for my sins, locked away for eternity. Embrace me into your prayers, so I can be forgiven.

Forever your loving servant; Reverend Samuel Carter.

Amen

Chapter Twenty-One

'Where's James, his phone's not answering?'

'What's the rush, Nick?' Fiona asked, hardly noticing Nick hurrying into the office, and heading towards the laboratory. He returned a few moments later, his face mirroring anxiety.

'Half an hour ago... an explosion on a yacht cruising up the river Dart towards Dittisham,' Nick explained. 'Reports coming in from first responders say it's big. I hope no tourists have been injured, being the start of the tourist season this could be devastating. I require help with this one, do you have time?'

'Sorry, I would help out Nick but I'm off to a pre-wedding shooting party; ah... in about twenty minutes. Actually, it's the wedding of the year: Stacey Maybury is marrying Sebastian Quinn-Harrington, it's all over the news.'

'Have him contact me the minute he drives in through the back gate,' Nick instructed, bolting out the side emergency exit almost bowling over Katie entering from the courtyard.

'He's in a hurry,' she remarked to her sister. 'Something up?'

'Massive explosion apparently, on the Dart,' Fiona answered, pre-occupied flicking through a bridal magazine. 'We'll know more soon.'

'Sounds like a job for the duty patho, what's Nick doing getting all…'

Katie stopped mid-sentence, interrupted by her mobile ring tone. 'What?' she demanded, visibly annoyed.

Fiona looked up.

'I've already told you to stop pestering me,' Katie shouted, before flinging the phone back in her bag and marching out the door.

Fiona sighed. *So much for a quiet morning. The Moorland Office was anything but peaceful.*

****

'Looks nasty,' Nick remarked, collaring a SOCO clambering onboard an outboard-powered police RIB from the Dartmouth embankment.

'Right, we have a few eye-witness accounts. They heard an almighty bang, just before eleven o'clock, and then saw the yacht explode into flames. Sorry can't hang around Nick, I'm on my way to the crime scene to retrieve any vital evidence. A marina salvage barge has lines attached but they're worried it will sink at any moment. I'll call as soon as I can with a detailed update.'

Nick, squinting from the sun's glare watched the rigid inflatable skim across the water towards the column of smoke visible downriver.

Senior forensic officer Lance Waring cornered Nick, briefing him on events. 'There were two people on board the yacht, thankfully no other boats were tangled up in the debacle. Bloody lucky; the River Cruise Paddle Streamer packed with sightseers was in the vicinity minutes before. Both victims will be transferred to the Mortuary in Torquay; a twenty-five-year-old exchange student from Amsterdam and a thirty-three-year-old male. Bodies are fairly intact but heavily traumatised receiving the full brunt of the blast. Death would have been immediate.'

'Do we know who owned the boat, or what the deceased was doing out on the water today?'

'Nope, not yet. A full-scale police operation is underway, we will have all the details shortly. What we do know is the boat is called the *Dartmouth Oyster*, a recently restored 30-foot racer, permanently berthed over at the Kingswear Marina. The Navy guys on a visiting Border Patrol Boat had a bird's eye view. They're saying the blast effect was like major ordnance.'

'I got here as soon as I could,' James informed Nick, joining both men by the water's edge. 'Any idea yet what caused the explosion and the extent of the damage?'

Nick shook his head. 'Soon as the salvage team can pump out the hulk and secure it at a marina we'll shoot over and take a look around.'

****

'You better sit down for this one mate,' Nick instructed James, joining him in the Moorland's lab, after five arduous hours attending the Dartmouth Oyster crime scene. He began fiddling repeatedly with the top button of his shirt, doing it up and undoing it, a habit of his when he was about to break disturbing news. Ready to board a police inflatable to access the damaged yacht Nick had received a disturbing SMS, instructing that James Sinclair return to the Moorland office immediately.

Nick placed his mobile on the lab bench. 'We believe the male victim on board the *Dartmouth Oyster* was Simon Greig.'

'What!'

'His kit bag was found in the bathroom lockers on the Kingswear marina, so we had a feeling he may have been on board.'

'There has to be some mistake,' James remarked. 'It can't be Simon Greig.'

'The marina hands spotted him taking the yacht out earlier and forensics recovered Greig's marina key and burnt licence on the remains.'

For the first time, Nick noticed James's hands shaking, fear in his eyes.

'There really isn't anything to worry about mate,' he reassured his colleague. 'So you happen to know of this guy, shit happens. No one is going to blame you for a boating accident. It's possible petrol fumes ignited from a leak or build up in the hold.'

James turned to stare out the lab window, all colour draining from his face. 'What did they find in his bag?'

'Car keys, wallet, sailing gear, the usual suspects.'

'Nothing else?'

Nick threw his hands up in the air. 'What the hell is this about James, your behaviour is bordering paranoia? The man gets himself blown up on a yacht, so what. The worst-case scenario is someone hated his guts, and this was an act of terrorism, don't beat yourself up on this one. Our forensic tests will uncover the truth and the bastard or bastards responsible will be caught.'

'Yeah, you're right.' James pushed back the lab stool, glancing nervously at his watch. 'Seven o'clock, how about an ale?'

Nick nodded, retrieving his jacket as the lab airlock burst open and two uniformed police officers stood framed in the doorway, accompanied by DCI Parker and a concerned Katie.

'Well, this is a surprise,' Nick commented, before noticing the grim look on Will Parker's face. 'I take it this is not a social call?'

Parker glanced directly at James. 'We've received a tip-off, indicating you were involved in a scheme to frame 2nd Lt Simon Greig for being in possession of a large quantity of cocaine. We also found your fingerprints on a document blackmailing Simon Greig for the sum of sixty thousand pounds. In light of this, we now suspect you to be directly or indirectly involved in his death. James Sinclair, we are arresting you on suspicion of murder. You do not have to say anything, but what you do say, may be used as evidence in a court of law.'